HONOR'S KINGDOM

HONOR'S KINGDOM

OWEN PARRY

WILLIAM MORROW

An Imprint of HarperCollins*Publishers*

This is a work of fiction. The characters, incidents, and dialogues are products of the author's imagination and are not to be construed as real. Any resemblance to actual persons, living or dead, is entirely coincidental.

FIRST EDITION

Designed by Fearn Cutler de Vicq

Printed on acid-free paper

Library of Congress Cataloging-in-Publication Data
Parry, Owen.
    Honor's kingdom / by Owen Parry.—1st ed.
        p. cm.
    ISBN 0-06-018634-8 (hc)
    1. United States—History—Civil War, 1861–1865—Fiction. 2. Jones, Abel (Fictitious character)—Fiction. 3. Undercover operations—Fiction. I. Title.

PS3556.A7637 H66 2002
813'.54—dc21

                                                      2001051820

02 03 04 05 06 QW 10 9 8 7 6 5 4 3 2 1

To that blessed young man from the blacking factory,
and to all his inky confederates

There is occasions and causes
why and wherefore in all things.

—SHAKESPEARE, *Henry V*

One

They found the dead fellow in London, balled up in a basket of eels. Chewed upon he was, and most unsightly. The Good Lord knows I have seen worse. In war and, once, in a church. But bad enough that one looked. Now, eels are nibblers and burrowers, so he did not lack great bits of himself as a corpse will that has been got at by vultures or pigs. To say nothing of dogs or jackals. No, he still had the proper shape of a man, if a bit whittled down and perforated. He would go in the ground almost complete. As for his soul, that is a separate matter. But he was not handsome on the butcher's table, even though the blood was long since out of him.

The body reeked of fish. A great stink filled the cellar room where the coroner's folk had laid him out, overpowering the smell of the lamps and lye soap. Twas mid-day, with the great city rumbling and grumbling beyond the damp walls, but within the morgue the hour might have been midnight. Young Mr. Adams looked as though his last meal had begun a revolution in his stomach and his pallor come near the typhoid.

"That," the elder Mr. Adams began, in a voice as calm as a Welsh Sunday, "is the Reverend Mr. Campbell, of Cleveland, Ohio. He called upon me at the legation some months ago. I believe he had come here to proselytize."

"Begging your pardon, sir?" the police inspector, a black-whiskered fellow named Wilkie, asked.

"To preach," Mr. Adams explained. "And to convert. It was a private undertaking, as I recall, conducted among the poor. He asked for a donation."

The United States Minister to Britain was not a tall man—though larger than myself—but he carried his shoulders like a grenadier and his face possessed the self-control of a veteran sergeant regulating a pack of young officers. A laurel wreath of hair wrapped round his baldness and a neat beard grew back of his chin. His collar was white and high, and cutting stiff. You would have thought him a high-born Englishman himself, for all the wintry dignity he wore. His eyes were hard as jewels. I had barely presented myself to him when the young swell from the Foreign Office appeared, police inspector in tow, to ask Mr. Adams to visit the morgue in his company.

And now we stood over the body, in the quiet the dead compel.

"Lord Russell will be dismayed," the Foreign Office lad intoned, in a voice one degree too haughty. Unwilling to steady his eyes upon the corpse, he was. His name was Pomeroy and he had feathery brown hair and a bare wish of whiskers. He was not the sort of Englishman who is permanently ruddy from sport and scented with hounds. More the club-room champion, Pomeroy seemed all narrowness, with eyes that lacked resolve, but his speech betrayed the impatience and expectations of a man who has never had to labor for his wages.

We were seven down in the morgue, not counting the dead man: the elder Mr. Adams and his son, Mr. Henry Adams, who looked the parlor sort himself and was suffocating a gag with a handkerchief pressed to his mustache; the young diplomatic fellow, Pomeroy; Inspector Wilkie, whose burst of whiskers rounded canine features; a brass-buttoned constable fingering his truncheon as if the dead man might rise up and attack us; a crooked-over coroner's assistant, happy in his work; and my Christian self.

When his utterance failed to draw a response, young Pomeroy added, "There will be questions, sir. Indeed, Lord Russell may be *extremely* dismayed."

Mr. Adams glanced at the boy, just for a twinkle, and said without emotion, "I appreciate Earl Russell's interest."

"In fact, sir," the Foreign Office boy pushed on, with more than a hint of petulance, "Lord Russell may be *extraordinarily* dismayed."

"Earl Russell's concern never disappoints," Mr. Adams said. "Please extend my cordial regards to the Foreign Secretary." A gas lamp flared. By a table of tools, the coroner's assistant gnawed furtively at a bun, for the hour had arrived for the midday meal and some men cannot regiment their appetites.

"*Sir,*" Pomeroy insisted, "I *mean* to say that Lord Russell will expect me to carry back an explanation. A letter addressed to you was found upon the person of this . . . this—"

"Upon the Reverend Mr. Campbell," Mr. Adams said helpfully.

"A letter, sir! Addressed to you, to the American Minister credentialed to Her Majesty's Government! Alluding to the gravest matters. Insinuating violations of . . . of diplomatic protocol!"

"I find that curious," Mr. Adams replied.

I almost began to suspect our representative of enjoying the exchange, for the young fellow was not his match, twas clear at once. Mr. Charles Francis Adams was the son and grandson of American presidents, see. America's answer to high breeding, that one. Formed out of New England's bitter winters, and firm as a block of ice.

"Her Majesty's Government will expect clarification," Pomeroy sulked.

Mr. Adams hinted a smile, as if the young fellow had been complimenting him steadily. "We shall all expect clarification of this particular matter, Mr. Pomeroy." He turned to the coroner's man. "When may the body be released for burial, sir?"

The crooked-over fellow lowered his bun and looked across the body to the police inspector.

Inspector Wilkie drew himself up in that rooster's posture that will pass for authority. "Begging your pardon, sir," he began, "seeing as it's murder clear enough, what with the back of 'is 'ead all crushed in for the eels to go in and out, and the poor parson a most evident victim of the criminal class amongst us, we shall 'ave to partake of the benefits of science a bit longer. To do up the inquest all proper, sir."

The inspector wiped a hand down the left side of his face, then repeated the gesture on the right. As his fingers smoothed over his whiskers, the fur bristled right back up as an animal's will. "My, my, sir, weren't it a sight, though? With them eels going in and out of 'im like worms through a cheese. Just dripping off 'im, they was, sir. Til a body would think 'e was a great eel pie, all baked up alive. But I doesn't wish to be morbid, sir, and I think we's got the last of the devils out of 'im now. Wouldn't you say so, Mr. Archibald?"

The coroner's man nodded briskly.

"Couldn't tell the eels from 'is brains at first, sir," the inspector continued. "The way they was all squirmed up together. But, speaking officially, sir, I doesn't expects as 'ow you couldn't 'ave the good reverend all to yourselves in the morning. Would that be in order, then, Mr. Archibald?"

"Oh, I should think so, I should, Inspector Wilkie," the coroner's fellow told him. "Yes, indeed. Tomorrow's all right. There ain't so much science to a feller once the back of 'is noggin's been bashed away. It'll be a disappointment to the medical college, though, for we've a shortage of paupers come in this week. The poor are fed up fat these days, and spoilt til they dies all reluctant."

"You'll want to be careful of the eels, sir," the inspector said, turning back to Mr. Adams. "In the event as there's one or two left in 'im. Sharp little teeth they 'as, sir, the bigger ones."

The elder Mr. Adams turned to the younger, who had lost his high green color and now looked blue as fresh milk in the pail.

"Henry, have Moran make arrangements for a proper burial. Something appropriate to the dignity of a religious office." He spoke again to the inspector, but somehow included the Foreign Office boy in his remarks. "We shall undertake to notify the family. In the meantime, the legation will assume the responsibility and costs for Mr. Campbell's interment." And then he looked at me. For he alone knew of my purpose in London at that hour.

"Major Jones? Have *you* any questions?"

Oh, didn't I plunge into the foolishness, the moment I had the chance? Vanity it was that turned my head. I was all puffed up with my recent successes in the field of confidential matters, see. But pride comes before a fall, as my Mary Myfanwy would tell you.

Had I held my peace that day, lives might have been spared, and torments avoided. But I was sick with pride and wanted humbling.

"If I might, sir?" I said, leaning on my cane to spare my bad leg.

Mr. Adams glanced at the inspector, then settled his marble gaze on Pomeroy. "Major Jones has just arrived from Southampton. He's been despatched by Washington to assist with legation matters."

"This is extremely irregular," young Pomeroy said. "He hasn't presented his credentials. He dare not act in any official—"

Mr. Adams nodded slightly, as if each nod were an expense to be tallied. "I shall present his papers to Lord Russell myself. Upon the next suitable occasion."

"Begging your pardon, sir," Inspector Wilkie put in. "But is the major some sort of a detective gentleman, then?"

"Major Jones is a military officer and a representative of the United States Government."

"If I might, gentlemen?" I asked, all too anxiously. Nor was it pride alone that made me hasty. The stink was on the fierce side, as if it had been gathering reinforcements, and young Mr. Adams appeared on the verge of losing his battle with the contents of his belly. Even I longed for daylight and better air, though, as a Methodist, I should find it elevating to ponder the mortality of the flesh.

They all looked at me.

"You said," I began, addressing Inspector Wilkie's indigo quills, "that the body was found here in London. In a basket of eels. And where, exactly, was the discovery made, sir?"

The inspector gave me a look as if I had gone silly as a drunken Frenchman. "And where in London's a fellow going to find 'im a basket of eels entire but in Billingsgate, Major? Oh, a gent might find 'imself a nice eel pie most anywhere, or a nice 'ot cup of eels to swally down. But a whole basket won't like to be seen nowheres but the Billingsgate fish market."

"And when, exactly, was he found?"

"Why, this morning and most early, sir, as it's Friday and the 'igh day of the fishmarket. Friday's a great day for eels, and not only amongst the Papists."

I shifted my attention to the coroner's fellow. "Now I will tell you, sir, and most respectfully, I do not pretend to a scholar's learning in these doings. Or to your evident skill, Mr. Archibald." You must use a fellow's name and praise him, see, if you want to soften him to you. "But I have been a soldier for more of my life than is sensible, and bodies I have seen aplenty. Now, I will ask your views, since you have knowledge of such matters. Hasn't this poor fellow been dead for a number of days?"

The coroner's fellow scuttled up close to the table and stuck a finger in one of the openings left by the eels. He wriggled the digit about most vigorously, testing the decay of the flesh.

Young Mr. Adams swept his head away.

"Right you are, sir, right you are," the coroner's fellow agreed. "I said it meself to Inspector Wilkie 'ere, soon as they brung 'im in. 'That one's ripe,' I says to 'im, 'ripe as a busting plum.' " He pushed his finger in deeper, added a second digit, and shook his wrist. "If it weren't for the eels opening 'im up, 'e'd be swelled up twicet over with gas."

"And how long would you judge he has been dead?"

The fellow shoved as much of his fist into the cavity as he could, then, satisfied, drew it out and wiped it on his trousers. "No less than two days that would be, sir, at the very least, and like unto three it's been since the murderers took an axe or somewhat similar to the back of 'is skull. It's my professional opinion as to 'ow the eels doesn't account for the missing eyes, Major. It's a curious thing how 'ard-enough blows to the back of a fellow's 'ead can put 'is eyes right out. I'd wager that's what 'appened. It weren't the eels what et 'is eyes, though they made a nice enough meal of the rest of the good parson." He smacked his lips. "Whoever bought them eels for 'is dinner has got 'im some fat ones."

Handkerchief balled at his mouth, young Mr. Adams hastened from the room.

"Inspector?" I began anew, only to be interrupted by young Pomeroy, who had gone more than a bit green himself, what with all the corpse-poking and reawakened stench.

"This is irregular, unacceptably irregular. The man's credentials have not—"

A last eel, disturbed in its slumbers by Mr. Archibald's prodding, slithered out of the corpse's side, slipped off the table and slapped the floor, then wriggled toward young Pomeroy's gleaming town boots. He followed young Mr. Adams from the room and we lost the benefit of his further opinions.

The constable settled the eel with a smack of his billy.

"Inspector Wilkie," I tried again, although my own bowels had grown somewhat mutinous, "if the eels were alive and capable of . . . of the efforts before us . . . then they were fresh-caught themselves, most like?"

"I'm not terrible knowledgable as to eels, sir, though I likes a nice eel pie. But I'd think as they was fresh caught. There's none won't buy eels rancid."

I tapped the stone floor lightly with my cane. "Then someone took the trouble to put a corpse that had already been dead for a matter of days into a basket of fresh eels."

"That's 'ow I sees it meself, sir. I couldn't of said it no better."

"And you found the accusatory letter sealed in oilcloth and affixed to the Reverend Mr. Campbell's person?"

"Sealed up all perfect, it was, and double tight. As if the parson was facing a storm at sea, Major. Next to 'is very skin it was, for safe-keeping."

"And you found a purse on him, but there was no money in it?"

"That's right, sir. Killed 'im and robbed 'im blind, they did. He didn't 'ave no watch nor chain, neither, though they left 'is shirt studs upon 'im." At that series of remarks, I noted the slightest flinch from the elder Mr. Adams. "And a gent such as a parson or vicar allus carries 'im a watch," the inspector continued. "Murdered dead 'e was, and robbed after. And them what 'as done it will be taken up and 'anged."

"The murderers took the money, but put his purse back into his pocket?"

"That's right, sir. Cool as Dandy Bill, they was. Typical of the more developed members of the criminal class, in my experience."

I nodded. "And your certificate, as I recall, lists London as the place of death."

"Well, 'e was found 'ere, sir, weren't 'e?"

"But the basket of eels did not come from London, I take it?"

"Not eels of that quality. No, sir. Them wasn't Thames eels, if I'm to judge. Though I 'aven't studied eels as I 'ave the criminal class."

"So he might have been murdered elsewhere? At any location within, say, two days travel of London? And," I pushed on, with a grimace at the body of the parson, "it would appear that he was put into the basket of eels some time before it arrived at the fish market, given the extent of the . . . desecration. It must have taken the eels some time to do their work, see."

Mr. Adams, who had remained steady as a statue throughout, grew restive of a sudden.

The inspector's eyebrows stood to attention, thick as a rank of bayonets on parade. Outposts of his whiskers, they were, detailed to guard his forehead. "And why would anybody, least of all the low, murdering sort, go to all the bother of that, now? That wouldn't be typical of the criminal class at all. No, sir, I'm afraid not. Why bring a fellow to London when 'e's already dead elsewheres and better 'id right there, and spare the effort?"

"I don't know. Unless it was important to the murderers that the body be found in London."

"And why might that be, Major?"

"I don't know that, either," I admitted.

Inspector Wilkie gave us all a superior look, as if to say, "There you have it—the little fellow's all bluster."

"Not to worry, gentlemen," the inspector assured us. "The Metropolitan Police will settle the matter, we will."

"Inspector," I pushed on, undeterred, "might you provide me with the name of the fishmonger who discovered the Reverend Mr. Campbell among his wares?"

"Oh, I expects we could do that, Major. Though the fellow don't know a thing about it, there's certain. For we give 'im a proper talking to. Shocked 'e was by the business, and none of the insolence of the criminal class about 'im, sir. Afraid we was going to seize up 'is basket of eels, 'e was, and cart 'em off and bankrupt 'im."

"But you didn't?"

"That's private property, sir. And I can't see 'ow as it figures. Eels is eels."

Mr. Adams cleared his throat. Now, when great men clear their throats, little folk such as you and I must pay attention. I understood he wished to end the interview, though I could not yet know his reason.

"A last matter, Inspector Wilkie," I said hurriedly. "May we take the letter with us until tomorrow? The one found on the body?"

"That's evidence, sir. But I can 'ave a copy writ up."

I shook my head. "No, I would need the original. But let that bide. May I call on you in the future, though? To examine the letter more closely?"

"That's what we're 'ere for, Major. Service to the public."

Mr. Adams moved to absent himself, and when our superiors go we are tugged behind.

As the rest of us fled that urban cavern, the coroner's fellow, Mr.

Archibald, retrieved the luncheon bun from his pocket and muttered, "Eels, now. I wonder what the old woman's bought in for supper?"

⌒

"Father, this is intolerable," Henry Adams said, with our hack caught in the swarm at the mouth of Bow Street and the summer's warmth shrinking our collars. I do not think the lad was twenty-five, though you might have thought him born aged forty by his manner. "It's the most shameless plot one could imagine. That letter . . ."

"Yes," Minister Adams said, "it *is* shameless."

"Surely, Father, something must be done. You *must* lodge a protest with Lord Russell at once."

Young Mr. Adams seemed to me the mindful sort of youth who would rather watch and judge than do, but a bit of pink had returned to his cheeks and he was badly vexed by the day's events. Matters of decorum excite such folk, though things of substance won't.

"Whether there are Confederate agents behind this," the young fellow pressed his case, "or English sympathizers with Richmond . . . you have to respond, Father." American he may have been, but he had chosen to decorate his speech with the tones of London society. "Really, you *must* make it clear the letter's nothing but a despicable hoax."

Outside our cab, which was larger than those queer-shaped hansom rigs, a hawker summoned passers-by to an exhibition of "the Celebrated Australian Fat Boy" and a costermonger cried up his greens. The walks along the shops were as packed as a chapel on Easter Sunday, though somewhat livelier, I give you. The air that drifted in to us was stinking, as a fellow expects in a great city during the summer, but it tasted fresh as April after the reek of the coroner's cellar.

"Really, Father. You have to respond at once."

"Calmly, Henry, calmly," the elder Adams counseled.

"But, Father . . . if *The Times* were to learn of this . . . or to publish that letter . . . "

Mr. Adams rested both his hands atop the silver ball of his stick, as if facing nothing out of the ordinary. "We must expect that, I suppose. Given young Pomeroy's attachments. Still, the Foreign Secretary will take a reasonable view of things."

"I don't like Pomeroy," Henry Adams muttered. "He's nothing but a Confederate lackey."

"Actually, I'm fond of Pomeroy," Minister Adams told his son. "He's too conceited to have any guile."

Our cab rocked to a stop again, for there was a great excavation in the middle of the street. A muscular navvy displayed half-naked strength, flinging dirt up to the surface, where it dusted a surveyor's shoes. The clutter and clamor of building anew seemed to annoy each last alley. All London was hammers and shouts.

"And what about Palmerston, Father? After the affront he gave you over General Butler? He's positively cheering on the Rebels, the old cad."

Pestered sufficiently, the parent told off the son. As calm of voice as ever, Mr. Adams said, "The Prime Minister is entitled to his views, Henry. Our purpose is to prevent him from acting upon them. At all events, Mr. Palmerston's bark is considerably worse than his bite. I would rather have him as he is, talking up the Confederacy and doing nothing, than supporting Richmond in silence." He looked at me and the very force of his gaze pulled my attention back inside the window. "Your first visit to London, Major Jones?"

Twas clear our minister wished to move the conversation along to matters more congenial. They were a curious pair, father and son. The elder had that solid Yankee quality that encourages you to place your money in his bank, while the younger struck me as nervous and weak of will, the sort of fellow who has every privilege and only disappoints. Doubtless, he read novels and attended the theater. And I wondered why a gentleman of good family and good health, in prime age for the army, was not back in America doing his part? But we must not be presumptuous in our judgements.

"No, sir," I replied. "That is, I was here for some days. Years ago, that was. I was only a boy, then, and looked without seeing." I gazed at the rippling wealth of the streets, unflawed but for a crippled soldier begging. "Grand, it is. I will say that."

"Yes," Mr. Adams said. "All the grandeur of empire. They're constructing an underground tunnel for omnibuses, at the moment. Hence the disruption." He waved at the world beyond our hack. "A project to control the course of the Thames is under discussion, as well, a permanent embankment from Westminster into the City." His lips spread ever so slightly, as if his smiles were rationed. "More impressive than our little Washington, I fear."

"It doesn't smell quite as bad," I agreed. "But look you, sir. I would rather have my American freedom and no monuments, than all the monuments in the world and Britannia's boot upon me."

Young Mr. Adams looked at me as if I had belched at supper. He was a curious sort, and as I come to know him better, I found that he liked the idea of America and did not shun the advantages of his birth, but he preferred the reality of England, or even, more's the pity, France and such like. But in that moment he peeved me mightily, for I am small and plain of countenance, and was not finely raised, but I will not be looked down upon by a pup. I have become an American, see, and I have fought for my new country on fields of battle, may the Good Lord forgive me. And as for any impropriety of manner, my Mary Myfanwy has seen to my public deportment, although I will never be the sort to please fine fellows who go out into society.

"You were born in Wales, Major Jones, if I'm not mistaken?" our minister asked, easing the conversation yet again.

"Yes, sir. I was born a Merthyr man. But I count myself an American now, for the past is all behind me."

I fear I verged on an untruth in my enthusiasm, for well I know the past is never behind us entirely. Would that it were. But let that bide. Twas his marking me as Welsh-born that confounded me. Look you. I do not think my speech betrays my origins, for I have studied the arts of elocution, and most diligently. Perhaps it is the Christian gravity of my demeanor that marks me as a Welshman.

"Well, we're in need of every good American we can muster," Mr. Adams told me. The hack rolled free at last and we passed into a neighborhood of fine town houses, where those afoot dressed swank and housemaids hurried along on daily errands. "Major Jones, would you dine with me just now? We shall dine out, if you have no objection. Mrs. Adams lacks enthusiasm for unexpected guests."

The son looked at the father in surprise.

The cabman called to his pair and the hack rolled to a stop. I recognized the American legation, where I had arrived that morning. Twas lodged in a good house, though hardly a grand one. Number 5,

Upper Portland Place, it was. And only rented, as I come to learn, for our minister's welcome was provisional.

"Henry," Mr. Adams said, "may I ask you to make my apologies to Judge Hagar, who is expected at three. See to it that Moran arranges for the acceptance of the Reverend Mr. Campbell's body, and tell him I want to see any dispatches that come in regarding the Number 290 matter. In fact, have him separate any correspondence from Liverpool, no matter the subject. And ask the driver to take Major Jones and myself to Galante's, in Oxford Street."

The young man gave his father a startled look. "Galante's? Father, that's hardly—" Then he looked at me again and his tone changed in an instant. "Yes. Of course. Galante's."

Obediently stepping down from the cab, Henry Adams turned and said, "Father, you won't forget that you're to call upon Mr. Disraeli? Before he leaves for the evening session?"

"I shall never forget Mr. Disraeli," Mr. Adams assured his son.

Our Minister stayed mum as they come during the rest of our ride, but he stared at me so attentively I might have been a portrait hung in a gallery. I would have thought him rude, had I not recognized that such as he know all there is to manners. But I could not stare back, for that would have been forward. So, I watched the streets as the hack crawled through the city.

How fine it all was, if stinking and dusty and hot. Eastward, where manufactories spit into the river and sky, it looked as though a child had streaked the horizon with charcoal. In the fineness of these West End streets, though, the sun come heavy and rude as a rich relation. A marvel of carriages thronged the ways, from phaetons and elegant sociables, with their hoods dropped to display fair complexions cooled by parasols, to fast young men jaunting along in gay two-wheelers, working the reins with one hand while tipping their hats with the other. Donkey barrows dueled for right of way with great dray wagons, and not all shouted sentiments were kind. Every one distinguished as a bank, buildings as high as seven stories shaded the pavings. And the crowds! A gentleman afoot could hardly pursue a straight line along the shop fronts, blocked as he was by fine ladies and their lesser sisters, all swelled out in a great competition of crinolines, if you will excuse my indelicacy.

Like painted ships those ladies were, maneuvering about a crowded harbor. Boys darted and called, swooping like gulls around galleons. A fellow got up in a motley attempt at gentility offered a refreshment of lemonade by the glass, while three strides on a newsboy cried a war in Servia, a land I did not know, where someone or other was having a go at the Turks. Treasures gorged the windows of the shops. All the world had come to London that summer, for in the railway coach I had read of the great International Exhibition just underway, attended by even the Pasha of Egypt, among a wealth of other princes and potentates, to say nothing of a wicked bother of Frenchmen. I hoped to see the exhibition's displays before I left, for they were reported to encompass every progress in the world and would surely edify.

London!

Sixteen years and more it was since last I walked those streets. A mere boy, I had sought my love, who had been sent away to keep her from me. I saw her face before me everywhere in my heartsick confusions, and failed to measure London or myself. Too soon, I went to Bristol in despair, where I signed for India and a scarlet coat. Thus began my young success, now rued, that let me bayonet myself up to a sergeancy, before misfortune put me in my place.

So much had passed, the years were heavy-laden. I was a different man. Not least, I was an American now, and in the very prime of middle age at thirty-four. And married I was to my lovely, peerless sweetheart, who had waited all those years. We had a son, our John. And a good home back in Pottsville, Pennsylvania, where I hoped to sit again at my desk in the counting house.

I had put on my blue uniform with the greatest reluctance, though now I wore it with a certain pride. I was no longer fit for field service. Bull Run had shattered my leg the summer before, and I limped a bit. I was no invalid, you understand, and walked me better with every passing month. Yet, run I never would again—not properly—nor lead men in a charge. Still, there are other ways a man may serve. The truth is I hardly regretted my little disablement. For I had seen enough of war to know it for the harshest of all mirrors. And there are things it does no good to see. I longed for peace and family and home, for a return to my ledgers at Mr. Evans's coal company, and chapel on Sunday, morning and evening both.

Still, London is a city worth a visit.

Oxford Street was a grand commercial thoroughfare, much remade in recent years by the look of it. A human river flowed between banks of shops. I did not see a plentitude of beggars, though some there were to put a claim on charity. Look you. I do not approve of such behavior by able-bodied men or even women, for begging is badly destructive of character, but I am an old bayonet and know something of the hardness of the world. The sight of a beggar in a soldier's coat gone shabby, a sleeve unfilled or left without his legs, will stir me. For well I know the role that sheer luck plays. I, too, might have been such a one as that.

Now, you will say, "It isn't luck but Providence, and Methodists should not paint life as a gamble." But I will tell you: In battle, Providence looks the other way. We shame ourselves before the eyes of God. Brute luck and bloody skill are all that save us. And so I felt an inner twitch as we rolled past a legless artilleryman croaking a ballad and dreaming not of glory but of pennies. We passed him by, but he would not leave my heart.

The hack stopped just past the Pantheon, by a sign reading GALANTE'S in golden letters and, in black, MODERATE PRICES, PUBLIC AND PRIVATE BILLIARD ROOMS.

Now honest prices are a thing I value, but proper Christians do not favor billiards.

Within, the bustle of the midday meal was slowing with the hour, but still the great room clattered like an ironworks. Twas fancy in that city sort of way that substitutes decoration for decency. A fellow decked out in a swallowtail greeted us, and Mr. Adams requested a private room.

Upstairs we went, leaving behind ranks of tables that set honest clerks down beside fellows dressed like racing touts on holiday. My leg was awkward, as it always is when I must get me up a staircase, but I smelled gravy and the scent of carvery beef, and that rarely fails to put me in a proper spirit. Food is not the least of the Good Lord's blessings.

The little room the restaurant fellow settled us in had but two chairs at table and a stained, red-velvet couch along the wall. Heavy draperies blocked all but the gaslight and the door could be locked from the inside. The smell did not resemble that of victuals.

Mr. Adams answered my perplexity.

"I'm afraid such cabinets are put to other uses in the evening," he said, as soon as the greeter had left us alone with the day's bill of fare. Our minister did not blush at the admission, but added, "My apologies, Major Jones. I needed to speak to you where we would be neither expected nor overheard. Even my private apartments wouldn't do, I'm afraid. The household staff are rather too attentive, and I'm not at all certain I'm their only paymaster. As for the legation offices . . . there are a few things my subordinates needn't know."

I listened to him with great attention, of course, but my mind had to struggle to do its duty. Startled I was by the prices on the bill of fare. "Moderate" they were not. The price of a beefsteak would have bought a cow back in America. And wanton expenditure is sinful. It wounds me.

A waiter knocked at the door, and Mr. Adams bid him enter. Our minister ordered a chop and I did likewise, since nothing on offer would answer to economy. As soon as the fellow closed the door behind himself again, Mr. Adams leaned across the table toward me.

"Why did you ask the inspector if you could borrow the letter?"

"I thought we might make a comparison, sir," I told him, relishing my cleverness. "You said the Reverend Mr. Campbell paid you a visit, see. I suspected you might have correspondence from him among your records, asking if he might call or such like. By comparing his note with the letter, we could prove the hand wasn't his, that he didn't write it. That the whole, wicked business is a hoax."

"It's not a hoax," Mr. Adams said.

I was nonplussed.

"The letter is genuine," he continued. "Were you to compare it with the correspondence in our files, it would be evident at once."

I saw a little way into the matter then. "That's why you wished to leave the morgue, sir?"

"Your questions had begun to concern me. Inspector Wilkie may be cleverer than he seems, though Pomeroy's oblivious." His wintry eyes judged me again. "You must have a great deal of experience in this line, Major."

"No, sir," I said. My voice come slow, though my thoughts were racing. "It is only that I have been involved in a few of these unfortunate affairs now. A man learns from his doings and his errors. I'm not a proper detective, sir, if any fellow of the sort may be called proper."

"Be that as it may, you were steering too close to the truth."

I fingered the cane I had propped beside my chair. "If the letter was genuine . . . "

"Genuine," Mr. Adams interposed, "but not necessarily accurate. It was something of a ruse. Do you recall its contents, Major Jones?"

"It said that the Reverend Mr. Campbell—would that be his correct name, sir?"

"Yes. Mr. Campbell served both the Lord and the United States. His vocation seemed an excellent disguise for an agent. It gave the late Mr. Campbell license to pry into all sorts of matters."

I wondered if such had not been a misuse of a reverend office, but let that bide.

"And," I continued, "the letter said he had learned nothing new, nothing at all, regarding Confederate activities."

"That may, or may not, have been accurate."

"It implied that you were his master."

Mr. Adams leaned so close I could see each separate hair in the fringe gracing his temples and every whisker under his chin, the texture of his skin and the veins broken by the years.

"Major Jones, you will be the only living person in this country, other than myself, to know what I'm about to tell you. Even my son is unaware. Henry's a fine young man, but he's better suited to stand for the St. James Club than to stand in the shadows of intrigue. And Wilson, the legation's secretary, is a political appointee, with all the deficiencies that suggests. Moran's competent, but he writes everything down."

He lowered his voice yet again. "Secretary Seward and I agreed that I would control a small number of agents to counter the Confederacy's efforts in Britain. To mask these activities, our Minister to Brussels has made a show of recruiting spies throughout Europe, including here in Britain. We hoped he might fix the attention of our enemies, while I pursued matters quietly. All seemed to be working as planned. Then I lost two agents, suddenly and only a few weeks apart—resulting in your despatch by Mr. Seward. Yet, neither of those deaths could be tied, in any way, to the legation. We had been discreet." He looked at me with a slight cant to his head. "Now Mr. Campbell's gone, but hardly anonymously."

"And the letter must be discredited."

"Ignored, for now. Unless it should become public. Then I shall deny it." He smiled that slight smile that was not a smile at all. "A man in my position may always make denials, Major Jones. It's expected. Not that a gentleman would do so under any other circumstance. But diplomacy is the one field of endeavor in which a gentleman may forget himself to advantage. No, there's something rather more important."

"Would it have to do with the watch, sir?"

That jarred him, it did. "How did you know that?"

"When the inspector spoke of the watch, you gave a bit of a start, sir."

Mr. Adams twisted his mouth. "Am I as obvious as that?"

"It is only a matter of paying attention, see. I cannot explain the matter properly, but I have always had a knack for looking in the right direction, sir. Even when all other eyes are elsewhere."

"Rather a useful skill, I expect. Yes. The watch. As I said, the letter was a ruse. Though a costly one, it appears. We had agreed that Mr. Campbell would always bear such a communication upon his person. To mislead, were he taken by Confederate agents or their sympathizers. It had to be addressed to me, you see, because anyone troubling to apprehend a reverend gentleman striving among the poor would only do so with a certain foreknowledge. The letter had to appear the height of authenticity, in order to mislead. That . . . had a price."

He looked about as if fearful of listening walls.

"The deception lay in the other contents of the letter, in the claim that nothing had been learned about any Confederate agents or their business here. The true message, Mr. Campbell's actual communication as to what he had learned, was concealed in a false compartment in the cover of his watch. Written in code. Were anything untoward to befall him, I was to claim the watch as part of his personal effects. Now it would appear that we have lost both Mr. Campbell and his intelligence."

I shook my head. Slowly. "Perhaps not, sir," I told him. Twas my foolish pride swelled up again.

He lifted an eyebrow.

"Might you tell me about the watch, sir?" I asked him. "Can you describe it?"

"A rudimentary mechanism, covered in simple brass. For Presbyterian humility, and to avoid the attentions of thieves. But, inside the spring cover, there is a scene done in enamel. An Indian temple, or something of the sort, by a river. With a tiny bullock. When the screw fixing the lid to the body of the watch is removed, the enamel disk separates to reveal a compartment capable of holding a few tissues of paper." He looked at me with the eyes of a hawk, or, perhaps, of an eagle. "Do you have reason to think you might recover it?"

"I will know one way or the other tomorrow. After I call on Inspector Wilkie and see to matters."

Our Minister's lips opened to shape a word and I knew he was about to ask me more about the prospect of retrieving the watch, but he swallowed the syllable he had begun to speak and only said, "You understand the inspector must remain in ignorance?"

"Yes, sir. I will attend to it."

"And you see the sensitivity surrounding the watch and its contents? An artless letter might be disclaimed as a hoax, but Her Majesty's Government would put a more serious construction upon a coded message. One containing the most sensitive information. My position . . . would become untenable."

"It is all right if they suspect you of fussing about with confidential agents—"

"That's what diplomats do, Major Jones."

"—but not if they have proof?"

"Exactly. Suspicions are the very nourishment of diplomacy. But facts make for a poor digestion between governments."

At that, our dinner arrived, with a knock and a flourish. Oh, the smell of a chop is a beautiful thing, lovely as Heaven on a Sunday. But I was to suffer a terrible disappointment. Although our meal was fit enough to be eaten, I had hoped for something handsome for my belly. Twelve days at sea on a Navy ship had meant my meals were plentiful, but not pleasurable. I would not be a sailor for all the world. And I had worked up an appetite since breakfast time.

Our meal had substance enough, but come short of savor. America had spoilt me, see. John Bull may keep the roast beef of Old England, and all the cutlets and chops that march behind. Once a fellow has become accustomed to the meat of America, he suffers when he sets his course abroad. My chop was drab and tough, though I consumed it.

After I had got a certain fullness in me, I asked Mr. Adams, "And what is it, sir, that the Rebels are doing in Britain? Buying ships to run the blockade, as I am told? And murdering now, are they?"

Mr. Adams had attacked his meal with a neat method and seemed perfectly content with its quality, though I will tell you: That meat wanted sabering. I have heard that the men of New England have a stoical bent and do not keep good kitchens on principle, but disdain common pleasures. Truth be told, I have even known Welshmen of such habit, who find a danger to the immortal soul in every innocent joy. But there is a great difference between a mortal sin and a good sauce, that is what I believe, and I have got my Gospels almost by memory. Our Savior offered his disciples a Last Supper, not a final fast, for he pitied us our prisons of flesh and blood. Every time I read about that Supper, I wonder what was served with the bread and wine.

"Yes. Murdering," Mr. Adams said. "Or so it would appear. But we must see through to what lies behind the murders. I believe it has to do with ships, well enough—but not only with the purchase of blockade runners. The South wants warships, Major Jones, and wants them badly."

Warships. To wipe our Yankee commerce from the seas. The Rebels were desperate for them, of course. I had got that much from the Navy officers who delivered me to Albion. Twas all they could speak about, dreaming as unblooded officers will of heroic engagements and fame, of prizes and promotions, should the Rebels manage to build or buy a fleet. But no one thought the British would sell Richmond warships. Commercial vessels, that much might be tolerated, for business never was accused of conscience. But the sale of fighting ships was cause for war.

Indeed, I had seen the evidence of Confederate deviltry with my own eyes. As the ship bearing me steamed through an Atlantic fog, we chanced upon the burning hulk of a clipper still trailing the Stars and Stripes. Twas a ghost ship, for the crew had been taken off by the raiders, and the flames made a haunting sight upon the water. We did not catch the Rebels, though we spent a day hunting for them and their ship, with our gun crews ready to open the moment we glimpsed a shadow in the mists.

The Rebels had done that much, and more, with third-rate vessels. Even in the far Pacific, so our Navy men told me, Southron privateers attacked our whalers. With proper ships, they might destroy our trade.

"And that," I said, "is why you asked young Mr. Adams to have the dispatches from Liverpool set aside. Because of the dockyards and such." I thought back. "Something else there was, too, some business with a number . . ."

"Number 290," Mr. Adams replied. "It's a shameless affair, absolutely shameless. The Confederates have contracted, secretly, for a fast warship. One clearly meant to serve as a commerce raider, built for the purpose from the keel up. In clear contravention of the 7th Section of Her Majesty's Foreign Enlistment Act, I might add." Our Minister had paused over his victuals and seemed nigh onto a fury, though an icy one. "Captain Bulloch, Richmond's purchasing agent, managed to keep the matter quiet for a suspiciously long time. British bankers abet him, I fear. None other than the firm of Messrs. Fraser, Trenholm and Company. And the shipyard owners lack the least glimmer of shame. A lesser vessel has already sailed for the Indies. But this Number 290 is meant to be a model ship of war. Built by the Laird yards—and old Laird means to stand for Parliament! The better to protect his business with Richmond!"

Still cased in arctic anger, Mr. Adams nodded to himself. "Our consul in Liverpool caught wind of it some weeks ago. Good man, avid as a terrier." He set down the knife and fork that had been frozen in his hands. "I've lodged official protests and even taken the matter to the courts—this contracting's not only against British law, but the Law of Nations, as well. Yet, many in Lord Palmerston's government prefer to turn a blind eye. There is great sympathy for the South in these isles, Major Jones. Many a lord, and many a lesser man of property, would like nothing better than to see our Republic successfully repudiated by the slave states. The United States seem to them a threat to their own system of hierarchies and privilege, given the recurrent clamor for reform in this country. And, then, of course, their manufacturers want Southron cotton. The blockade has been a hardship to the mills of Manchester."

Oh, yes. I knew that, too. For I had brushed against the business in, of all places, the snowy moors and vales of New York State. Where the truth had been as hard to find as warmth, and English interests ventured down from Canada.

"Might the loss of the Reverend Mr. Campbell have to do with this ship, this Number 290, then?"

Mr. Adams nodded again, slightly and somberly, but it was not quite a confirmation. "I begin to fear it. Yet, I cannot make sense of the deed. The Confederates—Captain Bulloch and his henchmen—know that we already possess a detailed knowledge of the vessel. Length, 220 feet. Breadth, 32 feet. Tonnage, 1040. Engines, two horizontal, of 300 horse-power each. Et cetera." He narrowed his lips to a pair of blades. "Our protests to the Foreign Office have been anything but secret, given the level of sympathy felt there for the Confederacy. Our approach to the courts has been public. Bulloch *knows* that we know. So, I simply cannot see the purpose of . . . of taking the life of a poor fellow like Campbell."

He looked down at the table and into his thoughts. "Of course, the first man was killed before we had the least inkling about the new ship. As for the second man and Mr. Campbell—why kill them to protect a secret that's already compromised? And risk perturbing Her Majesty's Government? After all, sympathetic or not, I would not accuse this government of the least tolerance of murder. At least not on British soil." Mr. Adams sat back, stymied by the hole down which his thoughts had fled. "I wonder if there isn't something more?"

I weighed the matter, wishing I had a powerful mind and not just a steady one. But we must be content with the gifts we are given.

"The first two agents . . . where were their bodies found, sir?"

Our minister had slipped into musings of his own and his eyes gave the slightest of starts when I spoke. "It's strange . . . the first man turned up in Scotland, floating in the River Clyde, right in the middle of Glasgow. Down in the Broomielaw, among the ships. I suspected he had learned of some smuggling effort—arms or other contraband. There are a good number of shipbuilders along the Clyde, as well, and shipping brokers by the hundredweight. I assumed Glasgow was the key and ordered another confidential agent to Scotland. But he never arrived. A hunting party discovered his body just south of York. Now Mr. Campbell's earthly remains appear in London . . . "

"In a basket of eels," I added.

"Yes."

"Well," I said, "you have confirmed this business in Liverpool, and publicly, so that is likely not the cause. There is true."

"Birkenhead, specifically. But let us say Liverpool."

"And if I were trying to hide a thing—a thing worth taking a human life over, or three lives—I would not want their bodies found near the thing I wished to conceal. Look you. Perhaps the first corpse was carried to Glasgow and deposited there, just as Mr. Campbell was carried here, to put us on a false scent? And Glasgow would fit, see, for then we would think of Scottish shipyards, not English. And here we might think of the London docks, hinted at by the basket of eels. Do you know if the first corpse was fresh, sir?"

"I'm afraid it's not a thing I thought to ask. But . . . what of the second body, the one found in York? Why call our attention to York? It's an inland city, without shipyards. Nor is there any industry that might supply the tools of war or other contraband to the Confederates. There's nothing suspect about York."

"Except that a body was found there."

"You have a suspicion?"

I shook my head above my disappointing, but emptied, plate. "I cannot say. Not yet." I was beginning to come to my senses, see. Remembering past errors made in haste and presumption. Hadn't I embarrassed myself at the start of the Fowler affair, blaming good Mr. Cawber? No, I had crowed sufficiently for one day. In the morning, I would visit Inspector Wilkie. Then we would see.

"Major Jones," Mr. Adams said, leaning close again, with troubled eyes, "my mission to Her Majesty's Government has three purposes. First, to avoid a war between Her Majesty's Government and our own. We barely did so last winter. Second, to dissuade Britain from diplomatic recognition of the Confederate States, with all the privileges and rights that would confer. That will come under discussion in Parliament in a matter of weeks, if I am not mistaken. And, finally, to prevent the British Isles from becoming the arsenal of the Confederacy. For today, let us concentrate on the last matter. The United States compose a trading nation, a maritime power. No matter how many victories our forces may achieve upon the land, we will have no credit in the eyes of the world if we cannot protect our commerce and assert our mastery of the seas. At present, our blockade of the South is hardly more than a sieve, if we are to be honest—although somewhat improved by the capture of New Orleans. We rely upon the acceptance by other powers that our war is, indeed, a civil matter, and that the interference of foreign governments is unwarranted and potentially of great cost to them. Thus, we cannot allow the Confederates to build or buy a navy for themselves, or to outfit themselves with ships superior to our own. We *must* command the seas to command respect. It is a matter of vital, of inestimable importance." He sat back a bit, a habit he seemed to have when summing up. "As a soldier, you will have to regard this . . . this curious sphere . . . as your battlefield now."

"Yes, sir," I said, all burdened by my thoughts.

"As to battlefields . . . may I ask your professional opinion, Major Jones, of the current operations before Richmond? Will General Mc-Clellan have the Rebel capital, or not?"

And, yes, I knew General McClellan, too, though I would not presume to say I knew him well. We only brushed past each other, in the course of a deadly business far from the sound of the guns. But I had judged him as a soldier will, and found him wanting.

"I will tell you the truth of it, sir. No man can foresee all the turnings of the battlefield, but I will be surprised if General McClellan is victorious."

"You think he'll be beaten?"

"No, sir. Not beaten, either. He is too cautious of his reputation to take the risks that lead to great victories, see. But he will fight well enough to avoid a complete defeat and all its shame." I smiled, a trifle bitterly, in remembrance. "In India, the rule was to risk everything, and to do so at once. To plunge in amongst the enemy and give him a

Cawnpore dinner, before he could so much as give us a wink. It rarely failed, at least against the natives. But General McClellan doesn't have that sort of spunk, sir. Forgive the comparison, but the general is like a boxer afraid to hit his opponent too hard, for fear of what he'll get in return. But he will not lose, either, for he is too vain ever to surrender outright. I do not think him the man to bring us Richmond. May the Good Lord prove me wrong."

Mr. Adams gave a small, but distinctly ungentlemanly, snort. "I'm afraid I lack any military faculties. I can't make any sense of that."

"War makes no sense," I told him, "until it is written down for the history books. That is the first thing to know about it, sir."

He looked at me with something near ferocity. Not that he had grown angry or even impatient with me, see. Twas only that there was a devil in him, too, behind the solemn mask of high diplomacy. I would have followed him into battle sooner than I would have followed General George B. McClellan, I will tell you. But let that bide.

"Well," Mr. Adams said, in a tone that marked the ending of our meal and our interview, "we shall allow the general to fight his war, and we'll fight ours. By the way, I would like you to accompany me later this afternoon, to visit Mr. Disraeli before he joins the evening session of Parliament. I want you to listen to what he has to say. The way you listened in the morgue today. Perhaps you'll hear more substance in his words than I do."

"Mr. Disraeli is a political fellow, I believe?" His name had graced the pages of the newspapers now and again, even in America, but I would be ashamed to tell you how little I knew of him.

"Perhaps the most political fellow who ever lived," Mr. Adams said. "He leads the Tory opposition, along with the Earl of Derby. To whom he pretends to be subordinate."

"The Tories are hostile to the United States, are they not, sir?"

This time, Mr. Adams's smile was genuine, almost full. "Not as hostile as they are to Lord Palmerston and his government." Then he mastered himself and straightened his mouth. "Do you have any clothing beyond your uniform, Major? I think we might be better served if you were dressed less conspicuously."

"I'm afraid I departed in haste, sir, and lacked the time to—"

A gentle rap tested the door.

"Yes?" Mr. Adams said, since we both thought it must be the waiter come to clear.

The door swung wide and two female creatures stood before us, painted thick and dollied up bright as heathens.

"As you gents is done with your dinner, would you fancy a pair of sweets?" With the speaker in the lead—a tiny, bird-boned thing got up in green—the women pushed their way into our chamber. Brazen as brass they were. "We'll give you boys a treat like you won't get back 'ome in Mayfair, and show you something what ain't in the Exhibition."

Mr. Adams, after overcoming his astonishment, shot to his feet. Red-faced, he was, and his tone was not diplomatic.

"Madame, how *dare* you suggest . . . the impertinence . . . *Waiter!*"

The second creature, bountifully rounded and decked out in organdy satin that was not unstained, grasped her sister in misery by the shoulder.

"Come on out, Lucy. Din't I say to you, soon as them two come in through the front door, 'ow they wasn't but two old spankers by the looks of them? Knickers down and whoops-a-daisy, that's them sorts."

The tiny creature elevated her nose and turned away as if she were a queen. "I know those likes meself, from Mrs. Marker's, and won't 'ave nothing to do with 'em. I bet they give each other the dirty freckles."

They disappeared and, shortly, we did, too. For virtue must not bide where vice parades.

We found ourselves another hack, for the legation studied economy and relied upon hire for its transport. As we clattered through the busy, blazing streets, Mr. Adams suddenly laughed aloud, startling me proper.

"It's dreadful," he said. "I really shouldn't say this—it's hardly diplomatic. But that little unfortunate in green, the one with the gift for oratory? She rather reminded me of the Prime Minister, Lord Palmerston. Although I expect her morals are somewhat better."

Twas the first time I saw Mr. Adams jovial. There would be but one other occasion when I would hear his laughter ring so rich and handsome. That, too, would have to do with Lord Palmerston.

Two

"*One always feels sorry for corpses,*" Mr. Disraeli said. "They do so resemble the Scots."

He twittered. Now, you will say: "That is a figure of speech. Men do not twitter." But I will tell you: Twitter Mr. Disraeli did, with a *hee-hee-hee* of delight at his own wit and a touch of the fingertips to his little goaty beard. Above two heavy crescents of flesh, dark eyes reflected the fellow's delight in himself. Yet, those eyes remained cold, for all their glitter. Suited up in black cloth of the best quality, he spoilt his dignity by wearing a waistcoat bright enough to please pandy. Not one, but two gold chains crossed his little belly, and his florid necktie hung thick as a noose. He didn't look English, either, but had an olive cast and oiled ringlets. He smelled of lavender.

For all his merriment and flash, he put me in mind of a cobra. I think it was the way his neck come up out of his collar, floating his head back and forth ever so slowly, as if awaiting the perfect chance to strike.

"You see my difficulty," Mr. Adams said, in a polite, but matter-of-fact tone. We sat in our host's study, surrounded by a rich fellow's heaven of books, all gilded by windowlight.

"But of course," Mr. Disraeli replied. "It really doesn't do to have corpses littering the path of policy and obstructing one's efforts. Yet, one mustn't over-estimate the importance of certain losses, as many of my parliamentary colleagues have discovered." The slightest of twitters escaped him. "The unexpected is the one thing we may fairly expect when diplomacy encounters politics, sir, and the most frightful crisis may simply evaporate. Indeed, it may vanish overnight." He leaned toward Mr. Adams. "I believe the Reverend Mr. Campbell will be allowed to rest in peace, without the indignity of reinvigoration by the press."

Mr. Disraeli's upper lip curled back. "As for the letter's ungentlemanly suggestions regarding your own activities, my dear sir, they are as infamous as they are impossible to credit." He fluttered his hand dismissively. Twas almost a feminine gesture, yet left a body with a sense of danger. His head shifted, and his serpent's eyes steadied upon our Minister. "I don't believe you need concern yourself, Mr. Adams."

Our Minister lifted an eyebrow, though not by much. For his part, Mr. Disraeli turned those hooded eyes toward me. I wish I could say he found himself impressed. But I am small, and neither fine nor handsome.

Mr. Adams read what I could not in that stare and said, "Major Jones is absolutely trustworthy. He has my confidence, sir."

" 'Absolultely trustworthy!' Oh, dear," Mr. Disraeli exclaimed, as if he were an actor on the stage. "Then I shall have to be especially cautious." He twittered and touched his little beard again. "But you haven't discussed the matter with Lord John?"

"I have not, sir," Mr. Adams told him. "I thought it wiser to seek your advice before proceeding. I am, however, considering a change in my plans so that I may attend Earl Russell's Saturday reception."

"Oh, but I should see no need of that at all!" Mr. Disraeli declared. "Generally, people change their plans to *avoid* dear Lord John's receptions."

He twittered.

"The Earl is welcoming Lord Lyons home from Washington," Mr. Adams said. "For consultations."

"Ah, Lyons. Our illustrious ambassador to your glorious Union! But, Mr. Adams, isn't 'consultations' the diplomatic term for 'utterly befuddled'? Really, you needn't raise the matter with Earl Russell. It will only confuse dear Lord John. I shall see to it."

"Thank you, sir," Mr. Adams said. "I shall rely upon your discretion."

Mr. Disraeli touched his fingertips to his beard. "Oh, dear, dear."

We sat quietly for a brace of moments. Look you. I got a lesson that night in how a man's silence may draw out more than his questions.

Twas clear that Mr. Disraeli expected Mr. Adams to say something further, to want additional assurances, but our Minister had spoken carefully at the outset, got what he wanted, and now he sat there like a Hindoo *fakir,* apparently willing to let the world proceed.

At last, Mr. Disraeli, who had a considerable appetite for his own speech, could bear it no longer. He cleared his throat and announced, "Naturally, Mr. Adams, you must be curious regarding the means at my disposal to allay your concerns."

"Not in the least," Mr. Adams said. "I have complete trust in you, sir."

But Mr. Disraeli was not to be dissuaded. It come out later that he was a novel writer, and those sorts always tell more than they should.

"I seem to recall," Mr. Disraeli said, "the slightest breath of scandal regarding young Pomeroy's sister. An event that occurred just at the beginning of the season, if my . . . acquaintance . . . may be trusted." Our host leaned foward from the basket of his chair and his collar swelled around his neck like a hood. "I do despise gossip, Mr. Adams. Doubtless, young Pomeroy shares my distaste. I'm certain he'll value my acquaintance's assurance that no one will overhear the slightest whisper regarding his dear sister's misfortune. After all, we must demonstrate compassion for the fallen." More the cobra than ever the fellow seemed. "As the beneficiary of compassion and forebearance himself, Pomeroy will hardly be intent upon embarrassing others."

"The letter may already be in the hands of *The Times,*" Mr. Adams said, in a voice suddenly gone cold as a north-woods winter. Twas as if a layer of snow had been whisked away to show the ice beneath.

Myself, I was dismayed at such untoward dealings. But I am only an old bayonet, and never made a study of diplomacy. Unless you count that bully Agamemnon, and the rest of Mr. Homer's sneaking Greeks, all of whom were nasty and wanted correction.

"I assure you," Mr. Disraeli said, in a voice like naked bone, "that young Pomeroy will redeem any such folly. More successfully, no doubt, than he has retrieved his error with a young seamstress in Lambeth, who has been the recipient of his sustained generosity. I believe he has since contributed a great deal to the prosperity of the medical profession, as well. Old Pomeroy would be mortified to learn of his son's charitable endeavors. Especially, given that gentleman's hopes for a peerage before he sheds his mortal coil." He sighed. "I do find that, these days, the sins of the son are more likely to be visited upon the father. There are certain gambling debts, as well."

"You astonish me, sir," Mr. Adams said in a toneless voice that did not sound astonished in the least. He would never be one for a Welsh choir, I will tell you, for the fellow showed less emotion than a board.

Mr. Disraeli twittered and gave his beard a generous, satisfied stroke. "I astonish myself, Mr. Adams. But may I offer you a glass of brandy? I find it a great facilitator of a parliamentary demeanor. And I do anticipate a long session tonight."

Mr. Adams declined, and our host turned in my direction.

"I have taken the Pledge, sir," I told him, "and partaking of alcohol is against my convictions, thank you."

Mr. Disraeli smiled. "It has long seemed to me, Major Jones, that the purpose of maintaining convictions is to extract the highest possible price for their alteration. But, then, I have never understood the Welsh."

⌐⌐

I wished my wife might have seen me. That is what I thought above all else. So proud she would have been, my Mary Myfanwy, though noting that pride comes before a fall.

Mr. Adams took me round the great lobby, introducing me first to a dozen members of Parliament, and then to a dozen more. Some had taken alcohol in quantity, and I do not speak solely of the members out of Ireland, but most were the pleasantest gentlemen. One Mr. Taylor seemed especially well-disposed toward our Union's efforts to reunite North and South, although a Mr. Lindsay brought Mr. Adams up short. As we moved on to other introductions, a fellow standing next to Lindsay commented, "If *he's* typical of the run of Union officers, I shouldn't think the Confederacy in much danger." It made me wonder why Mr. Adams introduced me to this Lindsay and his coterie, but I could not dwell long on the matter, for soon we found ourselves standing before Mr. Disraeli. I was introduced to him as though we had not met an hour before in his own study, which only made me wonder all the more.

Next, our Minister marched me up to Mr. Gladstone. He was a red and sputtering fellow, with busy, bulging eyes. Now, Mr. Gladstone was the Chancellor of the Exchequer, the chief clerk of the national counting house, which I think must be a fine job. Myself, I longed to return to my own clerking position, for numbers are lovely clear when men are not.

I knew a bit about Mr. Gladstone from my newspaper readings. He was reputed to be a great reformer and friend of the downtrodden, yet he showed himself cool enough to Mr. Adams and our Cause, for the English pity best where they are interested least. I wondered, again, why I should be paraded before such a fellow, though pleased enough I was by the attention. What value could I have to such high men? What profit lay in knowing Abel Jones?

I did not meet Lord Palmerston, the Prime Minister, for he and Mr. Adams had fallen out over General Butler's proclamation to the female residents of New Orleans, which explained to them that they must act like ladies if they wished to be treated as ladies, an eminently sensible position. But the English press sent howls of outrage Heavenward, and spoke of imminent ravishings by Yankee mercenaries, and Lord Palmerston liked to please the public temper. So he had assailed our struggling nation's dignity, just enough to make a nasty row, but not enough to compromise his government, as Mr. Adams put it. Lord knows, we handled the local women badly enough in India when I wore a scarlet coat, but the English like to look down on Americans whenever they may, and rare is the critic who glances into a mirror. I do not speak of the French, of course, to whom the mirror is a cherished companion.

Discreetly, Mr. Adams pointed out the Prime Minister across a vestibule, near where an elderly lady sold apples and oranges. And I marked at once the resemblance that had made him laugh that afternoon. Even by gaslight, you saw "Old Pam" wore rouge upon his cheeks. Nor was I certain his hair was entirely his own. He was great of beak and bent at the shoulders, with the profile of an underfed bird of prey.

Look you. I would not disparage the Prime Minister's lack of physical stature, for well I know a man small in physique may bear great virtues within him, but Lord Palmerston seemed a portrait of each and every decay as he stood there half in shadow, chatting with toadies. A man of the past he looked, a human relic. Yet, when he moved he showed a certain grace, even vivacity, although he was nearing his eightieth year of life. He carried himself like those men of the town who live below their years and beyond their means. And I will tell you, though it shock, that Old Pam was said to appear at unexpected hours, departing the abodes of women to whom he was not united by the bands of holy matrimony.

It is a curious world.

Oh, complain of the English we may, and even dislike them, but they will have respect from all the world. What power is mightier than the British lion? I was bedazzled, I will tell you, to have come so far in life that our Minister to Britain found it worth his time to guide me through the very halls of Parliament, from whence the greater part of the earth is governed. There was some damp, despite the summer's warmth, and a sewer odor haunted the outer rooms, but likely that was due to the neighboring river. I was puffed up with myself, I will admit to you, for Mr. Adams was as gracious to me that night as if I had been the Grand Chinee come calling. Oh, we were blessed to have him in that hour, for he knew his business better than men could tell.

The hall in which the Commons sat was not so grand as a fellow might expect, but about the size of a prosperous city church. All risen up like a phoenix the building was, since the great fire of my boyhood, and that room of opposing benches smelled of power and varnish. When the members all got going, the place grew as raucous as race day at the Lahore cantonment. We looked in on the floor, but Mr. Adams decided we were best-placed in the stranger's gallery.

I could not see it yet, although my brain was laboring, but Mr. Adams had accomplished all that he had set out to do that evening.

We stayed a goodly while, although our war and the blockade did not come up. The night's concern had to do with the ill-treatment of Jews in Russia. A pair of levied Hebrews had run afoul of the army's regulations, where such error was like to prove fatal. After a good bit of back and forth, denouncing the czar as a benighted autocrat and praising him as flawlessly progressive, an irate fellow got to his feet and insisted that Britain was obliged to stand against the persecution of mankind, wherever that persecution might occur. He did not mention slavery, of course, as practiced by the Rebels in our Southland.

I watched Old Pam, whose manner seemed shamelessly inattentive. Slumped down upon the Treasury Bench, with his hat pulled low on his forehead, he appeared to spend the evening rehearsing his eternal slumber. Only when the gaslamps provided the last light in the world did the Prime Minister doff his topper and rise to his feet.

All competing voices calmed, and the chamber settled down.

Twas then I got another lesson. Old he may have been, but Palmerston was canny. He made a little speech that seemed to give something to everyone concerned. Wonderfully artful it was. He agreed that the plight of the Jews abroad was a matter of concern, though I noted that he did not mention Russia specifically, and he thanked Providence that the honorable members were sitting in enlightened Britain. The latter remark met with cries of "Hear, hear!" from both sides of the House. *But,* the prime minister warned, no matter how dearly Britain, with its great traditions of impartial justice, might sympathize, no matter how the conscience of the splendid English yeoman might be troubled by such distant events, the Jew affair remained a matter internal to Russia, a sovereign foreign power. Her Majesty's Government *might* protest, but could not interfere without upsetting the established practice of nations. Lord Palmerston assured all present that the cabinet would address the situation in an appropriate manner, but did not elaborate as to how or when or with what.

The moment Old Pam resumed his seat, the passion drained out of the place. The opposition wore a collective expression resembling that of a young man who knew well enough that he had been cheated out of a small fortune at cards, but knew not how it had happened. Of course, we should not play at cards under any circumstances, for they are the Devil's device, and I record the image only for its exemplary value.

We left before the Commons dispersed, as the time had got near midnight. Mr. Adams found us a cab easily enough, for they lurked by Parliament in plenty, and he told me he would drop me at a hotel where a room had been engaged for me and my luggage deposited. He observed, politely, that my day had been a long one. Then we rode through a city not yet free of the day's thick warmth.

Shy of Piccadilly, music halls blazed. A street-singer, confident of the generosity of the Friday night crowds, bellowed, "Dolly Didn't See Him in the Corner (Even Though Her Mother Tried to Warn Her)," a ribald tune unfit for Christian ears. On lesser streets, where folk lived above the shops, men rested in the doorways in their shirtsleeves, sometimes companioned by drowsing women and children, come out to escape the heat of windowless rooms. In front of a noisy public house, a fellow sold tripe soup from off his barrow, offering tin bowls to wandering drunkards.

And then there were the women, abroad in ones and twos, and composing a multitude. But I will leave their purpose undescribed. I was only surprised, as often I have been, by the gaiety of so many of them. Their calling is a harsh one, yet they laugh. Perhaps they are like wounded men after a battle, telling jokes as they wait on the surgeon's knife.

"Mr. Disraeli does not look a typical Englishman," I said to Mr. Adams. I had waited as long as I might for him to speak first, for I would not be presumptuous, but he only sat there with that Hindoo holy-man calm of his. Perhaps that is why they call them "Boston Brahmins." Anyway, there were matters I wished to raise before I found myself deposited at the hotel. For I had been thinking as hard as I could and believed I had gained a little from the effort.

"You're not the first person to make that observation," Mr. Adams said, and seemed as if he would let things rest at that.

"Nor does his name sound English," I went on. "I find him a curious fellow, see. Though meaning no disrespect, sir."

"Respect," Mr. Adams said, "has not always been accorded Mr. Disraeli to the degree he might wish." He turned those marble eyes toward me, and they gleamed in the cast of light from the cab's high lanterns. "Nor is the name of English origins. 'D'Israeli.' The fellow's of Jewish descent. From a long and noble Spanish line, he claims, as well as from distinguished Italian merchants. He was baptized into the Church of England as an infant, but, of course, that's not good enough for many. Remarkable that the man has come so far. A credit to the English system, in its way. And to his own determination. The public seem to have accepted him, by and large. He's even been given the pet name "Dizzy" by family and friends, as well as by the press. Once Derby took to him, some measure of success was assured—though, nowadays, there are some who view the Earl of Derby as little more than a stalking horse for Benjamin Disraeli."

We passed a policeman admonishing an intoxicated fellow under a gaslamp.

"He didn't speak in support of those Russian Jews," I said.

"No. He wouldn't."

"Begging your pardon, sir," I pressed on, "but does Mr. Disraeli have . . . unpleasant habits?"

Mr. Adams looked baffled by the question, then began, "You've met him yourself. His manners are every bit as good as—"

He stopped. Perhaps he blushed, but the poor light would not show me.

"Nothing of the kind," he resumed. "Although I suppose his eccentricities might give one certain impressions. Really, Jones, he has a wife to whom he is absolutely devoted. As she is to him."

Well, I was glad of that. For no good ever comes of unpleasant behaviors.

"I know you explained, sir, that Mr. Disraeli shows you favor because he is in the opposition, even though the Tories dislike our Union. I would think he would use such events as the Reverend Mr. Campbell's decease to embarrass the government, rather than to help you. Even to bring down the government and lead his own party to power."

Mr. Adams nodded, and the street passed into a shadow between gaslamps. "I keep the possibility in mind. At the moment, however, Mr. Disraeli and the Earl of Derby don't want the obligation to form a government thrust upon them."

He glanced out at the darkened world, then turned his face back to me. "These are parlous times, and not only for Washington, Major Jones. London faces crises from the affair with the Taepings to the Tennessee River. India obsesses all parties in the wake of the Mutiny— I believe one of the reasons they've gone lukewarm on the anti-slavery issue is their experience of massacre at brown hands in Delhi and Oude. Nor are the French proving the most suitable allies. Louis Napoleon's activities, from Italy to Mexico, leave Her Majesty's Government a bit breathless. The Sublime Porte is misbehaving again, and the Turks appear feeble. The Russian fleet has become newly adventurous, despite the Crimean decision, while British observation of our

own operations has convinced them the Royal Navy is less than prepared for the demands of modern warfare—and Mr. Disraeli has made
a career of paring down naval expenditures, which is hardly fortuitous, under the circumstances. No, the opposition is content to let
Lord Palmerston be the first to embarrass himself." Our Minister's lips
thinned to the apprehension of a smile. "Should the embarrassment
prove great enough to break the present coalition, they might step into
office as the saviors of the situation. Otherwise, they'll wait for calmer
waters." He cocked his head to see me better. Or, perhaps, to see beyond me. "Politics isn't only about grasping power. It's about grasping
power at the right time."

"It seems an awfully deceitful world, British politics does," I said.

Mr. Adams gave a brief snort. "Our own politics are no better," he
said, with unmistakable bitterness.

He was already a disappointed man, although I did not know it
then, and this mortal life would disappoint him further. Despite his
professional dissemblings, which must have been difficult for him, he
was as erect a man as ever I knew. But I must not go too swiftly, or
leap ahead, so let that bide.

"Mr. Adams, sir?"

He turned his eyes back toward me as we bounced over broken
pavement.

"You did not introduce me around to be sociable, did you, sir? Especially not to the likes of that Mr. Lindsay. Nor did you take me to
meet Mr. Disraeli because you wanted me to listen to him. Meaning no
disrespect, sir, and all on the contrary, it seems to me there was a purpose in your doings."

He had been caught off-guard again and his eyes narrowed. Mr.
Adams was a man accustomed to surprising others, and such are not
fond of being surprised themselves. But I wanted him to know that I
saw what I saw, and that I understood and valued his efforts.

"It seems to me," I continued, "that if a fellow who has made the
acquaintance of members of Parliament, and of such high men as Mr.
Disraeli and Mr. Gladstone both, well, if such a one was to be murdered, say, there would be more of an explanation wanted than at the
death of a parson gone among the poor, or at the loss of anonymous
agents. Such a murder would be a greater embarrassment to the En-

glish than even to you, sir, since the victim was recently paraded in the very halls of Parliament. They would not see such a murder as in their interests, they would not. And you knew that the Rebels and their supporters would learn of my arrival, so you made it all public and turned the knowledge against them. You have wrapped me in invisible armor, and cleverly done, it was. If you will forgive the saying so."

Our Minister bore down upon me then, though his voice grew no louder. "Don't depend too much on any suit of armor, invisible or otherwise. Take care—take great care—Major Jones. After all, it wasn't Disraeli or that damnable Lindsay who killed Mr. Campbell. Tonight may have been a wasted effort. I merely did what lay within my power."

"But clever it was, sir. Begging your pardon."

"Clever or not, you're as exposed as Lear upon the heath," he said, as we turned back into the world of well-lit streets. "The men you met will have grasped the general purpose of your visit—at least those who take an interest in things beyond the breeding of their hunters. To the degree it may protect you, I fear it may also hinder you. You're known."

I shook my head. "I have never been a fellow for sneaking about, sir. It is not decent nor Christian. I have found that, if a body displays himself, any trouble that interests him will soon come round to call. It is a method I have used before, for secrets love to come out into the open."

The cab pulled up. "Well, let us both hope that you'll see any trouble coming in sufficient time to protect yourself," Mr. Adams told me. "Here's your hotel. There were no rooms at the Grosvenor, with the International Exhibition filling the town. And, to be frank, the legation's budget demands a certain discipline."

Now, that is as I would have it, and I told him so. We must not be wasteful with our government's resources.

He caught me as I stepped down. He did not need to touch me at all, but had the magic certain men wield and called back my attention simply by willing it.

"Major Jones," he said quietly, as two women of more enthusiasm than virtue strolled past the cab, "I dearly hope you can retrieve Mr. Campbell's watch."

"I will do my best, sir," I said, and meant it.

"Come see me Monday morning. Early. To tell me what you've found."

"Yes, sir. Monday morning."

I stepped back and the hack drove off with a snap.

The Empire Hotel appeared fine enough for my likes, although the neighborhood was livelier than I might have wished for my repose. The hotel sat on Baker Street, just along from MADAME TUSSAUD's and next to the ECONOMIC FUNERAL COMPANY (LIMITED), whose shopfront promised "funerals in the best style, and with superior appointments, at one-half the usual cost."

The hotel was clean, and that is all a Methodist demands. I do not like sheets that smell of a predecessor. My room was simple and small, yet I had me a table and chair for writing and pondering. Twas the modern aspect of the place impressed me most. Each floor had its own water-closet, with a pot of the sort that rinses itself to a purity.

Although my bags had been stowed in my room for hours, the porter insisted on showing me upstairs and demonstrating that splendid convenience at the end of the hall, which I allowed was a marvelous invention and a mighty step in the march of civilization. Of course, I had seen such before, and looked forward to the day when such a device might grace my own home, but such luxury in a hotel that appeared to cater to commercial men spoke well of British hygiene.

Cleanliness is a lovely thing, pleasing to God and man.

The porter seemed to have taken an odd liking to me, for he followed me back to my room after the demonstration. I shook his hand affably when he held it out, but he did not seem to want to go away. Perhaps he had a fondness for the Welsh. I began to unpack my effects and, at last, he put on a disgruntled look and stepped off with a bang of the door. He may have mistaken my weariness for rudeness. I am not at my best with help or servants, for I was not born high, though born most honorably.

I washed my face in the basin provided, then took me down the corridor to enjoy the splendor of that handsome sanitary appliance, which proved a salutary undertaking. Now, it is my habit to write to my Mary Myfanwy and our young John each and every night, and I had posted a baker's dozen of letters home in Southampton, as soon as

I debarked from my naval transport, but even a true heart sometimes fails in its duty. I stretched upon the bed to gather my thoughts, and fell asleep before taking up my pen. I fear I did not even say my prayers.

Mine must have been the heaviest of slumbers, for I heard no one enter the room. And I have an old soldier's ears. My life has depended on hearing the softest Pushtoon footfall below the Khyber, and sometimes I wake at the scratch of a mouse and alarm my Mary Myfanwy. But that night I heard not the slightest sound.

When I awoke, in yellow light, I found a box beside me on the bed. Twas a gorgeous thing of polished wood, inlaid most ornately, the way the Musselman artisans do in Lahore. I stared at the thing for a confused moment before I lifted the lid.

Inside lay a child's hand, bleeding and still warm, upon cream velvet.

Three

"Never seen nothing like it, I ain't," Mr. Archibald said. "Can't 'ave 'ad ten years on 'im."

"A boy, then?" Inspector Wilkie asked. "Not a girl?" His whiskers crept so high and black up his cheeks, and his hair grew so far down his forehead, that I could not help but think of a human monkey, though yesterday I had thought him like a hound. I do not mean such comparisons disrespectfully, of course.

"I would say a boy, Inspector Wilkie," the coroner's underling continued. "Although a body can't be positive certain in the case of a child. A lad of eight or nine. And poor, bless 'im. Look 'ere at those knuckles." The coroner fellow's large, deft fingers worked the hand that had not yet stiffened in its separate death. The deed was as recent as it was cruel. "See 'ow the fingers 'ave been scrubbed up, all like it was Sunday. Still, the dirt won't let go of the creases in 'is skin. And as it's 'is right 'and, it's all the dirtier, since 'e made more frequent use of it."

"Just what I was thinking meself," the inspector said.

"Took it off at the wrist, with one clean chop. Clean as the corner butcher might see it done. Not sawed through at all, but done clean-like. With a ten-inch cleaver, I'd put 'alf a crown on it."

"'A cleaver, then, Mr. Archibald?" the inspector asked. "And 'ere I am thinking the very same thing meself."

The stink of the cellar had settled overnight, though putrid enough it remained. Another body, that of a collapsed hag, had joined the Reverend Mr. Campbell in death's universal marriage and lay beside him on the next table. We worked over Mr. Archibald's desk, where a kerosene lamp reinforced the light from the gas fixtures on the walls. Bled pale, the child's hand lay on a bit of muslin now, removed from its ornate bed. Just beside Mr. Archibald's unfinished breakfast it was.

"Look 'ere now," the coroner's helper said, reaching out with his left hand. He took the inspector's paw and stretched it out for us all to see. Thick black hair grew downward from Wilkie's wrist onto the backs of his fingers. " 'Ere's just 'ow it was done. I bring down the cleaver like this." Mr. Archibald made a mock chop with his right hand, stopping just at the start of the inspector's wear-varnished cuff. "Cutting from the inside out, so to speak. That why it's cut on the bias, it is."

The coroner's fellow let go the inspector and bent low over the child's hand again. Making certain of everything. He seemed, indeed, a scientific fellow. He might have been a student of Mick Tyrone's.

"Just as I sees it meself," the inspector said. "Still, I'm troubled by the implications, Mr. Archibald."

"And why is that, Inspector Wilkie?" The little fellow's voice took on a wariness, as if his expertise might be impugned.

"It's just 'ow as this don't fit the 'abits of the criminal class, of which I 'ave made a serious study. As you 'ave yourself, Mr. Archibald. It's proven 'ow the criminal class misbehaves for only one of two reasons, when all is said and done. Either to attain a goal, which might or might not be the possession of an object, or in a fit of passion, drunk or sober. It's 'ard to see the passion 'ere. Your criminal class might bother a child most disgraceful, but they don't go cutting off pieces." We stared down at the tiny hand on the desk. "What could be the object or goal of such a deed?"

At that, the two fellows looked in my direction.

I was distraught, for reasons you will learn, but forced myself to go slowly and mind my tongue. Now, I have seen my share and more of life's cruelties, on the field of battle and elsewhere, but that child's hand disturbed me more than plague in the ranks and tribesmen surrounding the column. I know how to preserve myself in a scrap, and how anger poisons skill, while cowardice cripples. Many a day I have stood when I wanted to run, and kept myself upright with blood spattered over my snout. But there is a certain breed of man I fear beyond reason, the sort who find their joy in causing pain. I have known too many of them, and I have known them all too well.

Nor do I like that which is sometimes done to children by their elders. I do not like such cruelties, great or small. The man who hurts a child is worse than Cain.

But let that bide. I had to speak, for I owed an explanation. Hadn't the hand been found upon my bed? An incredible thing that wanted explanation?

I had rushed from the hotel half-way across London to Bow Street, clutching that box. Fair howling I come in, insisting that I needed to speak to Inspector Wilkie at once. I was not in full possession of myself, and am not sure I was more than half buttoned-up. I speak of my tunic, and not of my trousers, which were properly closed at all times. I fear I caused a fuss, but an English police sergeant possesses a beefy calm that sees things through. At last, the fellow behind the high desk decided I might not be a lunatic entire and he turned to a subordinate policeman with the order, "Go get Wilkie, Collins."

And now we were down in the coroner's cellar, and all my companions knew was that I had awakened to an unwanted gift tucked in beside me.

I am a fool in countless ways, but not in matters of viciousness or death. I knew the hand held a message, and a message addressed to me. But I could not see what that dreadful message might be. Only that, on my account, a child had been crippled. And likely killed thereafter. Twas not a pleasant thought for a man to bear.

Was it meant to frighten me off? Or to draw me in? To gain my attention? Or to confound me?

And there was more. But all that in good time.

"Mr. Archibald?" I began. "You said the wound was made by a cleaver. Might it have been another smooth-edged blade that did the work? A saber, perhaps?"

The coroner's man crumpled his eyebrows in imitation of his crumpled shoulders and chewed his lip before speaking. "I expects so, sir. So long as the blade was 'eavy enough to cut through at one go. A saber's got a weight to it, I believe. Although I 'ave observed that the criminal class, which Inspector Wilkie and I 'ave studied most diligently, 'as a preferment for the cleaver as an instrument. They'll employ most any butcher's knife what comes quick to 'and in a pinch, but when there's time to spare, they'll choose a cleaver. Wouldn't you say so, Inspector Wilkie?"

"I would, indeed, Mr. Archibald. But 'ear the major out." Surrounded by whiskers and hair, his eyes fixed upon me. "What's all this about a saber, now?"

"Gentlemen," I began, "I am in something of a muddle, see. A shock it was to wake to the box. As you will understand. But I will tell you a thing, if you will listen."

"Oh, we'll listen," the inspector said. "Won't we, Mr. Archibald? What with a parson dead in a basket of eels one day, and the 'and of a living child cut off the next. I'll listen all day and through the night to morning, Major Jones."

And so I told them of India. I told them of the pillaging of Delhi, after we took it back. I told them how the Seekhs and tribesmen who stayed loyal to our flag, not least for their own revenge against the Hindoo and the settled Musselman, went through the houses of the rich merchants, stealing with both hands. And when a great fat Hindoo fellow would not say where his jewels and gold were hid, the intruders began with the right hand of his youngest son, working up to the eldest, and hacking away until the poor devil squawked. For the left hand is defiled in the world of India, and only the right will do. And sons are precious.

No amount of begging would stop those dreadful amputations, and woe unto the family of the trader who had no gold. Mothers thrust their daughters forward, begging the soldiers to cut off the hands of their girls, only to spare their sons, but all was for naught. The worst of it was that the British soldier learns quickly. And when our own boys saw how well the low trick worked, they took it up themselves. I beat men with a rifle butt to stop them, and threatened to shoot others. I recall the baffled look on an Irish private I had knocked down. "Jaysus, Mary and Joseph," he cried, "they're only dirty niggers. Where's the harm?"

I do not paint myself a noble sort, you understand. I have admitted to crimes of my own, though each was done under orders. I was a devil myself. Until the day my will left me bereft and I became useless. But let that bide.

"I doesn't believe it a bit," Mr. Archibald said, after I had done telling and left a pause. "A British soldier would never do the like."

"Tut, Mr. Archibald," Inspector Wilkie warned him. "Our Teddy come back from the Cri-mee with tales would turn you green. Even tales of officers what done things."

"Nothing could have been as bad as India," I told them. "That would be impossible." I do not know if I was shaking outwardly, chilled as I was by the morning's wicked turn, but inside I was shivering in remembrance.

"Then you suspects this 'ere was done by a fellow what served in the Mutiny?" the inspector asked me. "Explaining the deed and the fancy box, besides?"

I nodded, but not forcefully. "I think it possible."

"Well," Inspector Wilkie sighed, "we 'ave 'Indoos and niggers of every description running about with the International Exhibition on. But you're not an 'Indoo gentleman, Major Jones. And I presumes as you're not 'oarding gold and jewels. I very much doubt you 'ad family ties to the victim. No, the criminal class likes a pattern, with all respect to your supposings, and I don't see 'ow this fits the pattern what you've described. Where would be the object? You said you received no threats nor communications. Every criminal deed must 'ave a purpose or a passion. A scientific fact, that is."

"The business didn't stop there," I said, reluctantly. "After we learned more of what had been done within the Delhi walls, or out at the cantonment . . . and, above all, at Cawnpore . . ." I sighed and shut my eyes, for it took a measure of strength to bear my recollections. ". . . we applied our powers of invention to revenge."

"Blew the buggers from cannon, I 'eard tell," Mr. Archibald said, "and the bloody niggers deserved it."

"Yes," I said. "We blew them from the mouths of our guns. Especially the Musselman, who has a superstition regarding dismemberment. Such like to go to Heaven in one piece. We stuffed pork fat down their throats first, and smeared the Hindoos with beef tallow. We made their high folk lick the floors we pissed on. We made them lick up blood, which is an immortal defilement, see. Then we killed them in more ways than you can imagine." I fear I let out a bitter little laugh.

"Although some men can imagine more than others. There was a unit of irregular cavalry, Hodson's Horse—"

"I 'eard of them. Dashing fellows, they was," Mr. Archibald declared. "All written up in the *Illustrated London News.*"

"Yes," I said. "Dashing. And brave. Undeniably brave. British-officered, they were, though the other ranks were mounted Seekhs and tribesmen. Hodson himself was fearless to the point of madness. Beyond madness, perhaps. My lads and I had been sent out to guard old Bahadur Shah's family, see, after the old man was taken out of the Hamayun to be judged. I was a sergeant, but trusted above my station in those days, and so many officers were dead of the cholera or cut down by the Kashmir Gate that I was left with the detachment under my own command."

I felt my eyes narrowing in remembrance. "One fine morning, Billy Hodson and his plungers come riding up. All pistols and plumes, they were. With him set to arrest two of Bahadur's sons and a grandson. Princes every one. When his doings drew a crowd and got them howling, Hodson had the princes stripped of their robes and unmentionables. In plain view. Then he took them a ways down the Delhi road, riding slow and unconcerned, although it stood two thousand against his two dozen. When the crowd followed after, cursing to bring down a thousand heathen gods and pitching clods of dirt, Hodson shot the princes with his pistol. Calm as a man potting rats. And didn't he ride straight into the crowd thereafter, and didn't they give him way like he was king?" I leaned on my cane and shrugged. "The high command ignored the day's doings, as near as I could tell. No doubt some thought him finer for the deed. We were not given to charity that autumn."

"No harm done, what I sees," Mr. Archibald said.

"Perhaps not. I cannot say. But look you. There is more. A certain Lieutenant Culpeper rode with Hodson. And if Hodson was fearless and cold, Culpeper was wild and cruel. He and a party of his tribesmen remained behind at the Hamayun, which, fitting enough, was something of a palace and a tomb at once, got up to honor dead princes. With other tombs rotting around it in their gardens, and the old Shah's followers malingering. Twas the screams in the night that brought me to my difficulties with Lieutenant Culpeper. Echoing, they were, for the place was a very honeycomb of stone, with handsome chambers above and cells below. Well, my boys had been there long enough to know the ins and outs of the place, for all its heathen tricks, and I had a dozen men beside me and more coming. Nearly had a battle all our own, we did, between my boys and his. And all of us Company men. For I found those great, tall tribesmen of his each holding onto a child of the royal family, as Culpeper went down the line with his saber, taking off their right forearms, one after another, with the light of Hell in his eyes. All this was in the *purdah* rooms, which had been forbid us and every other man."

Dear Lord, I saw it all so clear it pained me.

"Oh, the women pleaded and hurled their jewels at him. They even offered themselves, though he took no interest. He would not stop for God or man, this Lieutenant Culpeper. If even he heard me shouting at the first. Hardly more than a boy, he was, though tall and wide in the shoulders. Drunk with the joy of his doings." I felt a twitch inside me, as if that night were present in this morning, as present as my companions in that cellar. "Down the saber would come, and the blood would spurt. Then he would laugh and kick the fallen hand. As easily as if the action had been drilled into him. He liked the women's screams, I think."

I looked down. Not at the severed hand, but at my own past. "If a woman got away from his tribesmen and come too close, he cut her down, too. Several threw themselves at his boots, despite the fate awaiting them. I screamed at him, when shouting would not work. All this was a horrid matter of seconds, see. Lit by torches and grim as the Devil's Sabbath. Yes. Screaming I was. Fair shrieking. There was a madness brewing up in me in those days, though one of a different sort. But let that bide. Suffice to say I screamed as a sergeant must not do. Not at an officer. Not even at the lowest soldier, if he is a good sergeant. And Culpeper ignored me. So I had my boys rank up and prepare to fire. I would have given the order, too. But the devil paused just in time. We faced each other then, with his tribesmen loyal as could be and ready with cold steel—for they're loyal to the death to the officer who has won them over, no matter what he does to man or beast. Ready to rush upon us, they were, whether we had loaded rifles or no."

I must have been staring at the basement walls, but, really, I was looking through time. Backward through five years of flight from India and its demons. "He backed down. Purple in the face, he was, and I do not exaggerate. Purple. He swore I would be court-martialed and hanged, for interfering with an officer at his duties." I smiled, as we do when we ache at our own folly. "And he was nearly right, though he had nothing to do with the charges when finally they come round. No, he and Hodson's Horse rode on. I hear they did good service. But cruelly done, it was. And best forgotten."

"That one don't sound like a British officer to me," Mr. Archibald said, although his voice lacked its earlier confidence.

Inspector Wilkie ignored him. "And you suspect that this . . ." He pointed at the hand, which seemed even smaller now. ". . . this crime . . . is the work of a Lieutenant Culpeper you crossed in India?"

"That would be impossible," I said. "I heard he was cut to ribbons not long after."

Twas high morning and burning as we rode across London toward the fish market. Ahead, we saw the false storm clouds sent skyward by the manufactory chimneys down the river. Inspector Wilkie displayed admirable patience, I must give him that, for he had agreed to set aside the unspeakable business of the child's hand until I might give it more thought and his underlings could begin a proper investigation. Meanwhile, he took it upon himself to accompany me to an interview with the fishmonger who had found the Reverend Mr. Campbell mixed in among his wares, even though other policemen minded the law in the City Mile and Billingsgate lay outside of his purview. An ever-helpful man the inspector was.

We did not go immediately, for the duties of a policeman are many and varied. First Inspector Wilkie directed our rig to Jermyn Street where a dead man from the Argentine lay in his rooms. Reputed to be a maker of bombs, he had poisoned himself for love. Only after observing the anarchist's corpse could the inspector accommodate my desires.

Saturday or not, the density of carriages upon the streets was such that we had to turn down through Haymarket, where the Theatre Royal advertised *Our American Cousin*. Now, I will tell you: At times

I wish the theatre were not immoral, for I will admit to you, as finally I did to Mick Tyrone, that I would like to see the works of Mr. Shakespeare played upon the stage. But that is how our fall from Grace begins, see. With our succumbing to desires that seem most innocent. And then it is like a rout in the wake of a battle, where tragedy compounds with every step. We must be firm in the first instance, putting up a sound and constant defense against sin and evil. For once the barricade is pierced, late efforts go awry. So I content myself with reading Mr. Shakespeare, who is edifying upon the page, and true.

Evading morning drill, a Guards officer stepped into the street with a lady on his arm, confident the world would give him way. And we did.

Past St. Martin's church we went and along the solvent jollity of the Strand. The narrowness of the archway at Temple Bar delayed the succession of wagons and carriages, and an obstinate omnibus held us back for a time. Then we come free again and rolled down Fleet Steet, where the gutters flow with ink. Beyond the rotund wonder of St. Paul's, the fineness of the streets became less so, declining slowly and steadily to the east. After the proud facade of Mansion House, the ragged began to outnumber the respectable, though men of business were always to be seen. Public houses churned the damned by daylight, and sellers of second-hand clothes wedged their barrows between those hawking edibles. The competition of cries could have risen from a heathen bazaar. Along Cannon Street, a woman tugged at a man who smashed her face. I thought Inspector Wilkie would stop to intervene. But the woman only got up and tugged again, as if it were her custom, and we rolled onward.

A man could tell a poor lane from a fine one in pitch dark, by the smell of excrement. We had entered a portion of the city less salubrious. Yet, vivid with life it was, there was no denying. Navvies worked with rolled-up sleeves, pouring sweat in the day's young heat, and the children not set to work played in the streets, oblivious to danger.

I wondered if one of their brothers had lost his hand. There are matters upon this earth that only worsen as we think on them.

"Might I ask, then," Inspector Wilkie said of a sudden, "what it is you 'ope to learn of the eel-man?"

I needed to be careful. Yet the fellow was all willingness and assistance, so I had to tell him something of the business.

"He may not be a member of your criminal class, Inspector Wilkie. But I believe he knew an opportunity when it passed his way. I think that, upon finding the body, he had the presence of mind to empty Mr. Campbell's wallet, replace it, and take his watch and chain."

"And why would you think that, Major Jones?"

A girl shouted her plum duffs and tarts. Dirty she was, but gay.

"Those who killed Mr. Campbell were not robbers. Out to embarrass Mr. Adams, they were. With no wish to be misunderstood as thieves. No, I am certain the eel-seller took what money was in the purse, as well as any other effects of value."

"Then why did he put the parson's purse back in 'is pocket?"

I watched a row of shabby fronts trail by.

"Because he was afraid," I said coolly, "and a fool. He dared too much and too little at once, and such brings failure upon us."

"But he won't 'ardly admit to it."

I nodded, but half my mind was on that child again. I pictured him wandering the world missing a hand. Likely they killed him after, of course. I understood that much. But our minds are willful and strange.

"He will admit to it," I said, "when I make him an offer. I will tell him that a killer has been found and that he admits to the murder, but denies the robbery. That will unsettle him. Then I will tell him one of his friends betrayed him this very morning, and that we know all. Finally, I will offer him a bargain: He may keep the money, and good riddance, but he must produce the watch and chain for the parson's family, or at least tell where he pawned it. Otherwise, he will see the inside of a prison, if not transportation. A man who robs a corpse will not be steady, and will blabber before he knows he has been fooled. And . . . the family will have the good parson's watch. To remember him by."

Twas something of a lie, I know. And may I be forgiven. But that is how these things are done on earth.

"I was thinking the very same thing meself," Inspector Wilkie said. "All reasoned out in a scientific nature."

We passed the Monument and the air took on a startling tang of seaweed.

"If bright Lucifer could fall, so can a fishmonger," I said, as the sun lit up a glittering catch in a barrow.

"You're a philosopher, Major Jones," the inspector said.

"No," I told him. "Only a Christian who has seen more than he wished."

"Dead as a conked flounder 'e was," the porter declared, although we could see the eel-man's body for ourselves, "all purple and pinched in the gullet, Lord rest 'is soul. Slipped out to drain 'is willie, and they kilt 'im dead as a cod."

But I must not go too quickly.

We had drawn up short of the market, amid a welter of carts setting off with their purchases, and the seaweed smell had turned to a fishy cloud. A one-armed man grilled sprats at the mouth of an alley, where urchins pleaded for ha'penny carrying jobs. Inside the market— a great barn-like affair of modern construction—the stink became a miasma, for summer is no friend to a deceased fish. All vigor it was, though, with daylight and boat rigging showing out the back end, while countless hucksters barked their wares and prices. "Fine Yarmouth bloaters, praised by old Mayhew 'imself, and where's my buyer? Turbot, turbot, all alive! Fresh skate, fresh and good, go on and feel 'im, guv'nor. Prime flounders, a shilling a lot . . ."

Fish of all description were piled and heaped, or strung on lines like prisoners hanged in mass. Mounds of orange and brown shrimp twitched their last, while blue-black lobsters stared at men with hatred. A banty with a great basket strapped to his back come ploughing through, crying, "Give way, give way there . . ." Soaking he was, and faltering under the weight of his silvery cargo. An auctioneer sold off larger lots, formidable in the incomprehensibility of his language. I had to watch my going, for even with my cane the floor was treacherous. All slimed it was, and shimmering with scales.

Inspector Wilkie led me to the stall where the fishmonger sold his eels, but we found it unattended. The stalls next by were vendorless, too, though ripe with the fisherman's harvest. The inspector got on a baffled look.

Just then, a fellow tapped him on the shoulder. With the head of a cane, base metal polished up to look like silver.

"And to what do we owe the honor of this second coming?" the stranger asked Inspector Wilkie. He had the straight-backed posture of a constable, a boiled face and neat, but well-worn garments. "Now just 'ow is it we're graced with yet another visitation amongst us, and only a day after some 'igh and mighty ambassador bugger gets 'imself flushed up scarlet as Charlotte and they call for the Great, Grand Wilkie out of the west? As if we don't know our business 'ere without 'im? As if we was nothing but fools 'ere in the Mile? As if we don't know what to make of a dead man's arse?"

"Inspector Marjorie," Wilkie said, "may I present Major Abel Jones. American, 'e is, and looking into matters."

This Marjorie put on a skeptical mug. "Oh, and now 'ave we got Americans come to bother us? What'll it be next, Inspector Wilkie? Barbary apes and Roosians?"

"We just wanted to 'ave a minute with the eel-man what found the parson, Inspector Marjorie. A matter of a few questions, and no 'arm done."

Inspector Marjorie smiled. "Well, 'ave as many minutes as you want with 'im. 'E's just round back, in the piss lane. But I ain't sure you'll find 'im quick with 'is answers this morning."

Twas a damnable business. The man had stepped out on a private matter, in broad daylight, just where the boats crowd in and young Jews hawk silk scarves to the oystermen for their sweethearts or vend used shoes and guernseys. Down a close between two coffee houses he went, not half a dozen paces, where the danger was to your shoes and senses, but hardly to your neck. And, in a blink, he lay with his throat pinched in and his eyes wide open in wonder.

"It's beginning to seem like a dangerous profession, the eel trade," Inspector Marjorie said.

Inspector Wilkie was speechless.

"Dead as a week-old flounder, God rest 'is soul," the porter bellowed on. He seemed to like the prospect of an audience.

"Quiet, you," Inspector Marjorie told him, and the man slunk off.

"Might I take a closer look, sir?" I asked Marjorie.

"Peek up 'is arse, for all I care," the inspector said. He really was in a poor humor. "Cooper, Lumley," he called to the men in uniform by the victim. "Let this fellow 'ave a look and a good one."

I had a good look. And what I saw was like a club, beating upon my fingers, as I struggled to cling to the present. I touched the narrow welt upon his neck, although it was unnecessary. And I marked the differences where the blood had gathered, here a vein bruised blue, there an artery darkening brown. Twas needless, my fingering and staring, for I was already dreadful with my knowledge.

I rose and walked back to the feuding inspectors. I must have had the face of a man gone bankrupt. For if my pockets were sound, my spirit had failed me.

I am a steady man, that is my gift. But now I wavered.

"What I don't understand," Inspector Marjorie was saying in a tone almost of blame, "is 'ow the business come off right 'ere in the daylight. Nobody sees a thing, to 'ear them tell it. Yet, the sorts 'ereabouts sees more than they should the rest of the time. Always on the look-out, they are, and some of them with good reason." He folded his arms over his chest. A tall man he was. "But I suppose you've got a 'scientific' explanation for the matter, Inspector Wilkie?"

Wilkie gave a sort of growl and looked off through the masts that spiked the river.

"Aren't you going to tell us 'ow he was done for?" Marjorie needled.

"With a *Thuggee* cord," I said.

They both looked round.

"The welt," I continued. "I'll recognize it until my dying day. A *Thuggee* cord was the instrument. Who did the choking, I cannot say."

"*Thuggee,* now," Marjorie said, with the old policeman's suspicion in his eyes. "And ain't that to do with India? *Thugs* and *dacoits* and bandits and such? And what's India got to do with Billingsgate, if I may ask?"

I shook my head. "I cannot say," I admitted.

"Major Jones is something of an expert on India," Wilkie put in. "Out there during the Mutiny, 'e was."

"I thought 'e was an American? Though 'e sounds cod Welsh to me."

"Well," Inspector Wilkie said, as if I were not present, "it seems 'e was a bit of this and that aforetimes."

Marjorie eyed me skeptically. "And 'e says I've got black 'Indoos running around strangling people, does 'e?"

"I did not say any such thing, Inspector," I told him. "I only said a *Thuggee* cord was used. Perhaps by someone who learned the trick in India. Though queer it is. For the *Thugs* are more than bandits, see. It is all a ritual and a devilish worship to them, a sacrifice to their idols. It would be odd for a white man to learn the knack of it. And survive."

"And so we're back to niggers running loose?"

I began to speak, but found I had nothing to say. Which is burdensome to a Welshman. For words are our cakes and ale. The truth is I was rattled. And confused.

For flashes of an instant, I was not even certain where I stood. Had I closed my eyes, the boats and the boys in their canvas jackets and all the dockside tumult would have fled, and I would have smelled sandalwood and attar. Or the dreadful sweetness of the pyres along the *ghats*. The ripe perfume of a woman, tawny and loving, God forgive me, and the stink of a house struck by cholera. The smell of powder and blood. And the boundless reek of Man. When you have been young in India, see, you may leave it later on. But it will not leave you.

"I believe we'll be going along," Inspector Wilkie said to his counterpart. "It seems the major ain't used to the smell of fish."

But we did not go far. Wilkie guided me along the quay, past a scrawny artist who was sketching boats and whistling, to an establishment mere yards away. Rodway's Coffee House consisted of a large and crowded room, surprisingly clean and orderly, where an honest man could breakfast for a penny, and fill his belly properly for two. We sat down among the slurps and smacks and the clatter of tin and china. Now, my mind was mightily upset, and my spirits unruly, but my stomach was in perfect working order and, due to the day's irregular beginning, I had not had my breakfast. So I ordered the two-penny "tightener," although I am reserved in most expenditures.

Inspector Wilkie settled for the penny's-worth of buttered bread and coffee. Now, I will tell you: Once you have become accustomed to the coffee of America, the tepid, brown water they serve in Britain will not do. Twas as thin as English beef was tough. But I drank mine down, as not to waste. So let that bide.

We were finishing our victuals and chewing the day's events in a random manner, for there is a certain tiredness that comes upon the troubled heart when it pauses. And Providence descended. Fascinated, I was, by the serving gentleman behind the counter. He sliced and buttered bread with a smooth and ceaseless rapidity worthy of a modern industrial machine, and I wondered if we might not find ourselves remade as living engines in this day of infernal boilers and reckless speed. The age of steam is a frightful time for Man. Twas then the queer fellow sidled up and sat down without a greeting. An instant later, he leapt back up and asked, with extravagant politeness, if he *might* sit down. Then he plopped into the chair again without waiting for our answer.

Thin to a hurting, he put me in mind of the recruits out of the English slums who signed to serve in India, all spindly limbs and chests slight as Popery wafers. I could not determine his years for the filth of him, but he stank of decades of fish. His eyes flipped back and forth about the room, in imitation of the death-throes of a mackerel.

Leaning in across the table, he swamped myself and the inspector with the oceanic tide of his breath. His teeth were green and coated.

"I wun't talk to that Marjorie for the world," he said, "for 'e got no respect for an honest, working man." Closer still he come, displaying the myriad anthracite pores and emerald pustules on his face, and punishing our nostrils. "I noted as to 'ow you gents took an interest in poor Billy. 'Poor Billy Bounds,' says I to meself, 'strangled and dead all over.' And just last night, 'im standing tops of reeb to all the boys in the Lion and Lamb. 'Poor Billy,' says I, 'but that's what comes of chasing after flash girls and lording it over your mates, when everybody knows you've been doing dab for months and must of come by them show-fulls of money dishonest like.' Oh, I knew when I seen that tall gent this morning that Billy was up to 'is ears in it. I says to meself when I seen 'im, 'There's trouble a-day.' But I never thought they'd choke 'im dead in Piss Row."

"What tall gent?" Inspector Wilkie asked.

Another wave of Neptune's breath broke over us. "Why, the one that come in this morning and didn't buy nothing, but only 'ad at Billy for all to see."

"What did he say? What did he look like?" the inspector demanded.

"Oh, I only said as we all could see, not that we could 'ear. But going 'ard at it, they was, all nasty and hissing. As for 'ow the gent looked, 'e was tall and big through every living part of 'im." The fellow rubbed his cuff across his nose. "Looked like 'e could porter a double basket, 'e did, and keep an arm free to shove you. But then they all run big and bad, your Scotchmen."

"A Scotsman?" I asked quickly. For I had not forgotten the dead agent in Glasgow.

The little fellow twisted and turned. "Well, I couldn't say yes or no, not all and for certain, but 'e *looked* like a Scotchman, all red in the face and the 'air. And for all the size of them, there's a pinch to the way they does things."

"Did he go outside with the victim?" Inspector Wilkie asked. "With Billy Bounds?"

"Oh, no such thing, guv'nor, no such thing. There's the queer of it. No, off he goes, the Scotchman, like a peeler after a pickpocket, out of the market and headed to the other end of Thames Street."

Wilkie and I looked at each other.

"Oh, I told 'im, I did," said our informer. "I says to 'im right there, right on the spot, last night, I says, 'Billy, she ain't for the likes of us, and even if she was, Dutch courage won't 'elp you, no more than buying rounds you can't well pay for.' And 'Can't pay?' says 'e, bold as brass and all flaring upon me, and 'e pulls out a mountain of banknotes and says to me, 'e says, 'There's more where that come from,' says 'e, 'for me fortune's turned, just like I told Mrs. 'Epburn.' "

"Who," Inspector Wilkie put in, "did you mean when you said 'she ain't for the likes of us?' This Mrs. 'Epburn, would that be?"

The fellow shook his head as if we were great fools. And perhaps we were.

"Mrs. 'Epburn and Polly? That's a good one," he said, with a laugh so foul I feared it would coat us and follow us with stink throughout the day. "I was referring to Miss Polly Perkins, what sings in a penny gaff along in Eastcheap. Polly Perkins, the White Lily of Kent. Billy was deathly sweet on 'er, but the likes of 'er won't have nothing to do with an eel-man. The likes of 'er won't even stoop to a shrimpmonger or an oysterman with 'is own boat, not a flash bit like 'er. 'Er and Mrs. 'Epburn, that's rich. No, Polly paid Billy no mind, though she sings like a bird."

"Then who," I tried to clarify the matter, "is this Mrs. Hepburn?"

"Oh, she's the pawn-mother Billy was fond of trading with. For 'e didn't like to go pawning where familiar folk could see 'im. The sin of pride was all over 'im, and I pities 'im where 'e is now. Took whatever turned up to Mrs. 'Epburn, 'e did. She got 'erself a back-of-the-close shop over in the Dials, where I wouldn't go meself if you paid me a sovereign."

"The watch," I said, grasping my cane.

Four

The police rig retraced its earlier course, but our progress seemed wickedly slow. London is an ancient city, see, and not fit for the size and speed of modern conveyances. The weather promised to grow hotter than a city likes or the Englishman finds customary. Twas the sort of day when even the thrifty housewife sacrifices a ha'penny for the baker to cook the family dinner in his oven, sparing her family the heat of her kitchen stove. Of late, I had cooked in Mississippi, where even springtime boils, and I had stewed a decade in the clay pot of India before that, so my beef was toughened. But Inspector Wilkie had the look of a pig turning on a spit, although I do not mean that disrespectfully.

"We'll be blessed if the cholera don't come over us," he said. Then he thought for a moment and added, "Seven Dials is the Devil's own place in a cholera year. The worst sweepings of London turn up in the lanes and closes. Irishmen, too. Pig dirty, every one of them. No, the Dials ain't pleasant in the best of years. Provides all the social nourishment to grow up a criminal class. It's a scientific wonder, it is."

"And is this place in the City Mile, as well?" I asked. "Or does your authority extend there, Inspector Wilkie?"

"Even the City wouldn't 'ave their likes. No, the Seven Dials runs off St. Giles and, sorry to say, it's Bow Street's own green pasture." We jarred to a stop where a wagon loaded with tall crates blocked the way. "It's always like this," the inspector continued, "with the loads from the India docks coming in. And every what-'ave-you going back out in trade. One of these days, all London will come to a stop."

A boy called the latest news across the tangle of blocked carriages and carts, offering *The Times* for sale at thruppence. "Latest report from the Calcutta stock market, all just in," he cried. "Cotton prices up in India, Manchester all in a great anxiety, read it 'ere first, gentlemens."

Now, a good newspaper is an investment in our education, and its price cannot be counted as squandered. I waved him over and the lad dashed between wheels and horses and piles of waste dropped in his way. The edition was much thicker than our American papers, a dozen sides or more. I folded it up and put it in my pocket, for it is impolite to read in front of companions.

Wilkie watched the boy run off again and shook his head. "Now, who would cut the 'and from a living child, I arsk you that, Major Jones? Whether a fellow's been to India or not, I don't see 'ow as 'e could bring 'imself to do it." He seemed genuinely at a loss, although a policeman sees more of life than most. "I 'ave a boy and girl of me own, you know. My Albert's onto ten, and Alice seven. I wonder 'ow I'd feel if someone—"

"Tell me," I said, wishing to ease his thoughts and turn us back to business, "what do you think the chances are of one of your men bringing in news of the boy?"

Troubled enough I was myself, for I could not but feel I was to blame. Had Abel Jones not come to London town, that luckless boy might still have had his hand. And his life. But I have told you of that already, and must not repeat myself, for a tale wants proper telling. Yet, the thought of that child returned to haunt me constantly.

Wilkie shook his head again, and the eyes in his hairy face approached despair. "If there's not a thousand unwanted children in London, there's ten thousand. And if there's not ten thousand, there's twenty. Live like rats, they do. One won't be missed." Below the quills of his eyebrows, something glistened. "You wouldn't believe the 'alf of what I sees, Major. And the little fellows what earns a penny or two from their misery are the lucky ones. A body loses faith in 'is fellow man, 'e does."

"There is a higher faith that does not fail us, Inspector Wilkie."

He monkeyed up his mouth and disappointed me. "I'm not one for the church, Major Jones, for I can't see 'ow it 'elps. I only tries to live a scientific life, and to raise the young ones proper since their mother left us."

"I'm sorry."

He shook off his despondence and sat up. We passed St. Paul's again, in shifted light.

"You know," I began, for I had been thinking, "there is something that occurs to me. A thing I do not like."

He turned my way, with curiosity lifting his mighty eyebrows. Beyond his form, a rat-catcher preened down the walk in his velveteen jacket, tame rat on his shoulder, ferrets in their cage, and a battle-scarred terrier heeling.

"Do you recall," I continued, "how, yesterday, as we examined the late parson, I asked you if you might give me the name of the eel-seller?"

He nodded. "I does, indeed."

"And who was down there with us? Besides the parson, I mean. Who knew that I was likely to ask the eel-seller questions before too much time had passed?"

He understood me then. I let him think on the matter for a moment. His thoughts troubled him and his face showed it.

"Well," he said, as we passed a band of children delighted by a collapsed donkey, "there was you and me, but we don't figure. And your Mr. Adams and son."

"Above suspicion," I said. "And you trust Mr. Archibald, of course?"

"Mr. Archibald 'as devoted 'is life to science."

"What about the constable who assisted you?"

"Farmer? Sound as the Bank of England. Dependable as rain on a Brighton picnic."

"And that leaves?"

He did not answer me, for he was figuring the lie of things, although he knew the name as well as I did.

"It leaves young Mr. Pomeroy," I said. "Of the Foreign Office."

"Mr. Pomeroy," he began, carefully, "is a gentleman. You only 'ave to listen to 'im talk. And it's famous 'ow 'is guv'nor's got a pile. I don't see 'ow Mr. Pomeroy could figure."

"All the same, there is logic in it. He's known to have Confederate sympathies and—" I stopped, wondering if I had said too much. For some of my purpose must remain concealed.

Poor Wilkie could not go the final step in the corridor of supposition. He was an Englishman, see, and such cannot think past the power of a birthright. Oh, sad it is. Inspector Wilkie might look down and spot a plenty of criminals, but when he raised his eyes he saw his masters.

I let it go. For the present. I had been thinking with my tongue, and that is never wise. So I changed our theme entirely as we clattered westward and the principal streets improved.

"Would you happen to have heard of a great revolutionary fellow, a German sort, one Mr. Karl Marx?"

"Can't say as I 'ave. But what's revolutionaries got to do with this?"

"Nothing," I assured him. "It's only that my Washington landlady has a certain attachment to him and thinks him the greatest fellow in the world. He lives in London and suffers great deprivation, I am told."

"Well, he ain't alone, revolutionary or not. What's 'is name again?"

"Karl Marx. I believe he writes a great deal and wants to overthrow the established order."

"Well, we'll put 'im right, if 'e tries any nonsense around 'ere."

"Might you inquire, on my behalf, and see if his address is recorded? My landlady makes him sound an interesting sort, although my friend, Dr. Mick Tyrone, thinks the fellow's a fool."

"I should say so," Inspector Wilkie told me. "We'll 'ave no revolutions around 'ere, thank you. 'Er Majesty wouldn't allow it."

I left it at that, for all of a sudden we had turned into a maze of lanes so littered with filth and waste they seemed almost barricaded. I am ashamed to say I saw a naked child at play, of an age that wanted schooling and bodily concealment. Surrounded by boys and girls in rags, he did not seem to feel a thing amiss.

"Seven Dials," Inspector Wilkie said. "Where the Devil 'imself comes for dinner."

The ramshackle buildings, all tilted and tipping, snuggled as close as poor folk in the winter. Their ancient gables sought to meet above us, the way the weary lean in search of a shoulder. Fair blocking the light of day they were, and sheltering fetid odors of every description. Boards defended the street-level windows and makeshift rooms grew out of the upper stories, precarious as a drunkard's reformation. Beneath our wheels, the cobbles gave way to mud and planks and carcasses. The driver grew unsure of the wisdom of taking the rig any farther, so the inspector decided we might proceed on foot. There is trouble to understand this world, see. Twas the richest city on earth, encompassing souls in the millions, an achievement to dazzle Mr. Gibbon's Romans. Yet, here we were in Penury Lane, not far from Starvation Alley.

Sad it was to see a ragged mother sitting dull-faced on her tenement stoop, where the bit of sun that sneaked down was just enough to let her pick the nits from her child's hair. And the infant lacked the vigor to squirm and squawk. Hard the gathered women's voices were, and no tone under a shout come from their throats. Cursing a neighbor or calling a wayward child, they could not part their lips without profanity. Irish the half of them sounded, although I heard the lilt of Wales gone sour and plentiful English cackles in high complaint.

"And doosunt she get herself all tarted up, the minute her Tommy's gone cartin'? When that Tommy Boylan hears tell of her tricks, he'll beat her like Cromwell's drum. And she'll have it coming, the slut."

"Oi says to the old man, Oi says to 'is face, that Oim laving 'im out in ta gutter ta next toim 'e rolls back 'ere stinking."

"She stole it, I saw 'er, I did."

"Empty your shit-pot on my steps, will you . . ."

"Go on with you, Mabel. For I will not be told a single thing by the likes of you. I smelt the men all over her no sooner than she come in. And her always puttin' on airs with her fancy collars . . ."

" 'Two and six, or I'll 'ave you turned out,' says 'e. Well, 'e mought as well 'ave begged a thousand pounds, the dirty Jew. And then don't the filthy thing put 'is fingers—"

" 'Turn out the light,' 'e tells 'er, for 'e don't want 'er to see 'is shame. But she's been done dab times enough, and she lights up a match the moment 'e's bouncing and ready. And don't 'e just 'ave a great sore on 'is lum, and painting 'imself as the innocent . . . "

Such were the gentlest tones we heard, and the stench of the place was as vile as its spirit. Airless and lightless, the Dials teemed with the wreckage of Adam and Eve. There is poor, I will tell you, when you do not find a single public house on a street—although I do not approve of them, in any case—but in their place front-room affairs, with trestle tables and gin swilled out of jars.

"Go lively," a woman hissed to her sisters in poverty. "It's the tally-man come."

And there he was, indeed, alert as a scout on the cruel Northwest Frontier. Paging through his black book he was, hungry for overdue shillings and tardy pennies. The tallyman is fond when selling his wares, but fierce when wanting his payments.

The women disappeared, as if the fellow had plague and smallpox both.

Then we come onto a beggar, gathered against a wall in sightless squalor. Like boiled eggs his eyes appeared, where the ball of the yoke hints through the hardened white. His nose was ripe with sores and his lips were scabbed. We might have been in the worst lane of Lahore.

"You there," Inspector Wilkie said in an unhappy voice, "move along now. Begging ain't allowed, not even 'ere."

The beggar smiled up a blackness and made no move to rise.

"Begging? When did anybody see Old Joey begging? Following my perfession, I am, and werry skilled at it, too."

We paused. Although we did not come too close to the fellow. Oh, I am a sorry Christian. Our savior took men such as that to his breast. I call myself a Christian, but hesitate to touch him with my boot. And we content ourselves with feeling shame at our weakness, although our shame has never helped another.

"And what, pray tell, is this profession of yours?" Inspector Wilkie asked, not without a weary edge of doubt. The policeman's lot is one of repetition, enlivened now and then by sordid matters. I fear it is a life that cripples faith.

The fellow raised his boiled eyes toward us. "I'm a heel-reader," he said. "And the finest perfessional heel-reader in England, Scotland or Wales, if I do say so myself, your honor."

Now, this was a new thing to me. Although I have heard pattering in plenty, and am not unfamiliar with the conny-man, I had no inkling of the art of "heel-reading."

Twas clear Inspector Wilkie knew as little as I did. " 'Ere, 'ere," he said, "get along with your nonsense. I never 'eard of such a trade, I 'aven't."

The rotting face took on a dignified, even sniffy look. "Well, it's a rare craft, I give you that, your honor. A high craft and rare perfession. If a gentleman ain't born with the gift, it won't be taught in a lifetime. But Old Joey was born blessed. Try me, your honor. Just try me."

"Try you at what?" Wilkie asked.

"A penny to me, if I reads you right, a ha'penny's yours, if I tells you wrong."

Now, that seemed an unfair mathematics. "Look you," I intervened. "Whatever it is you do, my good man, it makes no sense that you should gain a penny entire by your success, but only lose the half if you should fail."

I have been a clerk in a counting house, see. And we Welsh know how many pence make a pound before we are out of the cradle.

"It's the premium," the fellow said. "For my perfessional services."

"I'll 'ear no more of your nonsense," the inspector told him. "Take up your cane and move along now."

"See?" the fellow said. "Knew two streets away you was a peeler. A man's walk allus gives him away. Allus. But it don't hardly make a proper demand upon my skills, a policeman's walk." He turned his crusted head in my direction, seeking to find my face with those dead eyes. "Your friend there, he's a werry different story. A challenge for even the finest heel-reader, that one. What with his cane annoying my perfessional sensibilities and distracting me of my concentration."

"You mean to say," I asked him, "that you can tell a man's profession by his walk?"

"What else do you think a heel-reader does, then? I can tell his perfession, and his character, too. I can tell you if he's happy or sad, young or old, a bachelor or a prisoner in his home. And plenty more, besides."

I fear I was taken in by his patter.

"All right, then," I told him. "If you can tell me the half of that, you shall have yourself a penny."

"Tuppence," he replied. "For you're a difficult case, your honor. Not like the peeler bloke you're dragging after you. Watch him, I would, if I was you. For he goes about unsavory."

"A penny," I said, "and not a copper more."

He shook his head. "See? I knew you wouldn't have your pockets raised, your honor. And not only because you're a Welshman. No, a man's heels tells it all, and yours say that you're careful of your purse. Werry careful, indeed."

As all men should be. Waste is sin.

He lifted a claw to his scruffy chin, as if in deepest thought. He even lowered his eyelids, as a man will who can see.

"Many's the year you spent soldiering," the fellow began again. "And sweating like a treadmill dog in a regiment of foot. But that's the easy part, guv. Crippled in a battle or worse you were. Within the last year, or mayhaps in a year and six. Still not comfortable with that third leg, are you now, your honor? All wishing you could run, and raging as you can't. And neither young nor old, but stump in the middle of your fourth tenner. Happy when home, for there's a married settlement to your gait. Your heels would turn homeward this instant, if only they could go. But there's something else, Lord, something else entire. Married the man may be, but he wasn't allus. No, not allus, not by a mile out on the high road. Not in the eyes of the law, with his pretty Nellie or Jane. Oh, you were a werry fiend for all your passions, your honor, though allus tender of a lady's feelings." He grinned like a cavern at midnight. "And as for your humor and temper, well, it's clear as you're God's own fool. Sometimes more the fool. But God's own, when it matters."

" 'Ere, 'ere," the inspector told him, "I won't 'ave the good major insulted."

The heel-reader turned his face toward the voice. "Insulted? I was giving him the goodness of his fortune. He's Johnny Luck out of a million. Not like you, Bobby Peeler. For you'll do dab twicet over before you're done. You'll fall down wicked, you mind me."

I feared an unfortunate exchange between the two and hastened to drop a penny into the fellow's palm. And then I dropped in another. Although I cannot say why.

"Now you've 'ad your way, 'aven't you?" Wilkie asked the fellow. "Just don't let me catch you begging, or you'll find yourself in the workhouse. Reading 'eels, indeed."

The fellow had closed his business with us and was slobbering over the pennies. I fear his symptoms were those of a dark disease of the sort men discover through vice. Such leads to madness. And madness will explain what science won't. I had a taste of that in cold New York.

But as we began to step along, I stopped and turned back to the unfortunate fellow. "Excuse me, sir. Would you happen to know where a certain Mrs. Hepburn conducts her trade?"

The heel-reader grinned. "In trouble, is she?"

"A simple inquiry."

His grin widened. "You're practically on her doorstep, gents. Step left on Quality Lane, just along there. Back of the first close and up the stairs. But don't believe a word she says, for she's got liar's heels if ever I heard a pair."

As we stepped along, the inspector gave me a gentle reprimand. "I intended to arsk a constable, the first one we might come across, for 'er address. Can't 'ave the likes of that one knowing our business, Major Jones."

Well, he was right, and I was wrong. Twas only that I was anxious. Besides, I know enough of poverty to understand that our business would be known by all in the neighborhood before the inspector and I were back in our rig.

As we stepped from Quality Lane into the appointed close, we surprised a brown-haired girl squatting down in the archway. Or, better put, the young lass surprised us. For she was no more concerned with our presence than with a pair of sparrows. She finished her doings, rubbed herself dry with her skirts, and moved along. We placed our feet carefully, for others had used the passage for similar purposes. The summer's heat awakened every scent, and flies feasted.

At the base of the first tilt of stairs, to the tune of a wailing child, we found a sign that read:

Mrs. Lucy Hepburn, Gentlewoman
Friend to the Temporarily Inconvenienced
Appraisals, Advances, Purchases
Confidentiality Guaranteed

And up we went, just as a golden-haired spark of a missy blazed out of a door and come down. Fair she was, in a flash sort of way, and gaily got up above the want around us. Her dress of lilac, inset with buttermilk satin, trailed on the steps despite her attempts to lift it—I glimpsed a pretty ankle, to my embarrassment, and raised my eyes as quickly as I could. She wore a summer hat of the palest green, with sufficient brim to mind her soft complexion. Trailing a gossamer shawl she was, as angels precede their wings, and its mint-green hue went handsome with the rest of her.

I stepped to the side, and Wilkie did the like.

Fury there was on the young lady's mouth, and her cheeks shone red with rage. Such a tempest was upon her that I do not think she marked us at first, although we stood there plain enough to see. Eyes to scorch a saint she had. When they burned our way at last, she paused to drop a veil over her features. As she brushed by, I smelled perfume and womanness. Her skirts rustled against us with the sound of a leafy tree on a blowing day. All to the tune of that howling child below.

And she was gone. Lovely she was, though I prefer a dark-haired woman, for such have deeper souls, I am convinced. Lovely, and yet she failed to seem a lady.

Dark of hair, spirit fair; pale on top, to Hell they drop. It is a cruel rhyme, I know. And one I had not heard for many a year. Not since my youthful departure from Wales. Yet, now it leapt toward my tongue unbidden.

Just below, in a shut-up room, the child howled on as if in fear and torment.

The inspector looked up to where I stood, with his whiskers quilled in wonderment. "That one ain't from the Dials," he said. "Though end up 'ere she might."

And we climbed on, with my cane digging splinters from the boards.

Mrs. Hepburn's establishment was the queerest thing. Now, my nose has not been stuffed with violets from the cradle up, and I have seen pawn-brokers from Pottsville to Delhi. At least through their front windows. And a fellow comes to expect a certain clutter. The interior of such a business is marked by a greater mess than a swag-shop, and piled with objects of even lower value. It is a place of dented tin, of discolored brass and iron rusted through. But Mrs. Hepburn's might have been a counting house, except for the absence of clerks. No single trinket lay on display, but all her goods were locked in chests and cabinets, with seaman's trunks stacked one atop the other. Twas one long room with a window smudged to gray at the distant end, a corridor of fastened drawers that led to the light and the woman.

And the woman herself was a very sight to see.

Mrs. Hepburn was spectacular in her rotundity. Sitting behind a desk at her embroidery, she must have had a specially constructed chair beneath her—although I could not see a trace of its wood. Her girth dwarfed that of the bountiful Hilda Schutzengel, my Washington landlady. Indeed, *Frau* Schutzengel seemed a child of famine by compare. Broader than the window spread behind her Mrs. Hepburn was. She loomed nigh as big as the elephants we used to cart our sick and sore upon campaign when the bullock carts gave out, in punishing India.

A most remarkable span of a woman she was. And bald as a lie in church. With a tiny white cap of frills that did not cover one-half the crown of her head.

Even in that dirty-window light, her scalp gleamed like the brass on a grenadier.

I do not mean this unkindly.

When she saw us coming down that corridor of chests, Mrs. Hepburn dropped her needlework, squared her great shoulders and said, "I'm a law-abiding woman, and I'll not be interfered with."

Perhaps she thought my uniform a policeman's garb—I needed to follow Mr. Adams's advice as soon as practicable and get me something plainer—or it might be that she read Inspector Wilkie's profession from his demeanor.

"Now, now, mum," the inspector said as we closed toward her, "it's only a matter of answering some questions."

She seemed to swell and darken, a leviathan set to attack, with only a flimsy desk to keep her from us. She stank, too. Although her dress was gray and most demure.

"I'm a law-abiding woman, and I only do business with law-abiding people. I know the law, don't think I don't. You have no right to come breaking in upon a decent woman."

We had not broken in.

Inspector Wilkie rose to the challenge. For he was a proper veteran of such matters.

"Act decent, now," he told her, with a steel edge to his voice, "or I'll 'ave you up on suspicions of running a bawdy 'ouse."

She looked at him in astonishment. Twas clear she had expected no such charge.

"I seen that young bit go down the stairs," he said. "The one all in purple and green. That's evidence enough."

"Ha!" the pawn-mother said, regaining her old confidence. "I never seen that baggage before in my life."

"The magistrate might take an interest in such claims, mum. I don't. And while we was allaying all suspicions of immoral activities . . ." He gestured at the ranks of chests and cabinets. ". . . we'd 'ave to inventory all what's in these drawers 'ere."

Oh, that struck home. I saw it.

"*And,*" the inspector continued, "I ain't certain all of your law-abiding customers would be tripping over themselves to do business with you, mum, after they 'eard the police was taking an interest."

Fit to bursting hot she was, for the inspector knew where to poke and prod and push. I do not mean that literally, of course.

I stepped up, for it seemed to me a time for mediation.

"Mrs. Hepburn," I said double-quick, "no one intends to bother you, see. It is only that I have come on behalf of a friend. To redeem a pledge that he no longer can. I am no policeman. And the inspector has only been my good companion. And there is true."

"What do *you* want, Tiny?" she said, in a voice that would not have disgraced a barracks bully.

"A certain Billy Bounds—known to you as William Bounds, perhaps—"

"I don't know any names," she said. "I don't ask names and my clients won't be bothered. I give them their tickets and off they go."

"Well, then . . . a certain gentleman, let us say, visited you yesterday, with a watch. Twas a simple brass affair, viewed outwardly. But, inside the cover, an enamel depicts foreign parts." I took a little breath and added, "It is a scene from India, perhaps."

"Ha," she said again.

"Do I take that to mean—"

"Ha," she repeated. "I wish I'd had me a dozen copies made of that one. Everybody in London wants their own." She looked at Wilkie and smiled as if about to consume him. By which I do not imply any immodesty. "That little bit of fluff you saw going off? The swanky bit in lilac? She was after the very same thing." She scowled triumphantly at the inspector. "Bawdy house, indeed."

"You sold it to her?" I asked in alarm.

"Not hopping likely," Mrs. Hepburn said. "It was already sold off this morning, hours ago."

"To whom?"

"I don't remember."

"You don't—"

"I don't remember any of my clients, Tiny. I trade in goods, not people. Don't even look at a one of them, I don't." She glanced at Wilkie briefly, as if he were a fly that had annoyed her. "Tell that to your peeler friend there. Him and his bawdy houses. There ought to be a law against his sort." Grunting, she added, "That one looks like he knows plenty about such houses, if you're asking Lucy Hepburn."

Wilkie opened his mouth to speak, raising his empty hand as if it held a truncheon. Which it likely had for many a year, until his promotion above the uniformed service.

I raced to speak before his words could blunder. "If you do not remember your customers, how is it you remember the lass who just went off?"

"She wasn't a customer."

"But you said she was after the watch."

"She didn't get it. So she isn't a customer."

"Do you know who she is?"

"Never saw her before in my life."

"Didn't she introduce herself?"

"My customers never introduce themselves. And a bit of that sort doesn't need any introduction."

Reluctantly and with a pain near physical, I drew my purse from my tunic. First I produced a pound. And then another. When the woman's eyes did not so much as flicker, I drew out a third.

Oh, that was hard.

I held the money just above the table. "And you do not remember a thing—nothing at all—about the purchaser of the watch?"

She gave me a dismissive snort, pondered a moment longer, then said, "In my business, reputation is all a lady's got for her advancement. A body needs to be trusted, front and back. And everyplace in between. Elsewise, she won't never see the best customers come to her door. An honorable lady of the merchandise business don't go telling her secrets, Tiny. Not for a stack of guineas." She gave me a look a duchess might aim at a footman found sloven and negligent. "Let alone for a sniffle of pounds."

Stymied, I did not interfere when Wilkie next leaned in. "Now, I 'ave 'ad enough of your nonsense, Mrs. 'Epburn. If that's your proper name, when all's said and done. What would it do to your great reputation if them as you trade with knew you'd sold off a watch that 'ad only been pawned the day before? Without giving the rightful owner a chance to reclaim 'is treasure?"

"He didn't pawn it," the woman said calmly. "He sold it to me outright."

Wilkie's nostrils, black with hair, flared out in a swell of anger. "Well, let me inform you of this, then: The former owner, Mr. William Bounds, is dead. What do you say to that, mum?"

Cool as mountain water, she answered, "Then it wouldn't even matter if he'd pawned the watch. Would it?"

With a look down at her embroidery, she added, "Can't you gentlemen see that I'm conducting business? You're interfering with my pursuit of lawful trade. After breaking in upon me rude as criminals."

Wilkie was hot. But, somehow, I led him out of those unhappy premises. Now you will say: "That woman was dishonest, such was plain, and she should not have been allowed to flout the law." But I will tell you: Even Colin Campbell knew when the hour had come to effect a wise withdrawal, and Wellington retreated to gain time.

I believed I had hit upon a strategy.

Down the stairs we marched, parading past the screaming of that child. Twas quite a wail, from lungs most inexhaustible, and I wondered what the little girl must look like to have such power of voice at her command. Then on we went, back through the filthy passage and out of the close, waving away those flies inclined to follow us.

"I'll 'ave her up, I will," Wilkie fumed. "I swear I'll find a—"

I laid my hand upon his arm to tut him. First of all, I am no friend to swearing, which is unChristian. Second, Wilkie was lurching off in the wrong direction.

"Look you," I said, for I needed his attention. Hot enough the fellow appeared to strike at me or anyone that drew near him. "Come with me for a moment, if you will. I want to try a thing that has occurred to me."

He followed, growling like a sullen hound.

I led him back to the beggar fellow. Or should I say, the heel-reader? For I hoped to have the benefit of his skills.

As we come up, the fellow turned his ruined eyes in our direction. His broken lips could not decide between a smile and a frown.

"Amazed by my perfessional skills?" he asked. "Astonished, as Prince Albert himself admitted he was when I warned him to put his affairs in order? Or is it Bobby Peeler come back to bother a poor working man, accomplished perfessional though he has proven himself this werry hour?"

"As a matter of fact," I told him, drawing out my purse again, which was happy to have regained those three risked pounds, "I find myself in need of your professional services, sir. Upon two counts." I brought out a shilling entire. "If you can satisfy me, you shall have a shilling for your performance."

"Now, if you'll forgive me, your honor . . . I ain't a performer of any kind. I'm a skilled perfessional. If you're wanting performers, there's a proper one just skipped on by us. A music-hall morsel, and proud as they come, all fancy and fussing and riled. Pained to step herself clear of the dirties she was. And not contented with her doings hereabouts, I'm judge enough to say. Why, didn't the little belter sound—"

"The White Lily of Kent!" I cried, all sudden. A shame it was, for I should have held my tongue.

Inspector Wilkie gave me a look of bafflement. Twas clear he had forgotten.

"I can't tell you her name or such, your honor, for that's not within the realm of the heel-reading art, but—"

I was excited, and that is never good. I cut him off: "You've already earned the half of your wages. Now I have a harder question to put to you."

He straightened his posture under his crawling rags. "I likes a per-fessional challenge. Go on, guv."

"How long have you been sitting here?"

"Hours. Except when I had to step into the close there." He ges-tured with a filth-encrusted finger.

"How many hours?"

He smiled a bit. Cracking open the scabs upon his lips. "I haven't been paying attention to my watch, now, your honor, but—"

Again, I plunged ahead in my enthusiasm. "Are you here-abouts regularly? Would you say you know the footsteps of the residents to a fair degree?"

"Well, now . . . a fellow what is lacking his sight, even a perfes-sional man, keeps close to what's familiar. I'm not a man to boast, your honor, but I think I know the steps of any man or beast this side of Covent Garden. And halfway up to the Tottenham Court Road."

"This morning, then. Did you hear anyone new go past? Any pe-culiar footsteps, perhaps? Someone who seemed in a hurry? A person on urgent business? Or anyone strange at all?"

I had high hopes, for there were only two possible directions legs could take a person going into or coming out of Mrs. Hepburn's close, and one, the more secretive way, led past the heel-reader. In the other direction, the lane ended in a bright commotion of trade.

"Well," the fellow said, "there was the Scotchman."

"A Scotsman?"

"And a big one he was, at that."

" 'Ere, 'ere," Wilkie intervened. "Now 'ow on earth could you tell if 'e was Scotch? I doesn't believe a word."

"Oh, a Scotchman's easy as they come, Bobby Peeler." Indeed, the fellow had the blithe confidence of a professional man, a doctor or a barrister or such. "He doesn't walk, but swagger, your Scotchman. Un-less he's broken down. Then he creeps along, clutching his purse. And the less there is in it, the harder he clutches. Gives him a funny gait, to make you laugh. But the big ones, now, they walk like they're climb-ing hills or slopping through their moo-ers. You can almost hear the heather brush their trows. When they got trows on proper." He cocked his head, all pride. "We always uses a Scotchman as a test, for him what wants to apprentice to a master heel-reader and embrace the high art himself. If he doesn't have the gift to tell a Scotchman right off, he'd only be an embarrassment to the perfession."

I dropped the shilling into his palm and started to move off, my thoughts a-boil.

"And here I thought you was an honest man," the fellow called after me.

I paused. "You have your shilling, sir."

"But I solved two questions for you, didn't I, your honor? And you said a shilling was my reward. So that would make two shillings."

The fellow was in the wrong, twas clear as day. And I do not misspeak when the matter concerns my funds. But I had such an excitement upon me that I gave him the second shilling without a quibble.

Wilkie led the way toward the bright end of the alley, I supposed to save us a trip back through the labyrinth of despair. He wore a look of discomfort, like a man whose bowels are tardy in their business. Clear it was that his thoughts had not kept up. And he did not like it.

"The fellow in the coffee house," I began, intent upon soothing him. For I wanted a friend and ally, not a foe. "The one with the stinking breath who pointed us here to begin with. He mentioned a certain Polly Perkins, if you recall. 'The White Lily of Kent.' A singer in a penny gaff in Eastcheap . . ."

Ah, yes. The light of recollection dawned.

"That was 'er, then," he said, in delayed astonishment.

"And don't you think there might be more to the business than an eel-man's unrequited infatuation? Now that we've seen her where he was rid of the watch?"

Wilkie stepped clear of a pile of waste and said, "I doesn't like the smell of this one bit."

The street at the end of the lane was bright and gay as a heathen bazaar, although it lacked the native's sense of order. Twas a market for secondhand clothes. And third- and fourth-hand, too, by the look of things. Smelling of attics and cellars, but active as ten-year-old boys, old, bent Jews sold all that might be worn. They bought, too, from rag-men and gentlemen out of pocket, from young sons troubled by secret debts and ladies so shy of being seen that they failed to haggle up to a proper price. But twas the Jews that captured my attention—at least as much as I had left to spare. A different race they seemed from my acquaintance, Mr. Moses Feinberg, of our Washington, whose trade resembled theirs only as a palace resembles a slum. Clean and light and orderly, M. Feinberg & Sons made purchasing almost a pleasure, although I am one chary of expenditures. But here all reeked of scanty margins and fears but half forgotten. It seemed to me a monument to America, that Moses Feinberg might come so far in life, and even dress him like a proper gentleman, while here his brethren wore black frocks cut long and big, and shabby hats, and forelocks out of Mr. Shakespeare's Venice. Of course, Britannia boasted Mr. Disraeli, who kept himself very fine. But he had turned from his ancestral faith.

I have grown fond of our American freedoms, where even the Jew may claim his lawful rights. We cannot blame a man for having faults, if we block every path that leads to virtue. Besides, I find the Jew a peculiar fellow. Ferocious when he bargains, he is honest to a fault when the deal is done. No Jew has ever cheated me, and I cannot say the same of Christian men.

I will admit I looked their barrows over, for I was in the market for a suit, and thought I might not need to pay full price. But all I saw were rags not fit for paupers.

How is it England conquered half the world?

Well, let that bide.

Guiding me through the thin-pursed crowd, Inspector Wilkie turned toward an avenue where we might rejoin our conveyance. But our progress was interrupted by the urgency of a constable in his swallowtail.

"Inspector!" he shouted across a brashness of boys. He pushed between a whisky-burned Irishman and a woman with the bitter look of a governess aged past her chances. "Inspector! Inspector Wilkie!"

Inspector Wilkie drew up by a barrow that catered to fallen gents. In truth, the inspector's own sober suit was worn from black to brown. I had marked him glancing over a display of re-whitened cuffs and collars and shirtfronts, although he had not stopped to look too closely.

Perhaps he was ashamed of his pocket's shallowness and would return when he might do business alone.

"What's the commotion, 'Iggins?" he asked. "Just what's all this commotion?"

The constable looked around at the crowd, which did not lack curiosity, then he drew us into an alley where cart mules bunched.

"We've all been put to find you," the constable said, "and to tell you they found the boy without 'is 'hand. The one what you was looking for. Under a bush in Regent's Park he was, where 'e scared Lady Wilmot to screaming."

"Dead?" Wilkie asked.

"Dead don't tell the 'alf of it, Inspector."

Twas then we might have made a dreadful blunder, for we shared an impulse to rush to Regent's Park. But there are times when I almost believe in the wisdom of Presbyterians, for some things seem predestined in this life. A gentleman of worn degree passed by the mouth of the alley, displaying a bulk to rival Mr. Barnaby, an acquaintance of mine and a champion doer at table. This strolling gentleman almost might have made a match for Mrs. Hepburn. A very John Bull he looked, and three times over.

Let me explain the importance of his passing.

With a boy cut up and murdered, it was left to me to make an idle comment. The girthy fellow had led my thoughts astray, as thoughts will go, despite our best intent.

"You must see all sorts in your duties," I said to the policeman. "That Mrs. Hepburn, the pawn-mother, for example." And here my spoken manners failed to answer, for I fear my words slipped out unkindly crude. "I've never seen a woman quite so fat."

The constable gave me a baffled look and even pushed his topper back off his forehead. Next, he lowered his whiskers down onto his collar.

"Mrs. 'Epburn?" he said. "Don't make me larf. Mrs. 'Epburn's thin as a tinker's dog."

I did not say another word to anyone, but took off at the closest thing to a run that a man with a bothered leg and a cane might manage.

The enormous woman was gone, of course. For we were not expected to return. She had taken her embroidery, but all else lay in place.

I looked down the long row of locked cabinets and chests.

"They will want opening," I said.

Wilkie, who lagged behind in his deductions, assumed a wary look.

"That's private property," he said. "We can't go—" Then he understood as well as I did. He even reached for a lock and began to tug it. But that would never do.

"Constable," I said to the fellow, Higgins, who had followed us as a good policeman will, "I presume you know the neighborhood. Might you find us an iron bar, or something of the like? Better still, two or three of them?"

He took off his topper and scratched his curls, then submitted his perplexity to Wilkie. "I'd 'ave to turn to a fellow suspected of all manner of criminalities, Inspector. A Grub Street 'ack named Peters what's gone bad. I know 'e'd 'ave all sorts of wicked implements."

"Well, do it, 'Enry. Go do it, for blue, bloody blazes, and stop wasting time," Wilkie told him. For he was hot now, too, and feared the worst.

Less determined fellows might have given up the task, for hard work it was. But Wilkie was my equal in perseverance. After the constable returned with the instruments required, the three of us broke open one trunk or cabinet after another, finding each as empty as the last. Except for the dust and insects, living and dead, there was nothing at all in any of the compartments. But we kept at our labors without pause, though it cost us many a pinch and bruise and splinter.

We found her in a seaman's chest, after an hour's sweating. It did not take an expert of Mr. Archibald's stature to see that she had not been dead a day.

"That's 'er," the constable confirmed. "That's 'er, all right. Lucy 'Epburn, that is. She won't be mourned, I can tell you."

The wizened body lay in the trunk, hardly larger than a child's corpse. The loose and ancient skin of her neck had been cut half through by the bite of the *Thuggee* cord.

"Well," Inspector Wilkie began, "and what am I to think now, Major Jones? Should I be looking for 'eathen 'Indoos what murders for pagan pleasure? Or should I be after Scotchmen with bagpipes and—"

My heart sank at the poverty of my mental faculties. I had missed one chance after another. With hardly half a dozen chests remaining, off I went at my crabby trot again, awkward on the stairs as I always am and chased along by the ceaseless wail of that child in the shut-up room. Out of the close I went for the second time that day, turning down the street in the direction that should have taken me straight to the blind heel-reader.

He was gone, of course.

A dozen things seemed too clear for my Christian comfort, yet nothing added up to any sense.

Was I supposed to chase a kilted phantom? Or look for Indian murderers in the alleys? Was I being put off one scent and onto another? If so, which trail was which? And who was who? I could not banish the thought of that child's hand. And now the rest of his body lay in wait.

I have a son of my own, our little John. I see him in every child that passes by. In this hard life of ours, so unforgiving.

Nearing despair, I caned my way down to a noisy clutch of women. I could not tell from their tones if they were having it out or just conversing merrily. Their chatter rang loud and harsh in a Welshman's ear, for we seek music in each whispered word.

"I beg your pardon, ladies," I said, which made them go all mum, though the youngest got the giggles at the sight of me. I am not impressive at a glance, not tall nor winningly handsome. "Pardon me, but did any of you happen to mark the direction that blind fellow took when he left here? The one who was sitting just down there all the morning?"

Every one of them looked at me, and I knew what they were thinking: What does that uniform mean to me? And what do I risk by answering?

At last, a redhead missing her upper teeth propped her hands on her hips and spoke. "That's a good one. Ain't it, girls?" The giggling bloomed into chuckles. "If 'e was blind, the Queen farts gold and silver. That's a trick as old as Methusalee's arse, them egg-whites over the eyes." She crossed her arms beneath her startling bosom. "Down the lane, 'e went, like 'e 'eard they was pouring free beer for every comer. No sooner than you and that buster went off to Jew Street."

My back come up. Now you might think that I had been fair beaten, and fooled enough to put me in my place. But no fight ends until a man gives up. I have fought my way, God forgive me, from Chilianwalla to Pittsburg Landing, and know that a soldier must see the crisis through. We do not know the victor until the finish. And this particular day was far from over.

And I was thinking clearly now. I saw that I had been stumbling blind—far blinder than the heel-reader ever was. I had been led along, for whatever reason, by those who knew far more of me than they should. There was many a matter I saw before me now, from here to wicked Washington, and I would have a talk with Mr. Adams. For he, too, had been duped, it seemed to me.

But first things first. I had much to assemble. And more to learn, beginning back in that close.

"They've made us into bleeding fools, they 'ave," Inspector Wilkie declared, though not so loud that Constable Higgins might hear.

"That they have," I said. "But we are not finished, nor will we be finished this day. Come with me, please, for we have a call to make."

Now, there are things a man cannot explain. At times, his blindness seems a thing remarkable. At other times, he has an inspiration, but cannot give the reason, try as he might. And I have learned to trust my soldier's instincts. Thus, I survived when better lives were lost. When the voice inside us shouts, we must pay attention.

I drew him back through the muck of the passage and into the little courtyard by the stair that led to Mrs. Hepburn's enterprise. The child was still at it, wailing to beat the band. Her throat was hoarse to bleeding, by the sound, but still she would not be comforted. If anyone was offering her a comfort.

I knocked upon the flimsy door that fronted the shut-up room. Inside, the howling redoubled, sparked to a terror.

A kind-featured woman appeared to answer my summons. Her face was even scrubbed, if somewhat care-worn.

"I'm sorry, sir, if my Jenny's been disturbing you." The haste of embarrassment colored her speech to a blush. "She's been done a dreadful fright and won't be told."

"I have not come to complain, madame. Only to put a question or two. If you will permit me."

After judging my unfamiliar uniform, she gave a thought to Wilkie, who looked like a mortician whose trade was slack.

"As you pleases, sir." But she was frayed. "Oh, Jenny, won't you stop, now?" she called into the shadows of her dwelling. Then she come back to me again. "If you'd like to come inside, sir? Mind the stoop."

We crouched inside. Twas no more than a closet of a room, where darkness triumphed over a single candle. Cheap wax sputtered, and the corners smelled of Mankind.

"She gets the terrors, she does," the mother told us. "Though never like today, not ever before." As if she read my thoughts, she added, "I had to shut up the window, for she thought they was coming to get her."

Watching us as sheep will watch their slaughterer, the child declined to a whimper, then to a sob. Her breathing was labored and she wore a fevered look. She did not move her eyes from me, not even to look at her mother. Twas strange, for usually I am a figure of fun to children. They like me, though I cannot tell you why.

"Who?" I asked. "Who did she think would come after her?"

"Oh, she's always making up her stories," the mother said. "The other children won't leave off her, for all the tales she tells. You can't believe a word the poor thing says."

"But what did she say today? What did she think she saw?"

The woman made a wry face, red with shame. "Oh, a fine tale this one was. Though she's a good girl, mind, my Jenny. Only fanciful, and special in her ways. Up early she was, and the pot was full from my George. So she let herself outside to do what comes needful—for she's never the one to mess, sir. And in she comes wailing and wild and all wet from herself. Screaming and jabbering tales of a great, big man out on the stairs, with a red mask over his face. And brown hobgoblins dancing along to his tune. He lifted up the mask, she said, and showed her the face of the Devil."

That should have been enough. Enough for one day, or a lifetime.

But Constable Higgins took pride in thorough work. Just then, he come bounding down from the pawn-mother's shop.

"They wasn't all empty," he cried. "I found this in a drawer. In the very last cabinet."

He stood in the light of the doorway. Holding out a plain, brass watch.

Five

I had to gain control of that watch, but Inspector Wilkie kept it from my grasp. Shifting it from one hand to another, as a child might do a ball of India rubber, he tantalized me. For he had come to realize that his suspicions did not match my own.

Back in the police rig we were, headed for Regent's Park and the dead boy's body. My thoughts were so intent upon the watch that I hardly marked the bustling world outside. That brass disk rolled from one of Wilkie's hairy paws to the other, then back again. I wanted to reach out and seize it.

A contest of intertwined carriage wheels delayed us by a rank of cabs and horses. The air smelled of hay and fresh droppings, and the day blazed.

Of a sudden, the inspector closed his fist. Hiding the watch to tease me.

"Now . . . not that I'm suspicious," he began, as the rig rolled free again. "For 'ow could I be suspicious in the least? But I can see 'ow it might strike a body that this 'ere watch is uncommon interesting to certain parties, Major Jones." He gave me a sideward glance, dark eyes peering through a thatch of whiskers. "Almost more interesting than people falling down dead on every side of us, what with eel-men and Mrs. 'Epburn and the boy. To say nothing of your own countryman, the Reverend Mr. Campbell, of which person we are now bereft." He opened his fist again, palm up, and regarded the timepiece. Plain brass it was, indeed. On the outside. "Now, 'ow is it that this 'ere watch is so interesting to certain parties, I arsk you?"

A Methodist must not lie. He dare not. No more than any proper

Christian should. But the world is real and, sometimes, out of accord. It will not march in step with men of faith. I wondered how much of the truth to share with Wilkie. Oh, now I understood the pain that Mr. Adams suffered from those dissemblings labeled as diplomacy. I did not wish to lie, no more than he did. And, yet, I could not offer all the truth.

"It will have great value," I said carefully, "to the Reverend Mr. Campbell's intimates. Think you, Inspector: Would you not wish a remembrance of someone dear and lost most unexpected? And what else is there left to have and hold of the fellow? Clear it is that Mr. Campbell was poor in worldly goods, for he was no high churchman or such like, but a proper Christian parson." I watched those black-haired fingers close over the watch again. "I cannot retrieve the little money from Mr. Campbell's purse. But I hoped to have his watch, see. For the benefit of those he left behind. Although the watch is a poor-enough thing in itself."

Wilkie snapped open the cover, which he had done enough times to excite me. "But look 'ere, Major. Look 'ere at all this enameling and the like. You seen the bit of fancy-work yourself. Don't it seem queer 'ow a plain brass watch—not to say outright 'ow it seems a most unworthy watch—don't it seem queer 'ow such a watch 'as got a fancy picture of foreign parts all 'id inside it? Why, it might even be a picture of your India. Of which you 'ave spoken yourself this very day."

Well, he was barking up the wrong tree there. For I had no connection to the watch beyond the one assigned me.

Oxford Street sketched past the window, bright and now familiar. With that crippled artilleryman begging on his corner.

"And," the inspector continued, "I must admit it did seem odd 'ow you was able to describe it all so perfect to Mrs. 'Epburn. Or to the Mrs. 'Epburn what really wasn't Mrs. 'Epburn. But you takes my point." He snapped the lid shut again. "Now, I was given to believe 'ow you never 'ad laid eyes upon the good parson before. Until you met 'im yesterday, in 'is belated situation."

"I had never seen Mr. Campbell in my life. Or heard his name."

"Then 'ow, begging your pardon, did you come to be a scholar regarding 'is watch?"

"Mr. Adams described it to me."

Wilkie's canine eyes narrowed, tensing up the flesh of that well-furred face. "And 'ow would it be that an 'igh diplomatic fellow like your Mr. Adams would know so much about a lowly parson's watch, then?"

"Mr. Campbell called upon him. He told you that himself."

"And showed 'im the watch? But why should 'e do that, Major Jones? Does Mr. Adams take a special interest in watches? Or only in certain watches, per'aps?"

"It *is* a curious watch," I pointed out. "As you yourself have remarked, Inspector Wilkie. Perhaps it held a special meaning for Mr. Campbell. And thus became a topic of conversation between them."

Wilkie nodded, but twas clear he was unconvinced. "It's only that a body 'as to wonder. Not that I means to imply suspicions, not in the least. It's only 'ow as this entire business confuses me. It just don't seem like the doings of the criminal class, with which I 'ave a lifelong association, so to speak. There's too much complication 'ere. Too much complication by 'alf, if you takes my meaning clear. Your criminal likes things simple, Major Jones. 'E sees what 'e wants and grabs it. 'E scratches where it itches. Even the murderer don't think more than two steps on, if that far. But 'ere we 'ave a series of commotions and complications like I never 'ave seen in one day. Or in a month, for that matter."

We clattered past another digging site, all a-chug with a boisterous steam-engine. It sounded as if its fat, iron belly might blow the world to pieces.

"Only think of it, would you?" the inspector rattled on. "I 'as a dead parson, to begin with, and tales of other Americans dead afore 'im. And this parson arrives drudged up from a basket of eels—which is not an 'abitual resort of the criminal class. An American major comes into town, all on that very same day. Just in time to 'ave 'im a sniff of the corpus delectable. And the very next thing, this American major—who is a fellow of a most peculiar background, by the way—'e finds a little boy's 'and chopped off in 'is bed. In a fancy box, no less. Then off we goes together to Billingsgate Market, to partake of a conversation with the eel-man. But the eel-man what found the parson is dead 'imself, back in the piss row. And nobody claims to 'ave seen a thing, though there's crowds enough for a racing day at Epsom and the sun is shining down so bright you could count the 'airs on a cat. And off we goes running after a watch what 'as been reported as given into pawn, but it seems a great arrangement 'as been made to fool at least the one of us. There's lies being told like it's Saturday night in Dublin, and there's blind men telling fortunes in the alleys. Except they ain't blind, and the fortunes ain't good. And don't the pawn-mother—the real one now—turn up deader than Raglan in the Cri-mee. And the 'andless boy's dead, too, amongst fancy neighbors, which we will shortly see with our own eyes. In the meantime, the pawn-mother's shop 'as been robbed of everything what was in it." He held out the watch, almost as if he were going to give it to me. "Of everything except the watch we 'appens to be looking for. About which the American major may know more than 'e 'as seen fit to tell a certain inspector of the police."

He shoved the watch into his waistcoat pocket, where I heard it clink against the fellow's own timepiece.

"What's a body to think, now, Major Jones? Even a body what ain't the least suspicious? Should I be looking for black 'Indoo buggers, snuck in from 'Er Majesty's rare and distant dominions? Or should I be looking for Scotchmen, as 'alf the population of London seems to want me to?" His smiled dissolved. "Or should I, per'aps, be considering Americans?"

"If by Americans," I told him readily, "you mean those loyal to the Confederate government in Richmond, perhaps you should be considering them, indeed."

"And just 'ow is that now, Major Jones?"

"Look you, Inspector Wilkie . . ." Oh, I was thinking fast in desperation, for I did not want to tell more than I should—and yet, I would not tell an outright lie, if I could help it. ". . . it seems to me that the Confederates would like very much to embarrass Mr. Adams. Plain enough that seems from the letter found upon the person of Mr. Campbell."

"A forgery, as I recalls. Didn't someone claim it was a forgery? Although I doesn't remember any proof."

"It certainly seemed," I said, carefully, "to have had a deceptive purpose. I do not think we could trust the letter's contents entirely." I turned full-on to Wilkie, conjuring the granite face I had wielded as a sergeant, when such as Jimmy Molloy stepped out of line. "Do *you*, Inspector Wilkie? Would *you* trust such a letter entirely? Given your experience of Mankind? And the circumstances under which the letter was found?"

He grunted, slow to find himself an answer.

I did all that I could to turn the tide. Or at least to shift the topic.

"The Confederates, see," I said to him, "are men. As you and I are men. Some are good, and some are bad, and most are in between. Some are brave as Johnny Seekh, and others are naught but cowards, for all their boasting. But the Rebel cause is a bad one, and there is true. Say what they might, they want to keep their slaves. And that is what our war is all about, Inspector Wilkie. No matter what you hear shouted from Richmond. Or even what you hear proclaimed from Washington." I leaned a little toward him as we passed a rank of high and fine town houses. "Do you believe men should be held as slaves?"

"I don't see what that 'as to do with matters," Wilkie said. "We ain't got slaves in London. Or even in Ireland."

"But *do* you believe that men should be held as slaves?" I pressed.

He twisted his face so his black whiskers bristled into a thousand quills. "Look 'ere," he said. "It ain't none of my affair, not that I can see. But if you 'as to know, well, then I'll tell you: I doesn't much care for black 'eathens meself, from what little I 'ave seen of them. But I doesn't think any man should be a slave. Why . . . why slavery's like putting a fellow in prison what 'asn't done anything criminal. It's worse than sending an innocent man to Australia." His lips grew narrow and hard. "No, says I, put shackles on the guilty, and do it proper. Give 'im English justice, front and back. But if I 'as to choose, I ain't for slaving. For there's them as wouldn't stop at chaining niggers."

That was, I learned, the very summary of the attitude of the English working man, who gained his daily bread through honest labor. Twas only the rich and high, those born to privilege or risen to power, who favored the Southron cause. But the working man's wishes do not have weight in Britain. It is the mighty men who will decide.

But let that bide.

Our course took us past the American legation on Portland Place, although we did not stop. I wondered if the inspector had taken us by it to hint a likely connection.

Shortly thereafter, we pulled to the side of the street by a fine green sward, which I assumed to be Regent's Park in name. Twas just set off from a crescent of handsome houses. A welter of policemen fussed about on the grass, between long ranks of roses. Sweating they were in their tight collars and high top hats, and when they bent over the tails of their coats spread out like the feathers of gamebirds. Measuring from here to there and back again, they strutted about importantly, sharp as clerks in a shop that serves the poor.

Beyond the iron fence rails, smart-dressed neighbors mixed with downstairs maids. All murmuring they were. For curiosity does not have a class.

Still grumpy—just as you and I might be—Inspector Wilkie led me across the lawn. A sergeant greeted us. He had that English sort of skin that looks as if it has been scalded and his whiskers were strawberry blond.

"This way, Inspector, if you please." His voice was somber and gruff. "And I'll show you a crime no Englishman would commit."

Two police fellows drew back a canvas to reveal the poor boy's ruin. Careful they were to keep the little body hidden from the good citizens pushing up to the fence. For this was not a sight for innocent eyes.

The boy had been mistreated in a manner I will not detail in full. Suffice to say there was blood upon him where there should not be blood on a boy. And, yes, his right hand was missing. His left had been hacked off, too, along with his feet. Small as roundshot for a six-pounder gun, his severed head had been placed near a battered shoulder, perhaps by the police. Still other parts had been torn away, but I would not dismay you more than needful.

A sin and a shame it was.

Wilkie turned away. With a look that paired sickness and rage. Fierce as a Pushtoon the fellow looked, when that tribesman's women have been glimpsed by a stranger's eyes. I dared not approach him for a considerable interval. Instead, I gestured to the policemen to lower the canvas again.

I tried to tell myself the deed might have been done even had I not been sent to England, that the crime might have been an action foreordained. But I could not believe it. The human beast who had done this thing had started out to send that hand to me, but the doing had only sparked his sickly appetites. And he had feasted on the child's misery. It could not be denied, though: I had been the reason why the killer raised his hand, although I still could not see through the purpose.

I felt a certain weight of blame upon me.

How could a human do such a thing and still walk upright among us? He should be down crawling in gutters and shrieking in horror. He should . . . but let that bide. I fear I am an insufficient Christian. For there are things I never can forgive.

Oh, how I wanted to find the man—or the men—who had done this murder. And yet, I wondered, what if that was their purpose? To divert me? To bait me with a child's death, to distract me from a war and secret plots?

Why not just kill *me* and be done with it?

He knew me, see, the one who killed that boy. He knew me better than reason said he could. The killer, or killers, whoever that might be, had made the day entire into a theater. Twas not like Mr. Shakespeare's stage of a world, where players strut and fret from wrong to right. All London had been nothing but a puppet show. And I had been the creature jerked on strings.

Let that bide. Oh, let it bide, for the love of our sweet Savior.

Walking away from the child's corpse, I thought of my son John. I went up to Wilkie, who stood beside a lovely burst of roses. With a thorn in his heart.

His rage had burned down to despair. When he looked at me, his suspicions paused and he spoke as a father, not as a policeman.

"I can't believe such a thing," he said. "Tell me, 'ow can a man believe it? Such a thing as that?"

I muttered something short of proper speech.

"It ain't as if I'm green," Wilkie continued. "Seventeen year a policeman, and a fellow's far from green." His fingers touched a rose, as if softness were wanted. "I know well enough what's done to boys. To little girls, as well. It makes a body sick." He raised his haunted eyes. "And still call themselves gentlemen, they do. A child of ten, still fresh, won't cost you 'alf a pound, if you ain't particular. The poor don't matter, Major Jones." Those eyes of his are what I will remember. Like two flames dying down behind a grate. "I can't believe such a thing was done. I seen it and can't believe it."

The man looked lost. At least I had the solace of God's map.

Now, I have heard it trumpeted that the Bible is not true, because the dates are wrong and stones say otherwise. It is the fashion of our times to mock. But dates are not the meaning of the Book, no more than mathematics explain morals. And rocks are rocks, though they be old or new. It doesn't matter if this earth is ten years old or a million. Let bitter men count up all those begettings. It is the tales in the Book that speak the truth, from Adam and Eve to Paul and all his wanderings. I read it as the Lord's report on Mankind, with worse things done than were done to that poor boy. Each and every one of us is Cain, and when we read the Word we find ourselves. The Bible is no book of calculations, where two and two makes four, all clear as glass. It is the very storybook of Man, not a clutch of numbers to be reckoned. When Jesus stopped to teach, He did not tabulate. He sat down in our midst and told us tales, so that our simple minds might understand. The Bible shows us who we truly are: Job and David, and Judas and Herod, too. The Marys and the Esthers. And the Eves. Numbers do not figure in the least.

If still you say the Bible is not true, I will say that no book is more honest.

Forgive me. I speak too much of things beyond my ken. But when I am sick at heart, I lift up mine eyes. Even on the cloudiest of days.

Inspector Wilkie would not be moved from his spot by the fragrant roses. Not one of his subordinates approached him. Perhaps he had a habit of bad temper, although he had not shown the like to me. In any case, they left us there. Apart.

"I thought," I began, hoping to lift him out of his slough of despond, "that we might go to the penny gaff tonight. To learn about this lass, 'The White Lily of Kent.' It must be done, see. Although I do not favor such entertainments."

"You go," he said, surprising me. His voice was changed and chastened. "You go yourself, Major. You go on. And be so good as to tell us what you find."

"But I'm not—"

"I'm going 'ome." His eyes had but the glow of embers now. "It's Saturday night, and I'm going 'ome to my Albert and my Alice." His voice was almost shaking, as if he feared he might find his own beloved children dead and abused. Twas frightful to listen to the man, who had been so diligent and strong an hour before. "I need to 'ave me a think," he told me, "and so I'm going 'ome."

I found I did not have a word to say.

The inspector held out his hand. " 'Til Monday morning, Major Jones. And do your best to stay clear of any more murders, at least for tonight and tomorrow. I think the town could use a bit of quiet."

I took the offered hand. And found the Reverend Mr. Campbell's watch in my palm.

"I'll know where to look if I needs it back," he told me.

Off he went, slumped, with his hands behind his back. One policeman took a step toward him, then thought better of it. Others wrapped the child's body in the canvas.

As I was leaving, I heard a newspaper fellow arguing with a constable. The scribbler was dressed as bright as a betting man and he claimed the public had every right to learn about the misdeed there in the garden. I wonder. I think our modern world lacks the benefit of decorum. We flock to hear of scandal, but those who suffer need a bit of privacy. Why do we want to know the worst of others, and rush toward any suffering on display? The truth is we are cruel as Joseph's brothers.

Let that bide, too. We must have faith, and go on, and do our best.

In the meantime, I had a tumble of things to do. The watch burned in my hand—I had to get me to a private place where I could unscrew the cover. And I would have to seek out Mr. Adams, though it was Saturday afternoon and reaching for evening. And I recalled that he had mentioned plans. Then I must get me a suit of clothing to replace my uniform, and do it before the shops closed for the night. For an officer's honorable garments must not be seen inside a penny gaff. And, frankly, I had come to feel conspicuous.

Next, I needed to bathe myself before proceeding upon my investigation, for twas Saturday, after all. Excuse me the indelicacy, but I believe the man who washes his every part most regular is a better man for it. The fellow who bathes himself once a week is happier and healthier, and doubtless a better companion to all he meets. Besides, my wife insists, and that is that.

I understand a bathtub is no Jordan. We cannot scrub away our sins with soap. But a good wash always seems a proper start.

~

I took me down along Portland Place, until I was out of sight. Then I slipped into a mews and took out the watch. Hard luck mine was. The screw that fixed the lid to the secret compartment would not be undone with a pen-knife or a fingernail. It wanted the tools of a watchmaker or jeweler. Now, I had nearly reached our legation and the afternoon was running away, with evening on its heels. High folk will not be at home on a Saturday night, for that is when they take each other's measure and call it society.

I decided to carry the watch to Mr. Adams, before he went off to his doings. We might open it together, for his wife must have a device to loose the screw. A good wife knows the tricks for finding out secrets, no matter how expertly they are hid.

I met with a disappointment. The servant who answered the bell was sour as vinegar, for he did not know me and he judged me slight. With a great sniffing up and an even greater looking down, he informed me that "His Excellency" had gone to the country and wanted nothing to do with the world until Monday. Only a general's arrogance rivals a butler's toward those he does not believe he needs to please. The difference, of course, is that servants have a purpose.

I stepped away and things picked up a bit. On my progress toward Baker Street I found a watchmaker willing to assist me. He would not let me touch his tools, but undid the screw himself. As he worked beside his smoking lamp, his tongue peeked through his lips at his laboring fingers.

The lid come off. And then the enamel layer fell away, just as foretold to me by Mr. Adams.

The compartment behind it was empty.

As I had feared.

"Well, there's a thing, ain't it?" the watchmaker declared. He gave me a knowing look I did not like. "The perfect hiding place for billy-doo." He winked. "A gent can't tell a rascal from a saint by looking, now can he?" He held the watch toward me in three pieces. "I can let you have twelve shillings for the ticker."

I bid him reassemble the parts, although it made him grumble. He charged me half a crown for his work, though it did not take a tuppence of his time. But that is London, where Mammon is enthroned.

Next, I found a tailor's shop that offered clothes ready-made. The proprietor was a Pole well past his prime, with a hanging mustache and billows of ashen hair. The whole world finds its way to London, see. He kitted me up in a black frock coat that almost fit and did not seem too dear. I matched it with a sober black waistcoat, but picked gray for my trousers, since he let me have them cheaper. Now, the Pole can be a gloomy sort, when not aroused by passions, but this old fellow was positively charming. He agreed to alter the cuffs of the coat and to hem my chosen trousers on the spot. I am strong in the chest and shoulders, see, but my arms and legs have no proportionate length. For I am small, though capable.

The winning grace was that I was an American. From the moment when I told him that, he would have altered the sun and the moon to suit me. He pinched a pair of eyeglasses onto his nose and set to work most fervently.

It come out the fellow was a revolutionist.

"Soon now," he told me, as he cut and stitched. "Soon now, you will see. Everybody will see. Poland will be free, there will be a free Poland. No Austrians, no Prussians. No black cossacks with the whip. Only Polish peoples. Then we will be free, like the Americans."

He looked up from his battered sewing table. "Socialism is coming, the revolution. All men . . ." he drew his needle through the cloth, which seemed to sigh, ". . . all men are brothers. Yes? As in America, I think." Biting off a thread, he confided, "In Poland, I am professor. In Cracow. In Jagellonian University." His eyes shone in remembrance. "It is very old, you know. Most old, our university. I am teaching the philosophy. Then comes the 'Forty-eight and the people say, 'Now we will have freedom.' But more of the Austrian soldiers come. Bang-bang. I go to Warsawa. To make the fight against the Russians there. But they are too many. So many killings they are making." The hot light in his eyes might have melted all the ice in all the arctic seas. "In the prison I have been. In Siberia. Very terrible, the things I see. Still, I go back. Poland must be free. No? Is that not true? Must not all men be free?"

I fear I was a disappointment to him. The truth is I know little enough of Poland and am not certain of its state of government, although I believe the Tsar has a heavy hand. Other foreigners were mucking about there, too, to hear that old professor and tailor tell it. But, while I do believe men should be free, I am no friend to uproar and disorder. As Mr. Carlyle has explained, most revolutions finish worse than they started. With dreams cut short, and heads cut off, and soldiers cut down by the thousands.

I began to speak of our own war and of slavery, but that only riled him the worse.

"Yes, yes! The black slave! He will rise up!" The fellow's mustache trembled with excitement. "And here, here in this England, the working man soon makes the revolution. Here, right here! In Manchester, I think. In such places. To be free of the rich people and the boot of the government. The system of the Capitalism—it all comes down. Very soon, I think. It cannot go on making only the poverty for the people. The worker is the slave of the Capitalism, like the Negro. Perhaps your American war becomes everywhere a war—and then the English worker rises up. Because he is told to fight against the black man, but he will not do that. Perhaps it starts this way, you see?"

I did not see. And I wanted no part of any bigger war. Our Union had enough to eat without a second helping. Worse, I knew full well what the English working man, given a bayonet, would do to a black or brown hide wherever he found it.

A thing occurred to me that might both please the tailor and aid myself.

"Would you happen to know," I asked, "one *Herr* Karl Marx, a German revolutionist?"

The tailor made a dismissive face. "I know. Yes. Him I know." The fellow shook his head. "He makes no revolutions, that man. Once, I think, maybe he does. But he only makes the talk and goes to the library. Every day to the library. To make his foolish writing no one reads." The tailor paused at his eye-straining labors. "The time of books is gone. Finished. I am professor, I know. Now it is time for the world revolution."

"Yes, but would you happen to have the fellow's address?"

He did. All written down in a book, which seemed an incautious practice for a conspirator. Mr. Marx might be found at 9 Grafton Terrace, in Kentish Town, which was just north of London and near the country joys of Hampstead Heath. Firebrand or no, he was not in hiding.

But the revolutionist tailor tried to warn me: "He wastes your time only, this Marx. Always talking. Talking and writing." He tapped his head. "He is more professor than me. Too much thinking. Now it is time for the war and the Socialist revolution! Here, take this. You try, yes? I think they fit you now, your coat and trousers."

They sat all proper and I paid the fellow. Although it pinched to count the money out.

Fortunately, I conserved the price of an omnibus, for Baker Street was but a stroll away. Before I went back to the hotel, with my parcel and my fears of what I might find, I bought a meat pie from a vendor and ate it in the street. I was determined to pursue a proper economy, see. All London was a horror of high prices, and I near expected to be charged a toll for walking and taxed for every breath I took of the air.

The pie made a good repast and was filling enough, although I spit some gristle on the pavings.

I went up the hotel stairs in trepidation. Concerned that I might find the boy's other hand—or worse—upon my bed. But my room was neat and orderly, though stuffy as the punishment cell in Delhi. Down I went again and asked the porter if I might have a tub of water in my room. Twas queer. The night before, the man had been gay and friendly, at least until he tired of our conversation, but now he was as sullen as a bear. He made it clear he did not want to be bothered, which hardly seemed a proper hospitality. To be fair, he doubtless had been questioned by the police about severed hands and dark-of-the-night intruders. Likely, I was no longer a favored guest.

Finally, he offered a tub of water. "Hardly used," he said, and left in a room just vacated by a lodger. Now, you may think me particular, but I will not bathe in another's leavings, except, of course, on bath day with my family. It required the production of some shillings—the city was extortionate to an outrage—to prevail upon him to haul up a tub, though a small one, and a bucket for me to carry my own water.

My bath smelled before I got in it, for London is a city poorly piped. Nonetheless, the experience was salutary. A cold bath always sets a man to rights. I drew on a change of linens and my new clothes, and started on my way to the depths of sin.

Six

The crush outside the penny gaff was shameless, with male and female pressed in a pack and hollering loud as recruits on pay-day night. I fear some were intoxicated and, sadly, not only the boys. Oh, colorful they were, that squirming mass of apprentices and laboring lads, of chambermaids off for the night and huckster girls freed of flower carts and fruit trays. Got up bright in cast-off clothes, a benefit of certain domestic employments, the best-appointed females paraded the fashions of seasons past. Some of the boys affected velvet coats, despite the summer's heat, while others, mannered worst of all, had stripped off their jackets and turned back their sleeves in public, with all the license of secluded artisans. But the herding together it was that struck me deepest, a mixing of the sexes indiscriminate, with bodies pushed up tight to one another, close as soldiers on a freezing night. Those young girls, some of them fair in the common way, did not display the least regard for modesty.

There were fights, of course. For some male hands explored beyond all permissible boundaries in that tangle. But, mostly, there was laughter and good feeling of a depth that proper folk would hardly credit. Twas Saturday night, and even joyless lives seemed full of hope.

"Which 'un was it, Mabel? Tell me, an' I'll put 'is teeth out 'is arse."

"Go on with you. Ain't you the fresh one, Charlie?"

"I told 'im, I did, 'e could put 'is lips right 'ere, but to leave 'is bloody 'ands off me."

"Oh, you din't!"

"I sent Bill off for an ice, so we got two minutes."

"Joanie? Where are you got to, Joanie-girl?"

"I put an 'alf couter down on the Lion of Lambeth, though I couldn't get no odds. Knock down Joey Bones, 'e will, so's the bastard won't get up."

"Don't be afraid to flash it, ladies. That's what we're all 'ere for."

Such was their talk, to the limits of my understanding. For many spoke true cockney, the maddening tongue of those born to the bells of St. Mary-le-Bow. The penny gaff itself appeared no more than a private house, altered to serve an alien purpose. Above that steaming rumpus in front of the doors, a great span of canvas displayed a painted female form, with blond locks and a finger raised to her chin. The lettering read:

Dr. Beezil's Universal Musical Theater Proudly Presents
For the Amusement of the Discriminating Public
Miss Polly Perkins
The White Lily of Kent
The Toast of Paris!
Newly Returned From Her Grand Tour
And Other Artists of Fame and Reputation

This seemed to me no venue for a Methodist. But let that bide. I had a task before me, and I would do it.

Tired I was, and sweated despite my bath, for I had sat crammed into a succession of omnibuses on my progress across London, confined in the closest quarters with ladies and gentlemen whose circumstances or good sense did not afford them private conveyances or the extravagance of cabs. On Saturday night, all the city seemed abroad, rushing here and there, to sample the world. Then, setting down by Mansion House and all its glittering glories, I had walked the last few streets to save the fare.

And I will tell you: For all the gaiety of those streets, there was plentiful sorrow, too. Public houses blazed with fancy fixtures, their gas jets sparkling on leaded glass and brass, even where the fallen looked weak in the pocket. The welcome-halls of Hell they were, foaming with damnation. The evening had gathered the warmth of the day and, although a clouding, darkening sky promised relief in the night, the city remained an oven to bake its children. It only made those weak souls drink the more, and though the light of day had not yet left us, the gutters counted men among their refuse.

Women of unfortunate profession walked abroad in startling numbers—passing in the omnibus, I had even seen them strutting in front of Newgate—and I could only wonder at the variety of their patronage. How many men must break their sacred vows, or lose their youthful health, to keep so vast an army of sinners marching? To say nothing of the fate of those sad women themselves. I even imagined I saw Mr. Gladstone pleading with one such in a shadowed nook, but doubtless the man I glimpsed bore but a resemblance.

Now I stood by the penny gaff—one of half a hundred in those streets—afraid I would not even get me in. For I did not see how the building before me could hold the swarming crowd.

When at last the chargers opened the doors, you would have thought the weak bound to be crushed. I edged forward, wielding my cane to keep me from unfortunate embarrassments, but could not get me anywhere close to the entrance. When Mr. Carlyle wrote of the Bastille's storming, his language failed to capture a penny gaff.

Girls squealed, some in delight. Nor were they shy of cursing any boy who stepped on their precious shoes or trailing hems. Their stock of words seemed drawn from docks and barracks.

I even think some made a game of touching.

Twas not that I wished to see the show, you understand, for I am one for hymns and not vulgarity. But I had to secure an interview with Miss Perkins. And that demanded entrance and a wait.

Near despair I was, when a fellow with a bright yellow neck-cloth come up to me.

"There you go, guv'nor, there you go," he told me, gesturing to the nearest door and shoving patrons roughly from his path. "A gent like you will want the two-penny row. The better to see what shouldn't be shown at all."

I did not want the two-penny row, for one penny seemed a sufficient contribution. And there were decided limits to what I wished to observe. But before I knew it, the fellow had me inside the lobby, such as it was. Thrusting me on like a prisoner bound for execution, he forced me through that welter of flesh and scents—above all, the scent of Woman, which draws as it repels—and I found myself faced with a line of chairs set halfway toward the stage. They were cordoned off from the rest of the room and raised up on a platform, with rows of benches in front and standing-room rearward.

My place was between a fleshy gentleman, who had brought along the drumstick of a fowl to fortify him during the performance, and a twitching fellow who smelled of paints and turpentine.

The tout in the yellow tie took off his hat, revealing a scalp time had begun to harvest, and thrust out his palm toward me.

"Tuppence for your placement, guv'nor. Though something additional wouldn't be taken amiss, between us gents."

I saw no choice and gave the fellow his two pennies. Then I added a ha'penny, for I wished the goodwill of all who might assist me on my way to Polly Perkins.

He rolled his eyes and took himself off to secure another victim.

Now I will tell you: Rarely have I seen a room so desolate. A proper theater it was not, nor was it clean, though that is a separate matter. It once had been a house, indeed, but the walls were all knocked through but for the brace beams, opening the space so the crowd could see the stage rigged down in front. Upstairs, the half of the floor had been chopped away to create a balcony. As the benches filled, planks sagged above my head. The walls had been painted with crude panoramas, suggestive of foreign parts and wild adventures, and the windows that lacked worn drapes had been boarded over, to keep the poor from having something free. Lasses offered ginger beer and papered toffees for sale as the youth of London rushed to claim their places. Rough their language may have been, but they got along in their way, I give them that. They reminded me a bit of fresh-made soldiers, bluffing confidence but raw yet in their hearts. Their manners were crude, but after my shock at their language, I found them a happy lot. And happiness is a rare thing in this world.

The proprietor packed the room as full as ever it might be filled, then a shabby curtain parted to a musical flourish. A little band of piano, concertina and fiddle served the house as an orchestra. And out stepped a fellow got up in a clownish exaggeration of the already-exaggerated dress of the males in the audience.

"Snarky Gifford," my neighbor explained, enjoying a bite of the drumstick as he spoke, "always makes me larf, old Snarky do."

The fellow onstage was a patterer. And I must tell you: Shocked I was by his language, but not half so much as I was by his physical gestures. He simulated the grossest of the body's habits and pantomimed acts that words may not report. In the course of his jokes and skits, he made noises, some of them purporting to be the most intimate of feminine sighs, while others would have made a milch-cow blush. He pleased the crowd, although he mocked its members—many of whom he seemed to know by name.

Next come an artless tenor, one Chauncey O'Dair, who gave us his rendition of "If You're After Mabel's Sweeties, You'll Pay Dear for Every Bite," followed by "Jimmy Stuck It Where It Shouldn't Never, Ever Go." The rhymes in the verses were as inventive as they were indecent. Then he gave us all a proper ballad, which was not so well received by the lads in the back, but put a glisten in the female eye. No great applause followed that melody of unrequited love, though. It seemed that those who paid had paid for laughter.

Then a fellow took the stage with a magical act. His tricks would not have impressed a Punjab villager. Only when his conjuring had to do with obscene matters did he win some brief approval from the crowd. But they were restless now, with the heat swelling up like a boil. Unruly, they began to stamp their feet, and to whistle and call cats. Plaster dust, and perhaps worse, sifted through the boards above me, dirtying the shoulders of my new coat.

Twas not only laughter that they wanted, though such amusement was welcome enough as a prelude. They had paid their pennies to hear, and to see, Miss Polly Perkins, the Toast of Paris, returned from her Grand Tour.

When she come out at last, they howled and screamed. I do believe I heard planks crack above me. And there she was, in pink trimmed up with lilac hems and ribbons, bare-shouldered, and flaunting her stockinged ankles for all to see. She curtsied, not entirely without grace, and blew kisses to her admirers. And while I would not associate such a creature with the lily, the lass was passing pretty, for all the paint on her.

They hushed, those half-wage boys and kitchen maids.

I fear I had been deluded in my expectations, anticipating some attempt at ennobling beauty from the girl on the stage, some lovelorn tune that sought to wrench the heart. Instead the piano plonked into a rollick. The concertina and fiddle joined in, and Miss Perkins danced like a sailor.

"Ain't that one the fondest bit of baggage?" my drumstick-sucking neighbor cried in my ear.

Modern youth is apt to be ruined by the spectacles allowed them. I do not see how discipline will hold. She kicked up her skirts as she leapt about, pouting and making a hundred kinds of faces. When a particular turn revealed bare knees above satin garters, I shut my eyes immediately. For I admit to an appreciation of Woman. God gave them beauty so we might admire them. And a man wants to have a look, when a look is offered, for such is our nature.

I am a married man, and blessed with every happiness. My wife is all the beauty that I need. It is not Woman's beauty that brings us down, but our greed in wanting more than we are given. I am a happy man when by my wife. I am content in her love. But Adam always lurks, in every man.

Miss Perkins began to sing at last, in the voice of a thrush, high and mostly true, though lacking force and majesty:

First, 'e tickled my twittle-dee-dee,
Then 'e wiggled 'is twittle-dee-dum,
And 'ere I thought it was just 'is thumb,
'E tore my innocent reputation down!
'E done it, 'e did, what should be 'id,
And I hollered 'is name, in my terrible shame,
And we shivered and shook to wake up 'alf the town . . .
Oh, 'e tore my innocent reputation down!

Now, I was but sixteen and unawares,
When Tommy follied me up my mother's stairs,
'E follied me into the privatest place,
With the queerest look on 'is 'andsome face,
And what 'e done to me can't be repaired . . .
Oh . . .

*　　*　　*

First, 'e tickled my twittle-dee-dee,
Then 'e wiggled 'is twittle-dee dum . . .

The audience responded with alacrity. They hooted and wiggled their forefingers in the air—I blush to say young ladies did it, too—and sang along on the choruses.

The White Lily bloomed in triumph, to a harvest of mighty applause.

Now, you will say: "You said you closed your eyes, in order to refuse the old temptation." But I will tell you: My eyes had opened all on their own, even against my will, for the floor shook under me, and the ceiling shook over me, and the walls shook around me, and, finally, I am a man and just as weak as you.

Judge me who will.

And it was a very good thing that I opened my eyes, see. For just as I wrenched my gaze away from the young gazelle on the stage, turning my entire head away to save myself, I saw the strangest fellow across the room, by the farthest door.

He wore a scarlet mask upon his face.

He saw me look and stepped back through the door. As if he had been watching me and waiting.

I leapt from my seat and went after him, pushing out of the two-penny row and through the crowd. My urgency engendered some dismay, I fear, for the audience was rapt upon Miss Perkins, who had begun another tune, this one with a tear or two in the melody. I shoved with my cane when begging pardon did not suffice, and the White Lily of Kent sang, "Oh, break, my heart, for Harry's gone away . . ."

I fair raged my way through that density of flesh and odors, though not without a nasty prick from a hat-pin when I had blocked a young woman's view and tread on her foot.

Out into the lobby I went, where the yellow-scarved tout was sharing a cigar with a colleague.

"Which way did he go?" I cried.

The two fellows gave me such a look of ignorance that I wasted no more time upon inquiries. I broke out through the doors, which near started a mad rush for the interior. As great a crowd had gathered to wait for the second show of the evening as had plunged into the first. Behind me, I heard the charger curse at me and at a boy who tried to slip in past him.

Free of the pack, I looked both ways along the street, but saw nothing. A gloaming had fallen over the city streets and a lamplighter clapped his ladder against a pole. People in plenty there were, honest of aspect and less so, but I saw no sign of a man in a crimson mask.

Then I marked the alley, set back between two shops.

Down it I went, stabbing the broken cobbles with my cane. I thought I glimpsed a figure at the far end and nearly tripped over a cat, whose scream reverberated between the old brick walls. On I went, through slops and slippery what-not, furious at my bothered leg and the weakness of the flesh.

The alley was a fetid place, where all the day's heat had gathered to make a last stand, yet there was life in it, too. Women too far gone to risk the lamplight of the streets lurked in black doorways. Quick to lay a hand on a sleeve, they stank of things infernal.

"You doesn't 'ave to 'urry, sweetie," a wretched voice proposed. Her long fingers sought me. "I lets a gent take 'is time."

Another said, "Give Mamie a try, why not? 'Alf a crown for any satisfaction."

Even in the murdered light, her face was a thing of horror.

I must have exploded from the other end of that corridor of doom, for I ran smack into a policeman.

"What's this, what's this?" he said, separating himself from me and laying a hand on his truncheon. A bull of a fellow, he straightened his back and thrust out his manly stomach, asking, "And why are we all in such a great hurry, do tell?"

He must have thought me in flight from a misdeed. But time was a greater matter than my pride.

"Did you . . . did you see . . ." I began, a bit winded, ". . . a fellow come by with a red mask over his face?" I got my lungs full and added, "Made of silk, perhaps? Or crimson satin?"

The constable inspected me more closely. " 'Aven't been sampling the gin, now, 'ave we?"

"Please. I'm serious. This may be a police matter."

"Indeed, it may."

"Did you see a man . . . in a red mask?"

Close enough he come to sniff my breath. "Can't say as I 'ave," he told me. "But I 'ear there's camels and ellyphunts over on Lombard Street. And lions and tigers in pairs, and a big brass band. So, why don't you be a clever gentleman and take yourself off? Go see the free parade they're giving on Lombard Street, where Constable Edwards 'as the duty. Maybe 'e's seen your gentleman in the mask."

You cannot change a policeman's mind, once he has made it up.

With failure attending, I turned back toward the gaff. I chose the long way round, down proper streets, although that did not spare me whispered offers. On a corner, a fellow with a barrel organ and a dressed-up monkey played and sang "The British Grenadiers," a tune for which I have an old affection. I gave the little creature a ha'penny for his cup.

I was burning money like kindling, and it galled me. But I did not rue the copper I dropped in the animal's cup, for which the tiny fellow saluted me. I had a pet monkey in India, see, though it favored Jimmy Molloy, who fed it sweets. Not all of my memories of distant service are cruel. Things of great beauty there had been, though they ended in greater heartbreak. But I will tell you of that another time. So let that bide.

Back at the penny gaff, the crowd was just let out, with the next lot thrusting themselves in through every door. I had some experience of matters now and meant to ease inside and take a penny seat, but the tout in the yellow scarf was lying in wait.

"Back again, is 'e? And 'im what couldn't bear the look of Polly Perkins in 'er golden beauty, but 'ad to run out and visit Clobber Alley for 'is relief."

A look of horror must have crossed my face at such a misapprehension, but another kind of shock entirely interrupted my denials.

I understood what had happened, see.

If the man in the red mask had not gone up the street or down, he could only have taken himself into that alley. And if he had not come out the other end, where the constable would have seen him sure, he must have made a rapid contract, of one nature or another, with one of those ravaged women. Either that, or he had a door of his own.

My heart sank. For I saw that I would need to take me back there, after I had finished my interview with the White Lily of Kent. Oh, it is one thing to glimpse a well-formed leg upon a stage, but quite another to visit the ruination of Eve in its final stages. And at night.

There were four shows in all and I sat through every one, for I did not intend to miss my chance. Each time, I had to pay for a two-penny seat, for the man in the yellow neck-cloth would have no less of me. Perhaps he took me for a wealthy man, which I do not pretend to be. In the strangest way, he seemed to know my purpose. For after the fiddler had put up his instrument and the curtains had closed on the stage for the final time, the tout pushed through the last mopers from the audience and stepped toward me.

"When a gent takes such an interest," he said, "I suspects 'e wouldn't take it amiss, was 'e to be introduced to Miss Perkins 'erself."

I found myself stammering in surprise, for I had steeled myself for an ordeal of persuasion. But strategy proved unnecessary. The fellow only wanted half a shilling.

He led me through that rancid hall of skewed benches and scattered trash, between the curtains and past a stumpy crone with a mop and pail, muttering toward her labors. Behind the stage there was only a smoky corridor and a cramp of rooms. Lead me along, he did, between the clown, who smelled of a muchness of drink, and the fiddler, who eyed me with a simper as he pushed back his long hair.

Just ahead, a door opened. As if bidden.

Instead of Polly Perkins, a gentleman rushed out. Cursing. In language salty enough to cure a ham. The sight of me reduced him to a stagger. I might have been old Banquo's ghost, come in to spoil the supper.

He made a sound like a wounded dog and began to shove his way by me, as if I were a cause of mortal terror. Refusing to meet my eyes, he thrust past roughly, then elbowed the fiddler, who cried, "You nasty *beast!*" He nearly knocked over the drunken clown, whose eyes were already insensate.

It was young Pomeroy, the rude lad from the Foreign Office. The one with Confederate sympathies.

He slammed a door behind himself, but his footsteps carried like thunder.

Of course, my impulse was to rush after him. But I restrained my-self, determined to stick to my plan. An impulse had led me astray one time that evening, and I did not mean to make a second error.

"Polly must've let 'im see 'er temper," my intermediary told me. "There's certain times, if you knows what I mean, when 'er temper comes up unnatural. And some gents makes demands what are impertinent."

Just then, the White Lily of Kent herself appeared in the doorway, lit from behind and gossamer in her loveliness.

"I bloody well want to know," she shrieked, "I damned well want to know what soddin' bum-boy let that bugger into my bleedin' chang-ing room?" She looked at my guide and companion. "Was it you, Artie? You sorry little bastard."

Forgive my frank report of her speech. I fear she was distraught.

"Good evening, Miss Perkins," I said, stepping forward. "I must say your performance was . . . extraordinary."

"Artie, what, are you out of your bleedin' skull?" she demanded, and not without a certain graceless tone. "Now you're dragging in cripples and buggering dwarves."

I am not a dwarf. I am not tall, but I am a man most regular. And I have served in a red coat and a blue, which says something.

"This one's a payer," my guide hissed, as if I should not hear. Or perhaps I was meant to hear it, after all.

"He don't look like he got a pot to piss in," the White Lily of Kent said. "With those Jew rags of his." Yet, I was not discouraged entirely by her observations, for her voice had grown more subdued. She flared, though, when she spoke to the fellow who had delivered me to her. "That bastard you let in my changing room? How'd you pick that one out, I'd like to know? Out of his bleedin' senses he was. Making demands like he thought he was Lord Kiss-me-arse."

She stamped her foot as a willful child does. "I don't have to stand for it, I don't. I'll have old Beezil pack off the bleedin' lot of you—or maybe *I'll* be the one to go, and you can just be damned. You won't see Polly Perkins again this side of Drury Lane, and won't you be sorry? Just you wait and see who pays to look up *your* (and here I omit an astonishing vulgarity) knickers. See who brings you their bleedin' pennies when I don't give 'em a peek and send 'em home with both hands busy in their pockets."

I found I lacked the words to interpose. She was a storm, and needed to rain out.

At last, her anger relented. "Oh, bugger it all," she said. And then she spoke to me. "You might as well come in and speak your piece, and get it bleedin' over with."

I followed her into the golden light of her chamber.

Shutting the door behind us, despite the impropriety, she finally got a look at me in the light. Paler she went than any theatrical paint.

"Oh, Jesus Christ! It's you! The bleeder from over the Dials! What are you, some useless, buggering peeler?"

"Now, now, Miss Perkins. There is no need to betray your better nature with such language. I am no policeman, no. But I would like to put a question to you."

"I don't know a thing."

"I have not yet asked."

"I tell you, I don't know anything."

I drew out a pound, then another, and laid the notes upon her table of paint pots, rags and scents.

"My intentions are the best, I assure you, Miss Perkins. I only want a little of your time and—"

She made a sound like a horse with feed up its nose. "That's what they all want. Ain't it?"

"—to ask a few simple questions."

"I said that I don't know a thing."

"Well, we will see. And I will risk your ignorance."

"I ain't ignorant." She drew herself up most proudly. "I just said I don't know anything."

"You went to see Mrs. Hepburn, the pawn-mother and—"

"That bleedin' cow. She doesn't keep a promise, I can tell you."

"What promise was that, Miss Perkins?" The room smelled of victuals left for days, and of night-pots.

"I don't have to tell you a thing," she said, with a glance at the two pounds lying on her table.

"Mrs. Hepburn is dead, you know."

That got her attention. Paler still she went.

"Now, if you would be so kind as to tell me what she promised you?" I continued.

The White Lily drew back a step. She seemed much smaller up close than she looked on the stage. Almost a child in size she was, though clearly a woman elsewhere. And wasn't it the queerest thing? Her features could not have been finer if she had been born to a baroness. Life does not scruple about our expectations, but loves to confound.

"What did she promise you?" I repeated, when Miss Perkins failed to answer.

"I didn't have nothing to do with it," she told me. "I couldn't have. I didn't even know her."

"But you said she made you a promise. And broke it."

"It wasn't her. I mean, it wasn't her that *made* the promise. A fine gent has been coming round every night. Though now he's gone off and no wonder. Likes to sit in that same chair he does, but I don't know why he bothers. For he don't take a proper interest in a lady, just sits and looks and patters. Then leaves a little gift for nothing at all. It's a shame he isn't after it decent like, for the bugger's bleedin' with money. But he just ain't for it, I can tell you that." She shook her head at the stubbornness of the world. "A girl can tell his type as soon as she sets her eyes on him. Not one for the ladies, if you take my meaning. But fine as they come and speaking all high and frilly, the way they do."

"Who?"

"Them."

"And who is that?"

"Oh, you know. Lords and ladies, like. And poofs. He seemed a bit of both, to tell you the truth. Reedy tried to make up to him, but Lord Bugger-Bum wasn't interested. He looked to me like the sort that likes a younger trade."

"And who is Reedy?"

She shrugged, as if I should have figured that much out. "The fiddle-scraper. Don't let him come in when you're using the pot. Or something'll go in where it should come out."

"And this 'fine gent' made you a promise? In Mrs. Hepburn's name?"

She looked at me as if in hard-learned canniness, but suspicion only made her more handsome. She was a pretty thing, though bound for ruin.

"Told me I belonged on a proper stage, he did, and said he was going to see me set up in the West End, in a proper theater, if I done him a little favor."

"Which involved Mrs. Hepburn?"

She nodded bitterly. "Last night he came by and told me I was to go at noon, and not a minute before or after, to see this Mrs. Hepburn in the Dials. Well, that seemed buggered to begin with, didn't it? I know the Dials well enough to keep my distance, I do, and his likes won't be seen there for love nor money. It's not a place for his sort of entertainments, if you take my meaning. The Irish are like to beat his sort to death. Though they ain't above a bit of the other from the missus, once there's brats enough to feed."

She scowled most handsomely. "I thought maybe that was why he wanted me to go for him, the sorry bleeder. Anyway, 'Go,' he says to me, 'there's a package for you to deliver. Mrs. Hepburn will give you the address when she gives you the package.' That's all it was, wasn't it? I was only to take up a package from the old cow and deliver it, that was all. Mrs. Hepburn was to pay me ten guineas for my trouble." Despair flitted over her face like the shade of a bird in flight. "And wasn't I just fool enough to believe it? As if they'd ever pay up for a thing like that. And ten guineas! Coo, I ain't never seen that much stumpy all at once in my whole bleedin' life."

"So you went?"

"As well you know yourself, for you saw me. And don't you pretend you didn't."

"No, Miss Perkins, I saw you and do not pretend otherwise. The vision was not a thing to be forgotten."

"Well, thank you, I'm sure.

"And then?"

"Then off I went, and paying my own clinkers for a cab all the way to St. Giles, where you have to pay the driver extra to go, and asking my way from every slut and sod in the Seven Dials until I found the old cow. With screaming brats on every side, no less. And in goes little Polly, more the fool. And wasn't it just the queerest place, this hocker of hers, with not a thing in it besides that fat old bitch? And I can tell you how that one lost the hair on her head, don't think I can't. And she sits me down, she does, just like we was all known and on intimate terms. And she starts passing the time, la-de-da.

" 'I've come for the package,' I tell her, 'and for my ten guineas.' But she only smiles and goes on passing the time. 'I'm here for my ten guineas and the package,' I tell her again. But she just goes on about her bleedin' ailments and pokes at her embroidering. But when I get myself up to go, all out of patience with her snorting like a pig, doesn't she grab me by the arm and pull me right back down? Fat that one may have been, but she was a quick one. There's men like that, too. Anyways, that cow won't let me go, and there I sit wondering, 'Polly, what have you got yourself into this time, girl?' When in runs the dirtiest little slut of a thing from the street, all out of breath like, and crying 'They're on their way, they're on their way!'

"All in an instant, the great cow lets go of me and tells me, 'Get out, you tramp. I've nothing for you. Get out.' And didn't I go, as fast as my legs could carry me? I was angry enough to take her up by the hair, if she would've had any." The White Lily paused. "Not that I did, acourse, for she would've broke my neck. I didn't do her any harm in the least, and couldn't have, for she must've been there when you two gents went up."

Oh, I was thinking now.

"The girl who ran in. The one who said, 'They're on their way.' Can you describe her?"

Miss Perkins assumed an indifferent expression. "Just a street bit. Like all that sort. Chestnut hair and dirty, every inch of her. Maybe fourteen. Won't have her teeth come twenty. Nor anything else worth having."

I recalled the girl who had squatted so shamelessly in the passage when Wilkie and I entered the close on our fool's errand. Quick of wit the child had been, when she failed to get away before our coming. Clever enough she had been to wield our own embarrassment against us.

"Miss Perkins, this is all quite helpful. Now, just a few more questions, if you would?"

"I think," she said, with a pout, "that I ought to have another pound for my troubles."

"Ten shillings."

She grimaced. "Ain't you all the same, the bleedin' lot of you? Ten shillings, then."

I dispensed the money. "Did this gentleman . . . the one who sent you to the Dials and promised you payment in return . . . did he happen to mention a watch?"

A moment of honest confusion wrinkled her brow. "Lord Bugger-Bum? He had a golden ticker he kept in his waistcoat, fancy as la-de-da. He always pulled it out just before he got up to go. Gave a little chime it did, when he opened it. Is that the watch you mean, then?"

"No. Not his watch. Did he say anything about another watch? In the package you were to receive from Mrs. Hepburn, perhaps?"

"Not a bleedin' word."

Now I would not applaud all aspects of her character. But I believed the girl and all she said. Had she seen profit in lying, she doubtless would have seized the opportunity to tell me tales. But I do not believe she did, though you may only think that I was smitten. Which I was not.

I was thinking—or trying to think—in a fog of new confusions and baffling clarities. Fair leaping from one view of matters to another I was, but I failed to think with the completeness that was wanted.

I stood up as if called to attention. For Miss Perkins had begun to disrobe before me. Likely, she wished to absent herself from her workplace and return to her mother and father for the night.

"Just one more question, please: The boy who left in a fury. The one you followed after, as I was coming in. What do you know about him? Was he involved with this . . . this high gentleman who had been calling on you?"

"The one what just went out? Him? I never laid peepers on that one 'til five minutes before you came strolling in yourself. All full of demands he was. Didn't even treat me like a lady. And when I didn't give him his satisfaction, off he went, with language that a lady oughtn't to hear. Without a by-your-leave, like I was dirt."

The young woman dropped an entire layer of clothing before my startled eyes. Before I could absent myself with propriety, she turned her bare shoulders and showed me the laces of her corset.

"Would you like to help a girl out?" she asked.

I suppose Miss Perkins was pleased with the payment she had of me, for she only laughed when I made a swift departure.

"Come back when you ain't so fearful of a lady," she called after me.

⌒

I stepped out into the sultry night, with the city crawling and noisy. Strange it was, how I had been led about. Had the fatality of Mrs. Hepburn, and of the eel-man before her, and of that boy, all been arranged so I might glimpse Polly Perkins in the Dials? And follow her trail to a penny gaff on Eastcheap Street? Where she could tell me, in so many words, that all of it was a game, if a brute and deadly one? I had no doubt that the appearance of the fellow in the red mask at the back of the theater had been purely for my benefit, as well.

Why?

Was young Pomeroy in it, or was he not? Was Polly Perkins lying about that part of the affair? Were they, perhaps, intimates who had only had a tiff? Was she protecting him? Was I a fool?

I saw already that I should have questioned her more closely. But I could not remain alone with a young woman determined to disrobe, although I suppose theatrical folk are accustomed to that sort of thing.

There was a dreadful lot to do tomorrow. But, first, I had a grim task left tonight.

I paused below a streetlamp and closed my eyes in prayer. It fortifies as nothing else will do.

Then I took me back into that alley.

I saw them all, a myriad now, shadows behind shadows. Creatures eaten by vice and set to devour. I could not mark the filth beneath my shoes, for I needed to watch the human wraiths before me. Calling to me already they were, the horrid sisters of Mr. Homer's sirens.

"Thruppence'll get you in, as it's so late, guv'nor."

"Anything you likes, as long as you likes it."

A hand, perhaps a claw, groped below my waist.

"Please," I said, stopping. I nudged her off with my cane.

"Oh, ain't 'e the polite one, Mary! I bet 'e's a proper gent what likes 'is usual."

I did not want to hear that name in such a place as this.

They clustered about me. Two, then three. I cringed before their touch.

"Ladies," I said, "if you please . . ."

"Oooh, 'li-dies,' is it? 'Aving more than one, are we? It's allus the little blokes as will surprise you."

They smelled of brimstone. And worse. One tried to set her lips upon my cheek.

"Please! Ladies! I only wanted to ask about—"

My life was saved by an accident of light. In the ravaged face that sought my flesh, the eyes reflected movement. Movement that was unnatural.

I did not mean to harm those ravaged women, but I shoved to clear myself a fighting space. And down I bent, in the instant before the cord would have caught my neck.

The old whores screamed and scattered.

And now I smelled the ancient scent of sandalwood. And India.

When the cord failed to snare me, my assailant drew a knife. His skin was coffee dark, even in that lightless glen of bricks, and his shape was foreign, confirmed by movements I knew all too well. He plunged toward me, seeking to drive in his blade. But I was once an instructor of the bayonet. I parried his thrust with my cane and gave him a knock. And a good one.

Staggering backward he went, and I thought I had him. His eyes shone white with the glow of human fear. I raised my cane to land its ball on his head.

God forgive me for the harshness of my judgements, it was one of those old Magdalenes who saved me. Again.

"Look out!" she screamed. "Look out behind you, dearie!"

I twisted about on my good leg, bringing up my stick like a steel-tipped musket. A blade hacked into the wood, but I threw it off. Then I gave it to that devil proper. With the alley naught but a screaming fair around us. Parry. Return to guard. I swept the ball of my cane up to his nether parts. It bent the fellow double. He was as lean and brown as my first attacker, though I could see he was dressed in Western garments.

I swept my cane around to catch the side of his head, but he managed to avoid me. Lithe those fellows are, and born to survive.

I fear I forgot the time and place. I thought I had a musket in my hands. With a bayonet fixed to it. I stabbed him in the chest. My God, if I had had my steel, I would have run him through. As it was, I dropped him down, although I very nearly tumbled after, for my bad leg sometimes throws me out of balance.

I was all set to put paid to him when I heard the other come up behind me again. All this was in seconds, mind you.

I turned with my stick raised up on guard. I saw the flash of steel coming down, where my rifle stock would have been but a cane did not reach. Bad leg or no, I side-stepped like the blood-stained sergeant I had been, letting my enemy stumble when he failed to find his mark. He sought his balance, but I swung my cane down and struck him hard.

My stick lacked the weight I needed to give him a finish, but the ball was just the thing to crack his skull.

Above the breath of my enemies and the cries of those wretched women, I heard the call of a bird. Of a kind I had not heard since I left India.

As if they were but phantoms, my attackers disappeared.

Seven

Cruel dreams assailed me. Whenever the cholera dead visit, I wake forlorn and frightened as a child. I do not think I am a coward. But darkness has a power all its own. All nights are haunted, even those spent in the bliss of love. Sleep disarms us and draws us back to the terrors of the cradle.

Do not misunderstand me: I love those dreams that bring me to my mother or, sometimes, to the aching shadow that was my father. I am a middle-aged man of thirty-four, and both my father and mother died at a younger age than I have gained. I was little above the age of four the year I lost them both. I suppose that is why I am soft toward orphans, although we must be guarded in our charity, for too free a hand corrupts. And given this cruel war, I often think of my young son, imagining his future were he fatherless. But I did not dream of our John. Twas my mother returned to me, only bitterly, for I saw her lying upon the floor again, with the vomit over her face and her eyes set wide, just as she lay for days in our poor parlor, behind the door whose lock I could not turn.

I dread the cholera, see. For it took more than my parents. There was a certain loss in India, too. But that is another tale, so let that bide.

I woke early, and broken, and all a-sweat. In that moody place between sleep and knowing true, a panic come upon me. Uncomposed, I battled with the linens, pawing about me in dread that another child's hand had been deposited during my slumber.

I had shifted a chest of drawers to block the door and balanced a water glass by the window frame, so that even the most skilled intruder would send it crashing to the floor. I wished I had my Colt revolver, but that had been left behind in Washington. The urgency of my journey was only communicated to me in the course of a visit to Newport, far from the smoke of battle and need of firearms, and I had left directly from Rhode Island. I was unarmed. In more ways than I knew.

As my eyes relearned the world, I saw naught was disturbed. Upon the writing table, the letter I had completed lay white and chaste. Twas to my Mary Myfanwy, my beloved, with a note for our young John, containing fatherly love and admonitions.

I gasped as deep as if I had fought a battle and tried to drive the last of my mother from my eyes. For the Good Lord knows I would remember her. But I would not remember her so.

She looked so frightful that it breaks my heart. Even now.

I got me up and sat by the window and read in my new pocket Testament, for comfort lies therein. I read the sorrowful bit set in the garden, where Our Savior doubts Himself and almost seems to share our mortal fears. Oh, there is strange. A garden is a lovely thing it seems to me. Yet terrible things transpire in such places, from Eden to Gethsemane. We always come up short when faced with paradise. Sometimes, when I feel put upon by Mankind, I wonder will we make a muck of Heaven?

I washed my face. It helped. And then I tidied myself to go to chapel, for this was a Sunday.

The hotel's dining room, all fragrant, bid guests in to breakfast. But I was wise enough to check the prices, which astonished. I went out into the cool of the morning, stepping over puddles from a night rain, and found a coffee stall along the street. I fortified myself with a bun. Then I set to the vital task of the day, finding a Methodist chapel. For I do not like churches grand and gaudy. I do not wish to worship golden altars or painted windows. I like a simple place for meditation, though I will gladly join a rousing hymn. I do not know if God first made the Welsh, then sent them hymns to sing, or if He made the hymns, then created the Welsh so He might hear the hymns sung true and proper. Music is a prayer deep in our blood.

I had to walk a bit until the buildings grew smaller and the streets narrower. Not far from Tottenham Court Road, with its competition of drapers stilled for the day, I found a little Wesleyan room. Twas humble, as befits our Christian prayers. But luck I was to have little in London town. We began with a hymn I favor, Mr. Bunyan's lyric of "Who Would True Valour See," sung to the martial strains of old "Monk's Gate," but the preacher had been called to the hard persuasion. The benches were at most a quarter filled, and twas no crying wonder. For that man of God had a fondness for Damnation, and thought we should be warned from first to last.

Now, I would be a good, God-fearing man. Nor do I favor any dissipation. But Jesus Christ come down to lift us up, not to give us a kick and start us fretting. Perhaps I am not proper in my Methodism. But I do not think John Wesley wanted cruelties shouted at the weak and wounded. And such they were in that unvarnished chapel. Old women crushed by life into a smallness and young girls plain and husbandless, old men bitter as the preaching fellow himself and little children brought to heel like dogs—such were my fellow worshippers, all black-clad, dry and joyless. The preacher made it sound as though we had no hope of Heaven. And I will not believe that, though I err. I most admire Jesus for His kindness. And for His good temper. Anger caught Our Savior only once, when He found that prayer had given way to grasping. That was in a church, where he upset things.

I let the parson rant and simply prayed. As I had prayed the night before, for those I love and then for all the others, living and dead, good or bad or middling. For a Christian must be particular in his habits, but not in his pleas to the Lord. All men need mercy. Last, I said a prayer for Mr. Lincoln, who is admirable.

I like to pray. It makes me feel an inch closer to Heaven.

I come out the doors in a faintness of rain, that slight wet you feel on your face but cannot find on the wool of your clothing unless you scrub a hand across your chest. Twas gone in minutes, the hint of rain, but great, gray-bellied clouds sailed over the city, leaving us cool and vigorous. The air was damp as a cellar. I felt that this, at last, was truly England.

I tapped my way to Oxford Street and along its drowsing prosperity. I meant to give a coin to that artilleryman, but he was gone from his begging place and so I saved it up. Twas reaching noon, for the parson's lungs had been possessed of stamina, and I hoped to visit the much-advertised picture by Mr. Hunt, "The Finding of the Savior in the Temple," which was on view at the German Gallery, in New Bond Street, some ways along. The admission was a shilling, which seemed high, but I would rather pay for my edification than for gratification. Thus, I had resolved to avoid the enticements of the International Exhibition until the conclusion of my purposes here in Her Majesty's domain. That visit would be my reward for work well done. Meanwhile, a nice religious picture seemed a proper entertainment for a Sunday.

Now, you will think me contrary, but, though I had to stand in a line and my entry cost a shilling, just as promised, I did not tarry before the painted scene. The mighty picture was a disappointment. It was as if the artist painted in sugar-icing, or covered over Our Savior's life with gauze. It was not real to me. Yet, Mr. Hunt is much acclaimed, and I am not, so I must be in the wrong. It is only this, see: I picture Jesus covered in sweat and striving, hungry at times, and hurt at last. Like us. And the Orient is hot and it is dirty. Nor are children anywhere given to neatness. Perhaps I blaspheme, though I do not wish to. But think you. By the end of a hard day walking the hills of Galilee, Our Savior must have been coated with dust and dirty. I know what it is to walk, see. And to thirst. Even as a child, at the young age when He took Himself to that Temple, Jesus must have had a jolly time or two and got Himself slopped up. In Heaven, He will wear His shining white. But, here among us, He must have looked a bit dodgy.

Let that bide.

I bought a paper cone of Spanish oranges and retreated toward Hyde Park. Oh, I had things to do and visits to make, Sunday though it was. But first I wished to have a little peace. To sit upon the grass and read *The Times,* which I had bought the day before and found no time to open. I did not want to think about the murders and such like, not for a little while yet. For I have learned a man can think too hard. Sometimes, when I have failed to look through things, I find it does me good to have a wander. Then, bursting out of nowhere, the missing bit I need will take its place. Thoughts are like young girls, see, and like to surprise us and come unbidden, though flummox us they do when we pursue them. I do not mean that improperly, you understand.

Then I was wounded, most unexpectedly, though not in the flesh.

The air was fresh and not as sooty, for the manufactories down the

Thames did not pour smoke on Sunday, and the breeze kept off the river's sewer smell. Open carriages streamed along Piccadilly, filled with bouquets of girls and the thorny mothers from whom they stemmed. The street seemed a rolling garden of roses, with parasols for petals and blooms of every hue of dyer's cloth. I noted that magenta was still fashionable and thought I should inform my Mary Myfanwy, who had undertaken a dressmaking enterprise back in Pottsville. The latest pattern books I would buy her, too, for the ladies of Pottsville like to go in style and think our town the center of the world.

A crisp young man trotted by on a horse as sleek as his master's boots. Oh, wasn't there a great tipping of hats and nodding of heads, as gentlemen greeted each other or a nosegay of ladies passed them by in a fine caleche or an elegant britzka with the canvas down? Handkerchiefs fluttered like butterflies strayed to town. And all these society folk were but the few who had not gone to the country for the week's end.

So gay it seemed! A far cry it was from the pleasures of Eastcheap Street, yet all these things sum up to make a city. And London was the city of them all.

Nor were these hours only for the wealthy. The working poor, got up in their Sunday propers, headed for the parks in family platoons, and strolling pairs of chums tugged their coatsleeves down over worn cuffs. Only, look you. There was ever a timidness to those of lesser fortune, as though the rich might notice them and call a policeman to send them on their way. They always gave way on the sidewalks, the poor folk did, and seemed prepared to flee at any moment. It is a thing of wonder how America changes a fellow's view of the world. Although our parks are not so fine, they are for every man. And each man knows it, and ready he is to tell you.

With the park spread green before me and half of London sauntering its paths, I spied young Mr. Adams coming toward me. He was bantering with a handsome group of acquaintances, all of them laughing in the quiet way gentlemen do. Then Henry Adams saw me plumb ahead. And didn't he turn the pack of them onto a side path?

Not once did he look back or hint a greeting. I might have been the serpent in the Garden, the way I worried him.

It saddened me. Now, I am not a grand fellow in appearance, but I keep myself clean and tidy. And Henry Adams was no English lord, but an American. Given his lineage, he should have been a good one. I did not wish to join his swank companions—only to be polite, see. But he would not pass a simple hello with a fellow such as me. Not if his English friends were by to witness it.

Now, you will say: "You should not be so proud. Better to be humble and turn the other cheek, like an honest Christian." But I will tell you: Each of us has something he is proud of, and I was proud to have become an American. Ours is a splendid country, see, as near to Heaven as this earth allows. And I wish to believe all of its promises, not least that we are equal in our dignities. Yes, I am proud of that. And I have done what I could for our good country, in war, when I would have liked to stay at home. And that young pup avoided me like a beggar.

Scorned. That is the word for how he made me feel. I burned inside to give that boy a lesson.

Well, let that bide. His father seemed a good man, and he it was who served as my commander, so to speak. And how the time was running away with every step I walked! Soon enough my Sunday would be gone. I had a call to make, on a business matter, but yearned for a bit of quiet Sunday leisure before resuming my endeavors. I told myself that I might take two hours.

I could not sit upon a bench, for fear of robbing a lady of her repose, should she wish to take it, so I spanked the last rain and dew from a stretch of grass and sat me down. Twas a great relief, for London is large and I had walked enough to bother my leg, which had been annoyed by the scrap in Clobber Alley. My bad leg had not failed in the fight, but now it wanted thanks.

I had an orange, and then another, savoring each burst of juice and the scent left on my fingertips. Finally, I opened up my newspaper.

Temptations aplenty there were. Not only did the International Exhibition spread out before my eyes, just across the Serpentine in the Kensington Gardens, but *The Times* told of a miraculous display at the Royal Colosseum where, for a shilling—which seemed to be the price of everything this side of Eastcheap—a spectator might admire dioramas of London by day and Paris by night, although a Methodist would skip the latter. Much of the news was commercial, rife with cotton worries. Indian prices had been driven up sharply. Of ships departing for India and similar parts, there was a plentitude. I counted eight vessels listed for Bombay, with fourteen for Calcutta—which made my heart come up—and two destined for Madras. Other ports of call included Rangoon and Kurrachee, Colombo, Singapore and Hong Kong, which is in China. Even the shipping lists were evidence of Britain's might and majesty.

I noted in the business news from America that railway shares were active and gaining value. That buoyed me, for I had holdings in a pair of railroads. Not as speculation, of course, but as honorable investments in the future.

News of our war there was, so much that the volume surprised me. Our English brethren certainly took an interest. I fear we read of war as women gossip, to enjoy the bitter misery of others.

But to the war.

General Halleck's authority had been greatly expanded in the west, and I hoped that might prove good news for General Grant, who had grit. Beauregard was at Tupelo and disorganized, although another report placed him at Grenada. The Rebels had retreated from Corinth, anyway, burning all that was useful as they left. Shiloh, as I knew, had left them bereft. I hoped that we would strike while we had an advantage, for Beauregard was no more than a peacock, but I read in the following lines that Halleck believed the Confederates superior in numbers to his own force. That was tosh, for I had seen them myself, and a sorry lot they were, if brave in a ruckus. But we had cautious generals by the dozen. The sort who will not lose, but cannot win.

The news out of Virginia was discouraging. McClellan was stymied before Richmond, after taking a great army south by sea. *The Times* said the general "declares that he is not in sufficient force to resume the offensive." Now, I will tell you what such statements mean: They mean a preening general is uncertain, and that the lives lost up to then are wasted.

I never have understood this business of calculating numbers in a battle. But then I was shaped by India, where you just pitched in and gave the devil to anyone in your way. We had to win, and we knew it. So we did.

In a little country town called Warrenton, a guerrilla party had raided the Union garrison, to great discomfiture. And there was high praise for the Confederate fellow Jackson, who had been marching all over Virginia. Finally, the newspaper gave grudging applause to Admiral Farragut, who had captured New Orleans for our Union in a masterstroke some weeks before. Twas clear enough *The Times* did not like Yankees, but they would not belittle things done proper.

I was just about to fold up the paper and rest my eyes on the clouds, when a bold-faced advertisement caught my eye. Twas for the Great Northern Railway, reminding travellers of the express train that had been running on the East Coast Route. Leaving King's Cross Station at ten in the morning, it daily reached Edinburgh at eight-thirty in the evening and Glasgow at ten-thirty. Now, that was a speed near miraculous, and Glasgow had been on my mind, of course. But it was not even the remarkable velocity of modern transport to Scotland that straightened my back and opened my eyes and pierced me.

There was, the advertisement said, "an interval of twenty minutes allowed at York for dinners."

York. Where the second agent's body had been found. I had almost forgotten those murders that had passed before my coming. But now I recalled the bafflement of Mr. Adams, who could not understand how our agent might have found himself in York.

The poor fellow had not *meant* to go to York. His body had been taken there by train! There it was before me, plain as could be: Three agents killed, including Mr. Campbell. One found in Glasgow, at the northern terminus, one at York, where the express paused for dinner, and one in London at the southern terminus.

There you have the good and bad of progress: Men may leave London after breakfast and sleep in a bed in distant Glasgow. And murderers can place bodies wherever they want them, with incredible speed. Face to face I was with modern crime.

I wanted to run to Mr. Adams, but he was still in the country, according to his manservant. And yes, his son's unpleasantness crossed my mind again, for I could not think of one without the other. But twas the father to whom I needed to speak. For here, at last, I had one bit of information that had not been dangled before me by conspirators. Finally, I had scratched up a hint on my own. I had no other fact that could be trusted entirely, but I knew at last how the corpses had been shunted about. As if they were on holiday, it was.

They, whoever they might be, had placed a body at York because it was an easy way to confuse us, given the speed and convenience of the railway. Kill a fellow in Scotland, and his carcass is still warm when you deposit him in the Yorkshire Dales. That is progress, I suppose. I suspected they had played the same sort of trick with the Reverend Mr. Campbell, dropping him in London to lead us astray. No, the first man had been found in Glasgow, and that was where I wished to take me next. For all three men might have perished in that city.

If any of the dead agents had been left on the spot of their demise, it seemed to me it would have been the first victim, before the conspirators had elaborated their plans and identified engines for their realization. Of the twin teasings I had been given in London—one tempting me to stay, one pushing me to go to Scotland, and one of them surely false—I now believed I had the means to choose between them properly.

I had to go to Glasgow. But I could not go without our minister's permission. And I feared I might not get it in time to catch that morning train, which would mean another day gone lost. Perhaps, more men, women and children would die for my amusement.

I wanted to go. I needed to go. I *had* to go.

Until that time, I had a call to pay.

The Pomeroy house was a grand affair, but the architecture interested me less than the address. It stood but a pistol shot from the spot in Regent's Park where the boy's body had been discovered. New suspicions piled upon the old.

The police at Bow Street station, who had developed a certain awareness of my relations with Inspector Wilkie, provided me with directions and I went by cab. My leg was much annoyed with me, and I with it. Now, I am a capable man. But, somehow in the scrap I had turned or twisted awkwardly. The aching wearied me, and gave me a temper. How hard it is when our body disobeys us!

The cab was not entirely an indulgence, though, for it saved me a muchness of time. Away from the parks, the streets wore a Sunday vacancy and I reached the Pomeroy house at the hoped-for hour, just after tea, when a young man was likely to be home at his leisure, if not gone out to the country until Monday morning. Twas the lull before such folk put on evening dress to sit them down to dinner or go out.

The hall-porter raised his snoot at the very sight of me.

"Government matters," I told him quick, and there was a good bit of truth in it. "I must see young Mr. Pomeroy, if he is in."

The fellow did not like my looks, twas clear. But he merely said, "Shall I take in your card, sir?"

I did not have a card, see. For I am not accustomed to making high visits. Not even in America.

"Tell him it is Major Jones," I said. "From the American legation."

"Yes, sir. 'Major Jones.' " He tasted the words and did not like their flavor. But he let me step into the cool gloom of the vestibule. His shoes clapped down the hall, leaving me in the care of an ancient dog that lifted an eyelid but could not lift itself.

Startling me, a door to my right tore open and a thick-cut man burst out. He had the look of a fellow happiest in the country with a horse and hounds or a shotgun, and it took me a moment to note the familial resemblance. And a moment was all he gave me.

He come out all a frightful storm of a man, clouding my view of the interior as he swept past. He liked my aspect less than did the servant.

"Who're you?" he demanded. "Another damned Jew come after Reggie for money? Well, he won't have a penny of mine to pay you bastards."

And the fellow blew out the front door before I could respond. Muttering a monstrous insult to all Hebrews, he gave the oaken door a royal slam.

At first, I was nonplussed to be thought a Jew. For though some Welshmen will show dark, we have a look that would not be mistaken. Then I realized what the fellow meant, for the ways of the world are common. All men after debts were Jews to the elder Mr. Pomeroy. Those of us lower-born had less identity to him than did his hounds. It is a blindness found in every nation. Even in America, I fear.

And the fellow was right about one thing: I had come to collect a debt from his wastrel son, although I had no interest in his money.

The servant reappeared, with an impassive expression lacquered over his face.

"Follow me, sir," he said.

I trailed along, between great hunks of mahogany and paintings gone dark with the years. He showed me into a study, all leather and globes and fittings of polished brass, where young Mr. Pomeroy was struggling to light a cigar. The boy wore his fear as plainly as a costume, and the costume was trimmed in hatred.

The servant left us. With that slight clap of a door that fits precisely.

Young Pomeroy glared at me. But there was no strength in it. He looked as frail as the head of the house was hearty.

"I suppose," he said, in an effort at sounding disdainful, "you've come to add your name to the list of blackmailers."

Now, you will understand my temper was near to failing me. My leg's lack of allegiance had bruised my spirit. Then I had been called a Jew, and now a blackmailer. No Christian has more than two cheeks he can turn.

"Look you," I said sternly. "I will not have you play the little lord with me, Mr. Pomeroy. Sit you down and listen. Or I will tell your tale where it will be heard."

He sat down on a divan, crumbling the cigar between his fingers. His spirit crumbled, too. I saw it. Still, I did not stop. For I was hot.

"Insolent you were with Mr. Adams, and quick enough with your 'Earl This' and 'Lord That' besides. You, a shameful boy who cannot pay his gambling debts. Not that any man should gamble, I will tell you, whether he can pay his debts or no. And next I see you all in a great passion, blowing like the north wind out of the changing room of a certain stage performer. All because she would not meet your base demands. You! A man who has already ruined the virtue of one young woman, a poor seamstress, and—"

At that, his face took on a baffled look.

"—you ruined her health, besides. For such as you are ever without shame. And selfish to the very depths of Hell." I gave him a look to chill the polar seas. "Now it's off to the doctor, is it? For both of you. Two ruined lives, is it? And you still chasing after singing girls.

With a poor lass out of Lambeth ruined forever, and where is she to go, your little seamstress? The one you have made sick with your misbehaviors?"

"Good God," he said. "Are you speaking of my wife?"

Yes, I had got it wrong. Though helped along in my error I was. The boy broke down in tears. He simply could not bear this sudden assault on his secret life. For secrets are not wives with whom we may grow comfortable in time. Secrets are whores—forgive me—and betray us when we are weak and poor in fortune. Secrets crush the spirit. And rob the purse.

"Sarah's from Hungary, you see," young Pomeroy continued the explanation he had begun. His red eyes wandered, but found nothing upon which to rest. Especially not the rows of books, which looked as though they never had been touched. "Her father brought her here. And he died. Suddenly. Sarah had no one. I don't know what would have become of her, if we hadn't met." He managed to look at me. Briefly. And pleadingly. "She's a good girl. You have to understand that. A wonderful girl. Sarah wouldn't . . . she isn't like some other women. She wouldn't . . . I had to marry her, you see. She wouldn't have me otherwise. She would've starved first. And I didn't want . . . I couldn't . . ."

I had taken a seat myself, fair knocked off my feet by embarrassment and mystification.

"Well, sir," I told him, "if you are married to the lass, there is good. But you have no business running after singing girls and such like."

He did look at me then. But he shook his head. With a bit of strength regained. "I wasn't running after any singing girls. Or anybody else. Nothing of the sort. Sarah's all the wife a man could ask for. I love her more than anything in the world."

"I was there, young man. I saw you last night, and heard a most unpleasant explanation from the woman you insulted."

"Insulted?" He seemed honestly bewildered. "What did she tell you? Did she say anything about the letters? Did she?"

"There was no talk of letters. What letters would these be, then? And if you are so innocent, why did you flee at the sight of me?"

"I thought you were mixed up in it."

"In what?"

"In blackmailing me."

"And who is blackmailing you?"

He shook his head again. Doubtfully this time. "I don't know," he whispered.

"That is a lie."

He raised his face as if I had given him a hard slap.

"Who is blackmailing you, boy?"

He moved his head, slowly, from side to side. As if it were the heaviest thing on earth.

"Who is it?" I insisted.

"I can't tell you. I daren't."

"Who?"

"I can't."

"Mr. Disraeli, is it?

We had gotten back to honesty again. For the look of shock on his face could not be feigned. I had guessed correctly. But I wanted him to answer me aloud.

"Answer me, boy. And perhaps I can help you. Is Mr. Disraeli blackmailing you?"

"Yes. No. I mean . . . he's one of them. Not the only one, it's all confused."

Now, there is trouble. When a fellow is blackmailed by more than one party. The thing of it was that the boy was weak. Twas plain. And weaklings are as game-birds to the world.

"Who are the others?"

"I don't know. The Earl of Thretford. Others, too. But they're all in it with him."

At that, it was my turn to be astonished. For he had spoken a name I knew too well. Arthur Langley, the Earl of Thretford. One of England's richest young men. And the inheritor of cotton mills in Manchester, of metal works in Sheffield, and of shipyards and manufactories in Glasgow.

In Glasgow.

Shipyards.

Oh, of all the lords and ladies in honor's kingdom, the Earl of Thretford was the one to whom I had come closest. Although we had never exchanged a single word. It all went back to a spirit girl and troubles with the Irish in the hills of western New York. I had seen him, once, in the flesh, in Rochester, dealing with a wicked man whom I pursued to his death. The Earl had disappeared, gone back to Canada. And on to England thereafter. I had thought such matters left behind, and good riddance.

Then I recalled another thing, overheard in shrouded winter streets. The Earl of Thretford had an indecent fondness. For street-boys.

"Don't you want to hear about the letters?" young Pomeroy demanded. For when we begin confessions, we do not like to stop until we are finished.

"Yes," I said absently. "The letters, then."

"I had a message. A note. It wasn't signed. That's how it usually is, you see. I was to go to see this singing tart, this Polly Perkins, after she finished performing for the evening. The note said she had my letters and would give them to me, that all I had to do was ask her for them." He shrugged and it seemed almost a sob. "I thought it was mad, of course. Why should the possessor of the letters give them back, just like that? But I was desperate. I thought . . . I thought that she might have gotten her hands on them somehow. Stolen from a lover's dressing table, perhaps. I hoped she was only after money." He raised his wet eyes to mine. "I'd do almost anything to have those letters back. They were stolen from my wife. Every letter that I ever wrote to her. I'd give anything . . . "

"And what," I asked, "is in these letters that is so frightful, then? What did you write to your wife that causes you so much shame?"

He sat up, almost bravely. "There's not the least bit of shame in a single word. None. I wouldn't take back a syllable. It's only . . . it's only that my father musn't find out."

"About what, then?"

"About . . . about Sarah. And our marriage."

I began to see it, but he made things clear.

"He really would disinherit me," young Pomeroy went on. "He'd never accept a marriage so far below our station. He wants his peerage, and he'd view any such union as nothing more than a plot to deprive him of it. He daren't take a false step, given the difficulties the family's already been through." He shifted. "The Queen is very particular, you know. She only needs to say half a word, or to make the

slightest tick with her pen. And her mourning's made things worse."
He looked away. And whispered. "They say she's half mad."

"So you are married. And your father must not know. Because your
wife was not born as your equal. And he wants to be made a great
lord."

He nodded, almost with a child's eagerness. "He wouldn't even
have her if she were a duchess. Not as long as she's a foreigner. He
hates foreigners."

"So," I said, with little enough pity, "you hope to conceal this
matter—your marriage—until your father dies. Is that it?"

He seemed to shrink. And I will tell you: Likely he had not thought
quite so far. Not clearly. Surely, it was in the back of his mind. And
perhaps it slipped toward the front now and again. But when we are
desperate and afraid, we only hope to survive the terrors of the day.
We do not think in years when we fear next week. We hope, blindly,
that somehow things will turn right.

"I don't know," he said. "I only know that he'd never accept her.
Or forgive me."

I looked around the splendid room, with its virgin books and
shelves of curiosities. We say that we would give our all for love, when
we are in a passion. But men and women like the things they have, and
would as soon maintain their every comfort. I am not a romantical fellow, but I would have liked the boy more had he been willing to take
a stand for his beloved. Perhaps his father would have liked him better, too. For the father had seemed an ogre when he passed me, but he
had the carriage of a bold and strapping man. The son was slender as
a book of verse.

"And what about your debts? And reports of gambling?"

He looked down at the Turkey carpet. "I was a fool. An incredible
fool. I thought I had a gift for cards. You know how it is, don't you? I
thought I could win enough to care for Sarah. To pay the doctors." He
lifted his face toward me as if his neck pained him. "We . . . we were
to have a child. But she became ill. The doctors . . . the expenses . . . I
thought I could win enough, you see. And when I lost, I borrowed."
He laughed. Bitterly. "I believed I was a prince in a fairy tale. I was
going to carry her off to a castle in the clouds. Now she's had to go
back to her lacemaking. And she's so ill . . ." Of a sudden, he con-

fronted me full on. "Haven't you ever loved to break your heart? Haven't you ever loved anyone, and failed them? Do you have any idea how that makes a man feel?"

Oh, I had recollections enough to sate me, and believed I knew more of life than the lad on the divan. But I whipped him on, for death had been prowling after me in the streets and a weak boy's troubles seemed of little consequence. "And the difficulties in which your sister found herself? What about those?"

"That's none of your business," he said, irately.

"I will make it my business, boy. Speak truly, and you may find that I will help you. Lie, and I will let you drop like a glass vase. Tell me of your sister and her difficulties."

"It wasn't her fault."

"I did not say it was."

"She's an angel."

"I did not say she was not."

"She found them. Together."

"Who then?"

"Her husband. And Lord Tye. She hadn't known a thing, you see. Although we all suspected. Father was all for the match, no matter what. Her husband's title goes back seven hundred years. And . . . when she found them, they were . . . they were in the act." His face, reddened by weeping, nonetheless changed color in a blush. "She hadn't known about it. Not a thing. She hadn't known such relationships could exist."

"And that is her shame?"

"She left him. But his grace put it about that *she* was the guilty party. The swine. He told everyone *he* had found *her*. That he found her with a groom. Before she could so much as whisper an accusation herself. So anything she said would sound like a vengeful lie. My father had to pay him to shut his mouth and take her back." He twisted up his face. "Seven hundred years of spending every penny they ever got. That's what it all came down to. Father had money enough, and Jasper had the pedigree. Now my father's afraid someone may have told Her Majesty. The lie about my sister and the groom, I mean."

"And where is your sister now?"

Hatred streaked from his eyes again. He laughed horribly. "Lord, you don't know a thing. Do you?"

"Where is your sister, Mr. Pomeroy?"

"I suppose I should challenge you to a duel or something. But then where would Sarah be?" He smirked. Twas dreadful to look at him.

I did not understand, see.

"Finish the tale of your sister, boy. For something is left unsaid."

"Have you no decency at all?" He swept his hand wildly about. "Adela's dead. For the love of God. She drowned herself in the river up at Bournely."

I had not known, of course. Mr. Disraeli, with his twisting and turning, had left out a great deal.

"I'm sorry."

He took no interest in my apologies. "My father loved her more than anything else in the world," young Pomeroy continued. "I was always a disappointment to him. Since Adela's death, he's been a monster. He even—"

I was hardly listening at that point. I pictured the lass as Ophelia, floating in a brook and free of this world. Mr. Shakespeare knew how frail we are. But let that bide. I had a task before me, and I would do it.

"These blackmailers," I interrupted him. "However many there are. The Earl of Thretford and the rest of them. Mr. Disraeli. What do they want of you?"

He thought for a moment. I did not think that it was calculation, only a move from one of the mind's compartments to another, for I had dragged him down to his sister's watery grave. And he needed to surface again to answer my question.

"Disraeli," he said, "never asked a thing until Friday evening. I wasn't even aware he knew I existed. I still don't know exactly what he knows. But I don't believe he's involved with the Earl of Thretford. It's all separate somehow. You see, the Earl never does anything in person, if he can help it. Not during daylight. I simply get these notes, delivered by a different boy each time. Another boy comes for the reply. But Mr. Disraeli sent his own carriage for me, so I could meet him after Parliament closed. It didn't seem the same thing at all."

"And what did Mr. Disraeli want you to do?"

"He made me tell him everything I knew about your Mr. Campbell's death. I had to get him a copy of the letter. I was amazed. That he knew so much about my circumstances, I mean." He made a wry face. "I'm beginning to suspect all London knows, anyway."

I, too, was amazed, but by other matters. "Didn't . . . didn't Mr. Disraeli say anything to you about keeping matters out of the newspapers? About protecting Mr. Adams?"

His face went blank. "Why on earth would he do that?"

"Nothing about Mr. Adams, then? Or keeping secret the letter found on the body? Nothing about keeping matters out of *The Times?*"

He shook his head. "Lord John had already seen to all that. Earl Russell has a certain fondness for Mr. Adams, you know. He does what he can for him. Lord John made it clear that he didn't want anyone to breathe a word outside the Foreign Office."

This was all awry. "But you," I said, "on Friday, in the morgue. You were positively insolent toward Mr. Adams."

He looked down like a child whose devices have failed. "I was afraid to go back to the office without an explanation of some kind. I didn't want to look a fool, you know. I suppose I was impertinent. But I didn't want to go back empty-handed and listen to them all saying, 'Old Pomeroy never gets it quite right, does he?' I thought there might be something I could learn, if I pushed a bit. Something that would show them all I could master a situation."

Abruptly, he leaned forward. "Don't you see? If I can't even keep my position at the Foreign Office, what will I do? If my father should disinherit me? I have no prospects. I'm in debt. Badly in debt. My wife's ill. I daren't lose my position."

I sighed. Perhaps he thought it was a sign of sympathy. If so, I did not correct him. Although the truth was that I just felt weary. And sick of more deceptions than I could count. Was anyone in England to be trusted?

Finally, though, the puppet-masters had made a miscalculation. Young Pomeroy had been lured to the penny gaff so I would see him and draw a false conclusion. Likely, that boy's hacked carcass had been deposited in the park nearby to add to my suspicions. I was to go on suspecting Pomeroy, see, conjuring a devil from a dupe. And he had not been expected to do the one thing of which an Englishman had begun to seem incapable: Telling the truth. I had simply had a stroke of good fortune, at young Pomeroy's expense. Even if I was God's own fool. I had caught the lad in a moment of weakness and given him the extra dose of terror that it took to break him down. And he had blabbered.

So the dark men pulling the strings had erred at last.

Or had they?

And was the Earl of Thretford behind the murders? I knew him for a man willing to shed blood. The blood of others, shed by other hands.

And he would have had some knowledge of me, imparted by Professor Kildare, the mesmerist behind the plot back in New York. That would explain some of my enemy's knowledge of me.

But what on earth could be the tie to India? To *Thuggee* cords and severed hands in boxes?

Young Pomeroy sat there, smaller than a grown man should have been. And I do not speak of physiognomy.

"Look you," I said. "What is this business I hear of your fondness for the Confederates and Richmond?"

He could not rise above his blighted slump, for he had been hit hard. By himself, above all. But he said, "It's just the fashion. None of the fellows I know thinks much of the American Union. Or of that Lincoln of yours. He's said to be little more than an ape."

I could have struck him. For well I knew the insults the whole world had ready for Mr. Lincoln. I would have liked to give them all a hammering. For if Mr. Lincoln was not high-born or polished after their society fashion, he was true and stalwart and good.

I mastered myself.

"So . . . you support the Rebels and slavers because it is the fashion?"

"I don't support them. Not really. The truth is I don't give a fig about your war."

"But you pass on information. Do you not?"

"To blackmailers," he said ruefully. "Not that they get anything from me they couldn't have free for the asking from anyone in the Foreign Office. Except Lord John. He keeps himself above things." The boy gave a one-note laugh. "He hardly knows the half of what goes on."

A weak reed he was, if ever one had sprouted. But young Pomeroy did not seem truly a wicked sort to me. Despite his many follies. For he loved his wife, who was ill, and he stood by her in his weakling's manner. That must have cost him all his reserves of courage. And more.

Twas nearly time for me to leave, for the evening was advancing. And now I had another call to pay. But I needed to clear up a final matter.

"The letters. Which you were to fetch from Miss Perkins, the singer. The letters to your wife. I take it the Earl of Thretford has them in his possession? Or is it Mr. Disraeli, do you think?"

He looked dull and drained. "I don't know. I only wish I did. Then I'd know where to start. But I doubt it's Disraeli. The letters went missing months ago. And I only heard from him Friday."

"Then the Earl must have them."

But he was not convinced of that, either. "He may have them. I can't say with any certainty. I only know they were stolen. And that I was told that little slut from Eastcheap Street was going to return them."

"Then these love-letters have not been used to blackmail you? At least, not yet? Not by the Earl of Thretford?"

"He may be holding them. As a sort of bank reserve. But he doesn't really need them, you see."

"Then what, in God's name, is he holding over your head, man?"

"He knows," young Pomeroy said, in the placid voice of a man worn-out completely, "that my wife's a Jewess."

Eight

I took me off to Mr. Disraeli's house, for I am rash when angered. Wet air darkened the alleys and twilight brooded above the chimney pots. Sounds carried. In a lesser street, I heard the play of children I could not see from the hack. To the clop of hooves and the creak of axles, their small, thin voices sang:

> *First comes the packman,*
> *Next comes the tallyman,*
> *Last comes the bailiff,*
> *One, two, three!*

Then we left the lanes of care and passed before fine mansions once again. Mr. Disraeli lived in a proper house, on a proper street, but I was unsure he was a proper man.

His windows were lit to a gaiety, giving the building's facade a luminous tone that suggested all was well and good within. I saw no forms from the pavement and realized we had reached the dinner hour. The Disraelis and their guests would be at table.

At least they appeared to be at home. Mr. Adams had mentioned to me that Mr. Disraeli missed no opportunity to play the country gentleman at a manor house provided by his backers. But Parliament was keeping the members in town with its plodding, which seemed to be my good fortune.

I should have waited, I suppose, for no man likes to have his meal disrupted. But I was hot, for I had been deceived, as had Mr. Adams.

And the misery of young Pomeroy affected me, although by rights I owed him nothing at all.

I pulled the bell. And gave the door a whack with my cane for good measure.

Instead of a sniffing porter, a serving girl answered my knock. Her hair was out of her cap and the lass perspired. After hardly a glance at me, she said, in a voice too loud, "Have you brung the oysters, then? For we're all at sixes and sevens. Though you'd ought to go round to the back where we take in the trade."

"Begging your pardon, miss. I am not in trade."

She gave me the up and down. "Collecting, then, are you? Well, you'll have to get in line."

"I have come to see Mr. Disraeli. My name is Jones and I am an American officer. The matter has a certain urgency. Might you ask the hall-porter to inform him?"

"You'll find no porter here, sir, for Sam's gone off in complaint of unpaid wages. Oh, ain't the four walls in commotion? For the guests are come, and the food's but arf-fixed, and nobody's brung the oysters. What shouldn't be et in the month of June, but no matter. For the master likes his rarities, he does."

I began to suspect that the course of Mr. Disraeli's household did not run smooth.

"Thought he'd be up the country, we did, so cook went off to Finchley with Mr. Grimes. Oh, we're all in a terrible uproar, sir, and I wish you had brung us the oysters, but the master carries it off with savwar fairy."

"Do you think," I tried, "that you could inform Mr. Disraeli of my coming?"

She looked at me again, as if she had to remind herself of my existence. "Oh, I can, sir, and I will, sir. It's only that I been sent to look-out for the oysters. What's like to poison us all, since the summer's upon us." She offered me a confidence. "You know, sir, that the month of June don't have no *r* in it. I'm worried the master will eat 'em and keel over dead. And me owed wages these three months and beyond!"

"Please, miss. *Will* you tell your master that Major Jones has come to see him? Upon a pressing matter?"

"Oh, I'm already gone to do that," she assured me. "I'm halfway down the hall. But would you be a right gent and look out for the oysters?"

I told her that I would. And she went at last.

In a brace of minutes, the lass come back, with a worried look on her face. I assured her that the oysters had not slipped past me.

"Oh, now I'm to show you in," she said, "but I ain't sure you should go. For when I said you was come, the master smiled. And he's always unhappy when he puts on a smile like that. He don't like seeing bill collectors on Sundays, sir. Not that he likes them any other day. But Sundays always set him off most awful. Would you happen to know, sir, of any decent households as wants a parlor maid? Although I'm not above a share in the kitchen."

I professed my good will toward her and, since the oysters still had not arrived, she cast her attention up the street, then down it to make certain, and hastened me into the study where I had enjoyed my first interview with Mr. Disraeli. He sat in the self-same chair, with the same little smile above his goaty beard, and his eyes were as dark and as deep in his flesh as ever.

He did not rise to greet me.

"How delightful!" he said. "And utterly unexpected! Won't you sit down, Major Jones?"

I took a chair, but found I could not look at him. For I was afraid I might not control my speech. Instead, I trailed my eyes over his books, whose gilded spines shone vivid in the gaslight. The room smelled of tobacco and pomade.

Dinner guests or no, Mr. Disraeli waited calmly for me to begin. With his head weaving back and forth, ever so slightly, above the points of his collar.

"Sir," I began at last, "you have been dishonest."

"Oh, dear!"

"You deceived Mr. Adams. And myself."

His face came forward, ever so slightly, as if he could strike out any time he wanted. But he only maintained that imperturbable smile. It did not alter even as he spoke. As though the man were speaking behind a mask.

"You have me at a disadvantage, Major Jones. I haven't the least idea what you mean."

"You gave Mr. Adams assurances."

His expression shifted at last. To a look that wished to appear amiable. "Ah, yes! I did, indeed. And in good faith." His face came forward another inch. "If I may ask—which of those assurances did I neglect, sir? The indelicate matter of your parson has been suppressed. Fleet Street has behaved admirably. I haven't seen a word in the press. Her Majesty's Government appears unconcerned. In what have I disappointed?"

"You implied that you would be the one who—"

"Ah," he raised his head higher, "there we have a fascinating word! 'Implied.' Perhaps you were about to say that I 'implied' I would effect certain results that Earl Russell saw fit to attain without my assistance? But why should I have duplicated his effort? As long as my assurances to your minister were fulfilled?" For an instant, his smile seemed almost genuine. "As to anything that may have been 'implied,' I believe that ears are in the habit of hearing what they wish, rather than what has been spoken for their benefit. I cannot interfere with human nature."

"You bullied that boy. Young Pomeroy. To find out all you could about the legation's involvement with the Reverend Mr. Campbell?"

"*Is* there an 'involvement,' Major Jones?"

"Your curiosity seems to—"

"Ah! 'Curiosity!' Another word that never fails to interest me. Curiosity, Major Jones, is a quality I find admirable under almost every circumstance. Curiosity leads us onward to knowledge. And knowledge . . . knowledge is the engine of progress, whether in the realms of industry, in the far fields of science, or in politics. Why, I believe a man in my position would fail in his duty, were he to decline the least chance to learn something new. Something," he said, with that masking smile upon him again, "that might prove unexpectedly advantageous."

"You preyed upon the boy's weakness!"

His smile was like the light on a field of bracken, when the weather is changeable and the clouds run. The moment I thought him in shadow, sunlight returned. But one thing was markedly different from our first encounter. He did not twitter. Not once. It made me think that matters had grown serious.

"Upon his weakness? My dear Major Jones! Weakness may be an explanation, but it is never an excuse. Weak men should not seek position, if they cannot withstand the strong. I think that is an accepted argument of our times." He stirred in his chair. "But I've been unspeakably neglectful. May I offer you a glass of sherry?"

Then he paused. For a sliver of a second after he had finished speaking, his mouth hung open. He looked just to the side of me and said, "But I forget myself. You abstain."

Twas clear that his slight forgetfulness annoyed him. And stranger still I found it that a man who had dinner and guests waiting would help himself to a sherry, as Mr. Disraeli did before my eyes. I do not think it is "done," as such folk say.

"I want the letters," I told him.

Before he turned to face me again, he said, "I find myself at a disadvantage yet again. What letters, Major Jones?"

I knew it in my bones, see. Pomeroy might funk a conclusion staring him in the face, but I would not. Disraeli had the letters the failed young man had written to his wife. That is how he knew enough to break him.

"Mr. Reginald Pomeroy's letters. To his wife."

He lowered his glass of sherry and constructed an amazed face.

"You must explain."

But I was learning his tricks of language, see.

"The letters from which you learned enough to make him sick with fear. Enough to make him dance and jump for you like a dog. The letters—"

"But my dear Major Jones . . . even if a gentleman came into the possession of such letters, which seems unlikely, he could hardly fail to—"

"Mr. Disraeli, I am not afraid to call things as they are. You have blackmailed that boy."

He sat down again, and neatly placed his sherry glass on a table topped with marble. "Is *that* what you Americans call it? When a fellow seeks to assist a young man who has strayed? When a gentleman . . . attempts to spare a threatened youth the gravest embarrassment? When a man of position tries, selflessly, to improve the performance in office of one of Her Majesty's officials? Is that called 'blackmail' in the United States, sir?"

"I will have the letters," I told him, "before I go."

He shook his head. Delicately, as a fine, high gentleman will. "Let us explore the dimensions of theoretical possibility, Major Jones. I will play Faraday and put a supposition to you. Now, if the first party possessed such letters, and party the second desired to come into their possession—perhaps for dubious reasons of their own, although that does not figure in our supposition—what might the second party offer party the first in exchange?" His smiled catted higher. "In what I believe the Yankee terms a 'swap'?"

I do not like games. Not games of cards, nor games with words. And I am not skilled in such matters.

Twas then I blundered.

"It seems to me," I said, "that the first fellow would be lucky not to be known publicly as a thief. Who stole a lady's letters while she was lying ill, and who used them against the loving husband who had written them to her. Such a fellow should be glad to save his reputation."

Mr. Disraeli made a steeple of his fingertips, feigning deep thought. Then he said, "But, Major Jones, I fail to recall any mention of thievery in our proposition. It was my unspoken assumption that the first party, far from annoying a lady and her property, had come by the letters in question in his customary role as a good angel. Rescuing them from less scrupulous hands, and keeping them safe and intact. But now we have begun to speak of motives, which are never as clear as they seem." He took a decidedly slow sip of sherry. "As for your suggested reward, the preservation of party the first's good reputation, I should rather expect that reputation to be enhanced, should the affair come to light. When it emerged that he had attempted, at some risk, to effect the best of deeds and preserve a lady's honor. Or, at least, the illusion thereof."

Now, I was in a muddle. I do not like to talk around things, or over and under them, but to say plainly what must be said.

"What are you suggesting, sir?" I asked, in a voice too near demanding for good manners. I have little polish, see, and Christian honesty will not do in society.

He rose, slowly, like a cobra from its basket. "Why, I don't believe I've 'suggested' a single thing. We have been speaking theoretically, nothing more. Even idly, one might say." He glided behind a desk and opened one of its drawers. "Yet . . . it happens, Major Jones," he said, bringing out a stack of letters tied up with a blue ribbon, "that there is a measure of reality to my proposition. I found myself enabled to defend the Pomeroy boy's interests and—at no small cost—I did what a gentleman ought."

He held the stack of letters out toward me.

I took them. And, sick with the vanity of my imagined cleverness, I pretended to count the stack I had been given. Though it was a fib of sorts, for I was merely guessing, I said, "The rest of them, too, sir. This is not all of them."

It seemed to me that such a one as Mr. Disraeli would not give all at once, at the first asking.

Obediently, he made a show of rooting through the drawer. And he produced another, smaller collection, bound up in a red ribbon.

"How good of you to remind me," he said.

I got myself up to my feet. "Thank you, sir. You have done the right thing, see."

"Oh, but must you rush off?"

I failed to anticipate him. "You . . . but you have dinner guests, I believe? Don't you—"

He waved such cares away with a jovial gesture and sat back down. "Mrs. Disraeli provides more than adequate compensation for my absence. No, Major Jones, now that you have 'bagged your game,' you must let me profit from your experience."

I sat me down again, with a feeling grown uneasy.

"Really, Major Jones! I have underestimated you frightfully! You must forgive me, I beg you." He leaned forward in that slight way of his. "I'm unspeakably relieved to know that those letters are in trustworthy hands at last. They've been a terrible burden to me. But . . ." He underscored the question with a tightening of his eyebrows. ". . . why do you think it is that Reggie Pomeroy's wife sold those letters in the first place? What benefit could she possibly have expected that might outweigh the risk to her worried husband? How much money do you think she asked?"

"Such a suggestion," I replied, "is abominable, sir."

"Ah," Mr. Disraeli said happily, "that is one point upon which your views and mine coincide. I have often found the truth abominable. Insistent, as well."

"She would not . . . no lady could have done such a thing!"

"But there we disagree, Major Jones. I have always found the fairer sex remarkably capable. Have you, by the way, ever *met* Mrs. Pomeroy? Young Reginald's wife? In whom you have taken so great an interest?"

"I have not, sir, but—"

"Another word that has changed the course of nations! Indeed, a sometimes-deadly word, infernal: 'But.' You have not met her, then? What a terrible pity."

"I believe she is ill and incommoded. And . . . if she did sell . . . *if* . . . perhaps . . . her health . . . perhaps she was in need . . ."

"I must plead ignorance," Mr. Disraeli said, as he emptied the final drop from his glass of sherry. "I had no idea Mrs. Pomeroy was in poor health."

"She has been terribly ill, sir. A child was lost."

At that, his smile grew unmistakably genuine. And cruel. "We do not speak, I take it, of young Pomeroy himself?"

"Sir . . ." Oh, there was a dreadful twisting at the bottom of my stomach, and not only from an abundance of Spanish oranges. ". . . if you please . . . the lady has a secret she must protect."

"What lady doesn't?"

"You must be mistaken . . ."

Mr. Disraeli assumed the expression of a benevolent elder, bent on imparting knowledge to a boy. "Major Jones, I have, at certain times in the past, occupied myself with the composition of novels, an endeavor evocative of the political field in that a man must condition himself to the keenest observation of manners and character. And it has never failed to be an inspiration to me how a young man, captivated by his passion for a particular woman, will believe whatever she may see fit to tell him, no matter its absurdity. Such young men demonstrate a magnificent faith in the veracity of the beloved, one that routinely strains credulity. But, then, I never have understood faith in any of its profounder forms. I take life as I find it, you see. And I cannot say I feel any the poorer for my deficiency."

"You expect me to believe that Mr. Pomeroy's wife betrayed him? And sold the letters he wrote to her? Knowing the danger in which her husband might find himself? And jeopardizing all their private matters?"

"Major Jones, I don't 'expect' you to believe anything. That is your affair entirely. I merely offer friendly observations."

"Friendly, is it?"

"You do seem to have some difficulty in sorting your friends from your enemies. Indeed, I've been holding out the hand of friendship to you with uninterrupted consistency. But you display a certain reluctance to embrace my offer."

What might I have said?

With a regretful wave of his head, Mr. Disraeli continued, "I recognized your value from the first, Major Jones. And let us be frank: Isn't mutual value the basis of all friendships? Although we like to paint them in finer colors? Haven't I entrusted you with those letters?" He pointed to the missives in my hand. "Would I entrust so delicate a matter to a man I did not believe I could trust without reservation? How *do* you Americans define friendship, if I may ask?"

I thought of Mick Tyrone, and of Jimmy Molloy. But let that bide.

Mr. Disraeli rose again, with a brief tut-tutting. He was the quietest man afoot that ever I did know this side of the Khyber. Save perhaps an American-Indian fellow, Broke Stick, who had crept through Mississippi—but that is another story. Mr. Disraeli seemed to glide across the carpet, and you heard naught but the hiss of his gleaming leather pumps.

"I believe," my host resumed, "there is another American expression, to the effect that 'seeing is believing.' I suppose I shall have to offer further proof of my consideration toward you, Major Jones. Just as you were so kind in your suggestion that my reputation wanted preservation from the public's misapprehensions. Indeed, circumstances have afforded me the ability to offer an identical service to you."

I did not know what on earth he meant. But I did not think I would like it.

"You are, sir," he continued, "a man of remarkable and varied accomplishments. I'm told you even served in the ranks, in India?"

"I did, sir," I said cautiously. "In a John Company regiment."

"And you served quite handsomely, I'm given to understand. Almost heroically, one might say?"

"That is not for me to judge."

142 / Owen Parry

"No," he said, in a thoughtful voice. "No, indeed not. Finally, it has been suggested—by a well-intentioned gentleman in the Indian Records Office—that you suffered a certain misfortune. As things were sorting themselves out in the wake of the Mutiny. The result of which was a medical declaration to the effect that you were no longer fit for duty. 'Mad of a fever,' I believe the examining officer put it." He had come quite close to me, until he almost hovered over my chair. "I must say, you don't look the least bit mad to me. Sitting there so pleasantly in a Morocco armchair. In mufti for the evening, but currently serving as an officer in the military arm of the United States."

"I am not mad," I said slowly. "Nor was I then." Although the truth is that I did not know what my condition might have been properly called. I only know the day arrived when I found myself helpless. I could not kill another unarmed man, which had become our vengeful occupation. I do not pretend to virtue in that regard. Twas only that I found myself unable. And I never had thought to raise my hand in the sin of war thereafter. America it was that called me back to service. Sweet America, and the sight of those helpless boys drilling.

"I was never mad," I concluded.

"Ah," Mr. Disraeli said, backing away as if to fetch more sherry. "I do find that a considerable relief! I will take you at your word and we shall declare the charge of madness an odious calumny. Really, it's an enormous relief! I had supposed myself in a dilemma, you see, but now there's no question of a madman let loose upon us. *With* the imprimatur of the Government of the United States. We need not fear embarrassment—or danger—on that count." He paused before the decanter, but did not touch it. Twas as if he were acting upon a stage. "And so I find my concerns reduced to one: If you are not and were not 'mad,' and I am myself confident of your sanity, Major Jones, then the sole liability we face is a charge of desertion."

He smiled and leaned his coat-tails against the front of his desk. "Might it not embarrass Mr. Adams, and your government—and, not least, yourself, sir—if someone of a malevolent nature were to misconstrue your actions? Imagining that you had perpetrated a hoax to avoid fulfilling your term of service? That you had made a wicked charade of madness out of cowardice in the face of the enemy?" He shuddered for my benefit. "With the best will in the world, I could hardly defend anyone against such a charge. Consider how your odyssey might appear to unfriendly eyes: Five years ago, you were a sergeant in an Indian regiment, who suddenly refused to do his duty. Who was deemed 'mad of a fever,' perhaps in lieu of hanging. Think of it, sir: Such a man returns to England, supposedly an invalid, only to leave, within months, for America. It might look like a case of flight, Major Jones. And now, astonishingly, our innocent returns to Britain's shores commissioned as a field officer in a foreign army. One whose interests are not entirely coincident with those of Her Majesty."

Dolefully, he regarded the curlicues in the carpet. "For the present, let us set aside selfish considerations, such as the prospect of your seizure and imprisonment. Let us consider only the public effects. I fail to see what I might do to help, were your history to reach the ears of those who might be anxious to misconstrue it. Lindsay, perhaps. Our 'Scourge from Sunderland.' I fear we would hear a speech about the matter in Her Majesty's House of Commons. Doubtless, from the Lords, as well." He raised his cobra's eyes. "What might that mean to your cause, sir? And to you?"

"I can explain," I said quietly.

"I am confident that you can, Major Jones. But, in my experience, explanations are as ineffectual as they are abundant. It is the accusations that interest the general run of mankind. Why, I myself have been the victim of calumnies, years ago, which will not be laid to rest. Although I am certain my explanations are every bit as worthy as your own." He smiled in a mocking display of sympathy. "No, sir. Our strategy must be designed to avoid such accusations in the first instance."

"What do you want?"

"Why, your friendship. What else might I desire?"

"What do you want me to do?"

"Nothing."

"What do you mean by 'nothing'?"

"Why, the same thing poor Cordelia meant: Nothing at all. We, too, must see that 'nothing shall come of nothing,' as her royal and dreary father liked to put it. Let us say, 'Nothing that would inconvenience a friend.' "

"Do you know who killed the Reverend Mr. Campbell?" I begged. "And the others?"

"No." He lifted himself from his perch on the edge of the desk. "Nor do I wish to know. I withdraw myself from any connection to this affair." He opened his palms toward me. His hands were long and shaped like flames. "I must be certain that no misunderstanding will associate my name with this sordid business. Not so much as a whisper. As my friend, you doubtless will attach the greatest importance to protecting my interests. As I shall protect yours."

"What do you know?" I fear my voice was not as brave as my intent. For I was shaken, there is true, and I will not deny it. For no man likes to bear a public shame, whether or not his shame may be deserved. And I thought of my wife and son, whose hearts would be broken. Oh, I felt empty as a leaky canteen at the end of a long day's march. "Can you tell me anything, sir?"

"I know," Mr. Disraeli said with refreshed aplomb, "that it will take the luckiest of men to emerge from this matter unscathed. And luck is an inconstant companion."

"Can't you . . . tell me anything else?"

He faced his bookshelves. I saw his narrow shoulders, the hood-like rise of his collar, and the shine of scalp through his hair. "I find," he said, "that I know more than I wish, but not enough to be of any value."

"Please," I asked, with a craven tone in my words that left me shamed, "will you just answer one question, sir?"

He turned toward me again. Somber now, his expression said: "Ask, and I shall see."

"Did you get those letters from the Earl of Thretford?"

He appeared surprised. "From Arthur Langley? Absolutely not. No, not from the Earl." He canted his head in frank curiosity. "You're acquainted with Lord Arthur?"

"No, sir. Not acquainted. I only saw him once. He was up to mischief."

Disraeli returned to his customary smile, part amused and part bemused. "Lord Arthur's always up to mischief. I'd stay away from him, if I could."

"But isn't he a member of your party? A Tory? Like you?"

"Arthur Langley is not in the least 'like' me. Major Jones, there is an abundance of members of both parties whose company is infelicitous. Political majorities are not built by an excess of particularity. One must appeal for votes, but we need not find the voters themselves appealing." Then he thought another step along. "You suspect the Earl's involved in this matter?"

"He may be," I said, for I was no longer certain of anything much. "I believe he has a tie with young Mr. Pomeroy. At least, the lad believes he has a tie to the Earl."

I wondered if I had said too much. But I dared not say too little. Far removed from my earlier confidence, I did not wish to be caught out by my host. I feared him in that hour, for I imagined he might ruin the life I had rebuilt so painfully, and that I might shame the country that had given me a chance to live in decency. Had Mr. Disraeli been less adoring of himself, he might have had of me intelligence I did not yet realize I possessed. I did not know the contents of my own pockets, see. But he failed to press me where he should have done.

"That," Mr. Disraeli said, "is a matter of some interest. I shall need to pay attention. Do you expect to remain in London a great deal longer, Major Jones?"

"In fact, sir, I hope to go to Glasgow. If not tomorrow, then on Tuesday." Oh, I was humble as a beaten dog. It shames me still to think on it.

"Glasgow," he repeated. Then he straightened his posture and declared, "You must have countless things to do. You mustn't let me detain you any longer."

He did not offer to shake my hand, or to open the door, but let me find my own way.

Just as I was set to step into the hallway, clutching the packets of letters, he spoke again.

"As your friend," he said, calling my attention back into the study, "I must say I'm surprised at your interest in the Earl of Thretford." He wore a smile now that I could not read clearly. It did suggest friendship, seen in one light. But when he shifted he looked like the very Devil. "I would have thought your interest would run more to his half-brother."

"His half-brother, sir?"

"Yes," Mr. Disraeli said, still smiling. "I believe he served in India, as well. Perhaps you know of him. A wild sort, I'm told, who rode with a unit of irregular cavalry." His serpent's eyes met mine. "Did you ever encounter Lieutenant Ralph Culpeper?"

"The man's dead." My voice wavered as I spoke.

"Is he?" Mr. Disraeli asked. "How odd. Someone told me he'd just been seen in Lambeth."

What was I to think? And worse to ponder, what was I to do? What sort of city was this, in which the dead walked and wives were said to sell their husband's letters? In which children were butchered and men sneaked about in red masks, where elaborate hoaxes dissolved into riddles more complicated still? Where the Confederate cause was advanced by everyone but the Rebels themselves, and a parson dead in a basket of eels had begun to seem as normal as butter biscuits?

Was I, indeed, mad?

I would not believe that. No, of that I would not be persuaded, although I will admit to a great confusion. I took myself along those unclean streets, with darkness pushing me forward like a broom. Were *Thuggee* assassins waiting in the next alley? Was a peer of the realm involved in a pawn-broker's death? Did I want to go to Glasgow to do my duty, or only to flee from London?

I had to speak to Mr. Adams, to tell him everything I could remember. And then I would need to talk with Inspector Wilkie again. And to pay another call, one which I dreaded out of all reason. Glasgow must wait until Tuesday, twas clear. For London would keep me chained for another day.

I felt so glum I walked all the way to the hotel, despite my leg's complaints. I went past men drunk on a Sunday night and past women offering more than I could bear hearing. I only wished that I were home in Pottsville, with my sweet wife and son. Safe. And far from the regard of the world. What had I to do with the contest of nations? I was a clerk, and wanted no higher calling. Let me have the honesty of numbers, the clarity of black ink on white paper! I would have liked to shout out my desire, and my grief. And my fear. But that would never have done.

I worried that I would be unable to write my daily letter to my wife, given my haunted thoughts. And the bitter love-letters stretching out my pocket. I wished me home beside my Mary Myfanwy, in the precious, mortal safety of her love. I wanted to read my Testament, and to pray.

A blind man tapped along as I turned into Baker Street. Leaning on my own cane, I felt as dull and visionless as him.

For all my years, what did I know of life? I would believe the best of men and women. But I do find it hard. And am oft mistaken.

Well, we must have faith, and go through.

The hotel porter had glared at me of late, grumpy at the very sight of me. But this time, when I come in, he gave me a little smile and the strangest wink.

Upstairs I went, full weary, and grown anxious to visit the sanitary appliance at the end of the hall. I fear I had consumed too many oranges after all, for I had eaten the last on my walk home, and my digestion was confounded. But first I went to my room to shed my coat. For modern plumbing does not ask formality.

The first thing I saw when I opened the door was a red petticoat draped over a chair. The second thing was Miss Polly Perkins herself, gone under the sheets of my bed in the guise of Eve.

Nine

"*Why, there you are, sweetie,*" the White Lily of Kent laughed. "It ain't polite to keep a lady waiting, you know."

"Miss Perkins!" I said, in abundant alarm, "I am going back into the hallway and I will close this door behind me. I will leave you alone for five minutes." I tossed my coat onto the dresser, far from that brazen petticoat and the scandalous array of nether-garments surrounding the bed. "For Heaven's sake, young woman, compose yourself!"

I fled back into the corridor, as shaken as a young soldier surprised in his slumbers by the enemy. The first thought—well, perhaps the second—that raced through my mind was that my wife was bound to hear of this somehow. Now, you will say, "That is a nonsense. How would she hear of goings-on in London? Anyway, you were innocent, according to your story." But I will tell you: All wives have a genius for discovery. My own beloved wife has a generous nature and an understanding temperament. She is the very milk of human kindness. But there is steel in her, too. In the end, she might believe in my innocence. But I could not relish the ordeal of persuasion. Even the best wife does not like to hear that her husband has shared his bedchamber with a kicking dancer from a music hall. And certainly not with one so out of costume.

I closeted myself in the sanitary room and found the experience calming. I began to formulate my questions. For the White Lily's presence wanted some explanation.

Then the queerest thing happened.

I felt a prickling on the back of my neck, and the hair went up on my forearms. The way it did on frontier campaigns, when you sensed an enemy not yet to be seen. I hastened to conclude my private endeavors and stepped back into the hallway. Ready with my cane.

There was nothing. Gaslights mottled the veteran paint. Cheaply framed pictures of coaches and huntsmen with hounds adorned the walls. The long parade of carpet, not immaculate, marched stairward.

Of course, I had reasons in plenty to feel disturbed, what with all that had happened since Friday and now the appearance of a guest so unexpected. Yet, the feeling that had come over me in that cabinet was different. I knew it. And, though it passed in a moment, of a sudden I feared for Miss Perkins. I wanted to find her clothed. But I did not wish to find her dead.

I rushed back to my room, practically vaulting over my cane. After fumbling a bit with the key again, I burst in breathless.

"Anxious now, is he?" Miss Perkins said.

She stood in the queerest posture before the dressing mirror. I fear she had not followed my instructions. Her condition of person remained what might, most charitably, be described as classical in form.

How pale she was!

I turned my back upon her with the requisite promptitude, but shut the door and locked it. Not to keep her in, you understand. But to keep danger out.

With my entirety faced away from her, I struggled to find words for my dismay.

"What's the matter with you, then?" she asked in a baffled tone. Under other circumstances, I might have described it as the voice of a little girl. "Ain't you the one told me to get up and pose myself?"

"Miss Perkins, I asked you to *com*pose yourself. To dress, madame!"

"Why ever should I do that?" Then she answered herself, with a knowing laugh. "Oh, that's it, then? You're one of them gents as likes to do his own unpacking. Well, I got all time in the world, so we'll do what makes you happy. Do you want me to put everything back on, or just my knickers?"

"Everything," I said, in the deepest mortification. "Please."

Behind my trembling shoulders, I heard the sound of bare feet crossing the carpet toward me. I am not sure I ever felt such a jolt of terror.

I wheeled about, holding out my hand against her approach. I fear I glimpsed her shame again, although I remembered my duty and shut my eyes hastily.

"Don't you look a funny one, sweetie?" she said. "If we're playing a game, I'd like to know the rules."

"Please. Just stop. Stop where you are. Cover yourself. Use anything."

I did not want her even one inch closer. For well I know Old Adam lurks in all of us.

I could smell her. The cheap perfume, likely from a bottle concocted in Stepney and labeled "French." And I smelled the womanness. That bidding scent they have.

"Please," I said, in a quieter voice. "Cover yourself. Use the bedsheet. Anything. And tell me when you're covered up."

"Well, what's this all about, I'd just like to know?" she said in a voice of wonder. But her footsteps retreated. And I heard the sounds of a great tampering with the bedclothes.

"Tell me when you're decent," I said.

Miffed, she declared, "I'm as decent as any girl *you*'ll ever know. And who says I'm not?"

"When you're covered, tell me. Tell me when you're covered up."

Condemn me if you will. I am the happiest of married men, the most fortunate. Still, my truant eyes wished to see what they should not.

Why are we made so? I am content in mind, and in heart. I love, and am loved. Why is this greed embedded in our flesh?

"Well, I'm all wrapped up like a baby in the cradle," she huffed. "So I guess you can open your peepers."

I opened my eyes. She was a pretty thing, you understand. No beauty, and hardly graced above her station. Yet, she was a pretty little thing.

Enrobed like a wife of Rome or a vestal of Troy, she sat down on the bed. She had blue eyes.

As careful as a man on the edge of a cliff, I eased into the chair behind the writing table. With a yard of oak between us.

"That's better," I said. Placing my hands sturdily upon my knees, I took a fortifying breath and continued. "Now, what exactly are you doing here, Miss Perkins?"

She rolled her eyes as ships roll on the sea. "Well, what does it look like, then? I'm here to please you, ain't I?" Then she huffed. "But I suppose there's some as won't be pleased."

"But *why* have you come? And presented yourself under . . . under such circumstances?"

She shrugged and the improvised toga slipped from a white shoulder. I readied a hand to slap across my eyes, should her similarities to Venus Aphrodite re-emerge.

"Oh, *he* sent me. He said you and him was playing a game with one another. Made it all right, he did, although I gave him a proper talking to when I seen him come strutting in. He gave me the twelve guineas he'd promised for my visit to the Dials and said as things hadn't gone just as he'd planned them. Then . . . then he gave me fifty more in gold. I couldn't believe it, I couldn't. Just to come and have a little visit with you. Fifty. In gold." She put on a knowing look. "Would've thought the two of you wasn't acquainted, to hear *you* tell it. But you must be thick as thieves for your friend to lay down enough to hire some little Jenny for a year and a day. Handsome, I calls it. Though I still think you ought to watch him, if you don't mind my saying so. For I don't think he likes the ladies very much, I don't." She laid her pale blue eyes upon mine own. "If you take my meaning."

Then she sat up in alarm. That devilish sheet slipped lower by an inch, revealing the first inkling of a swell of flesh. I tried to look away, settling my gaze first on her petticoat, until I realized the impropriety of that, too, then seeking out my coat on the dresser by the door. But her immediacy insisted upon my attention.

She looked like a Diana whose bow had inflicted a wound on an innocent.

"Oh," she said, raising an ivory hand to her mouth and tempting the flimsy cloth to abandon her bosom, "maybe you're that way yourself, not fond of the ladies. Well, I suppose *I* don't mind." Oh, she thought she knew more than she did. And she nodded. "So *that's* the reason I ain't been fondly welcomed . . ."

"It is not that."

"Playing a joke, is he? That friend of yours?" She snorted an indelicate laugh. "Well, let him, that's what I say. For fifty in gold, I'll play any joke he wants. Would you like me to pretend I'm a little boy?"

"Miss Perkins, please! He isn't my friend. This is disgraceful. I never—"

She lifted her proud chin. "Well, he, at least, is a proper gent, which is more than I can say for some as is present."

Of course, I thought I knew of whom she spoke: The Earl of Thretford. My new, and old, antagonist. But she had no need to know more of those matters. Indeed, she had come close enough to danger. I did not want her life plucked by cruel hands. For lilies may look strong, but they are fragile. Nor did I think her present behavior auspicious for her future, whether or not foul murder lurked ahead.

"Miss Perkins," I began again, "you are young . . . and impressionable. You must rethink your present course of behavior. This abuse of your sacred womanhood . . . you must not sell your virtue in the streets, and you—"

"What kind of girl do you think I am?" she demanded, for my well-meant words had riled her. "I ain't never walked the streets in my life. The wickedness of you! As if I ever would."

I feared she would leap to her feet and neglect her sheath.

"But Miss Perkins . . . you've taken money, see, and—"

"Fifty golden guineas, if a penny. And you won't find *that* on the London streets, I'll tell you and your guv'nor both."

I regarded her earnestly. "But . . . morally, you see . . . there's no difference in kind between a ha'penny piece and a hundred thousand pounds. You must examine your con—"

"Oh, ain't there? Well, I call that the biggest lie I heard since Barney said he fixed the Ascot races. Them what has money can do whatever they want. And they do it, don't I know it? But a poor girl's a slut for trying to make her way. Oh, I could tell you the difference between a half-crown got in an alley and fifty in gold for a ladylike visit, and none's the wiser." But, quick as the end of a summer shower, she calmed herself. "You really ain't for it, then? We could have us a lovely time, if you weren't such a silly."

I assured her I was not "for it."

She sighed. "I only hope he don't ask for his money back." She looked at me with an expression almost pleading. "You ain't going to tell him, are you?"

"Tell him what?"

"That . . . I didn't strike your fancy. That you didn't want me."

How little we know of the feelings of those before us.

"I doubt that I shall have the opportunity to discuss it with him, Miss Perkins."

"But if you did, I mean. You wouldn't have to tell him, would you? Fifty in gold . . ." Her eyes lit at the thought as they would never light for me. ". . . do you know what that means to a girl? And twelve more clinkers, besides, just for prancing through the Dials? I call that handsome, I do."

"Miss Perkins . . . my dear girl . . . you must think of your immortal soul."

She did not laugh, but looked at me earnestly. With those eyes the color of cornflowers.

"I can't afford to have no soul of my own," she said. "That's for them what already has their livings." She rose, but kept the sheet clutched to her person. No lily, the lass still might have made a splendid rose. "Please," she begged. "Don't tell him I wasn't pleasing to you."

I shook my head. "I won't. If ever I see him." For we would have more urgent things to talk about, the Earl and myself. If him it was, of which I felt near certain.

"And you want me to go, then?"

I nodded. Slowly. Exhausted as if I had fought a battle. "It would be best, see."

"Well, then, turn about. If you're not interested, I won't have you looking at me like I was a fish in the market."

I turned about, and listened to the vibrant sound of female garments slipping over flesh and over one another. There is music in the rustling, there is true. Forgive me this last frankness, and pray for me in my weakness, but it rends the heart, just slightly, to hear a woman dressing herself. That tune is lonely, and always sings of parting.

"I suppose you're great friends, the two of you," she said, as she warred with clasps and laces. "For all your will-he-or-won't-he's."

"No," I said. "We are not great friends."

"Well, maybe you can speak for yourself, but *he* seems to think you are. He even said I was to tease you, when I was leaving. To tell you something he told me. You can look now, I'm done up proper."

I turned and saw her, young and doomed. For even should she live a hundred years, we are all doomed. Sometimes, when I am not myself, I think it cruel of the Lord to have placed us here amid such a beauteous garden, only to tell us not to eat the fruit. And then to call us forth, with the beauty still rich in our eyes. I have faced death more than once, and I will tell you: The ugliest corner on earth is haunted with the shimmering glory of God. Perhaps it is the Welsh in me that wants to sing for joy and despair at once.

"And what was it you were to say to me?" I asked, watching her test her young face in the mirror.

"He said," she told me as she puckered her lips, "I was to ask you the price of a girl in a Lahore bordello. To buy one outright."

I did not see how anyone could know so much about me. For some things are not entered in the records. Some things would scorch the paper they were written upon, and break the cabinet containing them like a heart.

If everything were known about you, every close-clutched secret, would you be proud? Would every night that you have passed please under noonday scrutiny? I fear the saints are few upon this earth.

Yes, I bought her. And I would do it again. If I were not married. If she still lived. Mrs. Singh offered her to me, to spare the bother of an auction, for the poor child had taken a liking to me, though I know not why. Perhaps because I did not insist, the one time I was with her in that place, and only let her rest while I petted her hair. Perhaps she was sixteen, but likely she was not. Things are different in the East, see. Or perhaps they are not different at all. I only know that Mrs. Singh regretted taking the child in, for all the lass did was weep and would not please. She was not two weeks within those walls when I bought her out, although two weeks can mar a human lifetime. Sometimes a single hour will do the trick.

Who can say why we love? Show me the book, and I will read it and praise it. Even the Holy Bible, may the Lord forgive me, only tells us of David's errant passions, of mighty Samson's helplessness before his heart, and, always, of Adam. But not a word is written down as to why they loved, unless you count that catch-all reason: Beauty. But comeliness is no more than the start of an explanation, and never an end to it. Why lust unto death for one, and not another? Why does the plain girl fill the heart when the handsome lass won't do? How does the soul choose? What is it that we really love, when the animal act is done? And who stole Mary Magdalene's first, innocent kiss? How do we fall so easily into the darkness, when the heart would lift us, soaring, into the light?

I loved Ameera, that is all I know. As I loved the little boy that come to us, and our house by the river. She was my wife, my first, but no dark Lilith. And better she was than Eve, who heeded the Serpent. When the cholera took her and the child, I could have torn the Heavens into shreds.

"What's wrong with you, sweetie?" the White Lily asked. "Something you et?"

Unable to speak, I waved a hand at nothing.

My God, she put her hand upon my shoulder. That human touch was like a loaded fuse. But my charge was tamped inward. I was ready to collapse like a mine blown shut with powder. For Miss Perkins, the danger was all past. At least any danger from me.

"Having second thoughts, are we?" she asked. I do not think she was a wicked person. Only led astray. As we all are.

I shook my head. "It's nothing," I lied. "It will pass, see. In just a moment. And I will see you to a cab."

"Oh, there ain't no need of that. Really there ain't."

Of a sudden, the lass seemed anxious to go. Perhaps she found me fearsome then, sensing the bitterness of memory in me, the old anger revived. Mr. Milton had no idea of our struggle with the Heavens, I will tell you that much. There may be suffering in poetry, but there is no poetry in our suffering. I wished to beat my fists upon God's feet.

"I will see you to a cab," I repeated.

"Really, there ain't no need," she said, impatient as a child now.

"I'll just get my coat," I told her, rising.

"It's hot as an oven outside," she said. "If you have to come, come in your shirtsleeves. No one won't mind."

But a gentleman does not appear on the street in his shirt. I brushed past her, past that crippling scent of Eve, and covered myself.

She looked at me doubtfully, but out we went together.

I will say this for London: It does not take a fuss to find a hack, and in a pair of moments I had shut the cab door behind her. I even paid the driver, and somehow did not find the cost too painful. With a snap and a creak and a clobbering of hooves on the stones, the cab pulled off into the moist night, which was not hot in the least.

Back in I went, past the leering of the porter, who snickered and muttered, "I would've paid for the night entire with that one. But ain't the Welsh tight as the Jews?"

I lacked the will to respond to such indignities.

Laboring up the stairs, I felt unsure of whether this was London or old Lahore, today or then. My body perched upon those steps, but all of me that mattered had flown elsewhere. I am a small man, in so many ways, and lack a great understanding. But it seems to me the past is something real, that there is a merciless *now* to it, that we never can escape it, try as we may. Sometimes, of course, we do not even try. Some memories return to pierce us with rapture, as if we were rewarded while at prayer with a glimpse of Heaven. I do not know that this flesh is any more real than the meat of dreams. The Good Book is full of dreams, from innocent Joseph to Daniel in his dotage. The Lord sends dreams when He must speak to Mankind. And what are memories but our waking visions?

I led that child out of Mrs. Singh's establishment and she clung to me like a frightened little monkey. She was afraid of everything at first. Of the house I told her would be her own, and of the old woman who must do the worst of the chores and shelter her from the harshness the world reserves for young women left alone. But she was never afraid of me. It was so strange. Nor was she a child in certain ways. Once free of that place of sin, she displayed a boundless aptitude for affection. Of every kind. Twas I who was ravished, not the girl. Shocked into living at last, I learned joy.

I spoke but barracks nigger-talk in those days, although I got more words while we were together. Twas all regular, for I was a sergeant and had privileges, as long as each last duty was performed. And I was a devil for duty, a creature of polished brass and gleaming leather, of barked commands and bayonets thrust home. Then, freed of discipline and final inspections, I would go down to her, with my slightness of words, and she would love me in the immortal language of the heart. Call it sin, but I cannot. For I will not believe that love is sin. If anything is sin, it is love's loss.

Time is as undependable as it is bitter. I re-lived all this in the space of a flight of stairs, and got me to the landing wrenched apart. I was half-way down the hall before I saw him.

He stepped from the shadows by the sanitary cabinet. A man in a red silk mask.

This was no ghost. Nor was the revolver in his hand a tool of the spirit world.

"Give me the letters," he said, in a deep, charred voice. He was a big man, larger than I had realized from my glimpse of him in the penny gaff.

"What letters?" I said, pathetically.

He laughed like Death in a plague year.

"Give me the letters, or I'll spread your brains over the walls."

Now, in the books of Mr. Scott, the hero refuses all compromise. But I am not a hero, nor enamored of Mr. Scott and his fictions, and in this world of flesh and the devil a cane is no match for a pistol in the hand of a man twelve steps off. I wished to live. And had no great attachment to the letters. A small good deed was not worth a widowhood for my wife.

I reached into my pocket, where the letters had been tucked, and found naught but a loose thread.

He must have marked the surprise on my face.

"Come on," he said. "Give over."

"I don't have them," I told him, patting down my every pocket and then the lining of my jacket. Desperately. "They were in—"

And then I remembered the enthusiasm Miss Perkins had displayed for finding her own cab, and her reluctance to have me pull on my coat. The frock coat left in the room with her, when I stepped off to the sanitary convenience. And hadn't young Pomeroy come storming into her changing room the night before, demanding just such letters? She would have sensed their worth. And the White Lily took them.

"They're in my room," I told him, wanting time. For I would not betray a misguided girl. "I'll get them for you."

"Move, and you're a dead man." He laughed again, as that pale horseman might. "I've been through your room. Where are the letters, Jones?"

"Under the control of the United States Government," I told him abruptly.

"You little bastard," he said, raising the pistol.

A door opened between us and a plump man stepped out, half undressed and thinning hair awry.

"Can't a body get 'imself a bit of bleedin' sleep?" he demanded, looking in my direction.

A wraith between the gaslamps, the creature in the red mask slipped away. No one had seen him but me.

"Lieutenant Culpeper!" I called.

But he was gone.

Ten

I'm shut of it," Inspector Wilkie told me. "Finished and done. It ain't a bit of my business anymore." He sat there so distraught in his cubbyhole office that I would have thought him frightened, had he not been a police fellow. "I said to them, I did, that I didn't care if it 'ad to go up to Sir Richard Mayne 'imself, I wasn't 'aving no more to do with that murdered child." He looked at me, then looked away, then forced his eyes back to me yet again. "Even Mr. Archibald ain't never seen the like. I couldn't do it, I told them. I told them all I'd sooner go gathering pure in a bucket, I did. I couldn't 'elp seeing my little Albert lying there. Or my little Alice. And I wasn't 'aving no more to do with the matter."

Now, I myself had experienced a failure of the will, or of nerve, or of whatever you will term that quality that lends determination, so I could not be too harsh on the inspector. But I was disappointed, see. For I wanted aid and counsel, and found myself alone. Even Mr. Adams had failed me, in a manner of speaking, for I had gone first to the legation, as early as decency allowed, only to be told by Mr. Henry Adams that his father had been detained unexpectedly in the country and would not return until the afternoon. Young Adams spoke to me as to a servant.

But let that bide.

"Gleason's your man now," Wilkie added. "Inspector Gleason, 'e'll be in touch."

"I hope to go to Glasgow," I said. "Tomorrow."

Wilkie seemed only to want to be rid of me. "Well, then 'e'll be in touch when you come back, won't 'e? If not before, then after."

"I do not know when I will come back."

"Oh, sooner or later, no matter. There's plenty to do without you, ain't there? What with bloody murder every place a body looks. A gent just killed a serving girl in Chelsea, for serving 'is porridge too cold for 'is tastes and 'is liking. Oh, we 'ave work enough to do, there's plenty."

It did seem odd to me to be set aside so easily, since I had associations with these crimes as unwished and unfortunate as they were undeniable. But the police know their own business best.

"Look you," I said. "There is another matter. It travelled down the selfsame road, but it come in a different coach. Perhaps it is a separate doing entirely. Involving blackmail."

"Blackmail?"

I nodded. "That is how the matter looks to me. It is an affair of letters." And then I told him much, though not quite all. I left out my brief possession of the missives and their subsequent borrowing by Miss Perkins. For I planned to have them back from her, and no harm done to anyone. Nor did I think she needed more attention, even from the police, for her own safety's sake.

When I had finished my story, Wilkie said, "Don't that sound a rum business, now? 'Owever it comes out." He frumped his chin. "I 'ave looked into things enough to know old Pomeroy's as loaded as Lord Raglan's travelling trunk. Dripping like the Bank of England, 'e is. Though the family 'as a bit of a jinx to it." He gave me the full of his bewhiskered face to admire. "So the Pomeroy lad's got 'imself into a fix. And all for writing letters. I allus said, I did, that a man 'as to be careful if ever 'e writes things down what shouldn't be writ. Lord knows, I never writ a single letter to my late departed, and she was none the worse for it. No, pen and ink just gets a man in trouble."

"I had hoped . . . that you might go with me. To call upon Mrs. Pomeroy in Lambeth. A policeman would make it official, see. Otherwise, I do not see how I could call upon a lady to whom I have not been introduced or recommended."

"Oh, that's a different thing, it is," Wilkie said. "Blackmail. Now, that's a matter wanting more attention. No, I don't see why I shouldn't go along, if it's a separate matter and all completely different. For I 'ave enjoyed our discussions of the criminal class, I 'ave, Major Jones, and would gladly 'ave more profit from your devisings. So long as there ain't murdered little boys in it." He cocked his head, like a hound unsure of a brush-break in the distance. "A Cremorne dolly, is she? This Mrs. Pomeroy of yours? Is that the reason the father won't 'ave 'er for 'is daughter-in-law? A 'light lass of Lambeth,' is that the shame of it? A little less than spotless, is she?"

"It is not that at all."

"Then what is it, pray tell? If the girl 'as nothing she ought to be ashamed of?"

"She is of the Jewish persuasion. And from Hungary, I am told."

That lifted Wilkie's eyebrows. He thought for a moment, then said, "Well, I wouldn't worry about 'er, then. Your Jew allus lands on 'is feet like a scratching cat. Piles of money, every one of them. Although they don't let on when they line up at the charity ward."

I thought of the threadbare Hebrew boys leaping onto the boats at Billingsgate, in the hope of selling a jersey or a scarf, and I recalled the barrow clothiers by the Dials, whose faces looked worried half to death by life. But I said nothing.

"Of course," Wilkie continued, "everybody's equal before the law. After all, this is England, ain't it? But I wouldn't trust a Jew from 'ere to that wall. Especially not a foreign one, for they're the worst."

"But you will go with me, then?"

"I will, indeed," he told me. "I'd like to 'ave a look at the Jew-girl what 'as got 'er claws into a decent boy with prospects. Stinking dirty, the most of them, your Christ-killers."

Now you will say: "You should have called his language to account, for it was ungentlemanly, and some things will not suffer public utterance." But I will tell you: The only hope for the Hebrew is America, which is his promised land, though even there he is not always welcome. Still, I think he may find a place among us, as Moses Feinberg did, with his honest flannels. Nor does it help to chide when grown men speak, for you will only make them hate more deeply. And as for killing Christ, that is all tosh. A man as lovely as Our Savior would have been nailed to the cross wherever he was found, in Jerusalem, in Delhi, or in London. Such mercy and forgiveness are intolerable. We take up hammer and nails to show our thanks. And why not blame those Romans for their part? They were a nasty sort, according to Mr. Gibbon. Their bad behavior did not end with Pilate, either, for they went after Peter and Paul and the lot of them later.

The inspector agreed to go with me, but first he had other business to which to attend. I waited, thinking the interval would be brief, but it stretched on for over an hour. Notes were written and despatched by runners, constables were called in to clarify reports of theft and trespass, and, once, Wilkie excused himself to deliver a stack of papers to a superior. Police work is like the army, see, a very massacre of paper enemies.

I sat as patiently as I could, although I wanted to rush across the city. To be fair, I thought, I could not ask too much—for I had parsed my story and told the honest fellow little enough. The role of Miss Perkins was underplayed, and the appearance of that red silk mask in the hotel hallway went unmentioned. If he made me wait, twas no more than I deserved.

Twas noon when we were quit of the Bow Street station, with its smells of wax and worry, and its deep, brown light. Waiting for the fly to pull around from the stables, we took our mid-day refreshment from a street stall, where generous portions lauded the police. The city grumbled along under a gray sky, and summer seemed gone forever, although it was hardly begun. The wind had changed and the smoke-pot manufactories down the river smudged the air and put a sting in the nostrils, reminding all of the might of British industry. Then off we rode, in a plain, half-open vehicle. Crossing the Thames by Waterloo Bridge, Wilkie pointed out the new Westminster span, all scaffolded, in the distance past the bend. In between, the river was brisk with chugging engines and snapping canvas and oars drawn by calloused hands.

Lambeth, where I had not been, did not appear auspicious, but was a grubby mix of want and warehouses. Mrs. Pomeroy's address had been written brass-bold on the letters and we went to it straight, for the south side of the river was not trafficked so immensely, although we had interference enough from goods wagons and dray carts.

The street where Mrs. Pomeroy lodged was built all of brick and regular as a barracks. The houses might have pleased Mrs. Schutzengel's Communists, for all were equal, though equally undistinguished.

The street itself was cobbled, but not clean. The whole effect was of a cat's paradise, where there would always be something unpleasant to hunt. A few geraniums cowered in window-boxes and the air drooped with the sulfury smell of iron wrought in a furnace.

We counted the numbers as we rolled along, but, just as we come up on Mrs. Pomeroy's abode, I grabbed Wilkie by the sleeve and turned my face away from the row of houses.

"Keep driving!" I whispered. A hissing cat myself I was. "Tell the driver to go on, for God's sake!"

Wilkie gave the fellow a tap and said, "Go on, Michaels. Go on."

"As you like, Inspector," the fellow said.

"Have him turn the corner," I told Wilkie. "Out of sight."

"What's this, what's this?" the inspector asked.

"Did you see the fellow coming out the door? Did you see him?"

"The proper gent with the face like pink roast beef?"

"Yes. Him."

"And who would he be, now? What 'as got us in alarms and rushing around corners?"

"That was Mr. Pomeroy. The father."

Well, there was food for thought, it seemed to me. When a father who is not to know of a daughter-in-law's existence exits her lodgings at the start of the afternoon. And in my glimpse of him, he had not looked riled. You might have thought he had just enjoyed a meal.

I wondered what those letters had to say, and if it was at all what I expected.

And then, as we pulled up at the curb, a frightful thought coursed through me: What if we found Mrs. Sarah Pomeroy murdered? Killed by a father-in-law who would not tolerate her? Had the elder Pomeroy truly looked as calm as I had thought him?

"Well, you're anxious as a trotter waiting to run," Wilkie said. And he was right.

We stepped up to the door and I gave it a tap with my cane.

After a moment, footsteps padded within, followed by a woman's voice deep in the alto. Dusk and damask and languor, that was the sound of her.

"Are you coming back already, my lover?" the foreign voice asked the door. "Are you coming back again, you are so naughty!"

By then, she had the bolt undone. The light of day shone in, and she said no more.

We stood there, waiting for time to put itself right. If the woman's voice was dusk, her hair was midnight, and her green eyes promised depths forbidden the weak. Handsome she was, and vivid. Not least because she stood there in her unmentionables, chemise no more than half buttoned and her shoulders free of even a dressing gown.

"Betty Green!" Inspector Wilkie fair cried. "Why, Betty, I ain't seen you in I don't know 'ow long!"

She shut the door upon us.

Allowing her an interval to robe herself to a decency, I turned my perplexed face to the inspector.

"Call 'erself 'owever she likes," he told me, "but that's little Betty Green, what was the great beauty of Camden Town ten year ago. She wasn't fifteen before we all 'ad our eyes on 'er. Although there weren't nothing improper, I mean to say," he added hastily. "At least, not from the gentlemen amongst us."

"Perhaps she shares her lodging with Mrs. Pomeroy?" I said.

"Well, maybe she do, and maybe she don't, but that's our Betty Green, what went bad and found 'erself in a fix in Lisle Street, when a 'andsome young viscount took poison on account of 'er. Crawling around on the floor like a dog, 'e was, and barking, too. We 'ad to take 'im to the charity 'ospital, which was nearest to the establishment in which our Betty was positioned in her shame, and the doctors finished killing 'im soon as we got there. We 'ad to close Mrs. 'Opkins down for a month, which was an inconvenience to a great many 'igh gentlemen, although I don't say the old girl didn't deserve it. Betty come off with a promise to be good and a rash of new customers from the Inns of Court." He nodded thoughtfully. "I allus thought there was money must of changed 'ands, for a viscount's death would get most girls transported."

"But is she Jewish?" I asked.

Wilkie guffawed. "Jewish? Betty Green? Ain't that a larf? I used to see 'er from out the parlor window, as the old girl what got 'er the indecent way and then reformed all righteous went drudging

Betty off to the Methodist chapel. Every Sunday that was, for morning prayers and evening preaching both." He shook his head like a dog shaking off water. "Jewish? That's a good one, our little Betty." He looked at me. "She could of 'ad any man in Camden, but she aimed at 'igher things, that one." Then he corrected himself. "Any man but meself, I mean, for I was 'appily set up with the late Mrs. Wilkie."

I thought sufficient time had passed to try the door again. The truth is I was dazzled by my bafflement, and baffled to a dazzling. Nothing at all made sense in London town. But just as I was about to knock, a boy come whistling by in an old Dutch cap. He turned to enter the door of the house next by.

"You, lad," I called. "Who lives in this house?" I gestured toward Mrs. Pomeroy's door with my cane. I hoped to clarify matters somewhat, see. "Would you know, then?"

"Oh, that's the Jew girl," the boy explained. "Me mum says I ain't to speak with 'er, for she's a bad one."

"But do you? Speak to her?"

The boy glanced about himself. Seeing no one else, he said, "I said good morning to 'er once, but she told me to go pee off. The bloke what comes round to see 'er give me a penny, though. To fetch 'im a cab, though 'e mostly comes in a carriage."

"The man who comes to see her, how old is he, do you think?"

"Old as the bleedin' 'ills, guv'nor. 'E don't look like 'e could make it from 'ere to the gin shop."

And so the elder Mr. Pomeroy must look to a boy that age, although he seemed in his prime to developed eyes.

The lad glanced at Wilkie, then back to me, and asked, "Is that one there a peeler, sir? Is the Jew-girl come into trouble?"

"Never you mind," the inspector told him. "Or I'll tell your mother what you're up to."

"I ain't up to nothing, Bobby Peeler," the boy said almost ferociously. "And me mum would eat you up like 'er morning sausage."

He stuck out his tongue, and went in.

I knocked upon Mrs. Pomeroy's door again. With a certain firmness.

She opened, but only part-way. Covered up she was, but her flimsy gown was unsuited to greeting company. For a lady's dress is as regulated as a battalion of grenadiers. The mistress of that house would have failed inspection.

"You are not gone away?" she asked in that husky, foreign voice. "Why do such people come to me?"

"Oh, go on, Betty," the inspector said. "I've known you since you was short and stumpy as the major 'ere. You can't play none of your confidence tricks on Wilkie."

She flashed her green eyes round to me, but spoke calmly. "Who is this man? Is he a crazy one, from the asylum?"

"Begging your pardon," I said, "but would you be Mrs. Sarah Pomeroy?"

She graced me with those endless eyes for but a second longer, then considered Wilkie again. When she spoke, she looked between us and across the street.

"Who else am I to be, please? Now, you are going."

The door shut with the finality of a vault.

~

"I'll 'ave 'er put under arrest, and that'll be the end of it," Inspector Wilkie said. For he was miffed at what he thought was her insolence. Convinced he was that she was Betty Green, the belle of Camden Town, and late of a fancy house set up in Lisle Street. "It's clear as day, it is. I'll tell you just what kind of blackmailing she's up to. She's got something on old Pomeroy, and it's something 'e don't want told."

Not, indeed, if he was his son's wife's lover. If you will forgive me that awful supposition. But I did not see another explanation. I only wondered why the boy who lived next door had mentioned only an old man and not a young one, as well, if she was married to young Pomeroy.

If the woman was married at all.

I had more doubts than Thomas with his poking fingers. And far less likelihood of finding proof.

What was in those letters? Why had young Pomeroy told me about them? Were they truly his own, written to his wife? Or were they his own, but written to a woman *not* his wife, to his father's mistress? Or was his father's mistress the son's wife, after all? And what on earth had Mr. Disraeli to do with it? Was he an acquaintance of Mrs. Sarah Pomeroy? Or of Miss Betty Green? And how far had I strayed afield from the corpse of the Reverend Mr. Campbell?

Did any of this have to do with ships of war and Rebels and Richmond's schemes? If anyone in England had sought to divert my attention—and I suspected more than one Englishman of such designs—they had done a pretty job of it. For here I was in a swamp with no bottom, splashed by immoralities that were none of my business, while our murdered agents went forgotten and conspiracies plunged ahead.

I was unsettled.

The police rig took us back over Waterloo Bridge, where a handsome young man with anthracite whiskers darted between the carts and carriages, turning about to cry to a girl, "Julie, will you meet us at sunset, then? Just where you're standing now?" And the girl nodded and called, "At sunset, Terry, but not before, for I've got to see Davies off." Ash-blond she was, and radiant of complexion under her hat, with a lower lip born to pout. But here is the thing of it, why the trivial incident struck me so: Other lives go on, despite murders and betrayals and even wars. The bright boldness of this Terry and his Julie seemed to capture the spirit of our age, the turbulent sixties, with their progress, hope, immodesty and danger. But let that bide, for there is more to tell.

Wilkie pointed across my chest to the ramshackle buildings lining the northern bank. Motley they were, with their sagging roofs and worn advertisements lettered on their walls.

"All to be knocked down," he told me, "to make way for the great embankment. And a good thing, if you arsk me. For there's nothing along the river but crime and sin, from 'ere to Parliament."

Indeed, the Parliament buildings rose nobly in the direction of the new, unfinished bridge, but I was of a mind to correct the inspector. For I had begun to wonder if crime and sin did not extend into the Houses of Parliament themselves. But I said nothing.

"I wants to be there when they knock them down," the inspector told me. "Just to watch the rats with two legs outracing the rats with four."

He offered to take me wherever I wished to go, but I had consumed too much of his day already. He wished to part, twas clear. And I needed to think a bit. So I had him set me down along the Strand, with its restaurants and shops and human thickness.

Perhaps I only wanted people by me. To have a little taste of simpler cares. But this was no day for the soul's rest, for I always seemed to be looking past the smiles of the ladies and their beaux to the ravaged faces weaving along the pavement, ignored by those who would go home to cherished families and money in the bank. There was a great hurry of delivery boys bobbing under loads of packages, and the windows of the shops held such abundance it would have tempted a hermit into luxury. Sleek of waist above eminent skirts, ladies of fashion pretended to listen to each other as they went, and young men on the way up did not look down at the hard world at their feet. But I saw only the faces lashed by life and the broken hearts, the ragged girls and the cripples who could but envy my slight degree of lameness. A bit of rain come flirting, and the ladies crushed their starched muslins through shop doorways, while swains or squires—men of town and country—laughed to see them fearful of the elements. The gentlemen made a great to-do of tipping hats and holding doors and laughing. Always laughing they were, with a legion and more of beggars at their boots.

Dear God, I wished to see the last of England. And to return to my America forever.

"I want you to go to Glasgow," Mr. Adams said quietly, before I could offer a word of my own conclusions, "on urgent business. How soon can you leave?"

He had spoken hardly a word as we walked, bidding me hold my peace until we reached the breadth of Regent's Park, where only the grass might hear us. I had steered him away from the spot where the boy was found, since I was as haunted by the business as Wilkie and have my superstitions, I will admit. No sooner were we seated on a bench, with governesses leading their troops past in review, than Mr. Adams raised this matter of Glasgow, all on his own and without a bit of prodding.

"There is a morning express," I told him. "I can go tomorrow, but—"

"Then go. I've had a curious message from our consul in Liverpool. Everything appears in order on the Number 290 matter, the lawyers have filed and the courts are at work, so that appears to be that. But now he claims a rumor's circulating in the Birkenhead yards about a secret warship under construction along the Clyde, not far from Glasgow. I can't see how they would know of such a thing in Liverpool, but a Scottish yard is said to have built an enormous wooden tent over a vessel destined for the Confederacy. To hide their labors, you understand. The ship is reported to have a metaled hull that would render it formidable—perhaps, even unsinkable."

Our minister sat upright, with posture so perfect he might have taught comportment in a boys' school, and he spoke without emotion, stating facts. He turned his chin toward me, with that slow, iced-over dignity of his. "There it is, Major Jones. Glasgow. Where the first agent met his misfortune. It's Glasgow, after all, it seems."

I was relieved, for he had made a better argument for my going than I could. And yet, there was much left for me to tell him. And I was ready to tell him and waiting to tell him, but Mr. Adams had still more to say. Twas queer. For he seemed to me a close man, whose speech was measured and lean, yet that afternoon found him in a confidential mood. Perhaps he felt that I must be informed on every matter, or maybe he just felt a need to talk. Being a high diplomat must be a bit like leading men into battle, see. You must be strong for all, and hold yourself in, never showing fear or doubt or weakness. But all men need to speak from time to time. Our hearts demand it, though why I cannot say. And after we have talked, we do feel better.

"I had the oddest few days," he began. "Lord Parch invited me down to Fawes, which the English seem to think a signal honor. Frankly," he said, with his palms atop the ball of his cane and his eyes on the children playing across the sward, "it was a worse bore than dinner with Stanton and Chase at the same table. And I suppose I felt guilty, off in the country, watching the titled glories of England shotgun every living thing in a pair of counties while you were in town doing my work for me."

His lip wrinkled ever so slightly as he remembered. "The house was cold and miserable—I can't imagine what it's like in winter. I counted the minutes until it seemed a decent hour to take my leave yesterday afternoon, but just as I was about to have my bag brought down, His Lordship took me by the arm and insisted—'insisted' is the only suitable word—that I stay over for breakfast this morning. He claimed he had something he wished to show me. Well, I didn't want to offend the man—given his position—so I took my place at dinner between a fellow intent on explaining the merits of a dozen kinds of hounds and a lady who believes the Church of England must reconcile with Rome. Then, in the morning, when I went down for breakfast, the butler told me Lord Parch had already gone back to town on the early train. And who should appear—purely by accident, of course—but Earl Russell and Lord Lyons, who should have been in town themselves. They made rather too much of their disappointment at finding His Lordship missing, but insisted our meeting was more than a solace—that it was, indeed, fortuitous that they had ridden over to visit."

Mr. Adams sighed at the convolutions of the world. Or perhaps at the sight of a little boy thrashing his sister while their governess flirted. "You see, Major Jones, nothing can be done straightforwardly here. I might as well be at the court of the Emperor of China. Frankly, I expected a blistering about corpses and coded messages, but there was nothing of the kind. After our coffee, Lord John suggested the three of us stroll the grounds for a 'friendly chat.' Of course, I was glad to listen. Especially after I heard what they had to say—or what they implied between the two of them."

He nodded in satisfaction at the memory. "It appears we have turned a corner. They made it quite clear that England does not want a war with the United States, not now and not tomorrow. In fact, they hinted that the Prime Minister has other concerns entirely." He gave me a brief, sideward glance. "Of course, with Lord Palmerston you never quite know. But, far from chastising me, they seemed determined to enlist my backing, although they couldn't quite bring themselves to say precisely what might require my support. Nothing but mumbling about Old Pam at the tiller of state and a stable course amid the winds of crisis. They even offered a near-apology for the Prime Minister's remarks over General Butler, insisting that not a word of it was ill-meant toward me. It all seemed terribly slap-dash and not very English."

He poked his walking stick into the gravel. "At the same time, they seemed anxious to prepare me for a degree of turbulence in the future. They made a mystery of that, too, assuring me of their personal good intentions, but suggesting that not everyone, even in their own party, was fully subject to their control. On the whole, though, the conversation seemed all I could have asked. Lyons has even come around on Seward. Instead of the ogre all England thought him during the Trent affair, our Secretary of State now appears to be a reasonable gentleman who is not without a certain wisdom. I can't begin to convey what a change that is. They even told me Lindsay won't find any serious backers when next he offers a motion in support of Richmond in Parliament. Really, it was an extraordinary morning. By the end of it, I felt I might have asked for the moon and gotten, at the very least, a wheel of Stilton."

"Well, there is good, sir," I told him. "For a war with Britain would go hard."

"I should hate to see it," Mr. Adams said. "Enough blood has been shed between our two countries. After all, we're brethren, whether or not we enjoy the family resemblance." He not only turned his head toward me, but tilted his shoulders in my direction, which was a gesture of extravagant physicality from our minister. "And what have *you* learned, Major Jones? While I've been off watching the unintelligible shooting the inedible?"

I told him everything I could remember, about murdered eel-men and dead pawn-mothers, boys butchered like pigs in a slaughterhouse and phantoms in red silk masks, and a brass watch recovered with its secrets stolen away. When I handed him the timepiece, he said not a word, but slipped it into a pocket without examining it. Then I spoke of slums and penny gaffs, omitting only the lewdest utterances of Miss Perkins. He hardly interrupted, saying only, "Dear God," when I told him of the severed hand and the dead boy. But when I spoke of my visit to the Pomeroy house, he felt obliged to assist me.

"A difficult family, if reputation is to be believed," Mr. Adams told me. "This wouldn't be their first scandal. Although one shouldn't gossip, I did hear that a maternal cousin of the elder Mr. Pomeroy had difficulties in the West Indies in his youth—the family money comes from sugar, you see, and there were suggestions that slavery did not end on their plantations as promptly as the law declared it should. Anyway, this young fellow went out to the islands and married a creole girl, after which there were hints of every sort of horror, from miscegenation to madness. There was a child, too, at least one. The scandal became so much a public matter that the authorities ordered him back to England—quietly, of course—with his madwoman wife and the child. He seems to have retired to the countryside, somewhere in the northern counties, where he locked his wife in the garret and contented himself with seducing governesses. I believe there was a deadly fire, as well." Mr. Adams gave a faint shudder at the indecency of it all, then set his face in ice again. "Nonetheless, the Pomeroys count among England's wealthiest families. They lack only the title so desired by the elder." He looked at me. "Now, what had you begun to say about Mr. Disraeli?"

I told him of my visit the night before and of the letters gained then promptly lost. Not least, I told him of Mr. Disraeli's threat to embarrass us over my past, and of his mention of the Earl of Thretford and his half-brother. Mr. Adams listened quietly, until I had gotten through a tidied-up version of the White Lily's appearance in my room and the subsequent confrontation with the masked fellow.

Mr. Adams had been thinking all the while. And then he thought some more.

"I don't believe we need worry about Disraeli," he said quite suddenly. "That's not the way he behaves. If he intended to compromise you, he would never have warned you. He would simply have done it, surprising you when you least expected it." He leaned forward, just a bit, shifting the slightest fraction of his weight onto the walking stick implanted before him. "As a matter of fact, it sounds as if he's frightened himself. He must have wanted to get rid of those letters very badly—you didn't have time to review them, I take it?"

"No, sir. And, as a gentleman, I—"

"Disraeli doesn't think that way. If he gave them to you, he expected me to learn what was in them. I believe that's clear enough."

"Unless," I said, for I had been thinking, too, "it was merely a trick to appear to be free of the letters. Think you, Mr. Adams. How would the fellow in the red mask have known I was to have the letters? Unless Mr. Disraeli sent him word? Which also suggests Mr. Disraeli knew how to contact the masked fellow whenever he wished, whether he is this Lieutenant Culpeper risen from the dead or another person entirely. Might it not be, sir, that it was a nasty ruse put up to place the letters into the masked fellow's hands, by a roundabout route that seemed to be secure? Shifting any blame for future doings from Mr. Disraeli—and tying you to the letters, if such should prove to advantage?"

When next he spoke, Mr. Adams sounded chastened, although I had intended no such effect. "I'm afraid I have allowed my vanity to show," he said. "I find your supposition the more convincing of the two. Although I can't fathom the Earl of Thretford's involvement—unless the letters do lead us back to a Confederate conspiracy. From what little I know of the Earl, young Pomeroy would be too small a fox for Lord Arthur to hunt." He canted his head one tenth of a degree. "So . . . the man in the mask was to take the letters from you all along, but this Perkins girl interfered?"

"Yes, sir."

"Now she has possession of the letters. But the conspirators, whoever they may be, don't know that?"

"I hope not, sir. For her sake. But they have figured out a great many other things, so I fear they will come to that, as well."

Mr. Adams nodded. "Indeed. They seem to know a great deal. Particularly about you, Major Jones."

"I cannot figure it," I said. "Even if the Earl of Thretford knows everything this Kildare fellow back in New York had learned about me, it would not come to the half. And, dead or alive, Lieutenant Culpeper could know only bits and pieces."

"But the records, the files . . ."

"A military record tells certain things," I said, "but to understand it properly a body must know much more. And how did they know I would be the one to come? How could they have had time to prepare so much, all tailored to my benefit?"

"I'm afraid," Mr. Adams said, "that I may know at least part of the answer to that. You see, I had a telegraphic message—two, in fact—prior to your arrival. The first mentioned that a special agent would be despatched." He thought for a moment. "I don't believe it included your name. But the second one did."

"I thought the Atlantic cable had broken apart?"

"It did. Before the war even started. But Washington cables New York, a fast packet carries the message to the Irish coast, and the telegraphics are relayed from there. The cable between Ireland and England remains in order." He almost smiled, though it was a bitter sight. "I had the second message a full week before your arrival. Still . . . it hardly seems enough time, does it?"

"Unless," I said carefully, "there is a spy in Washington. Who learned my name early on and sent the intelligence by an earlier ship."

Mr. Adams shook his head and tapped with his stick. "I would hate to think that. Good Lord. It would have to mean a spy close to Seward himself."

"Or," I said, "close to Mr. Lincoln. And Mr. Nicolay."

"I can't . . . well, that would explain much, were it true. The code, for instance. In order to intercept the messages, they would need to have broken our code." He took a deep breath and let it out again. "I wonder what message was in Campbell's watch? They must have read that, too. What on earth might it have said? What could have been worth his death?"

"The secret ship in Glasgow, perhaps?"

"Perhaps. That may be. But, given all you've told me, I'm unable to feel certain of anything, at the moment." He turned toward me, almost sympathetically. "You made a remark—when you spoke of the use of the train between here and Glasgow—you said that we were faced with modern crime. Now it's a business of steamships and telegraphs." He shook his head almost as resignedly as a regular fellow might do. "I feel as if this age is passing me by. It all goes so fast, so terribly fast." He looked at me earnestly. "Where will it all end, do you think?"

Yet, he recovered himself in another moment and bore down upon our business once again. "What I suspect you've gotten exactly right is that there are two trains on separate tracks, if I may be allowed the description. They may converge, or they may simply be travelling in parallel. On one track, we have the affair of the letters, this blackmail business, in which Mr. Disraeli has mixed himself up and about which he now seems alarmed. Then there are the murders and a seeming conspiracy to build naval vessels for the South. One must be our paramount concern, while the other—intentionally or not—only diverts us.

But which is which? Is it possible that the letters might be even more important than warships?"

I did not know how to answer. For my mind told me one thing, while my instincts whispered another.

"But you had more to tell me," Mr. Adams said. "About this Jewess hidden away in Lambeth."

And so I brought him up to the present hour, with my report of the elder Mr. Pomeroy's visit to his daughter-in-law. If daughter-in-law she was, and not Betty Green.

"Extraordinary," Mr. Adams said.

"Yes, sir."

He sat back. "And here I was eating boiled beef among boiled shirts all the weekend. You've been a busy man. Tell me, Major Jones, if you had to draw a conclusion this minute, what you would make of the letters? Why do they have such value? If they're nothing but a boy's intimate scribblings?"

"I have made mistakes before," I said, "because of hasty conclusions. I do not know whether—"

"No, Major. Treat this as a requirement. As a command, if you will. You must make a decision this instant. What do you say about the letters and the Pomeroys and Disraeli?"

"Well, sir . . . it seems to me that Mr. Disraeli's banking affairs are not in perfect order."

"Indeed, they are not. The man's notorious for it. Always lives above his means. Go on."

"And Mr. Pomeroy—the elder—has a great deal of money."

"You believe the affair is exactly what it seems? Disraeli intends to blackmail old Pomeroy to settle his bills?"

"There is more, see."

"Go on."

"The elder Mr. Pomeroy wants a peerage. Before he passes on. And Mr. Disraeli has influence."

Mr. Adams snorted, almost like a tapster. "He'd like one for himself. Disraeli wants nothing more than he does a good title. Lord This or That."

"Perhaps Mr. Pomeroy advanced money to Mr. Disraeli. For his good offices in seeking a title. But there is no title gotten on the one side. And no money to repay the debt on the other. Perhaps Mr. Disraeli will present the recovery of the letters as a service to Mr. Pomeroy. Relieving him of a scandalous embarrassment—and canceling the debt."

"And the son? With his wife? Or his lies?"

"I cannot say. Not yet. But the boy is weak and would do as he was told by a stronger man. And he and his father do not seem to live in harmony."

"Do you think this woman's really young Pomeroy's wife?"

"No."

"Nor do I," Mr. Adams said. "And the woman herself? Is she a Hungarian Jewess? Or this Betty Green?"

"I would say Betty Green."

"Then why on earth make her out to be a Jewess?"

"It is a role, see. Making her a Jewess explains why she must be hidden away. By father or son. For a Jewish mistress would block an English title, while an English girl used thus might be overlooked." I looked down at the gravel path, as if it might hold answers. "Still, I do not rightly understand the business. For they would seem to be wishing harm upon themselves, with these tales of a Jewish wife."

"But why should the son make her out to be his wife at all?"

"Perhaps that was a lie told only to me. Because my role was to take away the letters. So the man in the red mask could take them from me. Twas only to send me off in a false direction. For whatever else he may or may not be, the son is under the thumb of Mr. Disraeli somehow. Nor is there any love lost between father and son. The boy himself could be the engine of the plot. Blackmailing his own father through a second party."

I let Mr. Adams ponder a bit while we watched a boy roll a hoop. That always seemed a tedious game to me, meant for boys who lacked the impulse to manliness.

"Yes," Mr. Adams said at last. "That must be the explanation. Sordid, isn't it?"

"Yes, sir."

"And the rest of the business, the greater part, will have to wait until you visit Glasgow. And make further discoveries."

"So I would think, sir."

"Good, then. Well done, Major Jones. Seward knew his man when he sent you out."

I was pleased by our Minister's praise, as you would have been. Of course, I had gotten the matter entirely wrong, leaping to the false conclusion that the old man of whom the Dutch-capped boy in Lambeth had spoken was the elder Mr. Pomeroy, and that the affair of the letters was the lesser concern. Neither of us saw what was right in front of our eyes. In a manner of speaking, I mean, for twas not there on the lawns of Regent's Park. But we were colossally wrong, the two of us, and time was running out to make things right.

"So," Mr. Adams said, "tomorrow you're off to Glasgow. A shame our consul's on the Continent. Gone to Homburg for the waters. He might have been of assistance with the Scots." He shifted to face toward me again, as he did each time he meant to change the subject. "What about Miss Perkins and the letters? Do you think we should simply extract ourselves from that particular affair?"

I had been coming to that. May the Good Lord forgive me, I was up to a bit of mischief. For I felt a bit of comeuppance was overdue.

"I must ask a great favor of you, sir," I began. "I feel we should not let those letters go, see. Soiled as they appear to be in their purpose. For we cannot say with certainty what is in them, and we may be in error. Worse, the lass may be in danger of her life, and only because she come into contact with me." I looked at the great man beside me, wondering if he would penetrate my deviltry. "I believe it worth our while to have the letters. If only to keep Miss Perkins from coming to harm."

"Well, then, I suppose you'll have to go and fetch them from her."

"I cannot do that," I explained. "For I am positive that I am being watched. Were I to go, it would only tell the world she has the letters, see. And maybe cost her life. No, sir," I said gravely, beginning to work my mischief upon that good man, "I think your son would be the man to go."

"Henry? Go to a penny gaff?"

"No one would suspect him, sir. And he's such a gentleman he would be admitted anywhere. Miss Perkins would be more trusting of such a one as him, since she would fear the sight of me, knowing I was after the letters. She might even flee. But your son could do it all in a wink, sir."

Oh, couldn't I picture the smug young pup packed into a penny gaff? I relished the thought of it, I did.

"I don't quite know if Henry's the man to deal with anyone as formidable as this Miss Perkins of yours," Mr. Adams said doubtfully. "He's something of a retiring young man."

"I would do it myself, sir, if only I could. But I cannot, and that's plain. Nor could you very well go yourself, Mr. Adams."

"No."

"He should offer her twenty pounds to start," I said. "But she might hold out for fifty."

"Good Lord!" he said, with such alarm I almost thought him Welsh. "Fifty pounds?"

"We do not know what the letters may contain, sir. But, doubtless, she will have read them, and she may sense their value. Their possession may bring us an advantage we cannot foresee. In other domains entirely."

It was my winning argument, and he agreed as we parted that his son would go to Eastcheap Street that night. Had we known what those letters had to say, we would have all gone together, and taken a hired army along, besides.

There is strange. I meant to have my joke on young Mr. Adams, and it come out the only thing that I got right.

I dined on a cutlet where working men ate, and had my fill at a price that was almost reasonable. Thus fortified, I took an omnibus in the direction of Hampstead. For I had another visit to make before I departed London, although it had naught to do with masks and murders, or with letters and immorality in Lambeth. I wished to call on Mr. Karl Marx, the philosopher, for I felt myself in need of moral solace.

Of course, the fellow was a Communist, which meant he had an appetite for uproar. But dear Mrs. Schutzengel, my Washington landlady, had always made him out to be a saint. And the lion in his den may prove less fierce.

I was curious, see. And hoped to have a pleasant conversation. I wanted to take my mind off other matters and grant myself an interval of refreshment. And what could be a greater source of renewal than drawing wisdom from a great man's lips?

Now, I was not familiar with all the boroughs and hierarchies of London, and knew only that *Herr* Marx had been frightfully poor— indeed, a child or two had died of want in the misery of his London lodgings, and I suspected Mrs. Schutzengel of sending him funds. But Kentish Town, when I stepped down, did not seem quite the vale of poverty I had anticipated. In fact, it looked quite nice and most respectable.

I asked my way to Grafton Terrace and spied out number 9. And didn't the sight of the place make me wonder? Twas handsomer three times over than my own little home in Pottsville, which was nothing to be ashamed of, though not grandiose. The house looked fine and new and suited more to a young barrister and his bride than to a driven, starving revolutionist.

A dark-haired lass, plain but pleasant, answered the door and looked me over with a certain trepidation. Now, I know it is rude to call unexpected, but my days and nights had not allowed me time for writing notes and asking permissions.

I cleared my throat and said, "Begging your pardon, missy . . . my name is Jones and I am from America, see. If a Mr. Marx lives here, I believe we have a mutual friend in *Frau* Hilda Schutzengel, who is my—"

She did not let me finish but fair dragged me into the hall. *"Mutti! Mutti!"* she cried to a presence somewhere behind the walls, *"der Herr kommt von der Hilda, von Hilda Schutzengel! Er kommt aus Amerika . . ."*

And wasn't there a great rushing to and fro after that? I heard a cry of *"Gott sei Dank! Vielleicht hat sie Geld geschickt . . ."* as I stood about, examining my environs. Now, quite the fashion the house may have been in itself, but the interior had a picked-over look, with rectangles pale on the walls where pictures were missed and a general sparseness of furniture, almost as if items had been sold off or pawned.

In a bit, an older woman emerged from back of the stairs to greet me—I fear I thought *Frau* Marx was the maid, so careworn she looked, with her hands all wet and raw. And her English had a want of specificity. She managed to pull up a certain dignity, though, as soon as she finished drying her fingers on a cloth. Your German keeps a straight back in adversity, see. We smiled at one another and jabbered a bit, but I fear we made little sense of one another.

The daughter—for such the plain girl seemed—insisted I was as welcome as a sunny day, although a Mr. Lassalle had been expected in my stead. A serving girl was dispatched to fetch the father, who was at a location I did not comprehend. I had lately applied myself to the German tongue, which I believe will become America's second language in the years to come, but my grammar book had not yet lifted me up to significant understandings.

The serving girl went off in a huff and a fluff, complaining of Heaven and earth. Even Communists have serving maids, see, and they are no happier than girls in service elsewhere.

Her mission proved unnecessary, for hardly a moment after she disappeared through the front door, *Herr* Karl Marx himself burst into the hall.

He was drunk. On a Monday night.

When he heard I enjoyed an association with Mrs. Schutzengel, he wrapped me in his great bear arms and slobbered over me. I fear he stank and wanted a proper scrubbing. His embrace drew me into his musty beard and showed me the violet carbuncles on his neck. He declared my arrival an event of notable magnitude, then he led me into his study, which was cluttered like an enchanted cave in a story, although his treasures were books and papers, pens and pipes. Dropping into an arm-chair that wanted pensioning, he barked out questions about America's readiness to dispose of the monied classes, whom he associated with a place called the Bushwa Sea, of which I knew nothing. I suspect it may be somewhere near Lake Erie.

Instead of listening to my attempted answers, he prophesied that our present war would spark a world revolution. He seemed a lively fellow, if smelly and dirty, but when he learned I had brought no funds from Mrs. Schutzengel, he turned grumpy and implied that America was a backward place, after all. He asked to borrow ten pounds, then five, and did not take my refusals in a comradely spirit. Though heavily filtered through his German origins, his English was not bad, but when I tried to put a question to him on moral philosophy, he merely belched and fell asleep in his chair.

It proved a less than satisfactory evening.

I should have foreseen just what would happen next. For when plans go awry, men try to fix them.

As I strolled the last steps to my hotel, through air damp as a scrub rag, a long face hailed me from a fancy carriage.

Twas Mr. Disraeli.

"Ah, Major Jones!" he said. "Might I desire the honor of your company?" He opened the carriage door toward me.

I had half a mind to tell him he might desire my company for a year and a day, for all the good it would do him. But we must not allow our feelings to become our masters. And he would be after the letters, see. Much is to be learned from men's excuses. Even when those men come short of honesty.

Get in I did, only to be surprised. For Mr. Disraeli had not come out alone. Young Mr. Pomeroy sat in a plush corner, just by a lamp, with a look on his face like a child in the midst of a whipping, as his master pauses to catch his breath and freshen his grip on the rod.

Mr. Disraeli tapped on the forward panel and the coachman bid the horses walk on. For a street or two, he and I only regarded each other, while young Mr. Pomeroy cowered.

"Last night," Mr. Disraeli began at last, "I suffered from an excess of generosity and entrusted you with letters not rightly mine to bestow. The gesture has cost me not a little embarrassment." His expression did not change as he spoke, but remained cool as a cobra's. "I must presume upon your good will and ask for the return of what I gave you." He sent the briefest of glances toward young Pomeroy. "Our mutual friend, Mr. Pomeroy, has applied to me for the return of his intimate property. Which no gentleman would deny him."

I was relieved. It meant they did not know Miss Perkins had the letters. Instead of replying, I let the carriage rock on.

"To reward your inconvenience," Mr. Disraeli continued, "I renew my offer to protect your personal and professional reputations from any misconstructions past events might inspire." His gaze tightened. "I should even provide you with documents the India Office need not retain. Papers . . . of which there would be no second copies available."

"There is nothing I am ashamed of," I told him. "Take your papers and hand them out to every scribbler in Fleet Street."

My reply was a degree too heated and only reinforced Mr. Disraeli's composure. Patiently, he drew out the finest of cambric handkerchiefs, embroidered white-on-white along the edges, and touched it to his nose, as if to remove a single drop of sweat. He shook it out with an artful snap and slipped it back into his pocket.

"Nothing of the sort! I shouldn't betray a friend in a thousand years! Not in an hundred-thousand!" He smiled, gone from cobra to a cat. "I must be frightfully poor of speech—you never fail to mistake my offers of friendship for something else entirely. On the contrary, I think," he renewed his smile, "we would all desire absolute discretion in these matters." He turned delicately. "Isn't that right, Mr. Pomeroy?"

Pomeroy looked at him warily.

"No, no," Mr. Disraeli insisted. "Far from wishing to annoy you, Major Jones, I only wish to offer my good offices. In return for the letters." His smile dissolved. "Which you certainly cannot construe as your own property."

"I do not have them," I said.

"Where are they?"

"Under the control of the United States Government." It was not true, not yet. But I hoped young Mr. Adams would acquire them before the night was up.

"That," Mr. Disraeli said, with a look of pain his efforts failed to disguise, "is a great relief to me. Surely, Mr. Adams will wish to return such an indelicate property to the only legitimate possessor."

"And wouldn't that be the wife?" I asked. "This Mrs. Pomeroy of Lambeth? Didn't he send the letters to her, making them her property ever after?"

"A wife's property is the husband's property. Under law."

"You told me yourself she sold them."

"I was in error."

"And you implied—"

"Ah, that troublesome word again!"

"Then I will not use it. Tell me this: Is your Mrs. Pomeroy even a Jewess? Or is she Betty Green, born in Camden Town and raised a Methodist?"

"Surely, Major Jones, given your own evolutions in life . . . you wouldn't deny a young woman the opportunity to amend the course of her life? To begin anew?" He flicked his fingers as if ridding himself of crumbs. "Let us say, she is a woman born without certain advantages, and who has made certain errors in the past."

"If I looked through every register in this city, would I find a mention of her marriage under any name at all?"

"The search," Mr. Disraeli assured me, "would require a great deal of time. Allow me to spare you the toil. The young woman in question remains unwed." He glanced at Pomeroy again, as at a beggar. "Modern youth is prone to an excess of enthusiasm, which sometimes manifests itself in insupportable exaggerations. Claims are made impulsively . . . that may not be warranted by the facts. Let us say— with the utmost sincerity—that the young woman under discussion enjoys the Pomeroy family's protection."

"I saw his father leaving her this afternoon."

"I do not doubt it."

"I have reason to suspect they are intimates."

"I defer to your greater knowledge."

"What do you want from him?"

"From whom?"

"From Mr. Pomeroy. That lad's father."

"Perhaps," Mr. Disraeli said, with his face swaying back and forth above his collar to match the rhythm of the carriage, "you should ask what the fellow wants of me."

"What does he want from you?"

"Nothing unusual."

"You never answered my question," I said.

"But which one? You ask so very many."

"Is she even a Jewess?"

Mr. Disraeli looked down at his walking stick for a moment. Sleek with lacquer, it rested against his trousers. When his eyes come up again, he said, "I suspect that was another of young Pomeroy's needless elaborations."

Twas odd to carry on such a conversation, with Reginald Pomeroy seated in our company. I would not say he looked like a mouse, but rather that he wished he might become so unobtrusive a creature. He stank of fear and regret.

"Why say she was Jewish?" I asked. "Why make such a wicked claim?"

Mr. Disraeli waved the question off, but answered it all the same. "Oh, I suppose he thought it might lend her a certain exoticism." He spoke blithely. "Tasteless of him, I will admit. But hardly without precedent. I believe the Jewess exerts a certain fascination over the Anglo-Saxon mind, a hint of . . . of dark riches, shall we say? Of private mysteries and all sorts of forbidden treats. From Shakespeare himself, down to the frivolities of Scott, the raven-tressed daughter of Judah is so often present—and ever compliant at the prospect of a Christian lad's attentions. She longs to be rescued from her own identity, if we are to credit the authorized version of the tale. And, of course, there is always an odious parent to be rid of, a creature positively thrilling with menace." He smiled. "The Jew may be deplored, but he compels."

He sat back, perhaps to see me better in the lamplit interior, with its hint of smoke and its smell of oil and horsehair. I wondered how a man must feel who has abandoned the religion of his forefathers. Certainly, we must rejoice when anyone robes himself in Christ's forgiveness. Still, a body wonders at the man who leaves the faith that runs in the family blood.

Mr. Disraeli might have read my thoughts, for he added, "Perhaps you know of my own peculiar relation to Judaism? One may weigh a certain pride against an inevitable distaste, you see. But I must send you one of my novels, Major Jones. *Tancred* would do, I should think."

I did not mention that I read no novels. For though I could not like him, one man's work wants no insult from another.

"So she is Betty Green from Camden Town, and not a Jewess from Budapest?"

"Really," Mr. Disraeli said, "I'm not completely certain *who* she is, at this point. She may not be certain herself. But why don't you ask her?"

"I did."

"And what did she say?"

"Nothing."

He smiled. "Perhaps . . . that is your answer?"

I shook my head. "It is not a sufficient one."

"For whom? For Mr. Adams?"

Twas then I made my error.

"I've read the letters," I told him. A man should never lie.

He laughed delightedly, ending with that twitter I remembered and touching the end of his little goaty beard. "No, you haven't. Dear me! If you had read them, you wouldn't be sitting here, I assure you. Oh, dear me. I have to wonder if you even have the letters at all? Whatever have you done with them, Jones? Lost them in some gutter?"

"You'll find out," I said lamely.

He smiled triumphantly. "I expect I shall."

In a humor much improved, he tapped the carriage's panel with his stick again, doubtless a signal to spirit me back to my lodgings.

"Really, Major Jones! I simply don't know what to make of you. So artful one moment, so . . . so charmingly plain the next."

Twas then young Pomeroy stirred himself to speak, although it clearly cost him a terrible effort.

"Tell him," he said to Mr. Disraeli, in a tortured croak of a voice. "Tell him what else you were supposed to say."

Mr. Disraeli gave young Pomeroy a look of such ferocious hatred that I wonder the boy didn't crumble into dust. It lasted but an instant, though, and the man who one day would become Britain's Prime Minister—and Lord Beaconsfield, to boot—composed himself.

"Of course! Thank you for reminding me, Mr. Pomeroy." He turned back to me as if truly grateful that his memory had been sparked. "In the event the letters *should* come into the possession of the United States Government, Major Jones, please convey to Mr. Adams that our gratitude for their return would prove unprecedented. Indeed, I would personally guarantee my own and my party's resolute determination to protect Washington's interests throughout the course of your present, unfortunate conflict." He looked at me with those impossibly steady eyes. "There is nothing he might ask which I would not grant, so long as it lay in my power. *Nothing,* Major Jones."

And I had nothing else to say, for I did not want to embarrass myself again. I had a muchness to ponder as it was. For Mr. Adams had told me that very afternoon how Lord Russell and Lord Lyons, both of whom stood high in the faction in power, had pledged their support of America's cause in return for some unspecified display of good will. And here sat Mr. Disraeli, the great engine of the Tory opposition, promising the same for a handful of letters.

I had not read them. Not only because I had lacked the time, but because a gentleman must not do such a thing. But England, I had begun to suspect, was hardly the place in which to behave as a gentleman.

If ever those letters fell into my hands again, I meant to read them through, although my Mary Myfanwy would not have approved. This world is hard and makes unkind demands on striving Christians. I would believe that virtue gives us strength, but fear I am so weak I could not prove it.

Well, we must have faith and go through.

I stepped down from the carriage just as the rain opened a skirmish.

"Remember," Mr. Disraeli said, before his carriage pulled away, "my party's unswerving loyalty for those letters. Pray tell Mr. Adams."

I nodded as he dropped the sash, then turned to the gassy brightness of my hotel. Half-concerned, but equally astonished at the ways of the world, I wondered what might be waiting in my bedroom, which had begun to seem the most public place in London.

I was not disappointed, for a gift lay on the bed. It was a handsome cane cut out of ebony, looking a bit thicker than was common. Fine and fancy the instrument was, though with the queerest top. The handle was straight and leathered, so that a man might grip it with his fist.

Glancing about to be sure I was not in the presence of *Thug* assassins or men in red masks, I took up the stick.

It had a weight to it.

And then I saw the latch below the handle. I released it and the ebony sheath fell away to reveal a rapier.

Once free, the sword had a lovely balance, and light as a bamboo stick it was in my hand. The blade shone and sang as I tried it on the air. Now, I had been a master of the bayonet and knew how to use an army cutlass, too. But that rapier was a thoroughbred compared to the plodding mules of my experience, and I feared I lacked the skills to use it well.

There was a note, too. It had been wound up tight around the blade. It flew off as I duelled with the air and dropped onto the floor.

I took it up and unrolled it:

I like to give a man a sporting chance. It keeps things jolly.

Eleven

All cities look unfortunate from the railway. The traveler sees their dirty linens only, and none of their finery. We left King's Cross in a blow of rain, and each bleak house and courtyard looked forlorn as we rushed past. Twas a gray world, painted a loveless tone, all grime and youthful dreams come up to nothing. The rain jeweled on the windows separating us from the rubbish heap of the world, and when a spark flew back from the locomotive it seemed the only light in all the land.

The companion with whom I shared the compartment looked morbid as the weather. Pop-eyed, with spectacles and prosperous whiskers, I judged him a government inspector on his travels, or perhaps the headmaster of a middling school. He was scribbling away and offered no greeting when the porter put me into the carriage from the platform—an English railway car is cut into separate boxes, see, little worlds that shun too much democracy—and my fellow traveller glared when the door clapped shut and caged us together. But soon enough he went back to his pencil and paper, snorting in satisfaction as he wrote.

I let him be, for I am not a chatterbox. Although a Welshman likes a pleasant talk, that I will give you. Instead, I watched the world go by, the falling away of the city, then the cringe of the groves and fields beneath the rain. A blowing willow caught my eye, sweeping its branches across a swollen brook. Then it was gone. Willows make me think of Mr. Shakespeare and that poor girl with her hair loose in the water. I have never liked Prince Hamlet, for he thought only of himself and not of others. He fussed about everything, and had no grip, and the sad lass died confused by all his nonsense. "To be or not to be" is a silly question. We are, and that is that, and we must make the best of it. I feel far more for poor Mark Antony, despite his doubtful morals, for well I understand the power of love. And we both were soldiers. Ophelia deserved a better fate. For she loved deeply, though she had her failings and went about too heedless of her deportment. But I cannot forgive that cold, young prince, who wanted a taste of honest work and a thrashing.

Let all that bide. Twas only the range of my musings as we throbbed across the lowlands, for I did not want to think of masks and murders, or of letters full of secrets. We cannot run on like a locomotive, but must pause.

Morning faded into afternoon, and the light was gray to break a fellow's heart.

The traveller with his scribbling showed no interest in aught else, so I watched the villages go by, and the dutiful shepherds wet under broad-brimmed hats, and the scooting of sheep when our passage made them nervous. I felt at once the miracle of speed and the loneliness that comes to us with distance. I did not relish the labors that held me captive in this war, and wished me home among my lovely ledgers. I hoped the boys in Mr. Evans's counting house were keeping up their standards. A colliery cannot run on ill-kept books.

The rain grew stronger. Across a sodden field, a pair of men stood over the smoky ruin of a fire. I knew not what they were about. Peatburners, perhaps. But they struck me as they watched us go, we creatures of privilege. Likely they felt jealousy at those who could afford a safe, dry life and all the many conveniences of progress. Or were we queer as creatures in a storybook? What did they see? I cannot say I wished to stand beside them in the wet. Yet, there was something to them that I envied.

At times, I fear our age is one of loss. When I was young, we walked and learned the world. Those with laden pockets might take coaches, or ride a horse they hired from a stable. But now the world is sealed from nature's blasts, protected ever more by grand inventions. I wonder if the day will come when no one but the soldier or the shepherd knows about the many weights of rain, or how the winter cuts and summer scorches. Perhaps it is that I am growing old, and that a man of thirty-four is uneasy with newfangled means of living. But, somehow, an ancient loveliness seems wanting.

At last, my companion snapped shut his notebook, put his jottings and his pencil into his travelling bag, and glared in my direction.

"You, sir," he began, "are impertinent! I don't know you from Adam, yet you've been staring at me this hour and more."

It was not true. My eyes, and certainly my heart, had been elsewhere.

"You are abominably ill-mannered," he continued, "and rude. But I suppose that's the way we live now." He snorted. "A fellow can't even have his peace on the railway!"

"I'm sorry, sir," I said, though I was innocent, for Christian meekness sometimes makes its way, "I did not intend—"

"Intentions have nothing to do with it! I will not have discourtesy. It's intolerable!" He reached back into his bag and drew out a book with a slip of paper sticking out as a place-mark. "Now, sir," he concluded, "if you are finished annoying me, I beg to be left in peace!"

I did not know what to say, so I said nothing. I watched the world again, for on such days, when the Heavens droop and the brooding weather pierces us as brightness will not do, we feel our slightness, and wonder how often we will see such sights again, and when we may be taken from this vale of rending loveliness.

I had read my Testament first thing in the morning, and got through *The Times* while waiting at King's Cross—more of the "cotton famine" and complaints of Northern "Hessians" pillaging and plundering the South, which was all tosh. The paper said French arms were in retreat in Mexico, a form of military adventure the Frenchman doubtless has perfected, and there was more fussing in Servia, with fighting at Belgrade. The Irish were up to murdering English landlords, which seemed to have become a Hibernian sport. I had digested all the news and even the advertisements. Thus, I had no pleasurable reading left, yet felt a growing guilt at sitting idle. So I put up my deadly new cane and took down the German grammar through which I had been laboring for a time. But I could not study it, despite my strong belief in self-improvement. My mind would not settle on *sein* and *werden* and *geworden*.

I sat entranced and lulled by our forward motion, with the country rising and the sky lowering, as if we were slipping down a funnel. The train clacked along, tooting like a proud and living thing, and the luggage shifted now and again on the roof of the car, as if the rain made it uncomfortable. The combination of rain, steam and speed fair overwhelmed me. I would have been contented in my reveries, and might even have drowsed, had the fellow on the opposite bench not punctuated the afternoon's sobriety with declarations spoken aloud as he read.

"Oh, that's dreadful!" he declared happily. "Impossible to credit! No one could believe such nonsense for a moment." And then, five minutes later: "He's certainly losing his talent, if not his mind. It's absolutely pitiable!" Happier and happier he sounded, although his outbursts seemed to tell of misfortune. "Rubbish!" he cried in delight. "He's finished! Such drivel won't last the season. His talent's run out on him, the fellow's done." He shifted and settled and read and exclaimed, "Ridiculous! As if rats and mice would have left a single crumb of cake after all those years! It's too absurd! And the child's insufferable! I shall get the tooth-ache from all the sweetness." He grunted, which I believe betokened a laugh.

I might have been a wraith, swirling in the smoke and wet beyond the window, for all the reality I seemed to hold for my coachmate. Although I am not unfriendly by my nature, I was a bit relieved when he got down at a station, bag in hand and topper on his head.

Only after the train pulled away, did I notice that his book still lay on the cushion. I picked it up, in search of an address, so that it might be returned to him, but found only the possessive inscription A. TROL-LOPE, which seemed to me an unbecoming name.

The book was *Great Expectations,* by Mr. Dickens.

It is the strangest thing how the mind surprises us. I was exchanging looks with a field of cows as we sped past, when I realized Mr. Adams and I had talked ourselves into a false conclusion. Foolishly wrong we were, twas damnably clear. The affair of the letters and that of the murders were unquestionably related, if not identical. They were not trains on separate tracks, but two compartments in the selfsame carriage. They fit together, back to back, they did. For the man in the red silk mask was a link to both, whether he was Lieutenant Culpeper resurrected or the Prince of Wales come out for a turn in the park.

How ever could I have missed it? The masked fellow had lured me out of the penny gaff before I had an inkling of the letters, and the slum-child had seen him earlier, going into the establishment of the murdered pawn-mother, where Mr. Campbell's watch was found. But when he come to me in the hotel, in the wake of Miss Perkins's unsettling escapade, he had wanted the letters of me. And now I had a sword-cane as his gift, if my suspicions were true. Why had I failed to see the clear connection? If not all of those involved with the letters had ties to ships of war, one at least was tied to both watch and correspondence.

A child would have seen it.

I am not cut out for matters of this nature. That is the sorry truth. I am a clerk, and a good one, not a detective. Why on earth did men place trust in me? I did not want it. I only longed to live a peaceful life, and perhaps to become an elder in our chapel, when I was ripe enough. To make my darling proud, and to raise our son, without shame or debts—that is what I wanted. And here I was hurtling to Scotland, without a proper plan or even a notion.

I saw another thing, too, thanks to Mr. Disraeli. He talked too much, enamored of his cleverness and voice. Declaring he knew I had not read the letters—mocking me—he had told me I would not be sitting there, in his carriage, if I had read them. So proud of himself he was, of his wit and his knowledge. He had not meant to tell me quite so much, I did not think. Not this time. No, he had revealed that the letters were not just a matter of amorous blackmail between a wastrel son and a wanton father.

And how she had convinced me, that Betty Green or however she might call herself. She had come to the door jabbering about the return of her lover, just after the elder Pomeroy had left. And I had fallen into the trap, even though I already knew that half of what had gone on in London had been got up for my benefit. I wanted to believe a lurid thing, see. They judged me all too well.

The elder Mr. Pomeroy was no more her lover than I was. He had been there on purpose, for me to see him. They were all in it together, father and son, Disraeli, and the Lord only knew who else.

The man in the red mask.

There was another thing I saw, a wicked thing that made my heart sink down. But I let that bide, for I had pressing, if less troubling, questions.

What had made Disraeli afraid?

Who truly wielded power over whom?

Why were those letters meant to be passed through my hands to the masked fellow?

Who had really written them? And what did those letters contain?

Who *was* the secret lover of the woman in Lambeth, the made-up Jewess?

Did she have a lover at all? Or was it something else entirely, a secret masked by lust and men's assumptions?

And what did it have to do with the Reverend Mr. Campbell?

There was a connection, but how deep did it run?

I felt too small a man for such intrigues, too slight of mind, too weak. I like to think that I am strong and sturdy, but life does not indulge our mortal pride.

I felt glum, I tell you. Fortunately, we drew into York just then, which meant I might look out for a bit of dinner. I always feel better, I do, when my belly is full.

Travel at such speed can muddle our senses. As I stepped down onto the crowded platform, with pie-men shouting their wares and a great to-do as we all hurried to secure our victuals, I thought I glimpsed a wild Indian tribesman at the edge of things, all got up like an Englishman, but dark-skinned all the same. I was reduced to seeing ghosts about me. When I looked properly, there was nothing. As you would expect.

Foregoing the expense of the dining saloon, I bought a sausage baked in dough and a pair of apples from a shawl-wrapped missy, then tapped my way back through the anxious crowd. The new cane put my balance off ever so slightly. It wanted getting used to, for its length would have suited a taller man than me.

The locomotive shrieked like a heathen demon. The advertisement had promised twenty minutes, but I did not believe the half was up.

At first, I thought I had returned to the wrong compartment when I saw those two young ladies sitting inside. But I was not mistaken, for the number on the carriage was correct and my travelling bag sat waiting on the rack.

A bit of drip-water from the roof of the car potted me as I stepped in. It struck me in the eye and made me stumble. The young ladies, all organdy and blue, did their best not to giggle at the sight of me. So young and fine they seemed, floating on their clouds of summer fabric. Their gauzy hats looked lighter than the air, and the beribboned parasols tossed in a corner spoke of the disregard for expensive things that sets the rich apart from those who labor.

And off we went, with the clouds dispersed and the evening refined to gold.

"Oh, Harriet," the lass in organdy said, in a haughty, South-of-England sort of voice, "you *shan't* marry him! I shan't *let* you . . ."

"I don't know," the beauty in blue said coyly.

I had taken up that book by Mr. Dickens, affecting to read, although it was a novel and wrong for a Methodist. I did not wish to intrude myself on the ladies, see. I sat as small as I could sit and, truth be told, they hardly seemed to notice me. But even a gentleman cannot close his ears.

"Well, I *do* know," Miss Organdy declared. "Why, you'd perish in the Highlands! Whatever does one do there? As if a week in Yorkshire hasn't been frightful enough."

"*I* think it sounds romantic," Blue Girl said. "After all, the Queen finds it quite the thing. All that walking and climbing about the moors with loyal dogs, and shooting grouches, or whatever those birds are called . . ."

"Harriet! You've never shot anything in your life. And you hate it when dogs bother your skirts. Why, you've never climbed anything higher than the stairs to a ballroom."

"But he *is* a laird. It all sounds like a tale of the Middle Ages. Like one of those lovely paintings one sees about these days."

"Fiddlesticks! I don't doubt they *live* as though it were still the Middle Ages. But you shan't like that one bit. Why . . . why, you'd be better off with John Grey. Cambridgeshire may be dreadful, but London isn't far off."

"I find I'm rather taken with the idea of Scotland," Blue Girl said, just a bit crossly. "Besides, I understand Mr. Grey is to be married to that impossible Vavasor girl. Not that I would have had him, of course. I prefer the thought of heather and Scottish adventures."

"Well," Miss Organdy told her, "we shall just see how you like the reality. You'll probably be made to read the Bible aloud to the servants and to sleep in a draught."

"Really, Josie, I don't see why you insisted on coming along."

Miss Organdy gave a harrumph that verged on the unladylike. "Well, you can be certain it has nothing whatsoever to do with that brother of his," she said, and turned her fair face to the twilight.

During our pause at York, the porters had lit the lamps within the carriages and we sat in a cheery glow. I fear I was in a dilemma, though, for as soon as the ladies fell silent, I found myself engrossed in the novel I held. It began frightfully, in a graveyard, with a convict's threats to a child who had been orphaned. The boy's protector, Mr. Gargery, seemed a lovely man, though weak. Twas obvious he cared for young Pip and would do what he could to protect him, but—

I realized I had been seduced. Low entertainments will not do for the conscience of a Christian. I know my Mary Myfanwy disagrees, and thinks me overly strict about the issue, although I let her read what books she will. But novels seem to me a form of gossip. What kind of man would make up untrue tales?

Let that bide. I decided I might, in fairness to my wife's earnest views, read just a bit more before I condemned the book. As an experiment, to know mine enemy. But in that embarrassed moment, when I wrenched my eyes from the page in shame at my weakness, I had noticed the queerest thing. One of the ladies had tucked a covered basket into the corner, just behind their parasols. Twas the sort of container used for a thousand things in the Punjab, not all of them good.

I fear my curiosity got the best of me. Perhaps I was a bit lonely, truth be told. But I let my manners grow forward.

"Begging your pardon, ladies. And excuse me for asking. But does one of your families enjoy a tie to India?"

The two girls looked at one another. Twas clear enough they did not take my point.

"It is only the basket there," I said, pointing into the corner. "It is from India, see. I thought there must be an association . . ."

Miss Organdy, who was the plucky one, said, "We thought it yours, sir."

I shook my head in denial.

"Someone must have forgotten it," Blue Girl said. "They'll be frightfully sorry. It's really rather lovely."

Miss Organdy spied about, as if faces might be peering in the windows. Which they were not.

"Oh, let's have a look, shall we? It might be a secret treasure." She reached for the basket.

I have a soldier's instincts, thank the Lord. Just as her hand touched the lid, I lunged and grabbed her, throwing her back into her seat.

"*Sir!*" she cried.

But her complaint was near-drowned out by the scream that come from her friend.

The snake slid over the edge of the basket with that vibrant smoothness they have. Long it was, til it never seemed to end.

"Get out of the way!" I barked. "Get up on the cushions."

We had seconds. For any man could see it was a cobra.

I grabbed for my cane and near sent it clattering. Had the snake not had its own moment of confusion at its new surroundings, one of us would have perished.

The ladies had more petticoats and crinolines and skirts than they wanted for clambering up on the seats. Clouds of pastel colors they were, and I feared the snake might disappear into their underclothes.

Its hood began to swell. Then it rose, all sudden.

I had no time to unsheathe the sword, but used the cane to parry the creature. For horrible seconds we faced off in that tiny box of a compartment. Then Blue Girl lost her footing and dropped with a scream.

The snake punched into her skirts. It is always a shock to see the force they have. They hit a man near as hard as a bullet does.

The screaming became general.

I brought my cane down on the back of the snake's hood in the frozen moment its fangs spent in her garments. I hoped to snap its backbone. But the creature only recoiled with a vivid hiss. I slapped the book toward it and the serpent struck the cover in midair.

Blue Girl fainted. I did not know if it was from fear or because of the poison.

Mr. Dickens rescued me. The fangs had gone through the binding and into the pages. The book stuck to the cobra's snout and the creature struggled wildly to free itself. For every creature on earth desires to live. The novel kept the snake occupied just long enough for me to crack its head.

Twas either dead or stunned.

I unlatched my cane. When the sword emerged, Miss Organdy gasped.

I made short work of the cobra after that. Although its body twitched about the compartment.

I had just turned my attention to the lass in blue, when Miss Organdy shrieked, *"There's another one!"*

And so there was. Slithering out of the basket.

I chopped its head off. With nausea rising in me. My breath labored to excel the locomotive.

I did not think the basket would hold another serpent, but I pierced it through with the sword a pair of times. I could tell by the basket's weight on my blade it was empty.

"Careful!" I told Miss Organdy. "The poison's a danger, even when they are dead."

She was weeping, near hysterical. "She's dead, Harriet's dead! She's dead! My God! She's dead!"

"No," I said, in a voice that wanted to calm her but was too wild by half, "she is not dead. Not yet. Stand you back. And help me lift her."

The girl seemed afraid to touch her friend. As if the poison—or death—were contagious. The dead snakes twitched at our feet, in bits and pieces.

"Oh, my God," she cried, "she's dead, she's dead . . ."

I was losing the lass in organdy, as well as the girl in blue. The way you lose a soldier who has broken, surrounded by imaginary terrors worse than the enemy before him.

I slapped her across her pretty face, although it was ungentlemanly.

"Help me, lass. Or your friend will die, and you will have failed her properly."

She declined to a whimper. But the intelligence had come back into her eyes. I made her help me, gingerly, as I lifted the sprawled girl across the bench of cushions. Then I had Miss Organdy climb onto the seat again while I undid the door and scooted the remains of the serpents out into the night. I got rid of that basket, too, although I could do nothing for the blood.

I shut the door again and told her, "Help me."

"What . . . what do you want . . . want me . . ."

Now this was hard for a married man and a Methodist, I will tell you.

"We must get her unmentionables from her. So I may see where the serpent struck her leg."

She looked at me, aghast.

"It is that, or her death," I said.

The girl began to quake again. I gripped her by her upper arms. Beneath the cloth they were but lengths of bone. I fear the thinness favored by ladies has become a thing unhealthy, for they are little more than walking skeletons. With fair faces, I grant you.

After a proper shaking, she bent to help me without another word. There was good. For I would never have made my way through those avalanches of starched cloth and stiffeners without irreparable destruction and much delay.

I fear I reddened in mortification as we neared the sanctuary of her flesh. Despite the obvious need for our urgent actions. In India, we cut into the flesh and did what little we could to drain the poison, although it only rarely saved a life. Had Mick Tyrone been with us, he might have taken off the lass's leg.

Blessedly, we did not need to shame her completely. But forced we were to draw her stockings off, and to fuss up to her stays.

Her flesh was absolutely clear, with only golden down upon her thighs, where the snake had plunged into her skirts.

A wonder it was! It seemed an English lady's garments were of sufficient depth to absorb a cobra's strike. Although they are not always so resistant to two-legged serpents, if you will pardon my frankness.

I did not touch her the slightest bit more than necessary, you understand, and I fear her companion and I were equally distraught at finding her most private of garments in need of a bit of a wash. But a grace and a glory it was that the girl was safe and had but fainted.

And only a faint it was. Just as I was finishing my inspection, she awoke. And spied me rooting deep within her petticoats.

She screamed worse than she did when she saw the snake. For death is not so frightful as dishonor, to a proper lady.

I must have jumped a yard, if I jumped an inch. I lost my balance and tumbled back into my seat.

There was a bit of confusion after that. Fortunately, Miss Organdy had mastered herself and, once she had calmed her friend, she explained the situation we had faced.

Blue Girl shut her eyes in shame, but she had been brought up proper, except for the importance of always wearing clean underthings, and she told me—eyes still shut to avoid mine own—that she was grateful for her rescue and my solicitation. Her voice trembled, and she did not say much more. I only hoped she did not think me nasty.

The rest of the trip was uneventful. The young ladies dismounted at Edinburgh. Thank me again, they did, the two of them. But I suspect they did not mind our parting. The one in blue never did recover her color.

The folk getting down from the next compartment gave the three of us a proper looking over. I blushed to think how they had deciphered the screaming. But we cannot undo a thing that is done, so I waited until the passengers had changed over, then switched myself into an empty compartment. Away from the bloody mess the cobras left. Relieved I was that the police had not taken an interest—and glad when the train began to move again.

I *longed* to get to Glasgow. For I faced pressing discomforts of the body after my sequestration in the train. And I half expected tribesmen with spears to drop through the roof and vault in through the window.

Despite all that, I will make a small confession. I had swept that novel out along with the serpents and the basket, for the first snake had not fully recovered its fangs from the pages. I believe we have an American expression about "sinking one's teeth into a book," and that the creature had done. But I fear I had sunk in a tooth or two myself.

I do not like to compromise my principles, and know that we must ever be on guard, yet I wanted to know what happened to young Pip, and if the convict fellow would make good his threats, and what the lad would have to do with the pretty little girl, and what the disappointed old woman meant to do. That decrepit, jilted bride put me in mind of a certain Mrs. Fowler, a lady of Philadelphia whose pride had killed her son. I feared I would succumb and purchase another copy. To give the Devil his due.

Well, fair is fair. Given the advantage the book had brought me in the struggle with the serpents, I felt I owed a debt to Mr. Dickens.

Twelve

That fiddler wanted a talking to, and I was the man to give it to him. Cobra snakes on trains are bad enough, but music played off-key will madden a Welshman.

At my morning prayers I was, in my room at the Hotel Clarence, which Mr. Adams himself had recommended, when the worst scraping on strings that ever was heard ensnared my words of thanks to my Redeemer and turned them into complaints at the ways of the world. I believe the fellow was attempting to perform a Highland reel of sorts, but it sounded to me like a battalion of cats undergoing torture.

The man played badly is what I mean to say.

I called "Amen" to Him above, and took myself below. I had slept well enough, and longer than usual, despite the poisoned air that come in through the very window glass. I could not say whether Glasgow stank like the bowels of a factory, or whether it reeked like a factory of bowels, begging your pardon, but the stench of the place was worse by half than that of Murder Bay in Washington. And that was an odor, indeed. Even my dreams smelled of sulfur and sewage and soot.

Out I went into the prompt and early bustle of George Square, with my cane fair thrashing the cobbles and the morning all teeming with bankers and high men of business and such. All set I was to make my complaint to the very source of the infraction, when the girl's voice stopped me, sure as the Hand of Heaven.

When we are led into that final garden, to receive our just reward—

should such be our lot—the angel that calls us to come will sound like her. I do believe it.

She gave the passersby a fetching tune, a ballad soft as down, and gathered a crowd. I crossed the street into the square, chased by carriages carrying Scotsmen stingy of their time, and joined the audience in time to hear the girl's light soprano gentle into "Annie Laurie." Oh, the fiddler was dreadful as ever he had been, and out of tune, as well, with his high string flat by nearly half a tone, but his bowing was no more now than a lesser devil's scratching at Heaven's doors. We all of us heard the angel, and not him.

I got me through to the front of the throng, and met a sharp surprise for all my fussing. No, I would not complain of the fiddler's doings, after all. Let other men insult him, if they had the heart. He was a veteran soldier, with a sergeant's stripes on his sleeves, his face burned half away and his two eyes gone. His scalp was raw, but for a few tufts on the left side, and his regimental walking-out cap seemed a very mockery, as if he were still young and jaunty, strutting off to the Saturday parade. What flesh he had was purple from his scalp down to the worn collar of his tunic, and the cloth on his breast was faded from the scarlet. His kilt hung limp and ragged as his stockings. Just at his feet, a rough sign spelled out:

INKERMAN

There are homes and hospitals for veteran soldiers, see. But those beds are never enough, and the waiting lists are long, and preference is given to the elder men who have served out full careers. Perhaps it must be so and should be so. But such a one as this would be pensioned on pennies, and left to scrape his living with his bow. The Crimea left old England with more maimed sons than anyone cared to manage. No common soldier finds his thanks when the war is over and done, though generals will have no end of handsome honors.

Perhaps that ruination of his visage, the blast or fire that had taken away his eyes, had done a damage to his hearing, too. For out of tune he was, and there is true. But the girl, who I assumed to be his daughter, had a pitch as sure as a good wife's heart, and satin and velvet where the rest of us have tonsils. Oh, a Welshman loves a well-sung

tune, and there is no denying it. I listened to that girl—twelve or thirteen I thought her, although the poor show small—I listened to her
with the deep attention we ought to reserve for sermons. And, really,
that performance was improper. For "Annie Laurie" is no song for a
lass, but meant for a man and a tenor. And at the end, singing that, for
the love of Annie Laurie, "I'd lay me doon and dee," the little thing
stretched herself out on the pavement, as if expiring of a broken heart.

Now, I have never been to an opera house, where all is gilt and finery, but I doubt if ever there was a more heartfelt round of applause
than we gave that girl. And to the brave soldier of Inkerman, though
his music deserved no praise.

But applause was nearly all the listeners gave, for the Scots go
about with their purses sewn shut and their souls are as strict as the
lines of a well-kept ledger. A pair of ha'pennies was all the lass had for
her brightening up of our morning. Until an old man come forward,
limping worse than me, with the sidelocks of the Jew about his ears.
Poor he looked himself, and bent, and a close record of his recent
meals adorned his lapels. But he cast an entire shilling into the brass
bowl the girl carried round.

"*So 'ne shayna Stimme!*" he told her, and I could not tell if he were
merely old or if tears afflicted his speech. "*Meen kleenes het je so
yesungen, meen kleenes Maedle. So viele Johren ist Die weg. So 'ne
shayna Stimme, hest Di, Kindeloin . . . Ach, die tumme Johren sind
scho' so viel . . .*"

The little girl curtsied to the old fellow, and off he went shaking his
head at his burden of yesterdays. Now, I had taken joy from her performance, although I wished that she had chosen hymns, and I could
not offer less than some Hebrew fellow. Although I am no companion
to extravagance.

I dropped a shilling entire into her plate. Just as the Jew had done.
It clanged on the brass and come to rest atop the old man's coin.

She curtsied for me, too.

"Thankee, sir. I do na deserve sich kindness, I'm sure."

She wore a woman's flowered hat, a bit the worse for wear and
twice too big, over flowing, tumbling hair the color of rust. Her face
was of that age when the prettiness of childhood has begun to fade but
the bones of the visage have not yet decided on beauty or plainness for

the woman she would become. A confusion she was, of childish sweetness and clumsy limbs, with a hint of a promise she might prove fair, indeed. Her face was clean, but the rest of her wanted a scrub.

I was about to ask her if she knew any of my favored hymns from Wesley or Watts, when the blind sergeant lowered his fiddle and growled, impatiently, "Have they na given ye this morn, Fanny? Lass, come o'er, and show us what they've na given ye." But that was all the language he could manage, for he bent into a coughing fit and nearly broke his fiddle on the pavings.

Sick the fellow was, twas clear enough. The girl rushed to him and tried to soothe his coughing with her coins. I left them so. For I had duties enough awaiting me, and the poor are legion in Britannia's streets.

"I could hae wept when I saw it," Inspector McLeod told me, although he did not look a weeping man. "In a' my years, I hae seen na sight so fit to break a man's heart, and a sinful waste it was. To throw him into the water that way, and with those fine boots still on him. I call that criminality of the worst degree, and sinful. To ruin so fine a pair of boots by throwing them in the water with the body. If ever a murdering bunch deserved to hang, it's that clan of them, whoever they mought hae been." He looked at me, as big and red as Wilkie had been small and dark, although both men shared an affection for powerful whiskers. "There's crimes are such a man will na forget them, though he live to be a hundred and a day. All my years, I'll see those twa fine boots all ruined from the soaking."

We stood along the Broomielaw, where the River Clyde enjoyed the tribute of nations. Below us, steamers and lesser boats adorned the northern bank, while the far side of the river harbored a density of shipping so great I did not see how the vessels could turn about to return to the sea. A forest of masts and funnels it was, all busy with human limbs and hoisted cargoes, and the black maws of the warehouses lining the quay seemed fit to devour the commerce of all the world. Whistles there were, and mechanical horns, and shouts in accents as foreign to Scotland as decency is to a Frenchman.

But let that bide.

"I thought perhaps you might tell me something of the condition of the body," I said to the inspector, whose blazing whiskers escaped from his hat like flames from an overfed boiler.

"Oh, there was na a thing to see of any interest. Except for those braw boots upon his feet."

"But you said he had been strangled."

The inspector nodded. "That he had. With the eyes bulging out of his head. He was na mindful of the law of the docks, which is ever to go careful and na to go anywhere useless in the darkness."

"Could you tell what sort of instrument had been used? To strangle him?"

The inspector's great pink face took on a wistful look. Thinking doubtless of those ruined boots. "Wire, I would say. His head was ha' choked off him."

"A thin cord, perhaps?"

Twas clear the inspector had no great interest in my questions and did not see their point. I had presented myself properly, as come from our legation to inquire into the circumstances of the death two months before of one Walter Quigley, late of Massachusetts. I did not mention any other matters that concerned me.

"Thin cord, thin wire," Inspector McLeod said. "I can na see the difference." At last, he forgot those boots and his eyes alerted with a first suspicion. "And why should it hae mattered?"

"Well," I said, "we are concerned about Confederate activities, see." It was no proper answer, I realize. But I was learning from Mr. Adams's art, wherein high diplomats respond to uncomfortable questions by saying nothing at all with the greatest confidence.

To my surprise, my answer perked him up. "Ah, your slavers," he said. "May the whole clan of them be damned twa times over. There's ever a brood with a grand fondness for the sufferings of others."

A dray wagon pulled up behind us, drawn by a blinkered team with unkempt manes. Three small men rolled barrels down from the bed. It looked as though the fellows must be crushed, but clever they were in their doings, jumping clear when the weight would not be resisted. From a deck nearby, a sailor cursed their lateness, and ship bells clanged.

"And is there nothing else you can tell me about the business, then?" I asked. The inspector had been good enough to accompany me from the police offices where I had gone to make my inquiries, but he would never have made a Welshman, for he had no love of words or joy in speaking.

"What would you hae me tell?" he asked. "There's precious little, as in a' these dockside affairs." He pointed behind us, to the Hotel Lord Byron, where the late Mr. Quigley had been quartered. "A laddie called late in the evening, and your Mr. Quigley stepped out with him. He did na return, and there he was found in the morning, snout-down in the river, floating by the wheel of the *Pride of the Clyde*."

"Was his purse taken?"

The inspector shook his head. "Another shameful matter there. For the murderers must hae feared themselves. They left his purse as cauld as they left his boots. With a' the banknotes ruined by the water. As ruined as those twa fine boots of his." The inspector's visage tightened in disgust. "Aye, murder's a wicked deed, that it is. But to murder and waste together, what could be more vicious and criminal than that?"

"So, you would say that it's . . . it's unusual, even unnatural, for a man to be murdered but not robbed?"

"I can na say it for America or London, but unnatural it is here on the docks of Glasgow City. For there's hardly a reason to murder a man, if he's na to be robbed for the trouble."

"And you say you have closed the book on the matter?"

"Aye. For there's na a thing more to be done."

Now, I have always found the Scots a people set in their ways, and you might as well debate a block of wood, so I let that portion of the matter bide.

We began to walk back toward the police offices, although public hacks abounded. We were both of us sensible men in that regard, see, and would not pay for the luxury of a conveyance unless it was sorely needed.

A great commercial city Glasgow was, though I wondered if the sun ever shone down upon it. A muck the color of a miner's tubwater slopped the sky, although it was not winter and no hearths burned. The clouds come from the wealth of manufactories that blackened the eastward portion of the city into a permanent twilight. The air smelled of burned coal, of rot and sulfur. But the streets were busy with money being made, from high commercial ventures to simple green-grocer shops. Of the poor, there was a plenty, but the bustle of the major streets seemed to force them back into their alleys by the sheer energy and thrust of well-done business. Success is a policeman above all constables, and money is another kind of law. Sober-dressed the place was, in comparison to London, and proud of money made in a busy lifetime and not passed down through wilted generations.

"Tell me, Inspector McLeod . . . do you know a great deal about the shipyard business?"

"I know there's wages to be had, if a man is na afraid to work."

"But are you familiar with the individual yards?"

He shook his head. "They're a' there along the Clyde or in the firth, and beyond the jurisdiction. Though there is a plenty of money to be made from them."

I was disappointed, see. For Glasgow was all new to me, and I was friendless, and the truth is I hardly knew where to start my looking. A true detective fellow would have known a dozen things to do, but I could only think of making a canvass of the docks and warehouses, of the chandlers and sailors and worse, from one weary end of the harbor to the other. Given the size and number of the establishments, I feared I would still be asking my questions when our war was over and done.

Before we had stepped too far from the river, I made my excuses to the inspector, pleading legation business and the like. He did not mind our parting, for doubtless he had many tasks before him.

"I will na forget those boots," he mused, as we shook hands on a corner. "I hae na seen twa riding boots more bonnie."

And so he went up the street, all the great tallness of him, with his flaming whiskers still to be seen over his shoulders. I turned back toward the docks. First, I went to the Lord Byron, where our dead agent had taken his room. The clerk in charge of the keys and the book had no interest in any murders and no memory available even for purchase. Nor was I better impressed with the Hotel Lord Byron than I have been with the tales they tell of the dead fellow from whom it had its name. He was not nice, and his poetry was intemperate. The hotel struck me as the sort of establishment where no attention is paid to misbehaviors that would lead to the immediate ejection of a guest in a better house. Soused with mildew it was, and it wanted a dusting.

Even the gray pall of the street was fresher than the interior of the hotel, and I steeled myself to set out on my labors. If duty so required, I would try every shipping office, warehouse and provisioner for information—about a warship I dared not mention outright, and on a great secret wooden enclosure that might not even exist. Was I only chasing after phantoms? I found myself at a loss for words, which ill becomes a Welshman.

A porter from the hotel overtook me. Plump he was, and past his prime, and his garments were far from immaculate. His beard showed a trail of snuff or such like, and his nose betrayed the decline of a drinking man. Had I been a guest at the Lord Byron, I do not think I would have trusted my bag to him.

"Will ye wait, sir?" he asked, all out of breath from the labors of rushing half down the block. "Will ye wait and listen?"

"Listen to what?" I asked him, pausing.

He finished buttoning his tunic as he stood before me, torturing the cloth until it closed. His mouth gaped with his appetite for air.

"For the answer to that ye were asking." He coughed. I fear I coughed along with him, as sometimes we do. The truth is that the Glasgow air was wretched. "Although," he went on, "I could speak a' the better, if I had a wee little dram to water my wheezer."

Shamelessly, he extended his palm. In daylight, on the street. Panting like a dog he was, for want of nourishing air.

I gave him a shilling and, when his hand failed to retract, topped the first coin with another. He made a fist and shook it in delight, then buried the coins beneath the worn flaps of a pocket.

"It's the murdered man ye're after? Mr. Quigley?"

"What can you tell me about him?"

The fellow shrugged. "Oh, quiet he was. 'The Quiet Mr. Quigley.' " He chuckled at his own wit, an impoverished cousin of Mr. Disraeli. "Nary a fuss, and manners a'most as good as a gentleman's."

"Did he have callers?"

"Niver. Not a one. But for the last."

"Do you know anything about his activities? What did he do? Where did he go?"

"He was a quiet one, Mr. Quigley. There's na telling aught with that sort. Only go off riding every day, he did, with a horse got from Cameron's stables, back of the house. Wasn't that an unco business, though?" He looked at me with pickled eyes. "Why would a man take city rooms, when a' he wanted to do with himself was go riding? It niver made na sense to me . . . but, then, he was an American. And they're every one of them quare."

"And what about that last and only caller? Did you see him?"

"Oh, to be sure, and I would na be like to forget that buckie, now would I?"

"And why would that be?"

"Well, we do na get a plenty of brown Indians in the Lord Byron. And we would na hae rooms free, if such was to come and ask. For we're a proper establishment, and don't allow whoring or niggers." He trimmed the slack from his lips. "Unco it was to see him standing there, all dressed up proper like he was a white man. And Mr. Quigley must hae thought so, too, for he bolted down the steps to go off, as soon as I said he was called for."

"And he never returned?"

"Sorry I was to hear of his misfortune," the porter said. "For he niver forgot the needs of a working man." At that, my informant extended his palm again.

I went around to the livery stable, Cameron & Sons, and asked if they knew ought of the late Mr. Quigley.

"A hard laddie on a horse," the old fellow told me, glancing over his shoulder toward the tremor and stink of the stalls. "Aye, that one was set to ruin the best of horses, given time. I don't know where he was going to day after day, but go he did every morning, only to come back as weary as the horse that was dragging him in."

There was no more to be had from the stable, and I did not want a horse myself, I promise you, having of late had horse enough in the wilds of Mississippi. But the information was sufficient, for now, in respect to Mr. Quigley. I had to wonder if the inspector had been so much the parsimonious Scotsman as he let on, with his concern about those ruined riding boots, or if he had tried to point me in a direction that he himself could not afford to take. Or was I only adding up numbers that belonged in different columns?

Certain it was, though, that Mr. Quigley had worn boots because he rode, and he rode because he had a place to go to on a horse, and that was a place where he could not stay at night, either for want of accommodation or in concern for his safety. But had he only been searching, or had he found what he was looking for on those hard rides? Had he found the wooden pavilion concealing the secret warship? And had he then been killed for his discovery? And here was India again, as unwelcome as ever, in the guise either of a murderer or of the murderer's emissary. And still there was no hint of a single Rebel. Only of deadly Hindoos and Englishmen up to trouble enough for a thousand. And did it have anything at all to do with the letters?

Was I being watched?

I had no reason to suspect it, beyond the logic of past events. But I wondered.

Back I went to a provisioner's shop just along from the Lord Byron. I started asking, as best I could, about shipyards and such like. Although the Scots are a careful, suspicious people, by the end of the afternoon I had learned the names of a dozen yards and the quality of their ships, details of the latest means of propulsion and the enduring need for canvas of good making. But never was there the faintest hint of a secret and mighty warship out in the slips.

I saw other things, too, and worried my bad leg in the course of seeing them. My search through the warehouses south of the river led me into a warren of twists and turns, and I found myself in a filthy place called the Gorbals, where the Irish had nearly driven out the Scots. The residents made those of the Seven Dials look plump and prosperous, and more than one house was limed to kill infection. The only hint of hope I saw was a convent school run by the Sisters of Mary. Now, the Church of Rome is benighted, and Christian only compared unto the Turk, yet I would be honest: There must be good in those who teach the children of the poor out of their charity. For the rich are born with the knowledge they need, but the poor must fight for every scrap of learning.

Well, let that bide. The Gorbals swallowed goodness as the crocodile devours a crawling infant.

Still worse lay north of the river, not far from the the offices of great firms and the banks. Near Glasgow Cross, where a high tower kept an eye on the comings and goings, there were alleys and closes as foul as any on earth. And up the High Street, with its buildings peeling away like a leper's flesh, pawnbrokers and drink shops surrounded the ancient buildings of a university. I stopped in the office of the Abstainer's League, which was the Glasgow branch of our Temperance crusade, but the starved old man with his yellowed tracts did not provide encouragement. I think he only wanted his pamphlets tidy. Most like, he had failed so oft at his conversions that his deeds had been reduced to sitting and waiting for the Lord to take things in hand.

The city even had a high Cathedral, all sooted and surrounded by skies as smoky as those of the nether regions, if Lucifer's portion has skies. Behind the spires, a fancy graveyard crowned a hill, with statues set to gaze down on our misery. They call such a place a "necropolis," for the rich are buried there and do not wish to rest in a simple boneyard. For all the rushing energy of the town, I could not like it much. For it took my breath away not by its beauty, but by the smothering foulness of its air. And I do not think I ever saw the poor in such numbers, or so lowly. Not even in the worst back lanes of India.

Weary I was by my dinnertime, and I took me back to George Square to wash my face and see to private matters. The girl was there again, dancing now to her father's fiddling, likely to save her voice for the evening crowds that would come by when the shops and offices closed their doors. I did not pause, but crossed the street, for I could not afford another shilling, deserved though it might be.

The fiddling followed me like an accusation. Nor did it blame me only for my caution with my funds. It blamed me for surviving battles that slaughtered better men, and for all the good fortune that ever I had that was denied to others. It accused me of having eyes to see, and of knowing I might have a plentiful dinner, if so I wished. In my room, the street noise nearly covered the scraping of his bow. But it did not hide his misery completely.

Tell me, if you know. Where does our duty end toward our brothers? Must we give all and burden our own lives with limitation and want to help our fellows to a bit of comfort? How much must a Christian do to be a Christian? I wonder at such things sometimes, but never find a satisfactory answer.

Well, we must have faith and go through.

And after all this rending of the soul, what did I do in penance? I ate a cut of mutton in the dining room, and had a sweet to follow. That, I fear, is how deep conscience goes.

I understand the poor must do for themselves. They must learn strength and discipline. Responsibility, too. And yet, I know life is a thing of chances. More so than any Christian likes to say. Our Savior does not speak of luck in the Gospels, for that would only have made things more confusing than they are, but His fondness for the poor suggests to me that He knew full well how chance may ravish our lives. Look you. Jesus could not very well tell us, "You must all behave and pray all your lives, but some of you are going to draw a rum lot, anyway."

I grew penitent in the course of my musings, and went out to put a few pennies into the girl's begging bowl. She looked as beaten down as a woman of fifty, dancing a ragged fling at the end of the day. Her eyes met mine, just briefly, and I saw that I was recognized as one who had been kind, but I could not bear it. I fled. And was followed by her father's dreadful coughing, which come so hard his bow would not stay fixed to his fiddle's strings.

I took me toward the Trongate and the Saltmarket region beyond, where the poor were squeezed in closer than men convicted. I hoped to find a simple chapel of the sort that gather in the poor on a Wednesday night. You cannot find such places among the wealthy, see, for they have other purposes for their evenings. But down among the poor you will find customers for a sermon and a hymn-sing any evening of the week, at least among the wives who are not drunk or in recovery from a beating. And Wednesdays always find a crowd at chapel.

And that was where my tale turned to its ending.

I went in search of a chapel, and broke a fellow's jaw. I fear the world does not respect our wishes.

I had wandered into Gallowgate, in search of a Christian altar, and turned into an alley I thought promising, for its mouth was wide and children were at play. But I did not yet know the ways and wiles of Glasgow, and found myself at the dead-end of a close, with Irish voices hushing on every side and ragged women staring down from stairways fragile as our hope of Heaven. The gutter in the courtyard had been used as a public cesspit, while a door hung broken from a closet intended for such refuse.

"Is it the gombeen man come?" a little boy asked his mother, but she hushed him quick and pulled him against her skirts.

Twas like I had stepped into a foreign country.

I turned myself about to make my exit, but a fellow tall as a grenadier, although without the posture, eased out of the shadows and stood astride the path that I must take. His shoulders were broad and thick, with the right one higher and heavier, as if he were long familiar with the pick-axe.

And then another Irishman slid from a threshold into the gauntlet of the passageway. This one had a West Country face, born smash-nosed. He shifted his weight from one foot to another and tested the size of his fist against his palm.

A fellow must never show fear to such as those two, and I did not. I stepped right along, careful only to keep my shoes and cane from the slops about me. The twilight had come upon us, although I doubt it was ever full day in that place, and I had to keep a certain watch over my going.

"If you lads will excuse me?" I said. "There is good of you."

The pick-axe fellow spread his legs, the better to block my path, and smash-nose smacked his fist in a steady rhythm.

Pick-axe made an astounded face, as Irishmen like to do, and said, "Well, if it isn't a little black Taffy come calling . . . and didn't I think it was only another Scotch rat?"

"If you will excuse me," I repeated. But I did not step aside to go around him, for that is a thing you must not ever do. Once a bully has his way, he will not give you yours.

"Here and I thought you was going to be nice and friendly," Pick-axe said, "but you'd take yourself off without a by-your-leave. *And*," he added, "without paying your toll."

Smash-nose leaned in and said, "Din't you see the Tollbooth Tower when you come gallivanting along with you? Sure, and everybody what comes into Flannery's Close has got to pay his coming-and-going tax."

I did not say a word, for you cannot argue. You must let such as those speak their peace until they are tired of themselves. I did not want a fuss, if I could help it.

"Now, I'll tell you what Taffy here's thinking, Kev," Pick-axe said. "He's thinking he's set to be robbed, for the Welsh all lack for decency and consideration. He's thinking he's going to be robbed, when the toll's no more than a voluntary contree-booshan. Which I can tell by the looks of him he's terrible anxious to pay. Aren't you, Taffy?" Pick-axe grinned. "For I know he don't want to go swimming down into a filled-up shitter, with his feet following after his head."

"You will excuse me now," I said calmly, as befits a Christian gentleman. "You have had your joke, lads, and I must be on my way."

"A joke, would it be?" He looked at his accomplice as if bewildered. "And have you been telling jokes when I an't been listening, Kevin, me boy? Have you been telling jokes to our little Welsh friend here?" He turned to me again. "Are the two of us funny, then, Taffy? Well, why don't we all have a good laugh together and look at what's struggling to get out of your purse and your pockets?"

All around us, leaning from windows and clutching the flimsiest bannisters in the world, women and children transplanted from Erin watched the goings-on. Not a voice was raised to interfere, nor were the children shielded from knowledge of such crimes.

"Gentlemen," I said, with my voice still calm and dignified, "I will ask you one last time to let me pass. Thereafter, I will go ahead. And you will not like it."

At that, Smash-nose made a grab for my cane.

And I gave it to him. Straight into a private place.

With a continuation of the same gesture, I put the metal tip of the handle into the very center of Pick-axe's chest. But he was a powerful man, that one, and did not go down but only staggered backward.

In the moment left me, I stabbed the tip of my cane—not the sword, mind you, for I did not think it necessary to unsheathe it—into Smash-nose's Adam's apple. With one hand still on his groin, begging your pardon, his other leapt to his throat, and he dropped backward against a wall with a gag and a gurgle.

Pick-axe rushed toward me. Swinging his right fist wildly, from behind his shoulder, as the clumsiest public-house brawler is like to do. I stepped aside, as I had done a hundred times in battle, and a thousand times and more upon the drill field, and let his own weight carry him after his fist. He smelled of use and gin as he went by.

My foot did find a bit of slime, but that was nothing compared to the gore of battle, and I kept my own balance well enough to strike. I gave him the metal bit at the end of my cane's grip with all the force I had at my command.

I meant to catch him on the chin and introduce him to a little sleep, but he was sloven in his inabilities, and he moved most unexpectedly, and I struck him along the line of his jaw. I heard the bone snap.

"*Jaysus!*" he yelled, as he went down. I could make out that much, despite the blood and bits of teeth that poured from his mouth. Flat on his back he went, rolling about in the muck and the slops, without the least regard for personal cleanliness.

"Jaysus," I believe he said again, "the little booger's kilt me." And he moaned. "He's kilt me half-dead, the little . . ."

His comrade had doubled up against the wall, gasping for his breath and wanting no more of my company. That one would make a recovery soon enough, although he might suffer damage to his voice. But, then, the Irish tend to talk too much. I was a great deal more concerned for the fellow whose jaw I had broken. For such destructions are not easily mended.

I was wondering if it might not be my duty as a Christian to see him to a surgeon, when the Irishwomen about the close began to curse me harshly. And then they started hurling the contents of their aprons in my direction. Fortunately, none of them was positioned close to the gutter, although a pair were moving in that direction. I did not want to have my new suit soiled. And not with Irish leavings.

I took myself back toward the street as fast as my legs and cane would help me go. Startled I was when that fine voice spoke to me, just as I reached the safety of the thoroughfare. I had been looking behind me, see, for retreats are ever dangerous maneuvers.

"Oh, well done!" he said. "I should have liked to put down a wager, Major Jones."

It was him. Every bit as elegantly got up as he had been the one time I had seen him, in Rochester, New York, on a winter's night. As fine as the Queen's own court on a day of high ceremony he was, although he did not wear a sash or costume. Twas only the confident way he had about him, despite his lingering glow of youth—he could not have been thirty. His frock coat followed his slender form as if it had been sewn upon his person, and his high hat glistened in the last light of the day. The fairest whiskers trimmed his girlish complexion. He made to tap my chest with the ball of his cane, just as I had seen him do to a man now deceased.

Just before he touched the cloth of my coat, he caught himself.

"But I shall need to take care," he told me, pulling back his cane. "You're rather a dangerous man, Major Jones. Isn't it curious how appearances deceive us?" He granted me a smile that pretended intimacy. Pressed together, his lips were thin as blades. "As a mutual acquaintance of ours was deceived." He gave his head a shake that was almost dainty. "But we must let bygones be bygones."

Just behind his shoulder, pulled to the side of the street, a fine carriage waited.

For him.

The Earl of Thretford.

If wealth and privilege share a smell, I'm certain it was on him. Although I got only a sniff of cologne water.

"You followed me," I said, and my voice was not even-tempered.

He frowned. Playfully. In that dauntless way the wealthy do. "I don't think I should put it quite like that. Indeed, Major Jones, I was *seek*ing you. Not following you at all. I'm afraid I missed you at your hotel." He held his cane just before his breast, as if he might give my chest a tap after all. "You've been inquiring about a shipyard and a mysterious pavilion."

He smiled, a fellow who never had cause to doubt himself, and the jewel in his stiff, white cuff exploded with radiance. "I'll spare you further bother. The structure in question is in one of my own yards. Hardly more than a pleasant drive from this spot." He tucked his walking stick under his arm and fussed with his gloves for a moment— such as he did not wish to be dirtied. "I think I should like to take you there myself." He settled his gloves and offered me the vacant beauty of his eyes—a woman's they seemed, though of the crueler sort. "But we mustn't loose the hounds before our horses are saddled. I thought we might begin by discussing your interests in shipbuilding in greater detail." He glanced at the decay, human and otherwise, that surrounded us. "Tomorrow, perhaps?"

"This is as good as any place, or any time," I told him, and my voice was surly and petulant.

"Dear me, no. This wouldn't do at all for the conversation we require. Nor would I burden you when you're so . . . distempered. Come to me tomorrow. Say, two o'clock?"

He handed me a card with a Park Terrace address, then glanced toward his coach with its liveried driver. "Hargreaves will call for you at your hotel. Just at two." He smiled, and his face was fine as tea at Windsor Castle. "I'm *so* delighted that we've finally met!"

Thirteen

I wanted the consolation of prayer with a new degree of urgency and resumed my search for a chapel. Retracing my steps toward the Cross, I turned down along the Saltmarket. The night fell down like a curtain. Weak as three-for-a-ha'penny candles, the gaslamps struggled against the sooty darkness, and the faces I passed grew crumpled, wary and stark. The false joy of public houses annoyed the Christian ear and troubled the eye, and beggars held out claws for drinking money. Nor were these fellows Irish, by and large, but Scottish as the pawns of Charlie Stuart. Glum they were, and sour as the air, and even the Magdalenes languished out of humor. Twas just the sort of realm held dear by Lucifer, for it makes a Christian wonder at God's plan.

But the faithful always find themselves a beacon, and I do not speak of those smoke-enshrouded gaslamps. I heard the strains of "Daniel and the Lions," boldly sung and true, from out a side street.

Twas but the smallest chapel of the small, its portals lit by oil lamps, not gas. But the hymn come rolling mighty in the darkness, as if belief might burst apart the walls and overwhelm the city like a flood.

Above the brace of lamps, a mounted placard told where I had come:

THE FIRST REGIMENTAL CHAPEL OF THE CHURCH MILITANT

Out of the spoils won in battles
did they dedicate to maintain
the House of the Lord
I CHR. 26, V. 27

Well, I was not quite certain what to think, for I would have my worship done in peace, and soldiering seems to me a separate matter. But in I stepped, for I never can resist a well-sung hymn and hoped to add my abilities to the bass section.

The room smelled of the honest sweat of workmen, and of milky women holding babes against them. Lit by lamps on walls but sparsely windowed, and plain, the congregation stood erect, as Christians need to stand upon this earth. Resounding with the power of that anthem, it seemed a place of perfect reverence, where ruined hands shared hymn-books, their pages lifted up to squinting eyes. For this was not a world of silver spectacles, or of golden pinch-noses, but of eyes shocked weak by forges or strained by needle-work in attic gloom. When they sang out, I heard "the cries of them which have reaped," and felt myself returned unto the Chosen.

And this was but a prelude to the miracle.

As mine own eyes were fixing themselves to the light, the hymn concluded. And straightened backs grew straighter, and slumping shoulders squared, as if at attention in a barracks square. Twas then the fellow who commanded the pulpit pivoted about from the choir rows and let me see the wonder of his face.

I stood back in the shadows in that moment, and he did not see me at first, but snapped his heels together and barked, "Compan-eee . . . *seats!*"

And down the congregation sat in unison, thumping pews of planks with their scrawny backsides. Begging your pardon.

I saw him, and could not believe my eyes. I staggered into the light, half like a drunkard.

And he saw me.

And I saw him once more.

He raised up his eyes, as if he needed aid to trust his vision, then lowered his gaze again.

I took another step. I do believe my mouth was hanging open, although it is a vulgar practice and much condemned by my beloved wife.

Then his jaw lowered, too, and could not close.

The congregation awaited his next command in perfect order. But when he only stared at me, as I was staring at him, they began to fidget a touch, as soldiers will when ranked for a parade, knowing an order to march must be forthcoming and wondering at the reason for delay.

He looked at me, and I looked at him, and we looked at each other til a tear come to my eye. For hadn't the fellow been good to me, when I was in my need?

But was it him? Or did he have a brother just as old? A perfect twin in every last detail? Only his garments were different, and his beard had grown out longer and was gray.

Him it was who finally broke the silence. He fell down onto his knees, as if at a vision.

"A miracle!" he cried. " 'Sing praises to the Lord, which dwelleth in Zion!' " Near gasping he was, and the lamps shone on his face. " 'And many of them that sleep in the dust of the earth shall awake . . .' " He shook his head, and I shook mine, and we shook our heads together. "A miracle!" he repeated.

Now, I was glad the good man found me welcome. But he seemed more the miracle than me. Twas queer what I thought, but that is in our nature. I wondered if my shirt had gotten dirty, either from the Glasgow air or the scrap. He always had insisted on clean collars.

He seemed to stammer and could not speak. He nearly choked, then found his voice again: "Sergeant Jones!" he cried at last. "Risen from the dead! Is it . . . are you . . ."

What fools we are, and vain. My impulse was to tell the good man I had come up a major in my pride. But I did not, and for a proper reason.

"Colonel Tice-Rolley, sir!" I said.

"Sergeant Jones!"

"Colonel, sir!"

"But . . . but . . ." Well, military discipline will tell, and the honest fellow mastered himself at last. He planted his heels, and squared his frame, and set off an imitation along the pews, where every slackness of posture was corrected.

"Compan-eee . . . Atten*tion!*" he called.

Up the congregation stood, as if they had been threatened with Sunday punishment. And, in a sense, I suppose, that was the case.

"Tonight's service is concluded," he declared. "When next the company forms, our theme will be 'The Sinner's March to Salvation.' " He faced half about. "Choir battery!"

The choir-master saluted and said, "Choir battery at the ready, sir!"

"Prepare to fire three rounds of 'Mine Eyes Have Seen, and I Believe in Grace.' "

The choir-master saluted and faced about, then gave his own commands, and hymnals opened up with astonishing speed. The choristers were like practiced gunners, indeed, serving their pieces in the face of the ultimate enemy.

"Choir battery, *fire!*" my old colonel barked.

"Battery, *fire!*" the choir-master relayed, and his charges roared to vanquish Satan's legions.

Above the voices raised in song, the colonel gave a sequence of commands, beginning with, "First rank . . . left *face,* forward *march,* left *wheel,*" and following up until every pew was emptied and the worshippers had paraded into the night. Then the choir stopped, and moved off smartly under their own master's orders, until I was left alone with the colonel—whose uniform was commuted to solemn black—and a somber fellow standing to the side, with a look on his face that hinted at bowel constrictions, despite his glowing eyes and earnest smile.

The colonel stepped down from his little platform and come toward me, staring as if I might prove an apparition. And I edged forward, though timidly, for much of my life had been spent in a world where colonels were at least of archangel's rank, and ready they were to smite down barracks sinners.

He approached me with those curious eyes that always had struck me odd, for an inquisitive nature is hardly the thing for an officer. Officers must be confident, see, and give the men the sense that they know everything—although the truth is most know little enough. But Colonel Tice-Rolley, commanding our "Old Combustibles," had always seemed to wonder at the world. I do believe the generals thought him lax. But he won his battles, and his wife was a marchioness.

I did not recall him as a religious man, though. For he was Church of England, and that is little better than a pagan.

He come up to me, and stared in my face, and looked as if he'd seen a dog play the fiddle.

"By George, you're dead," he told me.

"But I ain't, sir," I responded.

"Yes," he said, narrowing his eyes and stepping around me, as if inspecting the kit of an Irish corporal. "Yes, I see. Yes. A miracle, don't you know? A miracle of Great Jehovah's mercy!"

I fear that I was standing at attention. Old habits die hard.

Suddenly, his hand shot out to touch me. And drew back quick as a blade that has done its work.

"By George, it *is* a miracle!" he exclaimed.

"Kind of you to say so, sir," I told him. "But I—"

"Booth, come here," the colonel called to the somber gent behind him.

Dark as the bleak midwinter, the fellow strode up the aisle.

"Booth," the colonel said, "I want you to witness this. Not two weeks ago, this fellow was dead. Dead as left-over tripe, don't you know? And now he stands before us, hale and hearty. Is there no end to the Good Lord's tender mercies?"

Mr. Booth appeared a bit confused.

"Booth," the colonel said, "I want you to meet Sergeant Abel Jones—" He caught himself, and looked at me. "I suppose I must say 'Mr. Jones' now?"

I bit my tongue, for I wished to tell the man of my majority, but that would require a mighty explanation.

"As you please, sir," I told him.

"Mr. Booth, this is Mr. Jones, who is responsible for the very resurrection of my soul."

Now, that was a surprise as great as the raising of the dead on a Monday morning. When last the colonel and I had met, he had shown the grace to spare me a public hanging, and he it was who suggested to the surgeon that I be written down "Mad of a fever" and unfit for further service, although his number two was knotting the rope and would have liked to string me up himself. And speaking as a military man, I am not certain the colonel was in the right. For soldiers cannot decide they will not kill. But that is what I did, for I found myself incapable. The day came when I had massacres enough, and my weapon fell from my hands, and I could not slay another poor, old nigger. The Mutiny made devils of us all, and ruined men as sure as gin and a Jenny.

"Well done, Mr. Jones!" this Booth fellow praised me. And then he turned to the colonel. "Really, you know, this is unutterably splendid, sir. Everything you've done here . . . the organization . . . why, why it's a veritable army of salvation! That's exactly what it is," Mr. Booth fair cried, "a salvation army! I shall have to enact your practices myself." He thrust out his hand, and the colonel responded in kind. "Oh, I'm unspeakably, unutterably grateful for your example, Colonel Tice-Rolley. I feel positively uplifted! I'm going to try this very thing in England!"

The fellow left us, trailing inspiration.

The colonel looked at me, and I looked at him.

"Begging your pardon, sir," I said, "but who was the fellow told you I was dead?"

"Dead as a dog in a ditch, don't you know? Who was it? An American fellow, that's who it was. Called on me, oh . . . perhaps two weeks past, you see. Said you had gone to America and froze to death while drunk. Question of a small legacy to be paid to any survivors. Sought me out as your former commanding officer, asked if there might be dependents left behind in India." The colonel frumped his face to a bother, bemused by the ways of the world. "I told him there had been a woman and child."

He caught my look of astonishment, almost smiled, and said, "Oh, yes. Colonels know rather a bit more than the other ranks credit. But a wise colonel understands what he mustn't know too plainly, don't you know? Had to disappoint the American fellow, since I knew the woman and child were dead of cholera." He looked at me with unexpected kindness. "Often wondered if there wasn't a connection there, you see. Wondered if that loss wasn't the beginning of your turn away from the military profession. Of course, you were the regiment's mainstay during the worst of the Mutiny, and I'm not ashamed to say it. Never saw a man kill with such dexterity. Astounded me, the way those fellows followed you. Even the Irish. Why, I remember the

Kashmir Gate at Delhi. Gore from head to toe, as if you'd gone swimming in it. Cheatham with his nerves all blown, and the two lieutenants dead, and you dragging and driving that company through the breach. Screaming to spite the last of pandy's guns, 'Give 'em steel, you bloody, buggering bastards!' Never saw the like in all my years."

He remembered himself and stayed his old enthusiasm, for we both had changed and the fields of glory were far from the fields of Heaven. "Rum business, I suppose. But it saved you a hanging, don't you know? American fellow had a pocketful of other questions about you. Wouldn't be satisfied with just . . ."

He went on for a bit, but I had stopped hearing him properly. My insides had gone cold as an arctic sea. For I saw something welling from the shadows. A demon of a thought had risen before me.

"Sir," I interrupted of a sudden. "This American fellow . . . with the questions . . . did he have a name? Did he tell you his name?"

"Why, yes, of course. Scotch blood himself, don't you know? What was it? Oh, yes. Campbell. The Reverend Mr. Campbell. Seemed to know an awfully great deal about you. We shared a prayer for your departed spirit."

You see it, I know you do. For you are wise, and see it as clearly as I did. The Reverend Mr. Campbell was no martyr. At least not to our Union. For he had betrayed the trust of Mr. Adams, and every other trust he held besides. He had doubled his work to serve the other side, those Englishmen who sided with slavers and wished to furnish warships to the Confederates. He had not come to Glasgow in our service, or to look into the fate of Mr. Quigley, but to help a set of devils with their schemes. Whether or not he told them I was coming, or if they learned it from deciphered messages, he had helped them learn the tale of my life. Everything about us had been compromised.

But, then, who killed the fellow, after all. And who had stuffed him in a basket of eels?

Every time I thought I had gained ground upon our foes, I found they were behind me, and beside me, atop and underneath me, and blocking my path in front like a high, stone wall.

Who had killed the Reverend Mr. Campbell?

And why, when he had given them his soul?

Now, there is a bit when Mr. Shakespeare's Romeo, who was an inconstant lad and not worth a second look from that true-hearted Juliet, cried, "I am fortune's fool!" Or something to that effect. Well, fortune's fool I may have been, time and time again, but on this night I felt a fortun*ate* fool. And blessed. I do believe there is a hand that guides us. Laugh, if you will, and say I am old-fashioned, and unscientific. But it was more than luck that led me to that chapel and to my dear reunion with my colonel.

Walking me back to my hotel he was. The man insisted. He wanted to talk, see. For that is how we humans ease our hearts.

With the city grimy and grim and groaning around us, and scoundrels down the lanes and infants crying, he told me what he meant by his "resurrection."

"All because of you, Jones," Colonel Tice-Rolley said. "All because of you, don't you know? Oh, wasn't I the blindest of the blind? Positively enraged, you know. When I learned that you had disobeyed that order. Major Ricketts thought you needed hanging. As an example. But Georgiana calmed me down—she and I spoke of everything, you see, for she was an uncommon woman—and she had heard me speak about what a good influence you were on the troops, and rarely drunk, and never drunk on parade, and not once reduced in rank for dereliction. Why, I expected you to become the regimental sergeant-major one day. All in good time, of course. Oh, thanks be to God that my Georgie calmed me down, until I could see into things a little farther. Ricketts thought it was all a sham, of course. But I came down to look you over in your cell, and I don't believe you even knew who I was. Surgeon thought it might be a bad dose of sun. Makes men peculiar a hundred ways, when it don't kill 'em. But then you recovered your speech and told us, bold as could be, that you would not ever raise your hand against another man, not ever again, and no man on earth would ever make you do it, so help you God. Remember it plain as maggots on army beef."

Now, you will see why I felt some embarrassment and unease about the advent of my major's rank, for I had meant what I said at that time, and could not foresee the duty lurking in the future, or those poor boys drilling in Pottsville, and how I only meant to lend my skills to keep them from unnecessary harm. Before I knew it, we had crossed Bull Run. Then I was on a plank with a surgeon over me. And now I was a major, with a limp, and more blood on my hands than that Scottish shrew. How could I tell the colonel what I had done, and still have him believe I had been honest?

"Only made Ricketts madder, don't you know?" the colonel continued. "Lucky for you it was Ricketts. Half-poisoned himself with drink, if he didn't have a pig or a pandy to kill. Couldn't trust his judgement in the cantonment. Dear Georgiana thought I should draw a compromise and have you tried and sent off to the Andaman Islands. But . . . oh, I don't know, Jones. The Lord truly does work in mysterious ways, I suppose."

He paused before McIntyre's Spun Goods shop, just along the broken Trongate pavement, and gave me a look that masked his mind's machinery. "Never was one for gnashing at Bible verses and that sort of thing. Never thought it was quite-quite, don't you know? Seemed to me the vicar was getting his living to read chapter and verse on our behalf, so why should a fellow put himself to the bother? Only cloud things up, don't you know? Every so often, I slipped, though. Read the stuff, although I didn't really think it was good for me. On campaign, more often than not. Without my Georgie to tell me how sound a fellow I was. Nothing peculiar, of course. I'd just peek at a verse or two. Here and there. And when you planted your feet the way you did— chains hurt your ankles, I suppose?—and told us you weren't going to kill any more niggers or anybody else, well, I don't know. Put a worm in my ear, don't you know? Had a look at the old Book myself. Nothing too queer, of course. Not Daniel or Revelation, or any of that ranting sort of thing. 'Sermon on the Mount.' Always seems to do, don't it? And I got to the bit about 'Love your enemies, bless them that curse you, do good to them that hate you, and pray for them which despitefully use you, and persecute you . . .' Well, I thought of you standing there with more chains on you than a siege gun drawn by a train of twenty oxen, and damn me if I didn't send old Mahmood to get the surgeon out of bed and tell him I wanted to see him. Drunk as an Irish admiral, of course. Fellow always said alcohol promoted the effects of quinine. Told him you were mad of a fever, and if he couldn't see it, I could, and then I mentioned I'd heard of a vacancy in the plague hospital in Peshawar, which wasn't a position that had much appeal to the fellow, don't you know? Asked me if writing you down 'insane, but not dangerous' would do. Remember it clearly. Told him that was fine with me, as long as he put you on a boat for England before I changed my mind. Ricketts never did recover his temper, and I think he would have just as soon hanged me in your place. Died of a fit while eating his Christmas pudding. All for the best, I suppose. Would have been worse for the poor devil, if he'd seen me following in your footsteps."

We began to walk again. I had a thousand questions, but knew to hold my tongue. For I could tell he needed to tell his story, and he needed to tell it to me, above all others. This world is strange, a-tilt with pain and miracles.

"Well, we set off on the last punitive campaign of the season. Really, the pandies were all in. Didn't see the point of killing any more of them, don't you know? But Calcutta had its reasons, I suppose. Never settled into my camp routine, though. Worried I was getting a bad digestion. And then one night I sat there reading James, by the kit lamp. Moths and what not going at the glass like a charge of irregular horse. We'd burned a village that day—what there was of it to burn—and, damn me, if I didn't think of you that night, and hardly remembered to take my medicinal whisky. Moths popping against the lamp and sizzling and giving off that stink they do when the hot glass cooks 'em up, and I read that bit that starts off Chapter 4, don't you know? 'From whence come wars and fightings among you? come they not hence, even of your lusts that war in your members? . . . Ye lust, and have not: ye kill, and desire to have, and cannot obtain: ye fight and war, yet ye have not . . .' Well, I ain't certain I got the meaning quite right, and I won't say it don't matter. But those words blazed right up off the page and surrounded me. Just picked themselves up like Pushtoons waving their *jezails,* don't you know? Always wanted to be a general, you see. My ambition. Lusted after it. And there it was. '. . . ye kill, and desire to have, and cannot obtain . . .' There it was, don't you know? Thought of all the dead niggers it took to make me a colonel, and how many more it might take to make a general out of me. Damn me if I didn't write out my letter on the spot. Resigned. Sorry to leave the regiment, of course. But can't very well have one without the other, can we?"

He smiled as if one cheek concealed a sweet and the other a sour. "Georgiana was happy as a lark. Twenty-six years of India was quite enough for her, don't you know? Wanted to go back to the old house at High Belchgill for years. Stayed on for me, you see. Good wife. Perfect colonel's lady. Figured my bit of religion was just a fit. Only glad to be going home, don't you know? Talked about roses and what not halfway across the Indian Ocean. Tried to tell her I had a calling, you see. By that time, it all seemed clear. I was meant to convert the heathen, benighted Scots. Presbyterians, don't you know? And old Belchers ain't far from Carlisle, and Carlisle's almost a next-door neighbor to Glasgow, what with the railway. Georgie could have her roses, and I could introduce the Lord to the damned of Caledonia, and all that."

He looked at me again, but did not break his stride, which sorrowfully had slowed with the years, although his posture might still correct a subaltern. "How little we know of the Lord's will and devices. Poor Georgie never got to have her garden. Although she is in a lovelier Garden now. Lost her to a fever short of the Cape. Ship's doctor said another two days and the winds would have turned and blown off the miasma. Never got to have her garden of roses," he repeated, with a catch in his voice. "But the Lord's wisdom is above our understanding. And now I've found my peace, and thanks to you." He set his face toward the front, as I had seen him do in desperate battle. "But I'm chattering like Rosie O'Grady over the laundry. Terribly glad you're not dead, don't you know? Frightfully glad. But what on earth have you done to that bloody leg of yours?"

I feared to tell him. But I needed to tell him. And I *wanted* to tell him. For fair is fair, and he deserved the truth. But first I had a question I needed to put. On the chance that he might know what I could not.

"Begging your pardon, sir. There is a tale I must tell you, and tell it to you I will, if you will let it bide a moment. But first I must ask a question, and there may be more to it than a Christian man would like."

He paused again, and the Lord only knows what he thought of me. Glad I was that I was not in uniform, for I wanted to explain myself in a way that would make it clear I had not lied, and that I had never meant to kill again.

"Do you remember," I began, "Hodson's Horse and a big fellow that rode with them? One Lieutenant Culpeper . . ."

Even in the gloom between the gaslamps I saw the tightening of skin about his eyes.

". . . I had heard the fellow was killed," I continued. "Torn to pieces after some border skirmish. But now some have him alive and back in England."

It took him a time to answer, for old loyalties live on inside the flesh.

"Who told you Ralph Culpeper was alive?" he asked at last.

"Mr. Disraeli," I told him. "He was the first to mention it." I had determined to be honest, see.

That stopped him again, though. "Disraeli? The political fellow? *That* Disraeli?"

"Yes, sir."

"What on earth have you to do with Disraeli?"

"Well, more than I would like, and there is true. Begging your pardon, sir, things want telling in a proper order, and I will tell you everything. But can you say anything at all about Lieutenant Culpeper?"

"He never died," the colonel said. "Not sure I should be telling you this even now, don't you know?"

"Please, sir. Lives may depend on it. Lives, and even more."

"What on earth have you gotten yourself into, Jones?"

"More than I would have chosen, sir, if I had been given the choice. But please, sir. What happened with Lieutenant Culpeper?"

The colonel scowled. I did not even need to look at him to sense it. I fear his Christian tolerance had been breached. "Culpeper should have been shot dead. Or hanged. Or shot *and* hanged. That's what I have to say. Filthy man. Evil. A hundred and one times worse than Dirty Dick Burton. A devil on the earth. If he hadn't been half-brother to the richest young lord in all Her Majesty's kingdoms, I don't know that he would have lasted five minutes, once his fellow officers got their hands on him."

"But what happened?"

"What happened? I'm ashamed to even think it, let alone say it, man."

"But what became of Culpeper? Please, sir."

The colonel grunted. "They peeled the skin off his face, when they got their hands on him. His own brother officers. Rubbed curry into what was left. Old Rajput torture, don't you know? A captain among them had seen it done, but likely they made a muck of it. Don't imagine it was the pleasantest thing. Would've killed him afterward, if one of those political officers hadn't put a stop to it." Eyes that had seen a hard bit of the world glanced at me as we strolled. "They would've been glad to hang *you,* for refusing to kill a pack of *fakirs.* What mightn't they have done to a man sent to free a score of English children taken off during the Mutiny, only to kill the half of them in an orgy of shame that will not be described. And giving the rest to his natives to sell to the hill tribes. As a 'reward for their loyal service.' Telling us all that he hadn't been able to find 'em. But one of the children got away and made it to Lahore. Things hotted up quick enough, when Culpeper's mess-mates heard of it."

Abruptly, he laid his hand upon my arm. The grip was still as vigorous as a young man's. "It was all quietly done, don't you know? With the face skinned off him, he was as marked as ever a man could be. They gave him a horse and sent him off for the Khyber. Told him if ever he set foot on Her Majesty's territory again, he'd hang for certain. Last I heard, he was doing service along the Caspian, providing a bodyguard to an emir or such. Though that may have been no more than a rumor." He peered into my eyes, despite the darkness. "And now you say the devil's back in England?"

"So I am told, sir. And so I may have seen, but cannot be certain. I saw a man in a mask, but not a face."

He shook his head. "We were cautioned never to speak of him. Those of us who knew, or were suspected of knowing. Sworn to it. Now I fear I've broken my pledge."

"It may save lives, sir."

"Still . . ."

"I am in your debt. For telling me."

But his thoughts had roamed to that haunted land between the Ganges and Indus. "Last time he was seen," the colonel said, "the devil was on a horse, with his hands bound behind him and a bloodsoaked handkerchief tied over his face. And not a man in India wished him well." He gripped my arm again. Even more firmly. "And now . . . I think you owe me an explanation."

⌒

"Good Lord," he said, when I had finished my tale.

"I did not mean to go back on my promise, see," I repeated. "Or to mislead you, or to dishonor the regiment. And there is true. But none of us may see into the future."

"No," he said. "No, of course not. And now I suppose I should address you as 'Major?' "

"Well, that is neither here nor there, and you may call me what you wish, sir. So long as you will believe me."

"It's too queer by half to be a lie, that story of yours. How terribly odd, though. A sergeant in the Old Combustibles, and now a major in the American army." He sighed. "Anyway, it isn't as if you'd joined the French, don't you know? Although the frog-eaters would have probably made you a general. But a major . . . it's remarkable, really."

"A major of volunteers, sir. It is not the same as a regular commission."

"Still and all . . ." He brightened. "You know, the only army I wish to serve in now is the Lord's . . . still and all, it does reflect credit on the regiment, you know . . . from sergeant to a major . . . not quite the same jump in America, of course . . . still and all . . ."

Well, I was greatly relieved he had not scorned me. He was a better Christian than Abel Jones.

"Wouldn't old Ricketts just pop over dead to see it?" the colonel asked me. "If he wasn't dead already? To know you'd got up to the very same rank as him? I'd almost pay to see it, don't you know?"

I owed a special prayer of thanks to my Maker. For the good, old colonel had not only taken things well, but had done me a pair of services on the way. I now knew Campbell had been a spy for both sides, and that Lieutenant Culpeper might be more than a spook raised up to fright me.

Now you will say: "All this is pure coincidence." But I will tell you: I believe in Jesus Christ and justice. And, sometimes, in the goodness of my brothers.

~~~

We were stepping along in the strangest way, almost as if we were two old friends and not a retired colonel and his former sergeant who had been more trouble than he had ever been worth. This world holds such a wealth of possibilities that I cannot like the man who is ungrateful. Any man blessed enough to be able to choose between his cup of tea or coffee is already rich enough to feel himself a king.

But let that bide.

Colonel, Retired, Norbert Tice-Rolley was telling me of the wondrous things he had done, although he did not praise the deeds himself, but merely reported them. All his trophy money from the Seekh Wars through the looting spree after the Mutiny had been dedicated to his church crusade, as well as not a few of the rents from his late wife's properties at High Belchgill and Grapplethwaite. He not only had sobered up many a man, but found him work thereafter, and recalled a number of lasses from the streets. He even employed a pedagogue to teach poor children to read, although there were many who thought such skills luxurious and thoroughly unsuited to the poor. He did what he could for orphan homes, and to supplement the meals at the charity ward. And still he thanked me for sparking his conversion!

I was ashamed to call myself a Christian. A true one walked there by my side that night, forgiving even the sorry likes of me.

I only hoped to be rid of him soon.

I feared for him, you see, if any of my enemies suspected his involvement in my efforts. I did not want to see him come to harm, and though I was delighted by his company, and by his very decency of manner, I hoped to excuse myself from further meetings. At least until affairs had been resolved.

"And so you see," he went on as we entered the square, "it's all very simple, don't you know? The Good Lord gave us work so we might do it, and we can save ourselves through honest work. It's the very thing for the poor. Give 'em work and wages, and damn me if they don't begin behaving. Even give up drink, more often than not. It's a positive inspiration. Give the poor a spot of discipline, then find them a position that doesn't overtax their faculties, and before you know it they're bringing their neighbors to chapel."

Among the many grand things he had told to me, one was that he had joined the Abstainer's League and was given over entirely to the cause of Temperance. And the colonel had not been one to slight the punch back in the lines. Now I found his virtue had overtaken mine, for he even decried the stimulation of coffee, which is the very lifeblood of Americans. Had he not been called to found his own Church Militant, the colonel would have made a fearsome Methodist.

"The question of the poor is one that troubles me," I confided, "and glad I am—"

Twas then I noticed the crowd that had gathered ahead of us, just across the street from my hotel and shrouded in a fabric of filthy air. At first I thought the little girl, that Fanny, was performing late to please her thirsty father, but then I caught the hubbub and the cry.

"What is it? What is it, Jones?" the colonel asked me. For I had begun to quicken the pace without warning.

I knew what it was. I cannot tell you how, I simply knew. As veteran soldiers know things that will not be explained by all our mortal senses.

"Leg of yours hasn't slowed you down," the colonel complained, as he come following after me.

We crossed the street and I pushed through the crowd, and I found just what I had feared.

The old fiddler with the sergeant's stripes lay dead upon the ground, with his lungs coughed up, and blood down his neck, and his eyes wide as two moons. The girl had lost her hat and her hair was wild. But not so wild as her tortured voice. She stood above her father in utter dismay and howled like a beast at the darkness and the crowd.

"Keep off him," someone warned. "It mought be the cholera morbus laid him out."

At those frightful words, the crowd eased back.

It was not cholera. I know the look of cholera, see. You do not vomit blood, but watery gruel. And I had heard him cough to bring down a house. Consumption it was, or something of the like. And his rust-haired daughter refused to understand, and slapped at any hand that dared approach her, drawing complaints at the viciousness of the poor.

And then she saw me. The Lord knows what she thought. She come to life and broke to a run and launched herself against me. She hit me like the ball of an eighteen-pounder and nearly knocked me over on my back. I did not fall, but I could not order my senses.

She clutched me as a drowning man will clutch a bit of timber floating by. She clutched me as if I were life itself, and all hope of Salvation. Not one word did the poor lass say, and she only wept more fiercely, but her child's hands had the grip of a brawny gunner's. She cried until the tears soaked through my waistcoat, then through my shirt, and finally through my linens.

I do not know what children think, but they have a liking for me that is inexplicable. Perhaps it is that I am not made tall and still seem half a child to unlearned eyes. Or maybe it is only that I am fond of them, and know too well what a child can be made to suffer.

I would rather die myself than harm a child.

A constable arrived, and then another. Someone called for the dead car, and they hoisted the corpse away. I thought perhaps the child would want a look at him, a last look, but all she did was cling to me and cry.

The constables did not even ask about the girl, although they doubtless knew her relation to the dead man, for the two were much in evidence on the square. But the poor do not figure, unless they break the law. And before I knew, the corpse was gone, and the crowd was gone, and the constables disappeared. Leaving me with the weeping girl and a baffled Christian colonel.

"Missy," I said, petting her to soothe her just a little. "Missy . . . Fanny, if that is your name . . . you must tell me where you live, see. You must tell me that much, if I am to help you."

She did not, or could not, reply, but only sobbed. My shirt was soaked beneath my waistcoat and I could feel the warmth of her little face.

"Do you have any relatives?" I asked. "Is there anyone else, Missy?"

She wept, and would not speak.

"Is there a chapel you visit, lass?" the colonel asked, to a modicum of effect.

"Where do you live, Fanny? There's a good girl, just tell us where you live. Where's your home?"

She clutched me tighter than ever she had and squeezed out her first words.

"I canna gae ta hame without me faither," she sniffled. "He give me a knife for ance he was gaun off, for he knew he were set to gae. But I'm unco feared of Betts and Spanish Jemmy."

Fourteen

Her name was Fanny Raeburn, or so she had been called by those around her, and she lived off the High Street, in a room in the Old Vennel. The colonel tried to feed her a bun he fetched from the Hotel Clarence, but the lass would not let go of me to eat it. I managed to glean that she had no earthly relatives—at least none known to her—and the question of her age was inconclusive.

"I maun be twelve," she told me, "for that I hae been a time. Though I mought weel be a' thirteen, or a mickle elder."

"And this room of yours," I said, as I petted her hair. Great thickety, rusty locks she had, and lovely, though I felt a nit or two. "Can you sleep there, lass? Now, tell me true, and we will see you looked after."

She buried her head and tightened her grip and told me again, "I canna. For I'm feared of Spanish Jemmy. Me faither said he's waiting ta tae him a vantage."

Now, the colonel had ever been one for good solutions, pulling the regiment through a dozen times when every justice said we should have perished. And since he had attached himself to philanthropy, countless charities begged for his attention, as those in every sort of need will do, and he whispered to me that he knew the very thing for the lass: Miss Thumper's Home for the Elevation of Discommoded Girls.

"Miss Thumper and Miss Sharp will see her right," the colonel assured me. "Generous circumstances, Jones. Generous as could be. Institution adheres to the latest system. All terribly scientific. Science, with the very best of manners. Devil of a combination, don't you know? Child will find it a source of every joy. And all done Christian, too."

The little thing held onto me as if doubtful of every word, but after a bit she seemed to acquiesce. First, though, we would go to her old room to collect her things. I do not think less of the poor than I do of the rich and fine, but I know how the world is, all the same. An orphan's effects will go missing in a blink.

The distance to the Old Vennel was not far, but the difference between the elegance of George Square and the peerless squalor we found in that narrow alley was greater than any society should reveal—although I fear I sound like Mick Tyrone. A few high gaslamps, set above the reach of wicked boys and doubtless insisted upon by the police, set the walls to gleaming where the slothful had emptied their night-pots from upper windows, splashing the masonry until it crusted over. The stink would have offended a scavenger dog, and the poverty of the place was such that the sole prostitute we met was ancient beyond all tallying and so disheartened she did not even speak. A fellow, drunk or dead, had ploughed the gutter with his face, but Fanny only skipped over him, as if it were the commonest of customs.

I heard a fellow thrashing his wife, or at least the woman who shared his small existence, cursing her for a harlot, although the language he used was rather stronger. He hit her so hard we heard the blows below, and all she said in her own defense was, "Oh, cripes, do na hit all me taith out. Oh, Willie, just lea' me some taith . . ."

The child turned into a doorway that lacked any sign of a door. Had the colonel and I not been so long at our soldiering, we never would have found our way in that darkness. The black hall smelled of urine and decay.

Up a flight of stairs she bounded, to an upper floor built barely above our heads. The stairs cracked under my foot, as if they would not support more than a child, and the rats in the walls alarmed. Fanny waited until we were both come up, the colonel and myself. Then she pushed a door wide without knocking, for manners were kept differently in that place.

You would have thought the room a very meeting hall, if a tiny one. An old tuggle lamp bleared smoke from a table, spreading amber light so weak it faltered before it reached the walls or ceiling. Humanity slumped everywhere, from an old man with the ringworm and a mouth dripping streams on a wrapper of faded tartan, to children slight as if they had been starved and naked to a degree that would shame a Hindoo. Their arms and legs were mottled with welts, and one boy dangled a wrist broken sometime past. The room could not have been fifteen foot by ten, but there must have been twenty souls confined within it.

In the very center, at the table with the lamp, and seated on the only chairs in evidence, the king and queen of that domain presided. The woman was dressed in a gandy robe, of the sort cast off by prostitutes, and her face was so thick with moles and worse that it looked like a case of smallpox. Indoors she may have been, but she wore an old-fashioned bonnet on her head, of the sort dear Mrs. Griffiths used to wear in the years of my orphaned childhood. Her hands were pointed and scabrous, and busy scratching.

The fellow looked to be a back-street thumper, born to a meanness Christians disbelieve and proud of the swollen fingers his brawls had bought him. Dark he was, and too large for any room that would have him willingly, and hard as gunmetal. He did not seem a Spaniard to my eye, although he was unclean, but swarthy enough he was to earn the insult. I had no doubt that this was "Spanish Jemmy."

The woman got up and stretched out her claws, crying, "Oh, Dearie, we 'eard of your poor father's going off on you. Let your Auntie Betts be all your comfort."

"Ye are na me auntie," Fanny told her. She held to my coat so fiercely I feared for the cloth.

But the woman ignored her and spoke to the colonel and me. "Tain't it a kindness, when two such fine gennulmen brings back our dear, little Fanny, what's in want of 'er Auntie Betts to be 'er comfort."

The man stood up all belated, as men do when their minds are wrecked with drink. "Ye twa can gae," he told the colonel and me. "Fanny's taen care of by me an' Betts."

The child clutched me.

"We have only come for her things," I told them. "You need have no concerns for the child's welfare hereafter."

The dark fellow puffed himself up. "And 'oo set your little arse on a throne?" he asked me. "The wee thing won't be spiled by the likes of you. This is the hame she's allus kenned, and the only hame she's needing."

"We have only come for her things," I repeated. "Thereafter, we will leave you to your peace."

The big fellow stepped toward me, with a dismissive glance at the colonel, who stood to my rear.

I shifted my hand onto Fanny's shoulder, so I might shove her free, if such was needful.

"Aye," the fellow said, "an't it allus the same sang? Twa dirty buggers what think they're sae high and mighty, they mought come in amang daysunt folk and steal a bonnie bit like our Fanny awa'." He hovered over me, foul as a human sewer, puckering the crusts that served him for lips. "When we a' of us ken what's to be gat in poonds sterling for the privilege of introducing the lass to her womanhood." He slipped a hand into the pocket of a jacket pierced with wear. "Fi' poonds it is, for the spiling of Fanny's perfections. Fi' poonds to tae her off, and na mickle less."

"Fanny, get your things," I said, nudging the girl to the side.

The knife leapt out of his pocket. But the fool who held the blade in his hand was so addled he slashed at nothing. For I was already beside him, and the sword was free of the sheath of my cane, and the point was tickling his neck.

I backed him against the nearest wall.

The pox-faced woman screamed bloody murder, and the children began to shriek.

"Hold your tongue," I commanded, in a voice that rose from a ghost of drill-fields past, "and quiet the lot of them. *Now.*" I did not take my eyes from the eyes of the great, tall coward before me. For such he proved to be, all wet and blubbering.

It is almost shameful, how quickly the poor are cowed. In a moment the room was quiet again, but for some childish whimpering and the panting of Spanish Jemmy at my point.

"Fanny," I said, "go through to your room. Get your things."

At that, the woman cackled to rouse the dead. " 'Er room? Well, ain't that rich? 'Er buggerin' da and 'er sleeps in the corner."

Miss Thumper's Home for Girls stood off Blythswood Square, where the houses still had a fineness left over from the days of the German

Georges. Greekish and pillared they were by decoration, with high front windows, all cut from similar patterns. Except for the walls that contained Miss Thumper's establishment.

I would not say Miss Thumper's house was new, but it was not old. It was not large, though neither was it small. But it was odd. In that street of severe and handsome city mansions, just a bit dogged by the decades, Miss Thumper's container of fortunate girls seemed queer as an uncle who must be locked in the attic. It was not especially high, or meanly low, but all a-jumble, until you could not say whether it was wider at the bottom or the top. Afflicted with turrets, bays and gables that darkness turned to scars and warts and wens, the form of the place was awry, as if it had been built by the children it housed, without the benefit of wise direction. I half expected to find a maze behind the great front door, while the exterior must have been a delight to pigeons.

We stepped down from the cab—the colonel's largesse had provided us that commodity—and I must say that I paused a few seconds before leading Fanny up the front stairs by her hand. A fright of a place the building looked, and if it looked a fright to me, I could only wonder what the child made of it. Of course, a house is very much like a person, and should not be judged by the exterior, but by the qualities cherished and kept within.

Although it was quite late by now, the colonel gave the bell-pull a hearty tug. And he whacked the wood of the door with his stick for good measure.

After a second pull of the bell, and another crack with the cane, a maid appeared in her midnight disarray.

The colonel did not wait to be greeted, but spoke right up, as if a household familiar.

"Tell Miss Thumper that Colonel Tice-Rolley's come to see her." He glanced at Fanny. "On a most particular matter."

The maid gave a curtsy, narrowed her woeful face, and said, "Sor, the mistress is dape in her slumbers and won't be seen 'til morning."

Irish as oat cakes the poor girl was, and doubtless afraid of losing her position, but the colonel was no man to be deterred.

Perhaps it was his latest brush with the miseries of the poor, for such will ever ignite a fellow's conscience. Or he might have been out of sorts from age and weariness—his temper had been famous in the regiment, and even true religion won't turn an orange cat gray. Mayhaps it was just the habit of a man who all his life had been obeyed and did not like to be packed off by a serving girl. Whatever the cause, he unleashed a cannonade of language at that poor maid that would have persuaded the Roman Church to virtue.

The kindest thing he said was: "Get her now."

One effect of the colonel's barrage was to cause Fanny to cling to me as a frightened little monkey clings to its mother.

But wasn't there a great fumbling and tumbling thereafter? The colonel seized control of the entranceway, and as soon as he made his breach he led us inside. Gaslamps flared, and the flounce of night dresses brushed along high bannisters. Doors slammed. Voices squeaked, as if at an invasion of rodents. Footsteps pattered and clattered. And a disturbed murmur of femaleness swept the house like a tide.

"Why didn't you tell me at once?" a voice fresh off the whetstone cut the air.

I looked around the entrance hall, which was certainly Christian in its austerity. The few chairs looked hard as gun carriages, and the tables I saw were narrow as the hopes of a wounded man left behind in an Afghan pass. There were no decorations on the walls.

At last, two ladies succeeded so far in the matter of dress that they might descend the stairs. One behind the other they come, with wide skirts hiding feet that hurried along as if driven by steam.

The first was tall and alarmingly gaunt, and the second was short and slender to a concern. They looked as if they had spent their lives sharing a pauper's bowl of soup between them, without the benefit of an accompanying crust of bread. And those lives had not been short. If you will excuse my frankness, both these ladies were past the prime of life, if ever their lives had known such a thing as a prime. The taller one was dressed in black, the shorter in darkest blue. Buttoned up to the top of the neck, the closest to frivolity either of them approached was a quarter-inch of gray lace peeping over the taller woman's collar. She descended first, and she spoke to us first, and I figured the bit of lace for her badge of rank.

"Colonel Tice-Rolley!" the tall lady said. "What an unexpected pleasure!"

"What an unexpected pleasure, Colonel Tice-Rolley!" the shorter woman declared.

" 'Evening, ladies. Tip of the hat, and all that. This here's Sergeant—I mean to say, *Ma*jor Jones, don't you know?"

I bowed in the direction of the ladies, as a fellow is expected to do. Even then, the child would not release me. It lent my gesture some awkwardness.

"Major Jones," the colonel said, "that woman you see there is Miss Thumper." He gestured at the taller of our hostesses, as casually as if she were a boar's head hung on the wall of a gentleman's den. Although I do not mean that unkindly. "And that one," he told me, indicating the shorter, "is Miss Sharp. Do wonders with the girls, they do. Turn 'em into proper little ladies. Scientific methods. Christian, too."

Miss Thumper gave a bit of a curtsy, and Miss Sharp dipped down behind her.

"How kind of you to say so!" Miss Thumper said. "And we are honored beyond *words* to meet a comrade of our dear, dear colonel's."

"Terribly kind of you," Miss Sharp got in. "Positively honored."

I bowed again, and hoped I did not look a fool. For I have had to learn my social graces.

"Mesdames," the colonel said, "we have come on a mission of mercy."

At that, the two of them looked at Fanny. As if they had to force their eyes to do it. In truth, they had not seemed to see her previously.

Their faces took on the somber look of cabinet members threatened with war and invasion.

"This," the colonel announced, "is Miss Fanny Raeburn."

Miss Thumper leaned down, as if for a better look. She pinched her eyes, and narrowed her eyes, then pursed them to a squint.

"Is your name Fanny, child?" she asked.

"Is Fanny your name?" Miss Sharp reinforced her.

Fanny nodded her assent.

Miss Thumper straightened and Miss Sharp recoiled.

"Your name is *not* Fanny," Miss Thumper said.

"You name couldn't *poss*ibly be Fanny," Miss Sharp confirmed.

"Your name is Frances," Miss Thumper continued. "Fanny isn't a proper name at all."

242 / Owen Parry

"You are most definitely named Frances," Miss Sharp informed her.

"Fanny is a *pet* name, child. The *best* of your acquaintances may call you Fanny, *should* you permit them. But the common run of mankind must know you as *Frances*."

"Listen when your elders give you advice, Frances," Miss Sharp admonished the little thing affixed to my new coat. "Mankind always seeks to take advantage of a young lady. You dare not even be addressed as Frances, except by those awarded that privilege of intimacy, and only should you invite the familiarity. You are Miss *Rae*burn when you are out of doors."

"Or to those in service," Miss Thumper augmented. "Upstairs and down."

"Or to those who one day *hope* to be in service. Or to representatives of the professions. And, especially, to those who pursue a trade."

"You are Miss Raeburn, morning, noon and night."

"Even when asleep, you are Miss Raeburn," Miss Sharp said, with great moral emphasis.

"Miss *Frances* Raeburn," Miss Thumper stated conclusively. "That's who you are, and that's who you shall be."

"My name's Fanny," the child whispered.

"What?"

"What did she say?"

"Is she insolent?"

"Is she ungrateful?"

"Begging your pardon, ladies," I began, in a doomed attempt to soften their conditions. "Perhaps she—"

Before I could conclude my speech, Miss Thumper turned to the colonel and asked, "Don't you think this child would be better placed elsewhere?"

"Wouldn't you rather enroll her somewhere else?" Miss Sharp asked.

"She doesn't seem to appreciate her fortune."

"She doesn't appreciate anything at all."

"Damn me, ladies," the colonel roared, as if addressing two captains who'd botched a march, "you're trying my Christian patience. Where would you have me take the blessed thing?"

"There *are* institutions for the poor," Miss Thumper said.

"For the ex*cep*tionally poor and the diseased," Miss Sharp clarified.

"For those who have no interest in learning."

"Or in bettering themselves."

Throwing down her trump, Miss Thumper bent toward the child, who cringed still deeper into the folds of my coat.

"Can you *read,* child? Do you have *any* interest in working very, *very* hard and suffering for *many* years in order to learn what may be of *no* use to you whatever?"

"It may be of no use to you of any kind," Miss Sharp added. "But you may tell us, without the least shame, whether or not you can read."

"I hae me numbers," Fanny told them, employing the smallest voice upon the earth.

Miss Thumper fair exploded in triumph, and Miss Sharp stepped back to survey the conquered field.

"The child can't even read! And she must be eleven years of age. If not twelve."

"Or thirteen. Perhaps even fourteen," Miss Sharp judged. "And she hasn't learned to read!"

"She couldn't possibly be happy here."

"There are places for the hopelessly poor and the diseased."

Now, during this entire inquisition, the colonel's face had been reddening. As if he had returned to a place under India's fervent sun. I knew him well enough to take heed of that ever-darkening crimson in his cheeks, and the scarlet of his ears, and the deep and mounting purple of his forehead. I fear my old instincts even caused me to inch back from the present company, and to pull the child with me.

"Damn me from here to the Hooghly," he cried at last, "you're quick enough to come around asking for money, and all in the name of the poor."

"There are the poor, and then there are the poor," Miss Thumper said reasonably.

"We mustn't put the poor all in one basket," Miss Sharp explained. "We must speak of the deserving poor—"

"And of the unworthy, unwashed poor," Miss Thumper relieved her colleague. "I must not risk diseases in *this* house."

"Or insolence and disregard for learning," Miss Sharp concluded.

"Well, I'll be nackered to Ootacamund!" the colonel barked. "You call that Christian charity, the two of you? If the child can't read, you can damn well, bloody well teach her. What the blue, bloody blazes is this dungeon of yours for? Give her a wash, and teach her to read and to look out like a lady. Or you'll never see another pound from me."

He turned to inspect Fanny, who shriveled in fear, but the old fellow's face had turned from the blaze of a furnace to the warmth of simple kindness. "She don't look a bit diseased to me," he said. "And I could tell you tales of disease would give you the quivering vomits, don't you know?" I believe he smiled. "She's a pretty little thing, if you only had eyes in your heads. And the major here says she can sing like a choir of angels."

"We never said she wouldn't be admitted," Miss Thumper said hastily.

"We only thought we should clarify her situation."

"A lovely voice becomes a fine young lady."

"And we only elevate the finest young ladies in this house," Miss Sharp explained.

"The *very* finest."

"Although their origins may lie in poverty."

"Among the deserving poor, of course."

"They are nonetheless fine."

"Shall *you* want to be fine?" the two of them asked Fanny, almost in unison.

I thought the colonel about to return to the edge of apoplexy, but this time he limited himself to a briefer salvo.

"Damn me, I don't know what the poor deserve exactly, but I'm buggered if I believe it's what they've got. Christian charity don't mean pickin' and choosin' any way that suits us. Lepers and all that, don't you know? Fallen women. Thieves . . ."

At those concluding words, our hostesses turned their somber eyes, reproachfully, to Fanny. And allowed their silence to speak.

"Don't you read the bloody Holy Bible?" the colonel demanded of the ladies.

"Every morning," Miss Thumper said, affronted.

"And every night," Miss Sharp told us.

"And sometimes in the middle of the day."

"For moral sustenance."

"Then read it over again, damn me. And bring that girl up proper. Or I'll give my next hundred pounds to the Irish nuns."

Miss Thumper and Miss Sharp gasped at the immensity of the threat, and the matter was finally settled. Although I noted a look of satisfaction on the face of the housemaid back along the stairs.

Twas only that, with her future miraculously insured, Fanny did not want to let go of me.

She did not even look at the lot of them, but raised her face to mine. Now, I am not tall, and though she was small, the top of her head come up near to my shoulders. For all their redness, I saw the loveliest set of gray-blue eyes. Nor did they seem to me to lack intelligence.

"Can I na stay wi' ye, sir? I'm a guid girl, and I would na be a trouble."

"Now, lass," I said, "I am a man, and you are a girl, and we have no blood relation. Such would be improper, see. And I must tend to things that would not suit you." I tried to express a confidence I hardly felt. "These two fine ladies are going to do wonders for you."

"Wonders," Miss Thumper confirmed.

"And you'll have a nice gray dress, like all the other girls," Miss Sharp assured her.

But the child spoke only to me. "I would na be a trouble, and I'd work sae hard ye'd be 'stonished."

"I will come to visit," I told her. "Tomorrow. To see that you are properly bestowed."

Miss Thumper sniffed.

Miss Sharp snorted. Which I did not think ladylike to an excess.

At last, we got away, the colonel and I. Although I cannot quite say how. We left the lass in tears, with those two crows perched over her. Twas all for the best, of course. For rigor, within measure, is a blessing. But I know what it means to be handed to strangers.

There is ever a shortage of kindness in this world.

Well, better Miss Thumper's Home than the corner of a room in the Old Vennel for the girl. The poor thing had not even possessed a spare set of unmentionables, but had retrieved only a splintering box hardly bigger than a pencil case. And when I returned to my hotel, I would need to pick over my coat in case a louse or two had preferred my freshness to her familiarity.

The faintest of drizzles filtered through the dirty clot of air, but the colonel resolved to walk me to my hotel. And I was glad of his company, though I still felt a bit awkward about the old difference in our ranks. It did not seem to matter to him at all, now that everything had been explained, but once a man has been placed low, a part of him has trouble coming up. Perhaps I was his equal as a Christian, but I could not feel his equal as a man.

"Those two witches," he said abruptly, as a passing constable touched his fingers to his visor. The gaslamps wore damp haloes. "Have no fear, I'll see they treat her properly."

"I am indebted to you, sir," I told him.

But he was a true Christian, and did not look for thanks. He marched along, and muttered at the world, and confided, "Georgiana would have put the two of them right, don't you know? Never had any of that woman fuss from my Georgie. Miss her, I do, the old campaigner."

We walked in silence for a time, communing with separate ghosts. Then, of a sudden, the colonel said, "Sometimes I want to beat the Gospels into the whole bloody pack of them."

Twas gracious of the colonel to accompany me, but it tired him. When we parted before the hotel, he asked the porter to summon a cab. And off he went, through the warm and glistening streets.

I thought to go straight to my room, for I was weary myself, but the fellow who had the duty of the desk presented me an envelope with my key.

A telegraphic message it was. I stepped away to the privacy of a gas fixture and fingered it open.

It come from Mr. Charles Francis Adams himself:

AJ. DIFFICULTY OVER LTRS. HA LONDON TRAIN TOMORROW NIGHT. ACCOMPANIED. BG MURDERED. RP IN CUSTODY. DIVISIONS IN HP. REASONS UNCLEAR. CFA.

Of course, anyone might have understood the message, as you doubtless have done. I needed a code, and had none, and Mr. Adams had done the best he could to confuse our enemies.

There was a problem about the letters, and Henry Adams was coming to Glasgow the following night to enlist my aid, likely accompanied by a bodyguard, if not a police inspector, given the violent turn of events and the young man's lack of physical robustness. Betty Green had been murdered, and I saw the beauty of the deed at once: If anyone had written her compromising letters, that person would appear doubly compromised now, even if he bore no least blame for her demise. And woe unto him with political aspirations. A lover's murder may delight the public, but it will not please the sort who hold the franchise. Nor did I think it would amuse the Queen. And Reginald Pomeroy had been taken by the police, perhaps because he had botched a deed of which I would not have thought that young man capable. It doubtless would cost his father his hope of a peerage. Lastly, there were unexpected divisions in Parliament, the causes of which could not be understood by Mr. Adams, though worried he was.

That seemed enough for any man to sleep on. But the city of Glasgow had not yet had its fill of me.

When he tapped me on the shoulder, I leapt to defend myself. For I had not heard the big fellow coming up. He moved like a Pushtoon.

Inspector McLeod it was. His hat was in his hand, and his orange whiskers and hair taken together might have lit the room in the absence of the gas fixtures.

He gently pushed my cane aside until it no longer threatened his person.

"I hae heard you made braw use of that today. Down in the Gallowgate."

"I was set upon." For a moment, I suspected he had come to question me, if not make an arrest, because of the violence I had done.

"Weel, it does na matter to me, if it does na to you. A good thing that paddy won't need more jaw than you spared him, for young Doctor Russell says it'll serve as a lifelong reminder that he's to mind his manners around his betters. Tither one an't much for talking, either, though I'm na sure what you did to him." He glanced toward the guardian desk, where the clerk was hard at the ledger. "If you do na mind, I would like to hae a private conversation."

I recommended my room. And we went up. To tell you the truth, I was almost glad to have him along with me, for I was growing wary of British hotel rooms.

When we were alone—with no evidence of the severed hands of children, or penny-gaff Eves, or deadly gifts—I offered him the single chair and sat myself on the bed, though my legs were dangling.

"I hae also heard," the inspector said quietly, "that the Earl of Thretford appears to covet your company. Would that hae to do with your questions about shipyards, now?"

"Yes."

"And would it hae to do with dead Americans?"

"It may."

"And mought I ask what the Earl thought sae important that he lowered himself to the streets like the dirty thousands of us?"

"He wants to speak with me. Tomorrow. At his house in town."

Inspector McLeod nodded. "Weel, then you'll see a bonnie house. Though na sae bonnie as his hunting lodge in the hielands, which is na the quarter sae bonnie as the castle along over the muirs, which his father also bought with his English money. And though I hae na seen it myself, I hear the castle's as nought to the Earl's possessions south of the reivers. But you'll see a bonnie house, and that you will."

"A fine house, is it? Then I will mind my manners."

"Aye. And hope that he minds his."

"You take an interest in the Earl yourself, then, Inspector?"

"I would na call it a proper interest. Na more than I would call him a proper earl."

"And that would make him an improper earl?"

"Aye. Like his bluidy, black sire afore him. Wha bought his portion in the north and treated the land folk crueler than Stafford treated Strathnaver. Wha burned all that he could na break, and called for the Gordons when his hired men would na do. So that he mought gi' a portion to sheep, and hae the rest for his shooting. Twa thousand people put from their land. For sheep and the pleasure of shotguns. Aye, that would make a man an improper earl, and carry the impropriety down to his son and his grandson. Not that the true lairds did na betray their own, and by a multitude. But the sting gaes deeper coming frae an English wasp. Wha favors a grouse o'er man, or woman, or child."

"And in the time of the burning," I said, "would one of the children have carried the name McLeod?"

"Aye. One and more."

"And that is what you have come to tell me tonight?"

He shook his head. "I hae said more than I wished, and I hae said less. My purpose was to tell you to gae careful with the Earl."

I wanted a potent ally. Badly. So I asked him, "Then will you go along with me tomorrow? His carriage will call for me at two o'clock. Here."

He began to shake his head, then stopped and thought for a moment. "I can na say that I will gae along. Not now. For all things want their proper way of doing. But if you call tomorrow, in the morning, and find me at my desk, then you mought ask me for the courtesy of my company. Since you are from the American legation. Aye, that would be the way, all public and above an English suspicion."

He rose to go. Scotsman though he was, he could not stop himself from offering a final observation. "I hae thought, from time to time, I mought jeck up meself and go to your America. For when I gae through the streets of the city, I see a' ghosts upon twa legs, and I think of what mought hae been had sheep na been given the preference over men these hundred year. And then I'm angered, and there's na good will ever come of it."

Fifteen

There were no devils in my room, but devils there were in my soul. I dreamed of war. I killed and killed. Not only mine own enemies: Brown-skinned Sepoys, bronze Seekhs or leathery tribesmen. Nor only men in gray or butternut brown. I shot, and struck, and slashed at my old comrades. I could not find their faces, but they wore coats as red as mine had been, or the dusty-gray of the khakis we had at the last. I fought as if berserk, and they fell before me. I felt no pain and had no sense of danger. Remorseless as the juggernaut, I slaughtered every living thing in my path.

And there was a path. At the end of it was an icy, shimmering light. I needed to reach it. But a thousand times a thousand clamoring men defied my going. And the bitterness was not that I must kill them to reach my goal, that light at once compelling and wintry cold. The worst was that I *wanted* to lay them low. To make so great a butchery that all the fields of the earth should be bathed in blood. I tore at them with my bayonet, and slashed them with a sword greater than any I should have possessed the power to wield, and then I saw that I had many arms, like the cruelest idols of India, and I was death unto thousands, whirling my countless limbs to annihilate battalions and regiments. And still they came toward me, and I could not reach the light.

All the while, I knew this to be a dream, as we sometimes know, yet I felt a weight of wrongdoing that I rarely have had to bear in my waking life. I wished to throw off sleep, to stop the massacre. But my other soul delighted in the gore, and sought that frozen light, and offered it a sacrifice of thousands.

Then I saw the colonel's face before me.

I woke drenched. In as great a panic as the poor recruit who knows he was mistaken in his gambit, as he sees the blade descending to take his life.

Panting I was. And weeping. Nor could I stop the sobbing that watered me down to the bone. I felt as helpless as a little child.

I crawled from my soaking bed and found my knees, not without affecting my bothered leg. And I prayed. I crushed my hands together until they ached, and I prayed in that fractured manner that consists of broken words and shredded phrases. There was no meaning in it that I might explain to you. Twas a counter-madness, an animal repentance, if such a thing may be. The thrust of it was that I was sorry and begged to be forgiven. But even that is far too well-expressed.

When madness comes, it comes to me at night. Perhaps that drunken doctor in India was right. That I was mad, though he should not have blamed the madness on a fever. I had it in the marrow of my bones.

And you? I pray you have not known what I have known. But sometimes I suspect it comes to all of us in time, the old madness. It is only that some men build better barricades, and fortify themselves by light of day. Our forebears were not fools when they insisted that Satan's power lay in the dark of night.

I prayed myself sick. A man can do that, too. And I retched in the night-pot.

Then I slept.

In the morning, all that remained was the damp on the sheets.

I stepped out to find a less-dear place for my breakfast, and discovered Fanny drowsing against the wall. With the earliness of the city passing her by. Her dress was unfamiliar, but that rusty swirl of hair would not be mistaken.

I touched her shoulder to rouse her. After a moment's confusion, she leapt to me as my little monkey used to do in India. And as my first son had done, the tawny boy.

"Fanny, girl," I said, "what are you—"

Before I could finish, the porter interrupted me. With a tip of his cap. He looked the sort who has figured out what he must do in life, and would do no more and no less.

"Pardon, sir. But are ye Marcher Jones?"

I looked at him with a lack of understanding. "I am Major Jones," I told him.

"Weel, then, Major Jones. I did na ken the lass, for her speech is unco low. And sorry I am to talk so plain to a guest of the house, but the lass has been ha' the night asking for ye, and when I would na move to hae ye waked, she would na gae for a' the grief in the Gorbals. And it can na be, for the manager keeps a fine, high house, and a blessing it is that he has na been in to see it. I only let her be without beating her off, since I ken her for the singing girl, and her faither's only gone the past eve, to spare us the plague of his fiddling. Mought she be a relation, then?"

All the while, Fanny clutched me tightly.

"No. Only an orphan, see. I thought her bestowed in a proper home, and did not expect to see her."

"Well, please, sir, to tae her off afore the manager comes in. For he'd hae my position if I did na put a stick to her."

I led her away. To a breakfast nook off Buchanan Street. Twas difficult to peel her from me so that we might sit in separate chairs at table. And when she was seated, she brooded as if she might leap across the space that kept us apart, to fix herself to my person once again.

I ordered her toasted bread, with butter and marmalade, a softcooked egg and bacon, just the same as I would have myself. For I could not know the last time she had eaten.

As we waited for our earthly sustenance, I asked her, "Now, what is it, lass? Did they do any harm to you? Or frighten you, did they?"

In truth, she looked as though she had been nicely scrubbed, despite the lateness of her hour of delivery, and she wore a tidy gray dress that suited a girl placed in a young ladies' academy.

"Did they do you a hurt, Fanny? Something wrong, is it?"

At last, she shook her head.

"What is it, then?"

She looked down at the tabletop. It bore a cloth with a chronicle of stains.

"Come now, girl. Why did you leave your nice, warm bed like that?"

And in that instant, I recalled that I had left my own bed in the night. Nor had I forgotten the frightful dreams of my childhood. And the Good Lord only knew what that child had seen. What might we learn if we knew another's dreams? Perhaps it would bring about a reign of compassion. If it did not make us fear our brothers the more.

"What's wrong, Fanny?" I tried again.

She did not raise her eyes, but only said, "Can I na stay with ye? Please, sir?"

"Did anyone frighten you?"

Again, she shook her head. That ruddy storm of hair trailed after her face. "Please, sir? Will ye na tae me to ye? I'm a terrible guid lass, and I'd work sae hard for ye. Hae ye na wife to care for ye and tae up after ye?"

"Yes," I told her. "I have a wife, indeed."

She looked up at that, with those wondrous gray-blue eyes. "Oh, sir, I'll wager she's bonnie."

"You will do nothing of the kind," I told her, but gently. "Young ladies do not wager. Nor should anyone."

"I did na mean it wicked."

"I know you didn't."

"*Is* she bonnie, sir? Is she terrible fine and bonnie?"

"Well, she is 'bonnie' to me. And lovely as all the stars in all the heavens."

"And is she na here by ye, then?"

"No. She is in America. That is our home, see."

At that her face plunged until I thought she would weep again. "And . . . and must ye gae back to her, then? To America?"

"Yes."

"Soon will it be, sir?"

"Soon enough. That is why you must be placed where you are safe, Fanny. Where you may learn, and grow up to be a young lady."

"Could I na learn with ye, sir? In America?"

"This is your home," I told her. "And that lovely man who was with us last night? Colonel Tice-Rolley? With the red face and the beard like Moses himself? He is a very great friend to me. And he will be a friend to you. I have his promise. He will look after things, to see you are treated as you should be. You're not afraid of him, are you?"

"Nae."

"And it will be a very great thing to be able to study and learn. Education is the path of self-improvement, see. Why, I wish I might have had such an opportunity! My own schooling, what there has been of it, come by the barracks lamp and the candle in my tent. Oh, there is good, to have an education!" And then I saw a thing that might be helpful. "You will learn to read, and to write. Then we will send each other letters across the sea."

She looked as doubtful as she had before my little speech, but I was rescued from further argument by the arrival of our food. Now, if there is a lovelier thing upon this earth than the smell of well-fried bacon, or the scent of toasted bread fresh from the fire, then you may tell me of it and I will listen.

"Eat you now," I told the girl. "Everything looks better after breakfast." And I forked a cut of bacon to my mouth.

She would not eat. Not at first. I believe she was afraid of her surroundings, although they were not fine by the common measure, and she worried that my display of generosity could never be intended for such as her.

"The food is for you, Fanny," I assured her. "It is yours. All that lays on that side of the table."

Cautiously, she reached toward the bacon, perhaps emulating me in the primacy she accorded that great benefit of the pig. Her little hand went slowly as a cat creeping up upon its prey. She looked to me a final time, and I nodded, then she grasped an entire rasher in her fist. And when she had it swallowed—barely chewed—she stuck two fingers into the marmalade pot and spooned it so.

Now you will say: "The child needed a lesson in proper manners. We do not eat bacon with fists and jam with our fingers." But I will tell you: Time enough there would be for society etiquette. The little thing was hungry. Although I will admit that my own wife most likely would have taken your side in the matter.

Well, my sweetheart has put manners on me, although it took some time. I never was a sloven, you understand, and always kept myself tidy. But there are secret ways polite folk do things, and we must learn them if we wish their company. Still and all, old habits are a comfort. When my Mary Myfanwy is not there to watch me, I hold my fork the way I always did. Though I do not slop.

The child did not even know how to tap an egg, so I did it for her. She was an old hand at dipping toasted bread, though, and we played a game to see whose plate would finish the cleanest.

She giggled. Now you will think me a weak-minded man, and soft, but I could have wept on the spot. Twas the first glimmer of happiness, or of the simple pleasures of a childhood, that I saw from her.

When I paid, her eyes grew huge at the sum, although the establishment had no taint of extravagance.

I fear I forgot myself for a moment, for I needed to make an appearance at the police offices. Instead, I led her up the street by the hand—for she consented that we might go that way now, instead of clutched together. And then I thought of a thing.

"Fanny, would you say you are too old for a doll?"

I felt her shy a bit, and she did not answer.

"Have you ever had a doll, lass?"

After a pair of measured steps, she said, "I had a dolly ance. Flora Colley gae her to me, when she thought me faither mought come up high to his pension. She wanted Dolly back when she found she'd been fooled o'er, but Betts whipped her off with a belt and gae Dolly to her own wee bairn."

I stopped of a sudden, with the hurly-burly of the morning brisk around us and the streets alert to the prospects of the day.

"Fanny, what do you want, girl? And do not tell me that you wish to stay with me, for that is not what I mean. What would you like your life to be like? If the wishing were given you? It is a big question, there is true. But what would you wish of life, girl? If you had your wish and your way?"

She did not need to think so awfully long. Perhaps she had been thinking of such matters for years.

"I would tae a handsome jo of me own," she told me. "When a daysunt age comes on me. A handsome jo wha does na go beating me more than I deserve." By God, her eyes glowed when she said that to me. "And a house! A house with more rooms than people. That belonged to me and him. And he'd always protect me, and let none come in wha I would na wish to see."

When she finished speaking, her smile dissolved, and her eyes filled with doubt, and she looked as though she had asked for the sun, the moon, and the stars, but expected a clot of dirt thrown in her face.

"Well, I cannot say what the future will bring," I told her, "but let us see if we cannot find a doll."

And find one we did. I had to pick it out, for the child was terrified. Nor was the shopkeeper helpful, for he wanted to sell what he wished to sell, not what the poor girl wanted. I tried to sense her best desire, but frozen she was, even to the eyes. As if the abundance of that middling shop was a horror.

She would not even touch the doll until we were outside. I needed to thrust it into the child's arms. But when she took it at last, you would have thought it was her very own living child.

She held it as tightly as she had held to me. And though I should have been relieved, the truth is that I only felt a loss.

When I took her back to Miss Thumper's Home, those two gaunt spectres, tall and short, descended upon us.

"Where has the naughty girl *been?*" Miss Thumper demanded.

"Where has Miss Frances Raeburn been this morning?" Miss Sharp improved the question.

"And what's *that?*"

"What's that in her arms?"

"Is that a *doll?*" Miss Thumper asked, although the toy's identity was plain.

"What on earth would a young lady want with a doll?"

Fanny cowered again, bringing her warmth back to my side, and clutching me with one hand, while the other protected her dolly.

"Is this child to be *spoiled?*" Miss Thumper demanded. I am not certain at whom the question was pointed, for I never sensed that she was speaking to me. Twas as if a great, invisible arbiter filled that draughty hallway.

"A spoiled child is ever mean and ungrateful," Miss Sharp said.

Just then the Irish maid appeared, back by the stairs, in the tactical position maids prefer. And I had an inspiration.

"My dear ladies," I said, "you must forgive my interruption, see.

But I am late for my appointment with the colonel. He asked me to meet him at the Convent School of the Sisters of Mary—isn't that where those Irish nuns keep their orphans? Though I do not know why he should ask my advice about checques and monies and legacies."

There come a span of silence over the house, like the quiet when a battle is suddenly over and all those still on two feet return to sense. Miss Thumper looked aghast, as if surveying a field of the horribly wounded, and Miss Sharp appeared alarmed in the extreme.

"The colonel has never taken an interest in Catholic charities before," I added for good measure. Although it was a bit mean and most unnecessary, like slaughtering the wounded left by the enemy. "But, then, I do not believe I have seen him so angry as he was when we last parted. I feared for his health." I looked up at the gaunt Miss Thumper. "With his legacies undecided and so much in the balance."

"The poor man," Miss Thumper said.

"The *good* man," Miss Sharp added.

"The kind man."

"The *noble* man."

Miss Thumper plunged toward me, as if to grapple with me in deadly combat. I thought she would seize my arm, at least, but she only mauled the air.

"You *must* go to him at once, sir! You *must* not let those wicked Romans deceive him," Miss Thumper told me. "Oh, his heart's so open to the suffering of the world, the dear, *dear* man! And there's nothing those Catholics like better than stealing the bread from the mouth of an innocent *Protestant* child."

"Like this child," Miss Sharp specified.

"Like this *dear* child." Miss Thumper intensified.

"Like this dearest child," Miss Sharp conjugated.

"With her sweet little dolly."

They had by then positioned themselves on each side of the lass, who had been artfully edged from my side by the two of them. Miss Sharp petted Fanny's hair and I believe Miss Thumper meant to do the same, but only stroked the doll. I am not certain she could tell the difference.

"Go *forth*, sir," Miss Thumper exclaimed, as if she had been reading Mr. Tennyson. "Go forth and save him from the nets of Rome!"

"From priests and nuns and all that sort of thing," Miss Sharp added. "And tell the colonel—"

"—he must come by for tea," Miss Thumper assisted. "To see how happy the child is in our care."

"I cannot imagine that a child could ever be happier!" Miss Sharp stated emphatically.

Now, I suppose that servants must know their places, for that is the way of the world. But I do believe that Irish maid gave me a nod and a wink as I said my farewells.

Inspector McLeod was as good as his promise. A brief appearance by myself at his office was all it required to bring him to my hotel before two o'clock. When the Earl of Thretford's rig pulled up, the two of us were waiting outside in the gray air.

The coachman, Hargreaves, did not change his expression when I explained that the inspector would accompany me. "Very good, sir," was all he said, for he was English and had a servant's soul.

The carriage traveled St. Vincent Street, past a church that looked like a pagan temple and houses severe as crypts. The walks were crowded with men in somber dress, arisen from their middle meals to return to the Royal Exchange or their banks or firms. Glasgow was much the same as London in its preference for sunset over sunrise, for the farther west we travelled, the wider and cleaner were the streets, and the prouder the look of the people. We turned up a long rise of a road, then the coachman jollied his team to the west again, and we began a steeper, shorter climb.

The Earl of Thretford lived in a sort of community newly got up for the rich and rising. He did not have a mansion set off separate, but had taken the corner house of the handsomest town row I ever did see. Their stone was pale, buff with a hint of lemon, and those along Park Terrace each had five stories, if we count the servants' attic and cellar kitchens. On the other side of the street, the land declined into a green park, then stretched out to offer a view of the growing city and the furnace clouds that wrapped it like a shawl. All storybook castles perched up high, those clean-built houses seemed, as if to say: "Climb up here, if you dare."

Down we got, with the inspector hesitant of a sudden. I think I understood him. Among the men and women of the streets he might seem a lord, but here among great fortunes he felt a lackey. It is the way of things most everywhere, although it is less fierce in our America. It is only that, in America, every man thinks he just might get up the hill, while in Britain a fellow worries he may fall lower.

The servant who bid us inside would have seemed like a lord himself, had I not known better. He did not wear a livery, or any affectation, but black cloth better by half than what covered me.

"A moment, gentlemen," he told us, and left us in the brightness of that hall. For though the day was gray and stubborn without, the architecture had a trick of light.

How pleasant that house seemed. It made me jealous, and that is not my habit. It was only that I thought of my darling wife, and wished that she might someday grace such rooms. But I was not fool enough to think it likely.

I did not think I should like the Earl of Thretford, but our judgements must be fair. If wicked he was in his ways, I must allow that he had an eye for fineness. Now, I have seen a great plantation house—or part of it—built with the blood of slaves in Mississippi, and I have seen the palaces of India, when we tore into them like a red-coated storm. But I was old enough to know that what I had before me was taste of a different value, and a higher one. Nothing I could see begged to be looked at. There was no sense of money on display, or of any brash superiorities. Far the furniture and paintings were from the gilt and paint and colored glass of India, or the damn-all ostentation of our Southland. If the composition of a room could speak, those furnishings would have said—quietly—"We are the very best, and we know we are the very best, and you may take us or leave us, sir."

I especially liked a picture of two dogs.

The Earl come out, announced only by the opening of a door by a servant's hand that might have been disembodied.

"Ah, Major Jones. How very good of you to accept my invitation." He did not offer to shake my hand, for such folk don't.

Turning to my companion, he said, "Inspector, I'm grateful for your consideration, but I don't believe Major Jones has come here to threaten me. Really, I shall be quite safe. You may wait here. Spencer will give you tea."

And that easily, with the devilish knack the high-born have, he separated the two of us and had me inside a great, grand room of oddities, with the door shut behind us and Inspector McLeod left behind to pace and growl.

I did not know if I was in the finest of libraries or a museum of all the strangenesses of the world. As for the books that filled most of the walls, they looked to be specially bound in private Moroccos and blues. But elsewise there was all of nature's color, and some of her cruelty, besides. Stuffed parrots and predator birds I did not recognize vied for the eye's attentions with the skeletons of unknowable creatures and instruments of brass and polished steel. I fear my dear wife would have thought it a clutter, yet everything seemed comfortable in its place.

"Really, Jones," the Earl began, "this is the first time you've been a disappointment." He looked unspeakably confident, groomed beyond fine to a touch of elegant carelessness, in a long gray coat that looked as soft as a dove. "Did you seriously believe I meant to do you harm? And after sending my own carriage for you?" He floated his hand along a curious model of a building. "I had begun to think you cleverer than that."

Of course, he was right. I had been foolish. Had he meant to do me ill, he would have done it. Without the least degree of show or ceremony. And he would not have done it within the walls of his home.

He smiled. Perhaps because he had achieved the effect he wanted. "Tell me, Jones, what do you think of this?" He gestured toward the model, which was a thing of spires and steep rooflines. It made me think of one of those old cathedrals. "I'm told you take an interest in education. I'm thinking of giving this building to the new university. It's to be built just on the next hill, you see. I shouldn't like to look out and see something unpleasant. And I rather think I should honor my father's memory with a little gift. Lord knows, it's time for the university to move. Do you think I should accept the architect's plan? Or might you prefer something plainer and more to the purpose?"

I looked at the model, almost against my will.

"The architect describes it as Gothic Revival," he continued. "Personally, I'm not at all certain the Gothic wants reviving. The eye doesn't know where to settle. I should think something calmer might better suit an atmosphere of study. To be frank, I find the design a bit tasteless." He looked at me, as if we were two old friends deciding the matter. "What do you think, Jones?"

"I think this university will be glad of whatever you may give," I said honestly.

He smiled and turned away from the model, passing from muted light into the pale cast of a window. "Do you *like* it, though?" he asked me.

"No."

"Very good! You see, we're already in agreement. I don't like it, either." His lips widened in a brief display of mirth. "Perhaps I shall give it them just as it is. As our little joke. And you and I will always know how easily the tastes of Glasgow may be hired." He stepped back toward the model, returning to the softer light, and tapped the roofline with his hand. "I think that I shall add a tower here. Just here, you see? To make the building a resolute monstrosity."

With that, he turned to face me.

"You think I'm a monstrosity, don't you, Jones?"

"Why did you kill the Reverend Mr. Campbell?"

"Ah, I thought you were Welsh. And now I find you must have Scottish blood. Economizing even time and conversation." He passed to a globe and gave it a spin, as if he were the master of the world, then he raised his eyes to mine again. "The fact is, I've never killed anyone in my life." He frowned. Mockingly. "Really, do I seem the sort? A common murderer?"

"Then why did you have the Reverend Mr. Campbell killed?"

"Really, Jones! I'm not Benjamin Disraeli. I'm not given to playing these little games with words. I've never killed a man. Nor have I ever ordered a man be killed. Is that plain enough?"

"And in New York?"

"Those deaths were incidental. If I recall, it was you who did much of the killing. And Kilraine—perhaps you remember him as Kildare?—was crude. As the Irish are wont to be. I can't say I was sorry to lose him, you know. The fellow made a dreadful botch of things. I was frightfully angry at the time. Not accustomed to losing, you know." He smiled, and it almost seemed genuine. "He didn't give you credit, that was the thing. It caused me to underestimate you myself. I judged you a mere annoyance. And then you turned everything on end. I don't think I shall let that happen again."

"And Campbell?"

"Is he so important to you?"

"Yes."

"Then the suspicions about him must have been correct. To the effect that he was not only a double agent, but a triple one."

I did not understand the implication. Not then. "He was murdered," I said, too quickly. For I needed to think, instead of which I spoke. "And I believe you know who murdered him."

He gave the globe a rap and a spin, then eased behind a divan, spreading his arms and applying his hands to its wooden frame. "Now you're coming closer to the matter. Yes, I do know who lost patience with him. One may, in fact, serve two masters. But not three. In a just world, one might say he killed himself. The human instrument hardly figures."

"It was in your interest to see him killed."

"Was it?"

"Yes," I said, although my confidence was not all that it should have been.

"But even if it had been in my interest . . . I could hardly be blamed if some well-intentioned fellow believed he was serving me by acting in a manner that I had never suggested. Murder seems to me . . . a failure of the wit. An embarrassment, a tantrum. Like a child knocking over a game board when he sees he's losing. I should feel myself terribly inadequate, if I had to litter the earth with corpses." He lifted his hands from the back of the divan. "That's what soldiers do, isn't it? Kill, then lay the blame to some pompous cause?"

"And the boy? In London? Whose body was cut to bits?"

"I rather like little boys," the Earl said. "Unlike my half-brother."

Clumsy I was, and in a fragile temper. "I know exactly how you 'like' little boys," I told him.

"Let's not be indelicate. Although I am less ashamed than you might expect. I am in a position to facilitate my pleasures, and it might surprise you to find how fondly my pleasures are viewed by those who apply to me for attention. Do you really think children are made of sugar candy?"

"That is evil."

"Evil? Is it evil to share a pleasure that harms none, but virtue to slaughter one's fellow man under a flag?" He picked up a silver box from a table, then put it down again. "That was extreme of me. Forgive me. It's only that I so dislike that word, you see. 'Evil.' Need we really subscribe to the bigotries of a tribe of brute, old men who gathered in the desert some thousands of years ago? Who cobbled together a heartless set of rules to insure their own paramouncy would never be threatened? Shall we cast women into the desert, do you think, because they bleed where a man does not? Shall we put adulterers to death? Why, if we did, half the churchmen in the three kingdoms would be dangling from the gallows." He shook his head. "You've seen this city, Jones. I don't mean the terraces and crescents, but that alley you blundered into yesterday evening. Do you really think your god is merely testing those people, to see if they might be worthy of salvation? Sounds a bit capricious, at least to my ears. If he has the power to make the earth spin backward, why should he let those children that so concern you starve, or be beaten half to death? Or all the way to death, for that matter? Why doesn't he reach down and put things right?"

"We are given our opportunities on this earth, and it is up to us what we make of them. The Lord grants us every—"

"That's rot," he said. "Pure cant."

"—chance to better our souls."

"Our souls? Really, Jones. You seem such an intelligent man, in so many ways. I wish you had been allowed the privilege of a thorough education. You might have been a wonder of the age. But when you speak of 'immortal souls,' I rather think you must believe in ghoulies and ghosties." He paused before a handsome shelf of books. "I wish that I could see this soul of yours. Just once. Isn't it just a stick to beat the miserable into accepting their misery? What a cruel thing it seems to me, to promise a fellow eternal bliss, if only he'll throw away all chance of happiness in the only life he's got. Or ever will have. Even if there were a god, I shouldn't want any part of the heartless creature."

"Every logic in the world is nothing compared to faith."

"No, Jones. I won't accept platitudes. Really, I won't. If faith is all, and logic is meaningless, why did your god give us the mind and its logical abilities?"

"Logic is the devil's temptation."

"But you yourself use logic, don't you? In this detective work of yours? Would you be able to push these matters to a conclusion solely through faith?"

"I could not do it without faith."

"In God? Or faith in yourself?"

"If I have faith in myself as a Christian, then I have faith in God."

"That's doctrinally incorrect. In fact, it's a nonsense."

"Better men than you have argued against belief. Still, men believe."

"Doubtless. In regard to both points. But is the world a better place because of it? Or does it only crush our joys with fear?"

"This world is not the point."

"No, Jones. This world is exactly the point. If you have so great a disregard for the sufferings of this world, why should you bother finding a home for a girl you picked off the streets?"

"She does not figure in this. And I will not be threatened."

"Oh, bugger the Devil himself! I'm not threatening you. I have no interest in your little songbird."

"You have spied on me."

"And what are you? If not a spy?"

"You will not harm the girl."

He made a face so disgusted it crippled his gentlemanly demeanor. "I have no interest in harming the girl. I wish you pleasure of the little thing. Although I should not want my half-brother to hear of her. Cullie has rather a different sort of affection for children."

"And he killed that boy in London?"

"What do you think?"

"I do not even know if your brother exists. Or if he is long dead, and only a spook raised up to create confusion."

"Oh, Cullie's real. I assure you. He's deathly real."

"And would *that* be a threat?"

"No, Jones. It's a warning. And better-meant than you will credit."

For a ferocious moment, we glared at one another. But manners will tell. He softened himself and said, "I beg your pardon. I fear I take the metaphysical as a personal affront. The very notion of "god" insults my intelligence. And I've always been impatient with insults. Please sit down. Your leg must be uncomfortable."

"My leg is of no concern," I said, in a tone still surly.

"Please. Forgive me. Sit down. I quite respect you, you know. One rarely encounters such a challenging opponent."

"And are we opponents?"

"You never tire of the Socratic method, do you?" That smile again. "Of course, you know the fellow had rather a soft spot for young boys himself?"

Well, I have always thought those Greeks a bad lot. And I always suspected some monkey business between that Achilles and Patroclus.

We sat down. And to be honest, I did not mind it. For my leg is strong, but cranky.

"I will tell you something you may not choose to credit," the Earl said. "I'm going to win this match. You won in New York. But I shall carry off the cup this time round. And I shall do my best to protect you, although my means are limited in certain regards." His smile seemed especially cat-like as he spoke. "I should be disappointed by your death. I'd like to keep the game alive between us."

"A game, is it? When people are murdered? And lives are ruined? And still more fuel is thrown on the fire of war?"

"Of course, it's a game. It's the only game worth playing." He gave a barely perceptible quiver. "I suppose you would rather I joined a set and rode a hunter over hill and dale for the sole purpose of seeing a tiny animal ripped to death by dogs. No church here or in America would frown upon that sort of sport."

I looked around me, wounded in a way I could not explain. "For the love of God, why do it? You do not need the money. You have your pleasures, and no one to lay a hand on you for taking them. Why do such harm?"

"I told you. But you choose not to listen. Don't you understand, really? I dearly want you to be the opponent I require. I have great hopes for you." He gave a slight and gentlemanly shrug. "As for money, yes. I expect I have enough. Nor does power particularly attract me. Except in the most personal sphere." He leaned toward me, as if genuinely eager to persuade me to his view of the world. "Don't you see? It's the only game worth playing on this earth. The fear in the eyes of a fox is a travesty. But fear in the eyes of a man . . . doesn't that confirm the act of living?"

"Living is not an act."

"It's nothing *but* an act." He sighed. "I haven't offered you anything to drink, because I know you would not accept it. Not only because I've 'spied' on you. But because you and I have the same pride, the same rigor, despite the disguises we wear to deceive the world. The truth is that you're a furiously proud man."

"Then I am a sinner."

"Yes. By your standards. But by mine, you're only sensible." He waved the world away with a trick of his hand. "Without pride, we accomplish nothing."

"Humility is a virtue."

"Humility is a waste. Humility, Jones . . . is an excuse for letting the world do as it pleases to us. And I don't think you should like that very much."

"Some things are not to be understood."

He laughed out loud. "Oh, you don't believe that for a minute! I know you, you see. Your every waking hour is a struggle to understand things. To believe in things you cannot ever quite believe in. You speak of faith, but you desperately want to see through things. If it weren't so touching, I'd have to call it hypocrisy."

"All men are hypocrites."

"Yes," he said, happily. "On that we can agree. Well, I did not offer you my customary hospitality, because I knew you wouldn't accept it. But I should like to offer you something else. And I hope it will please you. Would you like to ride out with me tomorrow morning? To have a look at that great wooden pavilion that supposedly hides a dreadful, secret warship? I should like to spare you further waste of time."

"Why?"

"Because the game isn't any fun, if you're looking in the wrong direction. I should only like to get the game on track again."

"It isn't a game."

"Oh, but it is. It's a very great game, indeed. Will you ride out with me tomorrow? You may even bring your pet inspector, if you still doubt my intentions."

I wondered where the trap lay. For I was certain there had to be one laid.

"I will go out with you. But look you. Is there only one wooden tent? Or is there a second, built just to deceive me?"

He flicked the possibility from his fingertips. "That would be rather too shallow a device, don't you think? Shall we say nine o'clock? This time, I shall come in the carriage with Hargreaves. We'll go directly."

What could I do but agree?

"Have you any other questions, Jones? Any at all?"

I had at least a hundred. But he knew I could not ask them. Above all, I wanted to inquire about those letters. But that was a trap I did not mean to fall into. Young Mr. Adams would come on the train at ten-thirty o'clock. And then we would see where we stood, and where we did not.

"There is only one thing," I told him.

"Yes?"

"I do not want any harm to come to the girl. There is no reason for it."

"I have no interest in harming her. I give you my word. But others . . ."

"I will blame you."

"Then you will be unjust." He rose. "By the way." He nodded toward my cane, which rested beside me. "Since you've made such splendid use of that small gift of mine, I've taken the liberty of sending you another present."

He caught me in the act of rising myself. Of course, he read the surprise upon my face.

"But who did you think it was from?" he asked, as if honestly surprised himself.

"Your half-brother. Lieutenant Culpeper."

"Good Lord! Why on earth would he do a thing like that? He wants to *kill* you, Jones. I rather get the feeling he's wanted to kill you for a very long time. What ever did you do to him?"

"I thought . . ."

He tightened his face, in disappointment and wonder. "You really haven't thought things through at all. Have you? I hope you won't be a terrible disappointment."

"I do not need gifts from you," I said. Ready I was to give him back the sword-cane, too.

"Oh, but you do," he told me. "Don't be a fool. There is a point where even pride must stop." He turned away in an artful manner, so that I would have had to pursue him to give him back the stick. Or hurl it at him. "As I began to say—I've taken the liberty of sending a little gift to your room. If your pride disqualifies the giver, then I must insist you consider it an exigent loan. To be returned when the need has passed."

I did not say a word, but stepped toward the door. The truth is that I was afraid to make a greater fool of myself. I sensed that the Earl had had the best of me, from start to finish. And he was right—all too right—about my pride.

In the instant before my hand could touch the doorknob, the Earl rang a little bell. And the door opened before me.

I looked back at him. Perhaps because he wanted me to, and I could not resist. Or mayhaps it was the anger that I felt, for anger likes to look upon its object.

"Careful with my half-brother," he called after me. In that soft voice fortune conjures. "He's utterly mad."

Sixteen

I found a brace of pistols on my bed, in a box of the sort reserved for duelling pieces. But these were Colt revolvers, perhaps a souvenir of the Earl's American visit. Nor did the guns lack powder, cap and ball.

But I must not go too quickly.

I left the Earl's study and found no sign of Inspector McLeod in the entry hall. Outside he was, stalking up and down the pavement, with a cat-killing look on his face. He would not be persuaded to enter the Earl's carriage again, so I walked down the hill beside him. I understood. A man has his pride, and there is true. You must go very low in Mankind's order to find a level where pride does not exist. A fellow may as well be proud of a small thing as a great one. And the inspector was proud of his profession, and of the respect to be earned from duty well done. He did not think himself the Earl's equal, that I do not mean. But he would not be dismissed like a tinker girl come begging.

A great engine of a man, he fumed and he steamed, and he grunted and he smoked, so that the children at play in the park stepped out of his way and the ladies stared at him with indefinite tremblings.

"We'll see what tha' laddie has coming," was all he said to me in the course of our walk.

We parted in front of my hotel, and he still looked grim as a long march without water, but he added, "I'll hae a look into matters," and said no more, but roiled off. Half as tall the fellow looked as the statue of Mr. Scott out in the square.

Twas then I went upstairs and found the pistols. I loaded them. For a small fool is one thing, and a great fool another.

I thought that I might sit and search the Good Book, to find the refutations that I needed to cancel every one of the Earl's impingements. For he was wrong, and I knew he was wrong. But I could not find the words to make it right. Worse, the Holy Word lay flat upon the page, and would not live, not even when read aloud. That should have made me feel still lower, but I took it as a message plain and simple: My answer to the Earl could not be put into words, for words are open to challenge by the clever. At times I think that language is Satan's tool, though that is a painful thought to any Welshman. No, I saw that faith must be my answer, for you cannot fight riddles with riddles. And riddles were all that young man had to offer. Puzzles, with nothing at the end of them. We must believe, and go through. And that is that.

I closed the Bible and took me off to find my wife a gift. To give my mind a time for clearing, see. My sweetheart long had wanted a Paisley shawl. Which might be gotten cheaper in Glasgow than after it had journeyed to America.

I did not go to Buchanan Street, for I had seen enough to know its fancy shops were not for me and mine. I turned me north, up the incline, and studied the merchant offerings of Sauchiehall Street and environs.

I met naught but dismay. The loveliest shawls were priced above all reason, and the shawls of congenial price were less than lovely. Twas a great day for discouragements.

Now you will say: "We should not stint on gifts for those we love." But I will tell you: Love that does not stint itself need not rely upon gifts.

Still, I felt a bit of guilt at not making a purchase. And I wondered what the wicked Earl would have said, had he observed me. Perhaps that love is the cheapest thing in the world, and shoddy goods.

I felt so glum. Whatever I did and wherever I turned, I seemed to run into a mirror that reflected back the smallest man on earth.

By that time, I was hungry, and wanted a proper dinner before the hour arrived to meet the London train. But I did not go directly to my feed. Instead, I marched back to Sauchiehall Street and bought a scarf the price of which would have fed a hundred orphans for a week. And more. Twas green and gold, which I thought would suit my Mary, for her hair is that true Welsh black from up the valleys, and her eyes are green as the sea the day after a storm.

That made me feel better, and I dined upon a filet in thick blood gravy.

⌒

Just about ready to leave for the station I was, when the porter delivered a letter to my room.

"Police laddie said it maun gae to ye quick and ready," the fellow told me. Fortunately, he was accustomed to dealing with his fellow Scots and did not elaborate his expectation of a gratuity.

The note come from Inspector McLeod. Sealed close it was, and strange. Enjoining me to secrecy, perhaps because he meant to exceed official bounds, and asking me to meet him at one o'clock after midnight, in the Necropolis, at the foot of the statue of John Knox.

Now I will tell you of John Knox, for he had a great hand in making Presbyterians, who are the Hindoo variety of Christians. They believe that everything is made up in advance, see. I suppose he was more good than bad, for he stood opposed to Rome and gave a nasty time to that Scottish Mary, who seems a bit of a tart in the history books. But he also sounds as if he had a mean streak. And there is hardness a-plenty in this world, without our rendering Jesus into a tyrant.

But let that bide.

Of course, I was suspicious of the note. I realized it might be but a lure to lead me to a desolate place and work some mischief. With all the wickedness I had seen in Her Majesty's domains, I would not even rule out the chance that Inspector McLeod was in service to my enemies, and that his snub by the Earl was but a charade. The note might be an invitation to die.

But I would go, though not without a pistol and my sword-cane. For a soldier must always march to the sound of the guns. Ready I was to cooperate with the inspector, should he prove honest. Or to fight, if he was not.

No matter who wished to greet me in that graveyard, I would not disappoint them through reluctance. The truth was that I wished to put an end to things. The Earl had unsettled me, beyond reason. And weary I was of murders, threats and lies. When I loaded those revolvers, their heft had seemed all too comfortable in my hands.

I am a soldier. Perhaps that is what I am damned to be. No matter how hard I wish to turn away from such affairs. And patience is a rare thing in a soldier. A soldier is trained to action, and he believes that action will carry the day. I fear I was not steady in my judgement. Had I been invited to Hell that night, I think I would have gone, convinced that I should have a go at the Devil.

Whether I had business with a policeman who feared losing his position, or with a whole battalion of men in red masks, I had another duty that wanted completing first. I got me up Buchanan Street to the station, through the Thursday-evening wanderers and a singing drunkard or two. I bought my ticket to go onto the platform, and there I was when the London train chugged in and squealed to a stop on clouds of steam.

I did not see young Mr. Adams at once. For the first thing that I saw was Polly Perkins. Fair burst out of her compartment she did, and come strutting along the platform in a great huff. Twas then that Henry Adams appeared behind her. Juggling a fair tumult of luggage he was, and calling to a porter to fetch still more from the roof of the car.

Didn't Miss Perkins smile when she caught sight of me? Although she quickly re-attached her frown.

I was flummoxed.

Perhaps I am a fool in so many ways that they cannot be tallied, but I did not expect Miss Perkins to appear in Glasgow. Yet, up to me she stepped, with a great and grandiose folderol of bodily contortions. Her travelling costume included a rather alarming abundance of feathers, as if she had prepared herself to fly the rest of the way should the train break down. All in handsome green she was, with bits of cream lace planted here and there, and her hat was of a size to inspire awe. Her blond hair was put up, and she wore summer gloves that did not look quite fresh.

I would not tell you that she looked a queen, for she did not. Queens pursued a duller course than Miss Perkins. Nor did she achieve the elegance she wanted, to be plain. Even I could tell that much. Yet, every male head on that platform snapped in her direction, as smartly as if given a command.

Just as Mr. Adams come up beside her, with a look of infernal confusion on his face and the luggage precarious in his struggling arms, Polly gave me a smile as bright as sunrise. Although one of her teeth was just awry, which I had not noted previously. Still, it was not unbecoming, since the teeth looked to be her own, and that is something.

"Well!" she declared—indeed, hers was a tone of declaration—"It's good to lay eyes on a gentleman again, and one what don't think it's 'is right and 'is bleedin' privilege to take advantage of an innocent lady what finds 'erself cast on 'is mercies upon the railway!" She glanced cooly at Mr. Adams. "A gentleman what is unlike *some* people of which we 'ave a mutual acquaintance."

She extended her hand to me. Rather as if she expected me to kiss it. I gave it a friendly shake, instead, and welcomed her to Scotland.

Again, she aimed a haughty look at the luggage-encumbered slave to which Mr. Adams had been reduced.

" 'E's a dirty little cooter," she told me, "and wants watching every minute, don't think 'e don't." She sniffed. "You wouldn't think 'e ever met 'imself a proper li-dy."

And then she excused herself delicately, to answer the strain of her journey with a visit to the lady's parlor within the station, despite the intelligence I offered of the hotel's proximity.

As she took herself toward the bustling hall, Miss Perkins managed to seem an entire procession. With men and boys bowing and tipping their hats, and doing most all they could to beg her notice, Henry Adams put down the pile of travelling kit—not without dropping a bag or two about him—and admired his companion's triumph.

"Isn't she splendid?" he asked me. "I don't believe I've ever known anyone like her."

Of course, my primary interest was the letters.

"Oh, she has them, all right," young Mr. Adams assured me. "I've seen them."

"Well, what do they say, man?"

He looked perplexed, as if I should have known everything that had happened since I left London.

"She hasn't actually let me *read* them," he told me. "But she's shown them to me. Twice. She really is a wicked little teaser-cat, you know. Have you seen the way she dances when she—"

"What is the difficulty, then? Not enough money, is it?"

"Oh, no. Nothing of the sort." His perplexity multiplied, as if he thought me hopelessly ill-informed. "She hardly seems interested in the money. Although I suspect she'll take it, in the end. A girl in her position wants funds, of course."

"What is it, then? Why will she not give you the letters?"

Twas then his bafflement reached its apotheosis.

"She refuses to give them to anyone but you," he told me. "She says she's frightfully sorry she took them, and feels she has to make amends to you personally. I say, Jones. I suppose I should be more than a little jealous." He stepped closer to me, as men do when they intend to embarrass themselves. "But I don't imagine you'd be the sort to crowd the field on a fellow."

Just then, a porter come up with a trunk, and I told him we would make for the Hotel Clarence. Since Mr. Adams did not seem forthcoming of purse, I paid the fellow and added a tip. For safety. I did not wish to endanger Miss Perkins's wardrobe, see. For hard enough it seemed to keep her garments upon her.

As we followed the porter along the pier, through a great contention of ladies who lacked some precious parcel, young Mr. Adams edged close to me again.

"Jones, I find I must ask you something plainly. Man to man."

When fellows say that, they are up to something nasty.

"Have you . . ." he began, ". . . did you . . . has Miss Perkins ever . . . has there been any sort of intimacy between the two of you? I don't ask out of—"

I stopped and gave him a look to freeze the Punjab over in July. "I am a married man, Mr. Adams. And if you have the least regard for Miss Perkins, you will—"

"Terribly sorry," he said, fair jumping back. "Really. I *am* sorry. I knew better, of course. It's only . . . it's only that I'm afraid I've fallen in love, you see."

And there you have what comes of scheming mischief.

Our cab ride to the hotel was uneventful, except for the slap Miss Perkins gave to Henry Adams's hand when it accidentally strayed toward her skirts.

"Don't you be nasty," she told him, and I believe he blushed, although it was hard to see, for the cab was not lit.

The fellow at the desk had doubts about allowing a room to an unmarried lady, who was travelling without the benefit of familial supervision, but I convinced him it was a matter of legation business. He gave me a smirk or two, and he did take an especial interest in Miss Perkins's prancing about the narrow lobby, but in the end all parties had a room, and the luggage was sent up while Mr. Adams and Miss Perkins inked the registry. Young Mr. Adams received lodgings next to mine, but Miss Perkins was consigned to a separate floor, to suit propriety, with a caution not to come down to the lobby or enter the dining room unescorted. I thought the clerk's manner needlessly harsh, but the Scots are so wary of sin that they search until they find it.

Out of earshot of the clerk, we agreed to meet in my room in ten minutes. And that Miss Perkins would bring the letters.

"I can't 'ardly wait," she told me, with a smile and a blue-eyed wink.

When both of them made to separate from me, I held back Mr. Adams by his sleeve. Discreetly.

"Perhaps," I whispered, as Miss Perkins's form diminished up the staircase, "you should come to my room in *five* minutes. If it does not inconvenience you."

Mr. Adams agreed with alacrity. I do believe he was as eager to keep me from an intimate encounter with Miss Perkins as I was to avoid one. Twas queer to have the fellow jealous of me. But then Miss Perkins knew how to bait a man, if you will allow me the frankness.

I went to my room and moved the pistol case and the fancy-wrapped shawl to the top of the dresser, listening all the while to a fellow out on the square, who had been seduced by Satan's elixirs and was bellowing "God Save the Queen" at the top of his lungs. He could not find his pitch, which ever annoys me. I bent to the basin to rinse my face and hardly had time to look after myself before Mr. Adams come knocking on my door.

He did not beat Miss Perkins by a minute. And how she did it so quick I cannot say, unless it is a skill of the stage, but she had managed to exchange her green costume for a gown of sapphire blue. The dressmaker had economized on the amount of fabric devoted to the bodice, and her white shoulders led the eye lower still, to where a fellow's eye has no business going. She had dropped her hair, too, and might have taken the role of Guinevere upon the stage.

She had the two packets of letters in her hands, still tied with the same ribbons.

Disappointed she seemed that Mr. Adams had anticipated her arrival.

"I don't think as that one should be allowed to read 'em," she told me. "As 'e already seems to 'ave plenty of powder in 'is keg. Couldn't you pack 'im off til we finish our business?"

Mr. Adams's expression feared calamity.

"Surely, Miss Perkins," I said, "you wouldn't want to compromise your reputation by being alone with a man in his hotel room."

That pleased her no end. She lifted her nose and turned it to Henry Adams. "Always a gent," she said, "and considerate of a poor girl's reputation. Unlike some present company as might be among us."

"Please," I said. "The letters."

"Well, I ain't sure," she told me.

I searched for a response, but she continued without my interlocution.

"I don't know if anybody ought to be reading such dirty business." She blushed, and I do not believe it reflected the art of the stage. "I never 'eard the likes in my life," she told me. "Nothing but dirty filth it is, and not fit for the sewers, let alone being set down on paper, bold as brass. It's the wickedest business what ever I come across."

"Miss Perkins," I said, "the contents may have great importance. An importance that is perhaps beyond your—"

"Well, I don't see 'ow they could matter at all to anyone who ain't a stinker!" she declared. "Perhaps you ain't the gentleman I took you for. You all fancy and telling me 'ow I was to pose myself in your room and the like, and 'ere I thought you—"

At the turn in her discourse, I suffered a savage glance from Henry Adams.

"—wasn't a bit like the rest of them."

"Please. The letters, Miss Perkins. I assure you my intentions are not lascivious."

Tentatively, she began to extend them toward me. "I'm ashamed that ever I took them. And twicet ashamed that ever I read them. 'Ad to read them over and over, I did, since I couldn't believe the 'alf of what they was going on about." She lowered her eyes. "I didn't know a woman could do them kinds of things to another woman."

Henry Adams and I exchanged a glance that suggested we were not the men of the world we fancied ourselves. Out in the square, that drunkard still howled at the Lord to preserve the Queen.

"Oh, I know as there's bossy women and girls as like things peculiar," Miss Perkins continued. "But this is just the dirtiest! You'd think she was a man 'erself, the things she talks of doing to 'er sweetie."

"Miss Perkins . . ." I began, as I sought to force things back into a sensible order, ". . . you mean that these . . . these . . ." Of a sudden, I hesitated to take the missives from her. ". . . you mean these are love letters written from one woman to another?"

"And absolutely filthy," she said. "Nearly burned 'em, I did."

When I failed to grasp the proffered letters, Miss Perkins took matters in hand. For her temper was up just thinking of the injuries implied to her fair sex. She stepped to the writing table and pulled the first ribbon until the bow dissolved and the letters spread themselves in a fan. Choosing one at random, she unfolded it and spread it out for all of us to see.

When we proved shy of reading the text in her presence—given the immense nature of the perversity involved—she stared at us as if we were bad little boys.

"Well, I thought you wanted to 'ave yourself a look," she said to me.

"But . . ." I began again, trying to make all the pieces fit—where on earth was the value worth killing for, if the letters were not from a man of position, but from a woman? What woman in England maintained a position of such power and importance that she might be endangered by the existence of—

A wave of horror swept over me. And through me. And all around me.

". . . a woman," I muttered, seeing an august portrait in the air. Could it be . . . was it possible . . .

"Well, if you won't believe me, 'ave a look for yourself," she told me. And she picked up the letter and held it up to my face. "See 'ow the bleedin' cow signs it? Shameless as a slut on the docks, she is. 'Your Old Pam.' "

It is a most peculiar situation to find yourself relieved that the Prime Minister of Great Britain has embarrassed himself by scribbling obscenities.

Henry Adams made a grab for the letters, but Polly was too quick for him. She interposed a volume of skirts and swept up the papers and dumped them into my hands. Not without dropping a few of them onto the floor. Lord Palmerston was a voluminous correspondent.

"There," she told me. "If that's the sort of nastiness you prefer to a girl what was all ready to treat you proper, good riddance."

"Miss Perkins," I said, "Polly . . . these aren't . . . the letters are not from a woman. They're from Lord Palmerston, the Prime Minister. His nickname is 'Old Pam,' see."

She made a delighted face. "Coo, ain't 'e a dirty bird, then? The old bugger."

"Jones, really," Mr. Adams interposed, "you needn't tell her—"

"Polly, you're a good girl. A very good girl," I told her. "You're a very good girl, indeed. I . . . I believe I could kiss you!"

Of course, I did not mean it literally. And I regretted my speech the moment it was uttered. The words just come out, see.

"Well, don't stop yourself on my account," she told me, practically offering me one of those milky cheeks. "And to think 'e's still capable of doing things like that, the old leaker," she added. For even a penny-gaff songstress has some knowledge of the Prime Minister.

"Jones," Mr. Adams said, "do you realize . . . that those letters could bring down the government?"

"Or control it," I said, for I saw farther than he did.

"Coo," Polly said. "I shouldn't like to be 'im when 'is wife finds out."

⁓

And the night was still in its infancy.

You might have slapped my face and I would not have felt it. Fair stunned I was. Not only by the magnitude of power those letters offered the possessor, but by my blindness in the face of the obvious. I should have known days before who had written the letters, for the evidence had been hurled in my direction until it lay in piles on every side of me.

The risks that Mr. Disraeli had been willing to run had been too great to be caused by a stack of debts—in England, debts were the very badge of a gentleman. Yet, he had been willing to risk career and reputation—even prison, perhaps. I should have seen it could not be a matter of chasing after a peerage for the rich man who held his paper. And then Lords Russell and Lyons, who were no friends to Mr. Disraeli's faction, had come to Mr. Adams with their worries, implying that our Minister's help was to be rewarded, without the least willingness to enter into detail about the help required. There was the Prime Minister's notorious reputation as a fellow of more enthusiasm than virtue where the ladies were concerned. That boy in the Dutch cap, in Lambeth, who lived next door to the late Betty Green, had spoken of a tottering old man who come visiting. But I had leapt to the conclusion that he spoke of the elder Mr. Pomeroy, despite that gentleman's obvious robustness. Death had been piled upon death with pestilential abandon. The private indiscretions of some lesser figure could not have been the cause of such a massacre. As for Betty Green—or Sarah Pomeroy—twas obvious why they had made her out not only a Jewess, but a Hungarian one. For a Jewess would create an embarrassment of race, but a Hungarian mistress might be portrayed as the agent of a foreign power. In whose arms the leading man in England had taken his repose.

Those letters had the power and promise to draw the likes of Lieutenant Culpeper into the matter. A pawn-broker's life, or that of a boy, would be nothing against such stakes. Had Betty Green been wiser, she would have seen that death must be her destiny. For none who knew or suspected the secret, below the level of great social power, would be allowed to survive.

That meant that other deaths were in the offing.

I could have cursed. And I do not curse lightly, and wish not to curse at all. As much as I had deplored Inspector Wilkie's subservience, and mocked the English as a servile people, the taint was still deep down in my own bones. For I, too, had looked downward instead of up. And if I *had* cursed, which I did not, I might have laughed thereafter. For I had been proposed as a clever detective—although I did not make that claim myself—yet I had failed to look through a lamplit window when invited.

But what had Palmerston's follies to do with ships?

I had no more time to plod to conclusions, for the city's clocks already had given us midnight, and I was to be at John Knox's feet by one.

I turned to my companions. Young Mr. Adams had been as shocked as I was by the identity of the author of those epistles—perhaps he was even more shocked—but Miss Perkins expected less of the high and mighty, and she had taken upon herself the unbidden duty of examining the letters a final time, in case we had neglected some intelligence. Giggle and blush she did, and now and again she whispered, "The dirty old bugger . . ."

"Look you," I said abruptly. As if to wake myself from the thrall of a dream. "We must divide the letters. Mr. Adams, you will take one packet. Miss Perkins, might I ask you to retain the other stack until I return?"

"You're going out?" Mr. Adams asked me. "At this hour?"

"I have an appointment."

He gave me a look that I found inappropriate and said, "Why, Jones, you old dog!"

Miss Perkins also scowled her disapproval.

"No, no," I assured them. "It is a police matter, see. I am to meet a certain Inspector McLeod in the Necropolis, under the Knox statue. We must meet in secret, so that he will not be compromised."

"That sounds queer," Henry Adams told me.

"Yes. It does." I walked over to the dresser, took one of the pistols from the case, and tucked it underneath my frock coat. "And if it is as queer as I suspect it may be, I will be prepared." I looked at him a touch severely, for the young man wanted gravity. "There is another pistol in the box. And it is loaded. If you find you have a need . . ."

"Really, Jones . . . I know nothing of pistols. I couldn't possibly, you know."

"Well, it is in the case. If anyone comes asking for the letters. I suggest you take it with you to your room." I shifted my attentions to the White Lily of Kent, who now looked more alarmed than disapproving. "Miss Perkins, I recommend you stay here in this room, rather than returning to your own." When she looked a bit too eager, I added, "Until I come back. Then you may retire to your own chamber."

"I say, Jones. Shouldn't I stay here with Miss Perkins? For the sake of her safety?"

"And who's to protect me from you and your presumptions?" Miss Perkins huffed.

"You'll be just next door," I told Mr. Adams. "She can call to you, should the need arise." I took up my cane and my topper. "I must go now, see. Keep the letters safe. Mr. Adams, I do suggest you take up the revolver.

He still looked doubtful. Then, of a sudden, he put on the look of a gentleman who has found himself in the street without his hat. "Oh, Jones! I didn't mention—this morning, just before leaving, I heard that Reginald Pomeroy had hanged himself. In his cell. Really, can you imagine?"

The driver took me as far as the Cathedral, for that was as close as he would go at night. Clattering off across the cobbles, the hack left me alone. The tower and roof of the great stone church showed black against the sky, with that strange feel holy places have when they are unattended. The gaslights stopped, and there was not so much as a lamp in a gate-keeper's window to help me. Across the square, the clergy slept in their comfortable houses, battling the forces of darkness with their snores. Beyond, the land fell off. I knew there was a ravine, and an old bridge that crossed it to enter the place of the dead, for I had seen that much by light of day. The Necropolis was a steep lump of a hill. I remembered it studded with statues and crypts, with trees to cool the mourners and the mourned. But all I could see was a haziness, more a hint than a hill. The filth of the air and the moonless night did not make a man feel welcome.

Yet, faith is armor against the unseen world, if such a thing there is. And soldiers learn to cherish the night, if they survive long enough to learn its ways, for darkness is a friend to veteran infantry. I tapped along to a graveled descent, then onto the stones of the bridge.

A dog took up his barking in the distance, and other hounds basked in their noisy comradeship, making a competition of their howls. It sounded like all of the dogs in the city were at it.

But there was only silence where I walked, in the dank, black nearness. At the end of the bridge, a gate stood askew, from neglect or by design. I slipped me through and tried to take my bearings. The smoke of the day had lingered here, and I could not see a pistol shot ahead of me. I chose an upward path, only to find it led me down again. And then I found another that seemed to help me up toward my goal, for I had seen the statue in the daylight, and it stood just below the crown of the hill.

That track, too, veered off, and I picked a branch that promised—again—to aim me toward the crest. The air was so foul I could barely see the gaslamps of the city below. Weak stars they were, on a glowering night.

The path reached a dead end.

I retraced my steps, or hoped I did. Then I began to explore a slightly broader way I come upon, a lane the width of a mortuary coach.

After teasing me upward for a stretch, that course, too, turned down. As if the hill did not want to receive me.

The crypts that lined the trails were built into the hillside, some new and others of sufficient antiquity to have their marble and granite broken off and strewn where it might trip a careless man. The lingering smoke from the manufactories gave the place a fitting scent of brimstone. All in all, I did not like my surroundings.

Those dogs went at it with a force renewed. And, yet, they seemed a hundred miles away.

Path after path—perhaps the same paths retaken—all betrayed me. At last, I resolved to climb straight up the embankments, and I did. Only to find myself against a sheer wall of rock.

Back down I went, past a masoleum that harbored rats. They chirp almost like birds when you surprise them.

There is strange, how a man under threat can lose his fear in a welter of impatience. I might have been going to my death, but my caution had been replaced by a streak of temper at my inability to reach the place of appointment.

I tried my luck with a break in the brambles girdling the hillside between the crypts and monuments, and found myself on a higher path at last. Sweating I was, despite the coolness of that summer night. Now, I am a man who has a good sense of direction, and a hard-won feel for the features of the earth. But I could not have said which side of the hill I was on by then, or how near the crest. I tried to confirm the time, but the darkness would not let me read my pocket watch. When I replaced it, I felt the pistol behind my belt. Reassuring it was, though it is sinful to say so.

I climbed along the trail and found myself amid a field of graves. Interspersed with sepulchres and marble angels, the paleness of the headstones loomed up from the night in the moment before I would have stumbled over them.

I stopped. Not because I had decided to, but because my instincts—those of an old soldier—had decided for me.

I listened, and heard nothing but those dogs. Just quieting now. There were no footfalls, and no breaths but my own. I smelled only the dirty air, and damp earth, and some rot. Yet, there was a thing I did not like.

If McLeod was there, he should have shown a light. Even if he meant to betray me, he should have had a signal lamp to guide me to my fate.

The cathedral clock tolled one, and lesser churches added their metal harmonies. I worried that, if honest, the inspector might leave, deciding I would not come. But I no longer thought the business an honest one, if ever I had. I believe I only wanted resolution. But now, among the graves, I knew that not all of my sweat come from my climb.

To find the statue of Knox upon its pedestal, I began to make widening circles on the high ground, paying attention to the least dropping off to a slope. If I kept my rings neat, I would have to come upon the assigned meeting place, just off the crest of the hill. I poked along, trying to be quiet, and it seemed to me that my carefulness only made the rest of the world quieter still, as if it wanted to hear me.

I near fell into an open grave prepared for use in the morning. My stick it was that saved me, as another cane had saved me from a nasty fall in a Mississippi plantation house.

I stepped along the grass with still-greater care, wondering who the tombs around me memorialized. I know the poets find boneyards romantic, but I would rather be among the living.

More rats there were. I wondered at their diets.

And then a lovely voice broke into song. It was a voice I did not want to hear.

Fanny it was, singing "Annie Laurie." But her pitch broke, and her voice kept dying off. Then it would rise up again, as if she were being threatened and prodded and cursed.

She was not far away, and I went toward her. Yes, it was a trap. But a good man does not run away. Not when he knows what must live on in his conscience.

I wanted to call out to her, to tell her all would be well. But I knew better. I tried to keep a silence to my movements, as if I were patrolling the tribal frontier. I wished I might have had my boys from the regiment with me, the ones I chose when I knew the odds were mean. Molloy I would have taken first of all. Then a few others.

But I was alone.

Of a sudden, her voice broke off and left the world in silence once again. I only hoped they had not cut her throat.

I smashed my knee into a tombstone blackened to charcoal, and had to pause a minute to recover. My good knee it was. Now both knees were sour.

The night is a trickster, and memory is no better. You learn much through the years, but never enough. I sought to keep my bearings well enough to take me toward the ghost of her voice. But after twenty or thirty paces, I could no longer be sure of my orientation. The earth will lead your feet where it wants them to go.

I felt the ground declining. Slightly. And I had to make a choice.

I wheeled right and proceeded.

The spark of a match startled me, then a torch exploded. Near enough to dazzle my eyes near uselessness. And a second torch burst into flame.

"How long must a man wait," a scraped voice asked, "for the justice due him?"

The figure that spoke stood by a plinth and column. Wearing a gentleman's country garments. And a crimson mask. His sword flashed when he made the slightest movement.

Fanny stood behind him, held by both arms, with a tribesman to either side of her. The fear on her face brought back a sorrow of memories, from the days when I took pleasure in killing and called it a soldier's duty. The tribesmen were got up like English gents themselves, but the torches in their hands made them look like devils. Then one of them released his grip on Fanny, took both torches, and placed them in sconces fixed to the front of a crypt. After he returned to the girl, both natives drew their daggers.

"Do you think," the man in the mask said, "I should kill her now? Quickly? Or should we have a bit of sport between us first?"

"I should have killed you in Delhi," I told him.

"And I you," he said.

"And McLeod? Is he here? Or did you kill him, too?"

I thought I sensed a smile behind the mask. "I'm afraid I only borrowed the inspector's good name. I expect he's in his bed, dreaming of all the glories that were Scotland."

He whipped the air with his blade. Twas clear from that single gesture he was the better swordsman. My tools had been the musket and the bayonet, and the cutlasses we trained with now and then, in case we might be detailed to the guns. Culpeper had a young gentleman's training. And I come from a tan-yard and a mine.

I felt a fool for burying the pistol under my coat. Had I tried to reach it, he would have killed me before I got through the buttons.

"You first, I think. The child can wait." He sliced the air again. "Tell you what. Give me a proper go of it. Make this interesting. And I may only cut off her hands, and let her live. She can always sing for her supper." He stepped away from the plinth and took his ground in the open space between us. "After I introduce her to a few of the simple pleasures of the East."

I did not look at Fanny. It is a thing you must not do. You must keep your eyes on the eyes of the man who means to take your life. But I could feel her terror. Thick as the air that clutched us. I imagined how those devilish hands must feel upon her. But she was braw and bonnie, to use her words. She did not cry out or plead, or expect miracles. Perhaps she did not expect anything at all. And feared that I might think her of no value.

"Tell them," I said, "that if I win, they're to let her go."

He laughed. "Don't be a fool. If you should put me down—which I don't think likely, old man—you'll have to fight them after. Whether or not they cut your little gutter-bitch's throat first or not. And that will rather depend on how skilled you are."

He raised his sword. And I released the sheath from my own. Even had I possessed an equal skill to his, it would not have been a fair fight. For the grip of a sword cane will not rival the grip of a proper sword. Such a cane is meant for alleys and thieves, not for duels and fencers.

I stepped toward him. Quickly. Choosing my ground in the clearing. I had but one hope, see. And that was a slight one. My bad leg would not let me leap about—although my recent injury to the other knee was utterly forgotten in the excitement—so I would have to take my ground and stand to it. To retreat by half-steps when pressed, and to come back to where I started as quick as I could. Twas more a matter of fending off than of fighting.

"Even if you win," I told him, "you'll never get the letters now. They're in London."

He laughed. "I'd almost forgotten the letters," he told me. "I've dedicated this particular night to you. Anyway, I don't believe they're in London, old man."

He plunged toward me. Artfully done, it was. Had I not been quick, he would have pierced me through.

Back he jumped, before my own blade could chase after him. He stepped to the side. So that the torches were full in my face. But I knew that trick, and I stepped off and turned myself, although it left me with my back to the plinth and column.

He sizzled the air again, then thrust for me. I turned him off three times. Close enough we come for me to hear his panting above the crackle of the torches. Then we crossed blades again. He never was in danger from me, for all of my efforts went into parrying his attacks. Twas all I could do. Using my blade solely to block, with every hair on my skin remembering the hundred tricks of attack that near killed me in India.

He come at me fiercely, trying to bring his size and strength to bear. But coolness is better, and once I nearly cut him. It made him curse me savagely. But it also made him remember himself. He began to carry himself like a proper swordsman after that. Making me turn on one leg then another. Twisting me up. Applying his power at angles that challenge the defender's arm.

For a moment, he stepped back. Breathing richly. "Very good, Jones," he told me. "Keep that up, and I may only cut off one of her hands. Now, let's see if our little Welsh soldier's all bluff."

He rushed at me, but it was a trick. To bring himself close to me. When our hilts were locked, he reached up his left hand and tore off his mask.

No leper of India bore a face so dreadful. The dried and rotten beef of him was wet with unhealed sores. And I had been right when I suspected him of smiling. For his lips had been cut away, and smile was all the creature would ever do.

All this I saw in an instant. Then his blade slashed down my own face.

Had I not had the instincts of an old sergeant, he would have sent the tip of his blade through my eye. But I had turned me just in time. Not enough to escape him, but far enough to save my life. Still, I felt the sting and wet we feel when our faces are cut. I could not judge how much of my own meat he had laid open, but warm-cold gore poured down my cheek, and my left eye clouded with blood.

It goes so fast with a fellow like him that the novice cannot survive. The hard part of soldiering is getting through your first battle or two. After that, your chances begin to increase.

I was not fool enough to touch my face, or to try to clear my eye. I kept my eyes on his eyes. Struggling not to look at the rest of his face, which was a task near impossible. If he had possessed a monster's soul in India, now he wore a monster's visage to match it.

He did not laugh, but seemed to smirk. With that skull's smile disfiguring every expression.

"When a man kisses a woman. Or whatever he chooses to kiss. This is what he should see," he told me. "This is what we all are underneath. The beauty, and the beggar."

He did himself no favors by cutting me so. For I have scars a-plenty upon my person. But somehow I had ever preserved my face. I am no handsome man, and others have been known to put it less kindly still. But I did not like the addition of a scar to my face. It made me go strange. Cold, not hot. It put me in that killing place that lies beyond all morals and human decency. The place that spawns the deadliest of soldiers. And, perhaps, the murderer, as well.

We fought for a full five minutes more, which seems a time near eternal to the warrior. Just at the edge of death there is a place that cancels time, and we had found it. The blood rushed down my face and into my collar, for the head bleeds ever the worst, and I felt the slime on my neck and down my chest.

Our eyes took turns in the firelight. As we shifted and flashed our blades. I thought—feared—I felt a loosening in the handle of the sword-cane. Such implements are not made with duels in mind. But there was nothing I could do. I only kept him off me as best I could: One brief triumph after another, each canceled by the next attack.

We both were winded, but we kept at each other. Whether my sword broke first or I did myself, I knew I could not win against him now. But I would not give him any chance he did not earn.

One of the natives muttered something, and it nearly broke the lock of his eyes with mine. I recognized the old tongue of the barracks, but could not quite distinguish what the tribesman said.

I understood the next voice well enough.

And it was a voice I knew.

Commanding in that barracks tongue, as if we were in India and not Scotland.

The colonel barked at the natives to come to attention. And they nearly did before they regained control of themselves.

But Culpeper it was who suffered from the interruption. The colonel's sudden outburst startled him, and he looked away. Just for a slice off a second.

I put my blade through his heart. If heart he had. And plunged it in until it come out his back.

Twas all a great screaming then, with the colonel calling invisible men to the attack, as if he had our old, red regiment with him.

In another chop off a second I saw them, the colonel coming on waving his cane, and Inspector McLeod beside him with a truncheon. Miss Perkins was just on their heels, with Mr. Adams bringing up the rear.

The tribesmen released the girl and raised their blades. Beginning to scream their ancient battle-cries.

McLeod saw that his billy was no use and stepped him back. And

I saw Mr. Adams leap for the stony shelter of a crypt. I had no time to draw my pistol, for the colonel and the natives were already at it, and he was bound to lose.

I plunged into the melee with Culpeper's sword, while the inspector shouted at the lot of us that somebody was bloody well under arrest, blowing a whistle in between his curses.

The colonel was in the very worst danger. A wooden cane is no match for an Orient blade. And he was old, if brave.

I got one of them off him, but the fellow was all for chopping me to bits. I feared the colonel was nearing the end of his fight with the other tribesman.

And didn't a great, roaring pistol go off? Not once, but twice. The colonel's opponent went down in a heap, and I heard the voice of Miss Perkins, setting aside her demure temper and fair shrieking, " 'Ow d'you like that, you ruddy little bastard?" Twas then I marked the pistol in her hand.

The last of the tribesmen did not run. For such are brave and loyal. He knew he was dead if he stood his ground. But he stood it, and damn us all. I never faulted the men of India for want of bravery.

I only hoped that Miss Perkins would not fire again, for I suspected luck had given her all it intended to, and I was not certain who the next bullet might surprise.

The tribesman fought to evade my sword, while the colonel attempted to thrash him. I saw that final fear in the poor bugger's eyes.

Then the colonel shouted, *"Rally, the Old Combustibles!"* and he gave the fellow the ball of his cane on the temple, just as my own blade slithered into his entrails.

I recognized that final word they said, the "Allah" that comes out sounding more like "Ullah." He died with his brown eyes open.

Miss Perkins stepped up beside us, pistol fuming. I relieved her of its weight as swiftly as she would let me. Overcoming her ladylike timidity, she gave the poor fellow's carcass a poke with the tip of her shoe and said, "Let that be a lesson, you nasty thing."

Twas only then she noted my wound and cried out in alarm. When I assured her the cut was not mortal in nature, she bent to reveal her petticoat and tore off a great strip without hesitation. Come at my face she did, for she wished to bandage me. But the mess of my snout was a trivial thing at the moment.

Fanny had disappeared.

I called to her. Telling her it was me, and that the danger was past. Hoping she had not been injured in the fray. And hoping she had not run back to Betts and Spanish Jemmy, thinking their lair a safer harbor than any I was like to have on offer.

All of the rest gathered by me, including young Mr. Adams, who seemed quite charged now that the fighting was over.

"We did rather all right, didn't we?" he beamed.

But I could only think of the child. About to snatch one of those torches I was, though they were burning down. I would have scoured that hill, then the rest of the city. But I saw her storm of hair rise from a gravestone, then the white face.

"It's all right now, lass," I told her, in a voice much reduced. And up she sprang, and she charged for me. And she held to me again.

Twas then I found myself the object of a feminine rivalry for my attentions. Fanny did not intend to release me, but Miss Perkins wished to staunch the flow of my blood, with as great a dramatic performance as possible.

Twas then I noticed the shawl—my darling's shawl—spread over the White Lily's shoulders.

She followed the course of my eyes, as women do.

"Ain't you a dearie, though?" she said. "Such a sweet old bird, 'e is, to wish to surprise a girl with 'andsome presents. Don't you go getting your nasty blood all over it, now."

Well, if she had taken the shawl, she had picked up the pistol, as well. Miss Perkins seemed to have a sort of Communist's view of property, helping herself to everything lying about. But I found I could not chide her, or tell her that the gift was not for her. I owed her a shawl, and more. But I will tell you: Had I known she was to have that shawl for herself, I might have done my buying more economically.

And now I would have to buy another. Which galled me.

Thinking about those pounds and pence, I near forgot my wound. Until she touched it dead center. I jumped up near as high as old John Knox.

"You'll do for a good washing, when we get back," she told me.

All the while I saw Mr. Adams, eyeing the two of us dolefully, with a look on his face that as much as said, "Jones, you're a lying cheat at the game of hearts."

Innocent I was, and well you know it.

Oh, all this was but a matter of minutes, with the colonel picking over the dead and exclaiming, "Well, there's an ugly one, don't you know?" when he got a look at Lieutenant Culpeper's face.

Inspector McLeod wore a baffled look. I do not think such events were common in his experience. He muttered and muttered, as only the Scots can do.

" 'Old yourself still, dearie," Miss Perkins told me again. She brought her face so close to mine I could smell her youthful breath. I fear it was not as sweet as that of the damsels in romances. In fact, she smelled like cheese half-way coughed up. But pretty she was, do not mistake me. And I was grateful for her ministrations.

The more Miss Perkins went at my face, the tighter Fanny clung to me. Until I felt so pulled and poked I could hardly keep my balance.

"Fanny, girl," I said. "Give us a song, would you, then? A happy song."

When she did not separate herself from me in the slightest degree, I told her, "Miss Perkins here is a great singing sensation, you know. From London. I know that she would like to hear you sing."

Reluctantly, Fanny took one step away. Then another. Watching all the while in case I might flee.

"Do ye want me tae gi' 'Annie Laurie'?" she asked.

"No, girl," I said, for I would have no more laying down and dying that night. "Do you know 'My Love is Like a Red, Red Rose,' then?"

"Aye," she said, and she began to sing, by the last light of the torches.

Polly—Miss Perkins, I mean to say—interrupted her role as Miss Nightingale and stared at the child in wonder.

"Well, scratch my royal bum," Miss Perkins said, "she's got some lungs on 'er. And looks coming on, too. Use 'er, I could, in my musical revue." Vivid with excitement the White Lily was, with the torchlight dancing over her fair face. "I could tell 'em she was my sister, and none's the wiser."

Well, no one would have thought those were sisters. But no audience would find its judgement tested. For I had made a decision of some moment.

"No," I said as firmly as I could, "she will not go on your stage. Miss Raeburn has an engagement in America."

When all were satisfied that the dead were dead and that no more phantoms lurked by the crypts and headstones, we arranged ourselves for our descent to the city. Inspector McLeod was content to leave the corpses where they had fallen until they might be collected in the morning, although he observed they were like to give an awful fright to any gravediggers who took themselves early to work. He admitted he did not know quite how to explain the least of the slaughter to his superiors, but certain enough he was as to who was at fault. "It's bad enow with the Irish a' over the city," he said. "Glasgow is na place for devils frae India."

He had not written the note, nor had he heard of it. And the proof was that he had gone to my room for the very purpose the note described, to speak to me about events in private. When he appeared, Miss Perkins answered and soon engaged him in friendly conversation, for which she had a gift. And when it come out who he was and what he wanted, she remembered what I had said before departing, which deeply alarmed both her and the inspector. Fetching Mr. Adams, who had not been without certain misgivings as to the wisdom of exposing so delicate a party to the night air, among other considerations, they started from the hotel. And met Colonel Tice-Rolley coming in the front door. Which seemed rather a coincidence to me. Although that, too, would have its explanation.

Inspector McLeod knew the grounds and paths, and the torches had been a further aid to my rescuers, after which they heard our clashing blades. The inspector said he had heard me cursing, too. I told him he was mistaken and it must have been Culpeper. But the colonel piped up and said that it was me, indeed, and he never forgot a voice heard on a battlefield. After which he added, with an enthusiasm more fitting to the colonel he had been than to the reverend gentleman he had become, "Wasn't it like old times, though, Jones? Remember how we went over the guns on the flank of the 75th, at Badl-ki-Serai?"

The girl, of course, asked more than once if I really meant to take her to America. And I told her I did. Although I feared I had made a leap that would require some explanation to my beloved wife.

The inspector led the way back down, taking Miss Perkins by the hand to guide her over any treacherous pebbles that might conspire to her embarrassment. Truth be told, she was nimbler than the lot of us, and would have made an excellent subject for close-order drill. But then she was a dancer, and I suppose that even such wanton professions impart some useful skills. Mr. Adams trailed close behind the two of them, watching the inspector and his prancing charge with an attention that put me in mind of a Musselman mother watching out for a daughter come near the marrying age. Although I suspect Mr. Adams had intentions that might not be classed as motherly.

I went down with the colonel, with Fanny gay between us. How lovely it would be for us all, if we could recapture a child's gift of forgetting. You would not have thought her life had been threatened but half an hour before. Perhaps her singing helped her. Mine is a help to me, though I like hymns.

Pressing the shred of petticoat to my cheek with my left hand, I held Fanny's hand with my right. A goodness there is in a child's grip that the rest of us lose with the years. Her other hand had been taken up by the colonel.

"Just like old times," he said again.

"There is true, sir," I told him. "It is a very lion you were."

"And you were as great a devil as ever you were, Jones. Ran 'im through clean as gunner's brass, don't you know? Haven't lost your skills."

And then we both of us paused in our speech, for we had remembered ourselves. Our killing days were meant to be all past. And we had turned to a higher glory than any the soldier seeks.

I am not sure if we felt repentance, or only thought we should.

After a bit, as we approached the little causeway that would lead us back to the world of lamps and order, the colonel said, "You know, Jones . . . under the circumstances . . . and all things considered . . . I should be honored if you were to call me 'Topsy.' "

I near stopped in my tracks. Topsy?

"It's what all my dearest friends call me," the colonel explained.

"Sir," I said, "I . . . I would be honored." Although I frankly did not know if I could make the word come out. In the barracks, we had enjoyed a somewhat different nickname for the colonel, see.

"No," he said. "Not 'sir.' Topsy."

"Yes, sir. I mean . . . Topsy."

"And shall I call you Abel?"

"Yes, sir. Topsy."

"Oh, isn't this grand?" he asked.

As we entered the shadow of the cathedral, with the inspector ahead with Miss Perkins, defying the private ambitions of Mr. Adams and blowing his policeman's whistle to wake the dead, I stopped to give my bothered leg a rest. And I pulled the girl against me. Twas odd. I realized that was the first time I had done that unprovoked. Every other time, she had come to me. Now, she hugged me with the anxiety that is an aspect of a child's love.

As she clutched me and I petted her, I asked the colonel, "Topsy . . . there is a thing I do not understand, see. How is it that you went to my hotel? At such an hour?"

He did not meet my eyes, although I recalled him as a most ferocious staring man. Instead, he looked down at the cobbles and said, "Thought we might have a chat. Old times, and all that." And then he added, "Bit lonely, sometimes, don't you know?"

Seventeen

As promised, the Earl appeared at nine, in a splendid open carriage. He wore a black crepe band around his sleeve, but his disposition had not changed a bit. He greeted me with that little mocking smile.

"Would you like to see a physician before we leave?" he asked me, looking over my injury without the least embarrassment.

I shook my head and did not speak. The truth is that I was cranky. As for my wound, it was slight and I had prevailed upon Miss Perkins to sew me up with needle and thread when we returned to the hotel after the fuss. As I had done myself to a hundred men who did not merit a busy surgeon's attention. Although Miss Perkins's stitching was more regular. Still, my face looked a sight.

"Adams not coming?" the Earl asked, as he turned back to his rig. "I thought he might. I believe he hopes for election to my London club."

But Mr. Adams had not been invited. Not by me, or by anyone. Nor was Inspector McLeod present that morning. And Miss Perkins was still at rest in wholesome sheets.

"Good for you, Jones," the Earl of Thretford said as we mounted his caleche with a porter's unneeded assistance. "I see you've overcome your former dread of me."

Twas queer that he had chosen just that word. Dread. For that is what I felt, not fear. And my dread was not of his person, but of his personage. Arrived at the hotel, he had come in to fetch me himself, perhaps to show the common touch, and the orgy of fawning, if you will pardon my colorful description, and the celebration of servitude that greeted him made it clear that such a one as he would never be charged with a serious crime in any court in Britain. He might have butchered a hundred vestal virgins in front of police headquarters and all would have strained to look the other way, fulfilling their duty by telling any curious passersby to "Move along, move on there, move along."

We crossed the Clyde under skies so blue the smoke could not defeat them. We rode in silence, for he was waiting for me to speak, and I would not oblige him. I hated the way he made me feel so small, and I do not mean in physical stature. He had reduced me to a witless servant, one who had done a great wickedness for him. But let that bide for now. Suffice to say, I had slept little and badly, for I no longer killed with satisfaction.

"Cook says we're to have a splendid day," the Earl mentioned as we passed a grand building surrounded by squalor. "Doesn't keep much of a kitchen, I'm afraid. But I always go to her to ask the weather." Side by side we sat on the wide rear seat, and he leaned an inch toward me, as if to confide. "I think she's something of a witch, actually. In the classic sense. This morning she warned me I was to 'mind my company.' Fresh of her, but I rather like that."

"You *wanted* me to kill your half-brother," I told him.

He shook his head, bemused. "Always so forthright, so blunt."

"You wanted me to kill him. Didn't you?"

He seemed to have no concern for the driver, Hargreaves, who sat in front of us. "Well, that's putting it rather harshly, don't you think?" A brewery wagon passed us, bound for the city. "I will admit I hoped to even the odds. Had you been killed last night, it would have spoiled the effect I have planned for today." His smile expanded ever so slightly. "One doesn't enjoy winning nearly so much if the loser isn't present to make faces." He turned toward me as fully as the carriage allowed. "May not sound very sporting, but I believe it's commonly felt."

"You wanted me to kill him. Because you were through with him. And because he had become a danger to your plans."

The Earl shook his head. "No. You still haven't got it. Though I suspect you will, not terribly long from now. Fact is, I never 'used' him at all. Nor had he endangered my plans the slightest bit. On the contrary, poor, old Cullie rather furthered my designs with his blundering. It was all gloriously inadvertent." He laughed modestly, then resumed his poise. "I will also admit I found him an embarrassment. Too long under the foreign sun, perhaps. Although he always was an excessive sort. Enjoyed killing even more than you do, I think. And when he wasn't killing people, he was duller than David Livingstone. Of late, the poor fellow had grown simply inadmissible. Between us, it would have been quite the best thing had he remained in those distant harems of Mohammed. I should say his lack of judgement claimed his life. You . . . were merely the instrument, Jones. My own role was less than negligible."

"You can speak so. And he was your brother. If only a half by blood."

"We make too much of blood, don't you think? It seems to me a burden on dear, old Britain. The truth is that my mother never should have re-married. It was tasteless of her." He laughed. "A family wit says that my father died in childbirth, instead of my mother. And she hardly waited the year before she re-married. Gave a bad appearance. She might have had her pleasures without the formality. Worse luck, the man was a boor, and I always suspected disease—do I shock you?"

"No," I said. "You disappoint me."

"Oh, dear. I hate to disappoint."

A small bird swooped behind the driver's back and before our faces.

"It is not you yourself who disappoints me," I went on, for I would not have him feel flattered. "Not you in your person. It is with my fellow man that I am disappointed. You . . . are merely the instrument."

"Ah, point to you, Jones. Poor, old Cullie never realized what a delight you can be. Do you, by the way, have many German acquaintances?"

I thought of Mrs. Schutzengel, my dear Washington landlady, then of that disappointing fellow Marx.

"A few," I said, although I could not understand his interest.

He tapped me on the sleeve, as he might have touched a dear and valued friend. "They shall be impressed." His gloved hand gestured toward the slash on my face. "Once that heals, it's going to look like

the very best of duelling scars, I should think. Straight, and not over-
done. The sort received by the man who does not flinch." He tutted.
"Always seemed terribly childish to me, but my Berlin friends insist
that cutting each other up is the most important part of university life.
If you ever *do* go to Prussia, or any of the Germanies, I should be glad
to provide you letters of introduction."

"I do not plan to take me to Prussia. Or to any such places," I told
him in a sulky voice that peeved me as I heard the words come out.

"Ah, but we never know where life may take us, Jones. And though
I am rather a voice in the wilderness at present, I do believe the Ger-
mans capable of extraordinary mischief." His lips curled as if mocking
all of mankind. "Whenever anyone starts in on 'the world as will and
idea,' I suspect it means their idea is to employ that will against the
world. Watch that man Bismarck. He's clever."

"I have no interest in such matters," I said. "I am an American, see.
And we will leave your European wickedness behind."

"Will you, though, Jones? After all, you're here, aren't you? Really,
I'm fascinated by the question of America, and worry that we underestimate the Yankee. As I once underestimated you." He laughed. "But
do remember to let me know should you ever visit Berlin. It would
please me to be of service to you."

That is the thing about gentlemen. They know how to slap you
small with their very courtesy, and they give you no excuse to slap
them back.

We had left the proper confines of the city and travelled a road between villages and smaller settlements growing toward one another as
the city crept toward them. The Clyde appeared on our right when we
passed by fields or marshes, and shipbuilding enterprises littered the
rivers's banks, with swimming boys and fishermen in the intervals between the brisk commotions of hammers and hulls. I felt I saw a world
that was changing forever.

The sun felt lovely, and now the sky was of an unmarred blue, with
the soot and stink of the city left behind us. Twas one of those days at
the end of June when the Lord lets down his blessing upon the earth,
and the leaf trees shimmer in the breeze, and the heart yearns in desire
beyond words.

"I understand your singing tart was splendid last night," the Earl said to pass the time. "McLeod's put it out all over the police offices. I believe he's smitten with her." He gave the floor of the caleche a playful tap with his stick. "I wonder what he'd think of her if he knew she'd had a child and gave it up to an orphan's home? Without a backward glance?"

"That is cruel."

"Not enamored of Miss—Miss Perkins, was it? Not taken by her yourself, are you, Jones?"

"I am a married man. And happy in my—"

"Oh, but that has nothing to do with it! Marriage is simply a refuge—and a false one—for the weak and sentimental. For those afraid to accept their mortal lot."

"And what is our lot?"

"To be alone. First and last. And in between, any time it should matter." He smiled and his lips parted to show stained teeth that did not match the grooming of the rest of him. "How does it go? 'We must endure our going hence, even as our coming hither'? Have I quoted correctly? Really, Jones, you're much too strong a fellow to remain within the confines of marriage indefinitely. Sooner or later, you're bound to 'betray' your wife." He tapped me on the sleeve. "Remember me when you do."

"You do not know me," I muttered.

"But do you know yourself? Isn't that the thing?"

"I know what I must."

"That's a blatant lie. I'm ashamed of you. Tell me, though. What would you do if you didn't have a war? Or some other excuse to go about killing people whenever the mood struck you?"

"I do not need to kill."

"The opium eater insists he needs no opium."

"You do not know."

"No, not if you mean that I've never killed myself. I never have. I told you that. Nor do I intend to. It all sounds rather shabby. Encumbering to the spirit."

"Condemn me, if you wish. It will not move me."

"But I *don't* want to condemn you, don't you see. I simply want you to under*stand*. Look here. Although I don't know all you did in India, I suspect you've never taken a pretty little boy to your bed. No. I can see you haven't. So you don't know what it's like, what pleasures may be enjoyed by both parties. Yet, you're ready to condemn another's pleasures without hesitation."

"You twist things."

"No, I state things. The twisting goes on inside of you, don't you see. The Greeks—"

"We are not Greeks."

"And I find it a pity. We live in an age that flees from every pleasure. I expect that, any day, we shall hear of the invention of a machine with which we may inflict pain upon ourselves in regular doses. The inventor will become the richest man in England. And in America, I suspect."

"Your life is joyless," I told him, "so you imagine others have no joys. And you are loveless, so you see no love in others."

"Oh, that's trite. And inaccurate, by the way." He smiled the finest smile I ever had seen on him. "But here we are. I wonder which of us will have joy of what comes next?"

We had arrived at the gate of a bustling shipyard, perhaps halfway down to Greenock. I had no fears for my person, for half the population of Glasgow knew where I was going that morning, and the Earl had appeared in his open carriage to inform the other half. I knew I would return safely to my hotel. But I did not know if I would go back sound.

I saw it in the distance. A great wooden-sided structure it was, with canvas stretched over the roofbeam, like a vast exaggeration of the tents prepared for an army's winter quarters. Big enough that pavilion was to hold any ship of war I could imagine.

"There it is, Jones," the Earl told me.

"I want to see inside."

"Of course. That's why I've brought you here, after all."

"Is it that the ship is already gone from it? And you intend to show me an empty slip?"

He shook his head. "Too simple. We're playing chess, not checkers."

Then the servility started up again, with the guards at the gates, and workers and foremen, errand boys and lads set to glean scraps, all pulling off their caps and bowing as the Chinese are said to do, and some of them even cheering as we rolled by.

"I pay them a decent wage," the Earl said. "I find my fellow yard-owners simply disgraceful. With their parsimony. If you're looking for your beloved 'evil,' Jones, I rather think you should look there. Among the workers. And those 'dark Satanic mills,' although I do find Blake a bit much. More of a Coleridge man, myself." He tapped my forearm again. "You know, the first concrete act I undertook when I gained my majority was to raise the wages of every man and woman in my employ. And I'm all the richer for it, to be frank. I have the very best workers, and I've never lost a skilled artisan to another man's yard. Or to another's factory. I'm afraid I find most men of business benighted."

We stopped before a second barrier blocking access to the huge wooden hall. There were thrice as many guards about as there were at the front gate, and all were armed with clubs that would split a skull.

"Shall we walk in?" the Earl asked me, getting down himself.

I got me down, if awkwardly. My bothered leg was stiff from the ride, and the knee I had banged on the headstone had swelled as I slept. I must have looked a man of sixty following the Earl across that landscape of piled lumber and steaming pitch-pots. Although, at thirty-four, I judged I was but five or six years his elder.

The Earl paused for a moment, teasing me. "I wonder exactly what you expect," he said.

Of a sudden, I realized that I could not hear a sound from the great wooden structure. Around us, the yard was all banging and scraping and shouts. But it seemed that we had entered a vale of silence.

"Shall we?" the Earl asked. Smiling.

He flicked his hand and a great Scotsman opened a rough-cut door. The fellow looked the sort who had gone swinging claymore swords at walls of English muskets.

"Yer Lardship," he said, with his tam balled in his hand and his big head nodding.

And then we went inside.

The interior was empty.

Twas not that a ship had been built and discharged to the sea. The inside of the pavilion held nothing but dried mud and some grasses withered by the lack of sun. Otherwise, nature had been undisturbed, and I even saw a frog hop into the water at the end of the structure. There was nothing inside that building. And there never had been anything.

After he had allowed me some minutes of wonderment, the Earl said, "I suppose it was a rather shabby trick, after all. Playing with the expectations of everyone this way. But you must admit you brought this on yourselves."

He sighed, as a fellow does at the end of an abundant meal, when his buttons are popping. "Last night, while you were otherwise engaged—and your Minister was looking north to Scotland in expectation—a ship left the Birkenhead yards. You may know her as Number 290 and she sailed as the *Enrica,* but I believe she's to assume the name C.S.S. *Alabama.* Designed as a commerce raider. Oh, don't excite yourself. It's too late now. The ship's beyond territorial waters. She'll be armed before anyone could possibly move this government to act on the high seas."

"But . . ." I said, ". . . there is a law . . . Mr. Adams has filed in the courts . . ."

"As long as those letters of Lord Palmerston's were floating about, the government was not about to incense any party that might possess them. Certain hints were given. And the ship was allowed to go quietly. I've won, you see. All trumps, Jones!"

"But you do not have the letters. And never will."

"Nor do I want them," he said, with a sincere frown. "Can't you understand that, either? I value skill. I don't want to play with two queens when my opponent has none. Anyone can win that sort of game. I won't play unless there's an element of fairness between the parties, of equal risks. Bludgeoning poor old Palmerston with those letters would be rather like hunting rabbits with a battery of artillery. Don't you think it rather better to let people *fear* you have the letters— when you haven't got them at all?"

"You speak of fairness," I said sullenly, "and yet you have your wealth and position to back you."

"And you," he replied almost merrily, "have an entire government behind you. I should say that makes me more David than Goliath, don't you think?"

When I made no reply, he tugged his summer gloves to rights and said, "Shall we return to the rig? I expect you'll want to telegraph London."

And so we began our journey back to Glasgow. I was glum, as you will imagine, but the Earl was in excellent spirits.

"I don't expect you'd allow me to give you lunch?" he asked. "There's a not-bad inn just along here. No?"

"We will use those letters to further the cause of the American Union," I told him grumpily. Twas the start of a little speech I had prepared. But he forestalled me.

"Oh, I don't give a fig what you do with them."

"But you want Richmond to win."

"Couldn't care less."

"You want cotton."

"I'll have it from India."

"Not in time."

"Sooner than I'd have it from the Confederate States, to be honest. I have reasonable expectations, you know."

"But you have supported the slavers. By helping this ship get away. And in New York. You tried—"

"And failed. First match to you, second to me. I shall be interested to see who takes the next bout. Meanwhile, we'll just have to see which way the hounds turn. Why, you may even find I'm on your side, one of these days."

"You will never be on my side."

"That is ungracious."

"Well, if I lack in manners, I do not lack in morals," I told him.

"No," he said, "you've quite the highest morals of any killer I know."

"I am not a killer."

"By the tenets of your own religious profession, you're nothing less. But now I'm being ungracious. And I do think those old Jews should have added a commandment about that, don't you? 'Thou shalt not be a dreary conversationalist.' Or something to that effect. Are you quite certain I can't give you lunch?"

"Our Navy will find your ship," I told him, in the spiteful tones of a child. "And we will sink it."

"But it never was my ship," he said. "I was merely a good angel on its behalf. And as for your own fleet sending it to the bottom, that does sound like a game that's worth the candle. Shall we wait and see?'

I could not find another word, for the truth is I was chastened. And beaten. The Earl was right about that. I wondered if there would be another encounter between us. If such would come, I did not intend to lose again.

"Don't let it get you down too low," the Earl told me. "The truth is, I had better than average luck. When I sent that little tart to your room in London, I had no idea you'd have the letters just then. Or that she'd make off with them. I suspect she'll be had up for thieving, one of these days. Perfect candidate for Australia. Anyway, the effect was sublime. Pomeroy, Disraeli and that lot—and poor old Cullie—were unspeakably confused. And the confusion aided me, you see. All I wished to do was to keep the ball in play until the ship could get off." He clicked his tongue, which I am told is a vulgar habit. But earls can do most anything they like. "Really, it was a great relief when you finally came to Glasgow. I knew I could play you out for the last few days old Laird needed to get the ship off. I should say you did your best, under the circumstances. In fact, you did rather well, given your array of opponents."

"And you never wanted the letters? Not at all? Could you swear to that, if anything is left sacred to you upon which you might take your oath?"

"I fear I would embarrass you, if I laid my hand upon the nearest object I regard as sacred. No, the letters didn't attract me in the least. I should have thought it ungentlemanly to use them, you know."

The queer thing is that the fellow made me believe him.

"Hargreaves," the Earl called in his pleasantest voice, "let the horses show us what they're made of."

Of course, my failure carried an awful price. The *Alabama* played havoc on the seas, and cost our Union fortune after fortune. No man was better pleased than me when Captain Winslow's *Kearsarge* finally sank her off Cherbourg. But that is another tale. And we did not fare so badly in the end. For we won the war, and found ourselves a great power, much to our own astonishment. After Appomattox, when Mr. Adams and Mr. Seward claimed reparations from Her Majesty's Government for the *Alabama*'s rampage of destruction, John Bull paid up.

But all that was in the future, past seas of blood and landscapes soaked in crimson, and I have more to tell. So let that bide.

Henry Adams was so distraught he had quite forgotten Miss Perkins.

"Father's angry," he informed me, as soon as I stepped inside the hotel door. "I mean, the *min*ister's angry. Oh, I do so hate it when he's out of sorts. He's an absolute bear."

"Trouble, is it?" I asked, though I already knew. I would not need to telegraph my message.

"Oh, something about the sailing of a ship." He fished through his clothing. "He wants us to return to London immediately, though I suppose there isn't a train until tomorrow."

I had forgotten how little his father had chosen to tell him. I did not wish to pry into family matters that were no concern of mine, but I thought I understood the elder Mr. Adams. Young Henry had been born to disappoint. He had no gravity, as they say, and I thought him the sort who would mock the efforts of those who had the vigor to attempt what he would not. But let that bide. The failings of the day were mine alone.

He found the message in his waistcoat pocket and handed it over.

"It's addressed to you," he told me blithely. "I didn't think you'd mind if I opened it." Then he added, "He must be terribly angry about something. Not at you, I don't mean. You don't quite figure, if you don't object to my saying so. This must have to do with something important."

The telegram said simply:

AJ. SHIP SAILED. RETURN LONDON. CFA

I raised my eyes from the scrap to young Mr. Adams. "Yes, I know of the matter. But look you. How can you tell he is angry? From four words?"

Certainly, our Minister had a right to be disgruntled. For say what you will, I had failed to stop the Rebels from gaining their vessel. But I hardly could read any rage in that brief message. Curious I was.

"That's it exactly," Henry Adams told me. "Only four words. Whenever he gets terribly angry, he withdraws into that New England shell of his and starts growling about economies. His telegraphic messages get shorter and shorter—to conserve funds, he says—and the shorter the message, the more out of sorts he is. I'd hate to get a one-word message from him." Henry Adams sighed. "He drives us all mad at the legation with his counting pennies—although I suppose I shouldn't tell you that. But, then, after last night, we're comrades in arms, aren't we? He even expects me to use both sides of a piece of paper, and he won't hear of claret at dinner when he's like this."

Now, that sounded eminently sensible to me. But each man has his intricate form of anger. And the son must know its shape.

"Really," young Mr. Adams added, "he'd do better if he didn't insist on being so awfully American at times like this. He needs to take a lesson from the English."

Now, I was angry myself, about a thousand things and more, and I nearly gave that young fellow a proper talking to. For there is nothing finer than being an American. Even if we lack Britain's wealth and power.

"Where is Miss Perkins?" I asked, almost listlessly.

"Oh, that beastly police fellow took her off. He said he needed her written testimony about last night's affair." At that, Mr. Adams worked himself into a smart little huff. "It didn't take him five minutes to copy *mine* down. And *I* didn't have to leave the hotel."

"I'm sure Miss Perkins will give a good account of things."

"I say, Jones." He moved closer to me, as if to force more intimacies upon me, and his tone became more English than the English. "Do you believe Miss Perkins is a flirt?"

"Miss Perkins," I told him, trying to be just to every party, "is a survivor."

"That's really not an answer, you know."

But it was. And it was all the answer I intended to give him. I asked if he might book our journey to London for the next morning, and I excused myself. For I had a number of things I wished to do. And I wanted to walk. Bothered leg or no, a good walk helps.

"Don't worry *too* much," Henry Adams called after me. "Father's rarely severe with minor subordinates. He always takes the blame upon himself. And won't he be surprised to see those letters?"

⌣⌒⌒

Yes. The letters. Whether or not they mattered to the Earl, they would matter a great deal to many another man. I longed to see the elder Mr. Adams wield those letters as an avenging angel might, to lay into the lot of them with the shining sword of justice. Then we would see just who won what in Albion.

I did my duty first, which was to take me up to the police offices. Inspector McLeod had a look at my remembrance of the duel, declared it a "wee scrape," and pronounced me "the luckiest laddie from Largs to Lanark." He was glad to have my explanations down in ink, but even gladder he was when I asked if I might take my leave again. For the inspector had developed a great professional interest in Miss Perkins's abilities with firearms, and he asked her again and again to demonstrate how she had aimed and fired in the night's confusions. During those performances, the inspector stood behind her or beside her, rather closer than I would have judged necessary, and helped her support the tiresome weight of the pistol. Time and again, a great red bush of whiskers brushed her cheek. For her part, Miss Perkins seemed not the least bit incommoded by the inspector's attentions, and her laugh was jolly, not stern, when she told him, "Mind yourself now. And don't you go getting all sly with those 'ands of yours, Jock."

Twas clear her interest in me was much diminished. Which was only proper, I suppose. The truth is that she did seem a bit of a flirt.

Off I went to Sauchiehall Street, and I bought my beloved a shawl still more expensive than the one Miss Perkins had assumed to herself. You will think me wasteful, but I would not give my Mary Myfanwy a gift of lesser value than a music-hall lass got out of me. No matter that the present was unintended.

And I bought a copy of Mr. Dickens's book, *Great Expectations*. I wanted to know what happened to that young Pip. Now you will say, "Jones, you are the wickedest of hypocrites." But I will tell you: We must learn as we go in life, and give new things a chance. Suppose we had never tried the steam engine? Or the gaslamp? Nor did I mean to slight my Gospel readings. Although I was anxious to cut the novel's pages.

I took myself next to the colonel's chapel, where we had arranged to meet. Since I had been otherwise occupied by my duties, he had taken Fanny to see her father buried. The good old fellow had insisted on giving the deceased a bit of ceremony, at his own expense, and I understand he had a piper, too. I pictured him saluting, as he would have done at the graveside, for in the end all soldiers become brothers. The colonel said the girl asked him if he believed her father would be lonely after she had gone to America, and he promised he would go by the cemetery from time to time, if she would write him letters with news to be shared.

The girl was provisionally in the charge of Miss Sharp, who had been equipped with funds to outfit her for our journey, and the colonel and I sat in the front pew of his chapel and talked for hours. Or should I say I talked to him? The summer twilight had begun to settle in before I was done, see. I did not "make a confession" as Catholics do, for I will not go near the Church of Rome. Yet, I almost see a point in how they do things. A fellow likes to get things off his chest.

And we prayed together. For prayer is never wasted. And after the evening service, which was a wonderment of barked commands, devotions and hymns sung true, we shared a final supper. He would bring Fanny to the station in the morning and see us all off.

He seemed old and almost frail as we sat over the leavings of our stewed fruit. Yet, I recalled the lion he had been, strong when other hearts grew weak, and ever defiant. He had seemed to have no more fear of the cholera than he had of enemy lances or *jezails*, and men had died to seek his least approval. His bearing never faltered. Twas men such as Colonel Tice-Rolley who gave Britannia her empire, men who stood upright when others cowered low, and who lived on a mouthful of foreign dust while the timid dined well at home. I noticed that he had spilled a bit of soup on the front of his coat, and his thoughts wandered ever so slightly as he tired.

Cheery he was, though. He even said that he might turn his theological attentions to America, as soon as he had set the Scots to rights. And he seemed to delight each time I called him Topsy.

But the evening had to end, for the train would go early in the morning. And I needed to make certain those letters were secure.

"Rather thought you might have stayed a few more days," he said. "Jolly good to have these little talks, don't you know?"

He was a man long accustomed to directing regiments and judging men. Now he inspired the hearts of congregations. And, always, he enjoyed the world's respect. But admired by a thousand, he wanted a single friend. For the bones of those he had loved were far away, and prayer will warm the soul, but not the flesh. I believe the Earl of Thretford was wrong about most every clever and devious thing he said, but there was more truth than I liked in one of his suggestions: We are too often alone upon this earth. Sometimes I think that loneliness is the greatest of the plagues upon our kind.

But let that bide.

eighteen

"And to think," the elder Mr. Adams said to me, "that I almost declined to pursue those letters." The missives in question lay pale upon his desk. They looked deceptively chaste in the morning light. "Thank God you pressed me to send Henry after them."

"Sorry I am about the ship getting off, sir."

He grimaced. "Yes. Well, I'm sorry, too. My fault, not yours. Lord knows, you've done all that could be expected, and more. It was folly in me to trust to their wretched laws." He made a sound similar to spitting, and our Minister to Britain was hardly a spitting man. "Oh, they talk and talk about honor in this country. But that's all it is: Talk." He glared down at the letters, which his son and I had delivered the night before. "Had I had these a few days ago . . ."

"Sorry I am for that, too," I told him.

He waved a hand dismissively. "Done is done. I don't believe in looking back." He glanced at me. "Thanks to you, we haven't come up so badly, after all. That ship may be gone. But I'll make them pay for it." He picked up a fistful of the Prime Minister's errant communications. Holding them away from his person, as he might have handled a soiled cloth, he turned those wintry eyes upon me full. "I'll promise you one thing, Major. That injury to your face wasn't suffered in vain. The present government isn't going to declare war on the United States any time soon, nor will they lay one more finger upon our affairs." His voice was firm and inspiring. Yet, his stare broke, as if weakened from within. "They've lied to me. About that ship. I had Earl Russell's word." He lowered his eyes to the letters. "But I don't think they'll lie to me again."

"You said, sir . . . or implied . . . that gentlemen were allowed to lie in the practice of diplomacy."

"Not when they give their personal word. And Lord John gave me his."

Well, that seemed like splitting hairs to me, but I am not a diplomat. To me, a lie is a lie, and that is that. I regretted those that I had told myself, regretting the many necessities my unexpected profession had imposed upon me. I wished to be home with my wife, and my son, and my ledgers. But glad I was that Mr. Adams felt so great a confidence that we would not find ourselves at war with Her Majesty.

Our Minister gave the letters a tap. "These are more timely than you know, Jones. We've missed the ship, although I scorched both Russell and Lyons after I found out. But tonight that fellow Lindsay's to give a grand speech in the House encouraging the government to interfere in our war. In the 'interests of humanity.' And the interests of Manchester, of course." He almost smiled, although his face was not made for that exercise. "I intend to send a note to Lord John. Requesting a personal interview with the Prime Minister, before tonight's session opens." A smile fought to crack the marble of his face. "My note will leave the Foreign Secretary in little doubt as to why I wish to present my respects to Lord Palmerston." He gave me a look at his arctic visage full on, as if rehearsing the effect he would have upon Old Pam, and added, "I would like you to accompany me. It will unsettle Palmerston all the more."

He lapsed into a bit of quiet and let his eyes graze through a few of the letters. Yes, marble is capable of a blush, and Mr. Adams turned as red as a strawberry. Of a sudden, he gave out a deep breath and roused himself from his study.

"Lord Palmerston," he said solemnly, as if his sense of order had been ravaged, "appears to be an innovator in the development of the human body's mechanics." He brushed a hand through the white fringe of hair that wrapped round his reddened pate. "Astonishing, given the man's years."

No doubt I was mistaken, but I almost thought that last remark sounded hopeful.

"Mr. Adams, sir?"

He remembered my presence.

"Although it is not my place to ask favors . . ."

"What is it, Major Jones?"

"It is a personal matter, see. There is an orphan girl I have brought from Glasgow."

"That pretty little thing Moran shared his apple with?"

I nodded. "I intend to take her with me to America."

"A relation?"

"No, sir. More of an accident, see. But resolved I am to take her with me. To give her a decent chance."

"That's very noble of you."

I shook my head in denial. "Noble it is not. I *want* to take her with me, see. To do some good, after doing so much harm." I almost began to explain my understanding of a Christian's duty, but thought better of it. Our Minister would have things to do—as I did myself—and he did not need a sermon from the likes of me.

"I don't see that you've done all that much harm," Mr. Adams said. Then his head gave the slightest wobble, as if he had seen into the thing a little way. "A man's conscience is a curious thing," he said. "But what was the favor?"

"Might you keep her with you, sir? For a few days only? Until matters are settled? It would not be proper for me to have a girl of, perhaps, thirteen by me in a hotel. And her with no tie of blood, see."

He frowned, and I feared he would deny me. But he only asked, "Is she clean? She looks clean. But is she? Mrs. Adams is a perfect tyrant on the subject."

"She has been bathed, sir."

His head went into that slight wobble again. "Well, I don't see how I can refuse you. Or why I should. Especially, given all you've done for us."

"Thank you, sir. She's a good girl, and will give no trouble."

I only hoped she would not run away in an effort to seek me out at my hotel. Nor did I want her billeted with the White Lily of Kent, who had offered time and again to take the girl to her. I fear Miss Perkins was proving no better than she should be, although I do not mean that ungratefully. Twas only that she had spent the journey back to London showering me with attentions I thought insincere. I believe she did it to bedevil young Mr. Adams. And Fanny was not above a bit of jealousy herself, I had found. The child had a way of flaring her nostrils and setting her eyes that, surrounded with those swirls of auburn hair, gave her the look of a warrior queen out of Ossian. A lesser spirit than that of Miss Perkins would have crumpled under her glare.

With a minor straightening of his shoulders, Mr. Adams altered the mood in the room. It is a trick the great have to let us know when our time has come to leave them.

"I will expect you at five," our Minister told me. "Until then, I think you should have a well-earned rest—didn't you mention you wanted to visit the International Exhibition? Perhaps you could take your orphan girl along?"

"I cannot," I told him. "Tomorrow, perhaps. If you will allow me. First, there is a last thing I must do."

Men know when they are caught. When I appeared at the door of his cubbyhole office in Bow Street, Inspector Wilkie turned white as a flag of surrender.

"May I come in, then?" I asked him.

When he proved incapable of reply, I stepped into the tiny room, which was taller from floor to ceiling than it was deep or wide. It smelled of a bad dinner badly digested. The foul air seemed to make my cut burn under its plaster, and the stitches felt as if they hoped to rend themselves. Discomfort does not improve demeanor.

"I think I will shut the door behind me," I told him. "For I do not want your colleagues to arrest you before we are finished."

"I 'asn't got no idea what you're—"

"Will they hang you under English law?" I asked him. "Or will you have a hope of transportation?"

Doubtless, the wild Russians or stoical Eskimaux learn to distinguish between a hundred shades of white in their snow-swept lands, and even I had eyes to tell that Wilkie had gone distinctly paler than he had been not five seconds before.

"May I sit down?" I asked him. Although I recalled the wooden chair before his desk as uncomfortable, perhaps to worry criminals into confessions. We should have exchanged our seats, if such was the case.

I sat me down and looked across the desk at him. Those bushes of black whiskers seemed to wilt, and his eyes were dreadful.

"You made a very great fool of me," I told him. "Although I did my bit to help you along, and there is true. I should have seen it earlier, of course. But it is a weakness of mine to put faith in authority, and to expect better of a policeman. You must have thought I guessed the truth a dozen times, at least." I smiled at my own clumsiness. "That must have alarmed you. Surprised I am you did not try to have me killed."

"I ain't never killed a single—"

"No," I waved his concern away, "the murderers themselves are dead. Most, if not all of them. I do not think you have the liver for murder, Inspector Wilkie. But I believe the law will hang an accomplice, if it cannot apprehend the principal."

"I never 'as meant to—"

"I wondered how they did it all so artfully, guiding me to each next place exactly on their schedule. Leading me by the hand, as it were." I shook my head at myself, not at him. "I should have seen it that second morning, when you accompanied me to the fish-market—though not until the eel-man was safely dead. That other police fellow from within the City Mile as much as told me you had gone rotten, though he did not know it himself. When he complained of the 'Great Wilkie out of the West,' who had invaded his own territory without right. First to assume control of a corpse turned up in a basket of eels, then to bring along an American officer who could have gone to Billingsgate perfectly well on his own." I fixed my eyes upon the inspector's, and his failed to withstand my scrutiny. "Only the influence of the rich and powerful could have inspired your superiors to such a bending of the rules—oh, I don't believe they knew what you were about, not at all. But when the mighty hint at the desirability of so slight a thing as a temporary grant of greater freedom to a trusted inspector, one who's needed to smooth over some diplomatic unpleasantness, well . . ."

I shifted my behind, begging your pardon, for the chair was of miserable construction. "There was so much evidence in front of my nose. A blinded fool I was. When I raised the issue of young Pomeroy's attendance at the morgue, suggesting that he might have given information to the murderers, you defended him as above suspicion. Because he was one of the directors of your secret career. By the by, did the boy hang himself? Or did a greater power help him to it? No matter, I suppose. No matter to me, at least."

I had talked myself into a bitterness. "You it was who took me everywhere they told you I must go, from the Seven Dials to the lawns of Regent's Park." I mused for a moment. "I should have seen it there, if not before. An old police veteran such as yourself would not have been quite so shocked at the sight of that poor boy on the grass, unless there was more to it. Not a man with your great knowledge of the 'criminal class amongst us.'" I remembered the sight of that child all too well. "Now, I will credit you with this—you had not signed on for murder in the beginning, and you were soon frightened at the depths into which you had cast yourself. Then you saw the remains of that boy, and you feared the same could happen to your own children if you placed one foot awry—what are their names again? The names of your son and daughter?" I had not forgotten, but I wanted to hear him speak. For I knew those names would burn his lips like fire.

"Albert," he said, in a voice that might have come from a dead man. "And Alice."

"Your shock was far too great to be explained. Unless you yourself had something precious to lose. And I will credit you again—you tried to withdraw from the business after that." I looked at him as coldly as ever I have looked at a man. "They should have killed you then, before you could blunder so badly."

"I never knew, I swear. I never knew it was to be murder and the like. I never would 'ave—"

"Quiet you, until I finish. You know a Welshman likes to talk, and happy you were to listen to me before. To listen when I was telling you things you wanted to hear. So that you could relay them to Culpeper and the Pomeroys and the rest of them. Listen, and we will shortly make an end of things. Although I think you would benefit from patience. For when I am done, then you will be done, too."

He began to rock back and forth in his chair, gently but with great regularity, as I have seen soldiers do who have lost their wits in battle.

"Their mistake was asking you to do so much, while telling you too little. You did not know the importance of the letters. And you did not know of the involvement of Betty Green. You were not meant to go with me to the house in Lambeth, see, for you had begged them to let you off any further adventures and they decided to do so—doubtless to kill you later and keep things tidy. They cut you out in a moment, for they worried that you had weakened and might be a danger, and they led me along themselves, with hints and teasings from young Pomeroy, then from Disraeli. Had they tied me up and carried me to Lambeth to present me to 'Mrs. Sarah Pomeroy, the Hungarian Jewess,' they could not have been more sure of my going to find her. But *you* did not know of that part of the scheme. When I asked you to go with me, it come at you all of a sudden, and you feared you would be punished if you let me go off unattended. For they had relied on my own need of some secrecy, and saw no reason why I would ask you to go along. But you went, indeed. It is always the way of such things, see. The evil comes out, for it cannot be tied up in a neat little parcel. And you told me a thing I would never have learned on my own, that the fabled Hungarian Jewess was really Betty Green. Late of a house in Lisle Street, was it not?"

"You don't understand. You can't—"

"I understand that you will never see your children again. Whether you hang, or are condemned to Australia."

"But I did it for them, don't you see, Major? If only—"

"Perhaps they will be better off in an orphans' home. Or would relatives take them?"

"*Please.* You don't understand. You're off to your America again. But what 'ope 'ave my Albert and my Alice? What 'ope 'ave I got? When I ain't going no 'igher in my profession, because proper gents are brought in and placed above us. Gents what don't know a thing about police doings, who never 'ad to work for their—"

"Not so long ago, you seemed to have a very high regard for gentlemen. Even for gentlemen who were criminals."

"A bloke don't 'ave no chance 'ere, don't you see?"

"And then, how glad you were to be rid of me, Inspector Wilkie. You didn't even want me to remain in London long enough to give my testimony about a boy's hand in my bed, or to question me as to what I might have known about a series of brutal murders. The Good Lord knows I should have seen that was wrong. But I had taken the lure, and would not see what did not support my own prejudices. You have made a very great fool of me. Almost as great as I have made of myself."

"Please, sir. I'll do anything. You couldn't name me a thing what I wouldn't do."

I let him suffer a bit longer. For he deserved no less. Then I did a thing I never thought I would do upon this earth. I offered a criminal a chance to evade the law. On conditions I knew that he would find an immeasurable relief.

Now, you will say: "Again, you are a hypocrite, Jones. For you make such a to-do about justice and order." But I will tell you: We were at war. At war with our own brothers. And I had lost my taste for British justice. The justice that I wanted was a Union victory. And I had seen a way to further our cause.

I did not like it. But this world is not so simple as I wish it. I want to be a good man and a Christian. But every morning the struggle begins again.

I told Wilkie I would hold my evidence back for the present, then leave the details in the care of Mr. Adams. To whom the inspector was to report every incident rising to the attention of the Metropolitan Police that might in any way affect the United States, have to do with Americans—especially the Confederate variety—or involve anyone who even whispered the word "America." I fear it brought a deluge of reports to poor Mr. Adams over the next several years, but I like to think he found a few of them useful.

That evening I got a lesson in diplomacy that I wish had not involved such gross indecencies. For it deserved a page in all our history books.

When Mr. Adams and I arrived at Parliament, Lord John Russell, the Foreign Secretary, was waiting in the first lobby to greet us. He looked like a man who had eaten poisoned fruit, if you will pardon the implication.

Mr. Adams, for his part, was in the best of spirits. Which meant that his face had softened from granite to oak.

"How kind of you to meet me, Your Lordship," Mr. Adams said. "And even kinder of Lord Palmerston to receive me with so little delay."

"I assure you," Earl Russell told him, "the Prime Minister has only the very highest regard for Your Excellency. Indeed, he was honored by the prospect of your call."

For all his fine upbringing, Lord Russell could not quite keep his eyes off the leather portfolio Mr. Adams carried.

Now, I will tell you the queerest thing: Mr. Adams and Lord Russell were so alike in visage and stature that they might have been close brothers, if not twins. They even shared similar expanses of round, pink scalp when they tipped their hats. And I understand they did become great friends as time marched on. But friendship was not the foremost concern that evening.

Lord Russell ignored my presence, nor did Mr. Adams trouble to introduce me. I think he enjoyed the lack of clarity in my situation. As for the Englishman's opinion, I suppose the plaster upon my face and the damage my new suit had suffered in Glasgow did not recommend me to his highest opinion.

"Would you, please?" the Foreign Secretary said to our Minister, gesturing that they might go side by side.

I brought up the rear. From which position I marked the curious glances the two of them got as we crossed the great lobby and found our way to a staircase. The Foreign Secretary led us to an intimate smoking salon, in which a decrepit fellow sat alone. I recognized Lord Palmerston, "Old Pam." Small he was, and must always have been so, and he had more wrinkles than the seat of an Irishman's trousers. The sun of age had browned him, and he sat bent, as if an invisible bully were pressing his shoulders toward his knees. His teeth looked artificial, even from a distance, and I suspected that he was not the first of God's creatures to wear the hair that graced his august head. Like Mr. Seward, he had a nose the courteous would describe as Roman, though ailments had gnawed it a bit. He might have been on holiday from the tomb. Yet, he sprang up at the sight of Mr. Adams, agile as a man in the prime of life. He looked a relic of a bygone era, but perhaps of one that had been more enthusiastic about living. Not that I fault our age's preference for decorum.

"My dear, *dear* Mr. Adams! What a notable pleasure to see you again!" As he spoke, he nodded to Lord Russell, who promptly faded out the door, leaving the three of us alone. In a lingering miasma of Havanas.

Lord Palmerston turned an expectant face to me.

"May I present Major Jones, Your Lordship? He's been visiting our legation. The major's responsible for the opportune recovery of your effects."

I already knew Mr. Adams well enough to understand what he was about. He was no man for social frivolities or wasting time, and he had a knack for coming to the point. I wonder if, in New England, people have conversations of more than a dozen words at a time?

The Prime Minister's face shifted from an artifice of delight through a brief glimpse of anger to a mask of accommodation.

"But my dear Mr. Adams. I haven't asked you to sit down. How unforgivable of me!"

"I understand Your Lordship has business in the House this evening. I wouldn't dream of detaining you. My business won't take a moment."

I watched as Old Pam struggled to keep up that pleasant mask. Only half a century and more in politics could have given him the necessary training.

"Then let us address the issue, Mr. Adams. I believe you have come here tonight to make a request. Perhaps two requests. Or even more. I think you might know that the degree of friendship I feel toward your person, as well as to your American nation, is such that I am inclined to grant any requests to the best of my abilities."

I expected Mr. Adams to tear into the old rascal then. To give him what he had coming, and to lecture him about warships that were no better than pirates, and contraband, and threats of all descriptions. But that was when I got my lesson, for Mr. Adams had mastered his trade as few other men have done.

"Not at all, Your Lordship!" he said, in a voice at once wronged and almost jovial. "There must have been some error of communication. I only wished to return certain properties to you that accident carried into my possession. I could not think of associating requests or conditions with such a matter."

He held out the leather portfolio.

He trumped Palmerston, our Minister did! Old Pam may have been a master of the political arena, but he could not quite hide his astonishment in that first spatter of seconds. His mouth hung open as if he might start drooling.

But he took the pouch of letters, quick as a cat.

Then the Prime Minister got the beauty of it. I suppose he liked a good game, too. And he saw well enough that, had Mr. Adams strutted in with demands, he would have owed him nothing more, but now he was deeply in our Minister's debt.

"I have always found it a pleasure to deal with American gentlemen," Lord Palmerston told Mr. Adams. "Thus, it gratifies me to know that our future relations shall be entirely cordial, despite any minor problems that might annoy us. I speak of surmountable problems, sir. Of trivialities. Have I told you of the first time I met your father?"

I expected Mr. Adams to lead me into the visitor's gallery, so that we might hear what that Lindsay fellow had to say. Instead, our Minister took me by the arm and turned us toward the great doors that would let us back out into London.

"But Mr. Lindsay, sir . . ."

"Oh, I think we might let the Gentleman from Sunderland have his little say. Better to display our confidence by being absent. We'll read what he has to say in *The Times* on Monday."

We found we could not walk arm in arm, because of my hampered gait and the difference in our heights. But after we had come apart, our Minister showed no interest in the cab rank.

"I'm feeling absolutely splendid," he told me, although his face still looked as grave as a burial. "Major Jones, would you do me the honor of taking a turn with me? I thought we might stroll into Westminster. Or have a look at the progress on the new bridge."

We managed a pace or two, then Mr. Adams nodded to himself. "I wonder if the English won't have some benefit from all this themselves? They're apt at learning their lessons." His chin drew into his whiskers. "I doubt we shall ever see another such sordid affair in the British government."

The evening air was soft and not too grimy, and the city had slowed enough to allow a man a bit of peace. I was delighted to walk with him, of course. And proud. For I felt I had just witnessed a scene of greatness.

When we turned the corner by the great clock tower, he produced something from his pocket and held it out, closed in his fist.

"I thought you might have this," he told me. "As a remembrance. A pleasanter remembrance, I hope, than that injury to your face."

It was a plain brass watch. I knew what I would see when I opened its lid: Another reminder still, of a bygone life.

Glad I was that he gave me the watch, for it also gave me an opening. I had a thing to ask him, and it was not entirely delicate. But I am one for knowing each detail.

"Mr. Adams, sir. Begging your pardon. But there is a question I have."

"Yes?"

"It may offend you."

He gave me a curious look. "I believe I want to hear any question you feel obliged to ask. Especially one you fear might offend me."

"Mr. Adams, did you know Mr. Campbell had betrayed your trust?"

"Yes."

"And . . . was it you who then hinted that he had, in turn, betrayed those to whom he had betrayed you?"

"That's more than one question. But I'll answer it. Yes. I let the matter slip when I was talking to Moran in my own dining room. Poor Moran hadn't the least idea what I was talking about, but the butler knew."

"And did you expect them to murder him?"

"Yes. But you understand me, Major Jones. We are at war. And it is a war we must win. We cannot be gentle with traitors."

We passed a slump of aged walls, where new buildings crowded the old.

"You do understand. Don't you?" he asked.

"Yes, sir. I wish I did not. But I do."

"Are you perturbed that I kept the information from you? About Campbell being a traitor?"

"No, sir. I mean, yes. A bit."

"I did not want to prejudice your views, you see. And, frankly, you were unknown to me. Despite the recommendations from Washington. Having once been betrayed, and by a man of the cloth . . . I thought I should watch you for a little while."

Which was only sensible.

"And Mr. Disraeli? There will be no cost to him for all these doings?"

"Mr. Disraeli will do what it takes to survive. He is a spider whom men mistake for a moth."

"And Mr. Pomeroy? The elder?"

"You're full of questions tonight," he said, but not without some slight tone of amusement. Then he sobered his voice again. "Mr. Pomeroy has retired to the country, where I expect him to remain for some time. I believe his penalties have been sufficient. His only son is dead. And the sister was lost before him." He traced the tip of his walking stick across the pavement. "All because of this appetite for titles. I think perhaps the most important thing my grandfather's generation did for us was to avoid any sort of hereditary titles or patents of nobility. Although I don't think some of the Virginians would have minded a duke or two."

We had turned toward the river. The unfinished span of the bridge behind Parliament loomed in the deepening twilight.

"You've done a remarkable job, Major Jones. I won't forget it. And I'll see that Washington knows, of course."

"That is unnecessary, sir," I told him, though it bordered on a lie. For who among us does not like a bit of praise and respect when we do our best? Even when the results are sadly flawed?

"Necessary or not, I am indebted to you, and an Adams pays his debts." He seemed about to say something else, and I had an uncanny sense that it had to do with his son. But we had approached the bridge and Mr. Adams recognized a figure in the shadows. Someone who did not merit a share in our conversation.

It took me a moment to place the fellow, for he sat there in the gloaming half hidden by a sketching tablet. Then I fixed him as the man I had seen making a drawing on the docks behind the fish market.

"Ah, Mr. Whistler!" our Minister said. "My congratulations on the success of your 'Woman in White.' "

The young fellow was as surly as he was slender. A slouching man in a slouch hat he was. He did not even rise to greet our Minister.

" 'Evening, Adams. Thanks, I s'pose. But she ain't called 'The Woman in White.' That's all nonsense the gallery made up. Provoked by the success of that Collins book. Which is a piece of rubbish, I might add. My painting's titled 'The White Girl.' "

"Then I congratulate you on the success of 'The White Girl,' Mr. Whistler. All London is at your feet."

"I don't know," the artist said. "I wonder if I shouldn't just go back to Paris."

"London's loss," Mr. Adams told him, with a grim little ghost of a smile, "would be the gain of all France."

Mr. Whistler offered to do a character study of my head, for he said I might serve for a dust-man in a painting he was contemplating, but I declined his generosity.

We bid one another *adoo,* and Mr. Adams and I turned back toward Westminster Abbey, which wore a fresh garland of gaslamps.

"Impossible fellow," Mr. Adams confided. "Entire family are Confederate sympathizers, I understand. I'm told his mother's an insufferable Rebel." He made a sound surprisingly like a snort. "If he ever does a portrait of her, he'll have to limit his palette to shades of gray. Know anything about painting, Major Jones?"

"No, sir."

"Neither do I. Henry seems to know quite a bit, though. Had part of his education on the Continent . . . which may not have been the very best idea. Anyway, he doesn't think young Whistler will amount to much. Says his work looks like paint pots hurled at a canvas. Of course, with Henry one never knows if it's actually his own view one hears, or if he's echoing his London acquaintances."

We walked a bit, and my thoughts ached toward home of a sudden. London was a fine city, in its way, but my heart was across the ocean in dear, old Pottsville. I hoped the war would end soon. Meanwhile, I would content myself with a voyage back to our shores. With a new addition to our family, of whom I hoped my wife would not disapprove.

A carriage clattered past, drawn by high-stepping grays.

"Speaking of Henry," Mr. Adams said, with what sounded suspiciously like a paternal sigh, "I find myself dismayed. May I solicit your advice, Major Jones? Given that you're not entirely removed from the situation?"

"Yes, sir. Certainly, sir. Of course, sir."

"It seems that Henry has grown enamored of the Perkins woman. Who, frankly, might not prove suitable for him in every respect. Not least in regard to her . . . greater experience of the world, let us say. I worry that Henry may do something foolish." He stopped in the middle of the pavement to face me, with all a father's worry beleaguering his face. "You enjoy some acquaintance with Miss Perkins, I believe. What would you recommend I do?"

I pondered the matter for a bit, since I wanted to be helpful, and the great clock of Parliament began to strike the hour. Loud as the sound of guns it was.

When the tolling was done, I said, "Why not introduce Miss Perkins to Lord Palmerston?"

Twas the second time I heard Mr. Adams laugh out loud.

The adventures of Abel Jones will continue in:

The Bold Sons of Erin

Facts and Debts

*F*un is fun, but facts are facts. While this story is not true, I have sought to be true to history in every detail, save three. A historical novel, if written successfully, can fill in the human gaps left by the historian's footnotes, but the novelist should be as faithful as the historian to the setting. Thus, I feel obliged to expose the liberties I have taken.

First, the vessel that would take the name *Alabama* sailed from the Birkenhead yards at the end of July, not at the end of June, 1862.

Second, Inspector Wilkie, of the Metropolitan Police, would not have enjoyed the freedom of action allowed him in this book, nor were the London police at their best in 1862. The rigorous, slightly bumbling bloodhound familiar to us from countless films and period novels is really a late-Victorian and Edwardian type. Commissioner E.Y.W. Henderson, KCB, only began much-needed professional reforms (and allowed the police to grow mustaches and beards; previously, Wilkie's side-whiskers had been the limit) after taking office in 1869, and the famous Scotland Yard detective really appears with the development of the Criminal Investigation Division in 1878. Mid-Victorian writers created skilled detectives in their fiction well before plain-clothes sleuths were accepted members of the London force, an early example of life imitating art.

Lastly, I made one small alteration to the practices of the nineteenth-century House of Commons . . . but I will leave that as a riddle for Anglophile readers.

Any other errors of detail are unintentional, and represent a failure on the part of the author.

I must say a few words on sources, from sheer guilt at profiting so richly from the work of other men and women. Beyond a lifetime's interest in the literature of the period, I have been lucky enough to visit London many times since I first checked into a threadbare hotel off Baker Street in 1970, as a young, aspiring and very bad musician (so bad my only recourse was to join the Army). But the London we visit today is a very different city from the London of 1862.

The quarter century from about 1850 on brought enormous changes to the London cityscape, as more rail lines cut through, slums were demolished, the Embankment was constructed, bridges were replaced, the first underground tunnels were dug for horse-drawn buses, and the elders of the unique patchwork that is London began, reluctantly, to pay a bit of attention to sanitation (it didn't take immediately). In 1862, London was struggling out of its antique cocoon to become the first metropolis of the age, leaving the city of Dickens behind to become the city of Trollope. The mid-to-late Victorian period did more to give us the London we know than did the Great Fire, Christopher Wren, and the Georgian delight in building combined. It changed the scope and scale of urban life forever, much as the new suburbs of North America are doing today.

There are, literally, countless sources on the London of that period, not all of them in agreement. Of the many works consulted (and looted shamelessly), I must mention the two I found most valuable. First, *The Times,* so long the greatest newspaper in the world and now sadly eclipsed by a number of American and Continental papers, was a magnificent resource, offering everything from railway timetables to lengthy reports of Parliamentary speeches (their eloquence a painful reminder of a time when brilliant men still thought politics worth the trouble). The second source was the work of the incomparable (that is the only appropriate adjective) recorder of urban life, Henry Mayhew, whose *London Labour and the London Poor* appeared in book form in 1851. No other journalist or scholar has yet rivaled Mayhew's description of the men, women and affiliations that compose a working city. While a number of things cited by Mayhew changed between 1851 and 1862—some slums were cleared, a new building was constructed for the Billingsgate Fish Market (at the same location) and the adjoining docks were pushed back, and some of the odder professions dwindled—Mayhew remains the first source and inspiration for any-one who wishes to write about mid-nineteenth-century London. I have plundered his work with gratitude.

As to Glasgow, there are many fine works available, but not one is a substitute for walking that resilient city's streets. Today's Glasgow is a vivid, muscular, spirited place, a sort of Chicago-on-the-Clyde, with hustle and great character. It has survived dreadful social (and archi-tectural) experiments with a robust sense of humor. It deserves as many visitors as Edinburgh, its prettier, shallower sister. Specific refer-ence works worth recommending are *The Second City* by C. A. Oak-ley; *Glasgow, The Forming of a City,* edited by Peter Reed; *Glasgow's Doctor, a biography of James Burn Russell, 1837–1904,* by Edna Robertson; and, above all, the magnificent period photographs of Thomas Annan, recently collected by James McCarroll under the title *Glasgow Victoriana.*

For those who like their Civil War undiluted, I would recommend several works on the secret struggle for Britain's favors and on the un-derappreciated, vital Charles Francis Adams. The most useful are: *The Journal of Benjamin Moran, 1857–1865,* edited by Wallace and Gilles-pie; *Charles Francis Adams,* by Martin R. Duberman; *Great Britain and the American Civil War,* by E. D. Adams; *The Secret Service of the Confederate States in Europe,* by James D. Bulloch; and *Confederate Finance and Purchasing in Great Britain,* by Richard I. Lester. *The Ed-ucation of Henry Adams,* written in the third person by and about Henry Adams, is an acquired taste that I have failed to acquire. On Disraeli and Gladstone, there are numerous biographies available, but fewer on Palmerston, who was, to me, the most interesting of the lot. Old Pam may be criticized for a hundred things he did or failed to do, but he was never afraid to enjoy the banquet life spreads before us.

Lastly, I must thank a few of the living. My editor, Jennifer Fisher, though merciless as only those of auburn hair can be, is patient, dili-gent, wise and incisive. Carmen Capalbo, the copy editor on this se-ries, would have been accorded "hero worker" status in the old Soviet Union; the copy editor's job is always vital and too often unremarked. And then there is Sara Hanks, an English rose transplanted wonder-fully to the soil of America, who took time from the thorny legal pro-fession to save me what embarrassment she could by weeding misshapen speech and improper terms from these pages. Remaining errors of nineteenth-century English usage lie at my feet alone. Sara's efforts were as gracious as they were helpful, and she never told me directly that I was a fool (Lonnie, you done pretty good for a boy from Arkansas).

—Owen Parry

Presented to:

By:

Date:

Occasion:

Warner Books Edition
Copyright © 2001 by Joyce Meyer
Life In The Word, Inc.
P.O. Box 655
Fenton, Missouri 63026
All rights reserved.

Warner Faith

Time Warner Book Group
1271 Avenue of the Americas, New York, NY 10020
Visit our Web site at www.twbookmark.com.

Warner Faith® and the Warner Faith Logo are trademarks of Time Warner Book Group Inc.

Printed in China

First Warner Faith Edition: October 2002
10 9 8 7 6 5

ISBN: 0-446-53210-X
LCCN: 2002110837

THE JOY OF
BELIEVING PRAYER

Deepen Your Friendship With God

JOYCE MEYER

WARNER
Faith®

NEW YORK   BOSTON   NASHVILLE

$\mathscr{C}$ONTENTS

A SIMPLE, BELIEVING PRAYER

*If we don't pray, the best
thing that can happen is
nothing, so that things will
stay the way they are,
which is frightening
enough in itself. We all
need change, and the way
to get it is through prayer.*

GOD'S WORD FOR YOU

And when you pray, do not heap up phrases (multiply words, repeating the same ones over and over) as the Gentiles do, for they think they will be heard for their much speaking. [I Kings 18:25-29.]

MATTHEW 6:7

one

SIMPLE, BELIEVING PRAYER

or many years I was dissatisfied with my prayer life. I was committed to praying every morning, but I always felt something was missing. I finally asked God what was wrong, and He responded in my heart by saying, "Joyce, you don't feel that your prayers are good enough." I was not enjoying prayer because I had no confidence that my prayers were acceptable.

Too often we get caught up in our own works concerning prayer. Sometimes we try to pray so long, loud, or fancy that we lose sight of the fact that prayer is simply conversation with God. The length or loudness or eloquence of our prayer is not the issue. It is the sincerity of our heart and the confidence that God hears and will answer us that is important.

We must develop the confidence that even if we simply say, "God help me," He hears and will answer. We can depend on God to be faithful to do what we have asked Him to do as long as our request is in accordance with His will. We should know that He wants to help us because He is our Helper (Hebrews 13:6).

Simple, believing prayer comes straight out of the heart and goes straight to the heart of God.

GOD'S WORD FOR YOU

Two men went up into the temple [enclosure] to pray, the one a Pharisee and the other a tax collector.

The Pharisee took his stand ostentatiously and began to pray thus before and with himself: God, I thank You that I am not like the rest of men—extortioners (robbers), swindlers [unrighteous in heart and life], adulterers—or even like this tax collector here.

I fast twice a week; I give tithes of all that I gain.

But the tax collector, [merely] standing at a distance, would not even lift up his eyes to heaven, but kept striking his breast, saying, O God, be favorable (be gracious, be merciful) to me, the especially wicked sinner that I am!

I tell you, this man went down to his home justified (forgiven and made upright and in right standing with God), rather than the other man; for everyone who exalts himself will be humbled, but he who humbles himself will be exalted.

LUKE 18:10-14

HUMBLE PRAYER

For prayer to be sincere, it must come from a humble heart. In this lesson on prayer taught by Jesus Himself, we see that the Pharisee prayed "ostentatiously," meaning that he prayed pretentiously, making an extravagant outward show. There was nothing secret or even sincere about his prayer. It even says that he prayed "before and with himself." In other words, his prayers never got two inches away from himself; he was all caught up in what *he* was doing.

The second man in the story, a despised tax collector and a "wicked sinner" in most people's eyes, humbled himself, bowed his head, and quietly, with humility, asked God to help him. In response to his sincere, humble prayer, a lifetime of sin was wiped away in a moment. This is the power of simple, believing prayer.

Build your faith on the fact that humble, believing prayer is powerful. Believe that you can pray anywhere, anytime, about anything. Believe that your prayers don't have to be perfect or eloquent or long. Keep them simple and full of faith.

We receive the grace of God by humbling ourselves
before Him, casting all our cares upon Him,
and trusting Him to take care of them
as He has promised in His Word.

11

GOD'S WORD FOR YOU

And I tell you, you are Peter [Greek, Petros—a large piece of rock], and on this rock [Greek, petra—a huge rock like Gibraltar] I will build My church, and the gates of Hades (the powers of the infernal region) shall not overpower it [or be strong to its detriment or hold out against it].

I will give you the keys of the kingdom of heaven; and whatever you bind (declare to be improper and unlawful) on earth must be what is already bound in heaven; and whatever you loose (declare lawful) on earth must be what is already loosed in heaven. [Isa. 22:22.]

MATTHEW 16:18-19

AUTHORITY THROUGH PRAYER

Since we are not only physical creatures but spiritual beings as well, we are able to stand in the physical realm and affect the spiritual realm. This is a very definite privilege and advantage. We can go into the spiritual realm through prayer and bring about action that will cause change in a situation. *God is a Spirit* . . . (John 4:24), and every answer we need to every situation is with Him.

Jesus told Peter that He would give him the keys of the Kingdom of heaven. Keys unlock doors, and I believe those keys (at least in part) can represent various types of prayer. Jesus went on to teach Peter about the power of binding and loosing, which operates on the same spiritual principle.

Jesus was also speaking to Peter about the power of faith in verse 18, and we know that one way faith is released is through prayer. The power of binding and loosing is also exercised in prayer.

When you and I pray about deliverance from some bondage in our lives or in the life of another, we are, in effect, binding that problem and loosing an answer. The act of prayer binds evil and looses good.

Jesus has conferred on us the power and authority to use the keys of the Kingdom to bring to pass the will of God on earth.

GOD'S WORD FOR YOU

Now Peter and John were going up to the temple at the hour of prayer. . . .

ACTS 3:1

THE HABIT OF PRAYER

Many people feel vaguely guilty about their prayer life because they compare themselves to others. God is a creative God and wants each person to have his or her own individual prayer life. It doesn't have to be just like that of anyone else.

Yes, there are definite principles of prayer that need to be followed. As we see here in the book of Acts, the early disciples set aside certain hours of the day when they would go to a designated place to pray. That is good self-discipline, but that should be the start of prayer and not the finish. We should discipline ourselves to establish a prayer schedule that is individually suited to us and then stick to it until it becomes such a part of our lifestyle that we do it without even thinking.

All day we can continue to communicate with the Lord, praising and worshiping Him, thanking Him for His presence with us and asking His help in all our problems. Then just before we go to sleep at night, we can offer up a final prayer of gratitude for the blessings of the day and a request for a peaceful and refreshing night's sleep.

God wants prayer to be a normal part of our lives.

GOD'S WORD FOR YOU

Be unceasing in prayer [praying perseveringly].

Pray at all times (on every occasion, in every season) in the Spirit, with all [manner of] prayer and entreaty. To that end keep alert and watch with strong purpose and perseverance, interceding in behalf of all the saints (God's consecrated people).

EPHESIANS 6:18

PRAY WITHOUT CEASING

The *King James Version* of this verse says, "Pray without ceasing."

I used to wonder, *Lord, how can I ever get to the place that I am able to pray without ceasing?* To me the phrase "without ceasing" meant nonstop, without ever quitting. I couldn't see how that was possible.

Now I have a better understanding of what Paul was saying. He meant that prayer should be like breathing, something we do continually but often unconsciously. Our physical bodies require breathing. Likewise, our spiritual bodies are designed to be nurtured and sustained by continual prayer.

The problem is that because of religious thinking we have the mistaken idea that if we don't keep up a certain schedule of prayer we are missing the mark. If we become too "religious" about prayer, thinking we must do it one way or the other because that is how someone else does it, we will bring condemnation on ourselves. The important lesson about prayer is not the posture or the time or place but learning to pray in faith—at all times, unceasingly.

It is the Holy Spirit Who will lead you into prayer without ceasing.

GOD'S WORD FOR YOU

Do not fret or have any anxiety about anything, but in every circumstance and in everything, by prayer and petition (definite requests), with thanksgiving, continue to make your wants known to God.

And God's peace [shall be yours, that tranquil state of a soul assured of its salvation through Christ, and so fearing nothing from God and being content with its earthly lot of whatever sort that is, that peace] which transcends all understanding shall garrison and mount guard over your hearts and minds in Christ Jesus.

PHILIPPIANS 4:6-7

PRAYER PRODUCES PEACE

In this passage the apostle Paul does not say, "Pray and worry." Instead, he says, "Pray and don't worry." Why are we to pray and not worry? Because prayer is supposed to be the way we *cast our care* upon the Lord.

When the devil tries to give us care, we are supposed to turn and give that care to God. That's what prayer is, our acknowledgment to the Lord that we cannot carry our burden of care, so we lay it all on Him. If we pray about something and then keep on worrying about it, we are mixing a positive and a negative. The two cancel each other out so that we end up right back where we started—at zero.

Prayer is a positive force; worry is a negative force. The Lord has told me the reason many people operate at zero power level spiritually is that they cancel out their positive prayer power by giving in to the negative power of worry.

As long as we are worrying, we are not trusting God. It is only by trusting, by having faith and confidence in the Lord, that we are able to enter into His rest and enjoy the peace that transcends all understanding.

Make a decision now to cast all your care on the Lord and begin to watch Him take care of you.

GOD'S WORD FOR YOU

Come to Me, all you who labor and are heavy-laden and overburdened, and I will cause you to rest. [I will ease and relieve and refresh your souls.]

Take My yoke upon you and learn of Me, for I am gentle (meek) and humble (lowly) in heart, and you will find rest (relief and ease and refreshment and recreation and blessed quiet) for your souls.

MATTHEW 11:28-29

For we who have believed [adhered to and trusted in and relied on God) do enter that rest.

HEBREWS 4:3

PRAYER PRODUCES REST

If we are not at rest, we are not believing, because the fruit of believing is rest.

For many years of my life I would claim, "Oh, I'm believing God; I'm trusting the Lord." But I was not doing either of those things. I didn't know the first thing about believing God or trusting the Lord. I was anxious, panicky, irritable, and on edge all the time.

Just as we can be involved in outward activity, we can be involved in inward activity. God wants us not only to enter into His rest in our body, He also wants us to enter into His rest in our soul.

To me, finding rest, relief, ease, refreshment, recreation, and blessed quiet for my soul means finding freedom from mental activity. It means not having to live in the torment of reasoning, always trying to come up with an answer I don't have. I don't have to worry; instead, I can remain in a place of quiet peace and rest through prayer.

If we are truly believing God and trusting the Lord, we have entered into His rest. We have prayed and cast our care upon Him and are now abiding in the perfect peace of His holy presence.

You can speak His Word to your raging soul
and tortured mind just as Jesus spoke to the wind
and waves and said, "Peace, be still."

GOD'S WORD FOR YOU

Through Him also we have [our] access (entrance, introduction) by faith into this grace (state of God's favor) in which we [firmly and safely] stand. And let us rejoice and exult in our hope of experiencing and enjoying the glory of God.

Moreover [let us also be full of joy now!] let us exult and triumph in our troubles and rejoice in our sufferings, knowing that pressure and affliction and hardship produce patient and unswerving endurance.

And endurance (fortitude) develops maturity of character (approved faith and tried integrity). And character [of this sort] produces [the habit of] joyful and confident hope.

ROMANS 5:2-4

PRAYER PRODUCES PATIENCE AND HOPE

It is easy to say, "Don't worry." But to actually do that requires experience with God. I don't think there is any way a person can fully overcome the habit of worry, anxiety, and fear and develop the habit of peace, rest, and hope without years of experience.

That's why it is so important to continue to have faith and trust in God in the very midst of trials and tribulations. We must steadfastly resist the temptation to give up and quit when the going gets rough—and keeps on getting rougher over a long period of time. It is in those hard, trying times that the Lord is building in us the patience, endurance, and character that will eventually produce the habit of joyful and confident hope.

When you and I are in the midst of battle against our spiritual enemy, every round we go through produces valuable experience and strength. Each time we endure an attack, we become stronger. If we hang in there and refuse to give up, sooner or later we will be more than the devil can handle. When that happens, we will have reached spiritual maturity.

*We serve a God Who is so marvelous
that He can work out things for our good
that Satan intends for our harm.*

GOD'S WORD FOR YOU

All of these with their minds in full agreement devoted themselves steadfastly to prayer.

ACTS 1:14

UNITED OR CORPORATE PRAYER

Whenever believers are united in corporate prayer, there is great power present. Jesus Himself said, "For wherever two or three are gathered (drawn together as My followers) in (into) My name, there I AM in the midst of them" (Matthew 18:20).

Throughout the book of Acts we read that the people of God came together "with one accord" (Acts 2:1, 46; 4:24; 5:12; 15:25 KJV). And it was their united faith, their corporate agreement, and the presence of Jesus by the power of the Holy Spirit that made their prayers so effective. They saw God move in mighty ways to confirm the truth of His Word as they gave testimony to their faith in Jesus.

Then in Philippians 2:2 we are told by the apostle Paul, "Fill up and complete my joy by living in harmony and being of the same mind and one in purpose, having the same love, being in full accord and of one harmonious mind and intention."

Paul is giving us an important principle about corporate prayer. If we will heed these words and come into harmony and agreement with one another and with God, we will experience the same kind of powerful results the first-century disciples enjoyed in the book of Acts.

When you come together to pray,
expect God to show His power!

GOD'S WORD FOR YOU

*And the Lord said to Moses, I have seen this people,
and behold, it is a stiff-necked people;*

*Now therefore let Me alone, that My wrath may burn
hot against them and that I may destroy them; but I will
make of you a great nation.*

*But Moses besought the Lord his God, and said,
Lord, why does Your wrath blaze hot against Your people,
whom You have brought forth out of the land of Egypt
with great power and a mighty hand?*

*[Earnestly] remember Abraham, Isaac, and Israel,
Your servants, to whom You swore by Your own self and
said to them, I will multiply your seed as the stars of the
heavens, and all this land that I have spoken of will I give
to your seed, and they shall inherit it forever.*

*Then the Lord turned from the evil which He had
thought to do to His people.*

EXODUS 32:9-11, 13-14

GOD CHANGES PEOPLE THROUGH PRAYER

Moses' intercession for the children of Israel is a stirring example that depicts how sincere prayer can change God's mind.

There are times when I can sense that God is getting weary of putting up with someone who is not obeying Him, and I will find myself being led to pray for God to be merciful to that person and to give that individual another chance.

As Jesus told His disciples at Gethsemane, we should "watch and pray" (Matthew 26:41 KJV). We need to pray for one another, not judge and criticize each other. If we watch people, we can see when they need encouragement, when they are depressed, fearful, insecure, or experiencing any number of obvious problems. God allows us to discern their need in order to be part of the answer, not part of the problem. Remember we are not the potter. God is, and we certainly don't know how to "fix" people.

People who are hurting don't need someone with a spirit of pride trying to *fix* them; they need acceptance, love, and prayer.

Pray! Pray! Pray! It is the only way to get things accomplished in God's economy. If we do things His way, we always get good results.

❧

We need to do the praying and let God do the working.

GOD'S WORD FOR YOU

For we are fellow workmen (joint promoters, laborers together) with and for God; you are God's garden and vineyard and field under cultivation, [you are] God's building.

1 CORINTHIANS 3:9

Do you not discern and understand that you [the whole church at Corinth] are God's temple (His sanctuary), and that God's Spirit has His permanent dwelling in you [to be at home in you, collectively as a church and also individually]?

1 CORINTHIANS 3:16

WE ARE THE PLACE OF PRAYER

Under the Old Covenant, the temple was the house of God, the place of prayer for His people, the children of Israel. And no expense was spared to beautify the temple where the people came to worship the Lord their God. In 1 Kings 6 we have a description of Solomon's temple, which contained the ark of the covenant, God's pledge of His presence.

Under the New Covenant the apostle Paul instructs us that God's presence is now a mystery revealed of Christ in us, "the Hope of glory" (Colossians 1:27). Because of the union we now have in Christ, we are God's living temple. We are indwelt by the Holy Spirit, a building still under construction, but nonetheless His house, His tabernacle. That is why Paul goes to great length to tell us to live a holy life. We are a temple of the living God.

Whereas the children of Israel had to go to a specific place to offer their worship with detailed instructions, we have the incredible privilege of worshiping God anywhere and at any time. Therefore, we should be called a house of prayer.

We become the sanctuary of God because of the presence of the Holy One in us.

How to Pray Effectively

*There is nothing more powerful
to change our lives and
the lives of those around us
than God's hand moving in response
to our heartfelt, continued prayer.*

GOD'S WORD FOR YOU

The earnest (heartfelt, continued) prayer of a righteous man makes tremendous power available [dynamic in its working].

JAMES 5:16

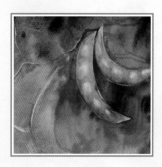

t w o

HOW TO PRAY EFFECTIVELY

 reached a point in my prayer life where I felt frustrated, so I began to seek God about it. I wanted the assurance that "the earnest, heartfelt prayer of a righteous man makes tremendous power available, dynamic in its working." I wanted God's power made available to change that situation or bless that person's life over which I was praying.

If we're going to learn how to pray effectively, we have to say, "Lord, teach me to pray." He will show you the keys to praying more effectively. Keys lock and unlock. Keys reflect authority. Whoever has the keys has the authority. When we pray this way, we're asking the Lord to reveal His prayer principles that will make our prayers effective.

I encourage you to start seeking God's will when you pray, because there will be an anointing on prayer that is in line with His will. God showed me that to pray fervently means to put your whole self, all of your attention, your mind, your will, your emotions, all of you into what you're praying about. He is more concerned with the quality of prayer than the quantity of prayer.

Be shamelessly persistent in prayer.

GOD'S WORD FOR YOU

The effective, fervent prayer of a righteous man avails much.

JAMES 5:16 NKJV

The heartfelt supplication of a righteous man exerts a mighty influence.

JAMES 5:16 WEYMOUTH

. . . The prayers of the righteous have a powerful effect.

JAMES 5:16 MOFFATT

FERVENT PRAYER

For prayer to be effective it must be fervent. However, if we misunderstand the word *fervent*, we may feel that we have to "work up" some strong emotion before we pray; otherwise, our prayers will not be effective.

I know there were many years when I believed this way, and perhaps you have been likewise confused or deceived. Look at some of the other translations of this verse that may make its meaning clearer: "fervent prayer . . . avails much"; "exerts a mighty influence"; "have a powerful effect."

I believe this scripture means that our prayers must come out of our heart and not just our head.

At times I experience a great deal of emotion while at prayer. Sometimes I even cry. But there are plenty of times when I don't feel emotional. Believing prayer is not possible if we base the value of our prayers on feelings. I remember enjoying so much those prayer times when I could *feel* God's presence, and then wondering what was wrong during the times when I didn't *feel* anything. I learned after a while that faith is not based on *feelings* in the emotions but on knowledge in the heart.

Trust that your earnest, heartfelt prayers are effectual because your faith is in Him, not in your own ability to live holy or pray eloquently.

GOD'S WORD FOR YOU

. . . The effective, fervent prayer of a righteous man avails much.

Elijah was a man with a nature like ours, and he prayed earnestly that it would not rain; and it did not rain on the land for three years and six months.

JAMES 5:16-17

THE PRAYERS OF A RIGHTEOUS MAN

James tells us that the fervent prayer of a "righteous" man is powerful. This means a man who is not under condemnation—one who has confidence in God and in the power of prayer. It does not mean a man without any imperfection in his life.

Elijah was a man of God who did not always behave perfectly, but he did not allow his imperfections to steal his confidence in God. Elijah had faith, but he also had fear. He was obedient, but at times he was also disobedient. He loved God and wanted to fulfill His will and calling upon his life. But sometimes he gave in to human weaknesses and tried to avoid the consequences of that will and calling.

In 1 Kings 18 we see him moving in tremendous power, calling down fire from heaven and slaying 450 prophets of Baal. Then immediately we see him fearfully running from Jezebel, becoming negative and depressed, and even wanting to die.

Like many of us, Elijah let his emotions get the upper hand. He was a human being just like us, and yet he prayed powerful prayers. His example should give us enough "scriptural power" to defeat condemnation when it rises up to tell us we cannot pray powerfully because of our weaknesses and faults.

Never underestimate the power
of effective, fervent prayer!

GOD'S WORD FOR YOU

And when you pray, do not keep on babbling like pagans, for they think they will be heard because of their many words. Do not be like them, for your Father knows what you need before you ask him.

MATTHEW 6:7-8 NIV

SHORT AND SIMPLE

I believe God has instructed me to pray and make my requests with as few words as possible. If I can keep my request very simple and not confuse the issue by trying to come up with too many words, my prayer actually seems to be more clear and powerful.

We need to spend our energy releasing our faith, not repeating phrases over and over that only serve to make the prayer long and involved.

It has actually been difficult for me to keep my prayers short and simple. I began to realize that my problem in praying was that I didn't have faith that my prayer would get through if it was short, simple, and to the point. I had fallen into the same trap that many people do—"the-longer-the-better" mentality. I don't mean that I am advocating praying only for a short period of time, but I am suggesting that each prayer be simple, direct, to the point, and filled with faith.

Now as I follow God's direction to keep it simple and make my request with the least amount of words possible, I experience a much greater release of my faith, and I know that God has heard me and will answer.

If your prayers are complicated, simplify them.
If you are not praying enough, pray more.

GOD'S WORD FOR YOU

Keep on asking and it will be given you; keep on seeking and you will find; keep on knocking [reverently] and [the door] will be opened to you.

For everyone who keeps on asking receives; and he who keeps on seeking finds; and to him who keeps on knocking, [the door] will be opened.

MATTHEW 7:7-8

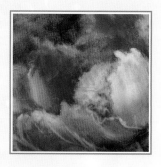

How Many Times Should I Pray?

I don't believe we can make any strict rules on the subject of how often to pray about the same thing. I do think there are some guidelines that may apply to help us have even more confidence in the power of prayer.

If my children need something, I would want them to trust me to do what they asked me to do. I wouldn't mind, and might even like it, if they occasionally said, "Boy, Mom, I'm sure looking forward to those new shoes." That statement would declare to me that they believed I was going to do what I promised. They would actually be reminding me of my promise, but in a way that would not question my integrity.

I believe sometimes when we ask God the same thing over and over, it is a sign of doubt and unbelief, not of faith and persistence.

When I ask the Lord for something in prayer, and that request comes to my mind later, I talk to Him about it again. But when I do, I refrain from asking Him the same thing as if I think He didn't hear me the first time. I thank the Lord that He is working on the situation I prayed about previously.

Faithful, persistent prayer builds even more faith and confidence in us as we continue to pray.

GOD'S WORD FOR YOU

And this is the confidence (the assurance, the privilege of boldness) which we have in Him: [we are sure] that if we ask anything (make any request) according to His will (in agreement with His own plan), He listens to and hears us.

And if (since) we [positively] know that He listens to us in whatever we ask, we also know [with settled and absolute knowledge] that we have [granted us as our present possessions] the requests made of Him.

1 JOHN 5:14-15

BELIEVE GOD HEARS YOU!

When you pray, believe God hears you!

In John 11:41-42, just before Jesus called Lazarus forth from the tomb, Jesus prayed: "Father, I thank You that You have heard Me. Yes, I know You always hear and listen to Me, but I have said this on account of and for the benefit of the people standing around, so that they may believe that You did send Me [that You have made Me Your Messenger]." What confidence!

Satan does not want us to have that kind of confidence either. But I encourage you one more time: *Be confident!* Make a decision that you are a believer, not a beggar. Go to the throne in Jesus' name—His name will get attention!

Because my ministry is broadcast on TV, a few people know who I am, and some people like to use my name. My employees like to say, "I work for Joyce Meyer," and my children like to say, "Joyce Meyer is my mother." They think those they are approaching may give them more favor if they mention my name.

If that works for us as human beings, just think how well it must work in the heavenly realm—especially when we use the name that is above all other names—the blessed name of Jesus! (Philippians 2:9-11).

Go to God in prayer—boldly. With confidence. In the name of Jesus.

43

GOD'S WORD FOR YOU

Then He was praying in a certain place; and when He stopped, one of His disciples said to Him, Lord, teach us to pray, [just] as John taught his disciples.

And He said to them, When you pray, say: Our Father Who is in heaven, hallowed be Your name, Your kingdom come. Your will be done [held holy and revered] on earth as it is in heaven.

Give us daily our bread [food for the morrow].

And forgive us our sins, for we ourselves also forgive everyone who is indebted to us [who has offended us or done us wrong]. And bring us not into temptation but rescue us from evil.

LUKE 11:1-4

KNOW GOD AS YOUR FATHER

For many years I prayed the "Lord's Prayer," and I no more knew God as my Father than anything! I didn't have any kind of a close personal relationship with God. I was just repeating something I had learned.

If you want to be effective in your prayer life, you need to know God as your Father. When the disciples asked Jesus to teach them to pray, He taught them what we call the "Lord's Prayer," which is a spiritual treasure house of principles for prayer. But foremost, Jesus started out by instructing them to say, "Our Father Who is in heaven, hallowed be Your name."

Jesus was showing them the importance of seeing the privileged relationship He came to bring to every believer. He told them they needed to have a relationship with God as their Father if they expected to go to Him in prayer. Don't go to God as some ogre that you're afraid of, but develop a Father-child relationship with Him. That intimate relationship will give you liberty to ask Him for things you would not have asked for if you had a starchy, stiff relationship with Him.

Our heavenly Father longs to give good gifts to His children.

When you pray, remember you have a loving Father Who is listening.

GOD'S WORD FOR YOU

And He said to them, Which of you who has a friend will go to him at midnight and will say to him, Friend, lend me three loaves [of bread],

For a friend of mine who is on a journey has just come, and I have nothing to put before him;

And he from within will answer, Do not disturb me; the door is now closed, and my children are with me in the bed; I cannot get up and supply you [with anything]?

I tell you, although he will not get up and supply him anything because he is his friend, yet because of his shameless persistence and insistence he will get up and give him as much as he needs.

LUKE 11:5-8

BECOME A FRIEND OF GOD

The key to this scripture is *friendship*. The man in the story went at midnight to get bread for his friend in need. If the person you're going to isn't your friend, you will not shamelessly persist. Jesus was telling His disciples that God is much more willing to give us what we need than the man in the parable was to give to his friend.

Jesus said, "You are My friends if you keep on doing the things which I command you to do" (John 15:14). We're talking about a right heart attitude, that you're going to obey God no matter what it costs you. That's one of the criteria for being a friend of God. You also become His friend because you spend a lot of time with Him.

Isaiah 41:8 says, "But you, Israel, My servant, Jacob, whom I have chosen, the offspring of Abraham My friend." What an awesome thing to have God call you His friend. When God was going to bring judgment, He said, "Shall I hide from Abraham [My friend and servant] what I am going to do. . . ?" (Genesis 18:17). And as His friend, you can expect to have firsthand knowledge about what God is doing.

The closer friend you become with God,
the more boldness you have when you pray.

GOD'S WORD FOR YOU

Let us then fearlessly and confidently and boldly draw near to the throne of grace (the throne of God's unmerited favor to us sinners), that we may receive mercy [for our failures] and find grace to help in good time for every need [appropriate help and well-timed help, coming just when we need it].

HEBREWS 4:16

BE BOLD!

When you and I pray, we need to make sure we approach God as believers, not as beggars. Remember, according to Hebrews 4:16, we are to come boldly to the throne: not beggarly, but boldly; not belligerently, but boldly.

Be sure to keep the balance. Stay respectful, but be bold. Approach God with confidence. Believe He delights in your prayers and is ready to answer any request that is in accordance with His will.

As believers, we should know the Word of God, which is His will; therefore, it should be easy for us to pray according to God's will. Don't approach God wondering if what you are asking is His will. Settle that issue in your heart *before* you pray.

As you and I come boldly before the throne of God's grace, covered with the blood of Jesus, asking in faith according to His Word and in the name of His Son Jesus Christ, we can know that we have the petitions that we ask of Him. Not because we are perfect or worthy of ourselves, or because God owes us anything, but because He loves us and wants to give us what we need to do the job He has called us to do.

Jesus has purchased a glorious inheritance for us by the shedding of His blood. As joint-heirs with Him, we can pray boldly.

GOD'S WORD FOR YOU

But you, beloved, build yourselves up [founded] on your most holy faith [make progress, rise like an edifice higher and higher], praying in the Holy Spirit.

JUDE 20

PRAY IN THE SPIRIT

Just as Ephesians 6:18 tells us that we are not only to pray at all times with all manner of prayers, we are also told here by Jude that our prayers are to be "in the Holy Spirit." The apostle Paul tells us in Romans 8:26 that when we don't know how to pray, the Holy Spirit knows how to pray in our weakness.

It is the Holy Spirit of God within us Who provokes us and leads us to pray. Rather than delaying, we need to learn to yield to the leading of the Spirit as soon as we sense it. That is part of learning to pray all manner of prayers at all times, wherever we may be, and whatever we may be doing.

Our motto should be that of the old spiritual song, "Every time I feel the Spirit moving in my heart, I will pray." If we know we can pray anytime and anywhere, we won't feel we have to wait until just the right moment or place to pray.

When we are praying in the Holy Spirit, we can know that our prayers are reaching the throne of God and will be answered.

Ask the Holy Spirit to get involved in everything you do. He is the Helper, and He is waiting for you to ask.

GOD'S WORD FOR YOU

For God did not give us a spirit of timidity (of cowardice, of craven and cringing and fawning fear), but [He has given us a spirit] of power and of love and of calm and well-balanced mind and discipline and self-control.

2 TIMOTHY 1:7

PRAY AND FEAR NOT

God wants us to pray about everything and fear nothing. We could avoid a lot of problems if we would pray more, worry less, and fear less. Timothy says that God has not given us a spirit of fear. So when we feel fear, it is not from God. Any kind of fear—little fear, big fear—is not from God. It's from the devil. And the devil will try to intimidate us with all kinds of fear so that we do not pray.

If Abraham or Joshua or David had bowed their knee to fear when the task before them seemed overwhelming, they never would have experienced God as their abundant provision.

Prayer and God's Word will give you power to overcome fear. Memorize scriptures so when you feel fear, you can open your mouth and confess those scriptures out loud in faith-filled prayer. In fact, I think one of the most important things that we can do in our prayer time is walk around and confess the Word.

So often when we have something that we've got to confront and deal with, we start to dread and fear and wonder and reason what to do. Fear must be confronted. You can't wish fear away. You have to confront it with the Word of God.

Put on the armor of God through prayer and stand against all the enemy's fiery darts of fear.

THE TYPES OF PRAYER

*As believers we have spiritual
authority to do God's will
on earth through prayer.*

GOD'S WORD FOR YOU

First of all, then, I admonish and urge that petitions, prayers, intercessions, and thanksgivings be offered on behalf of all men,

For kings and all who are in positions of authority or high responsibility, that [outwardly] we may pass a quiet and undisturbed life [and inwardly] a peaceable one in all godliness and reverence and seriousness in every way.

For such [praying] is good and right, and [it is] pleasing and acceptable to God our Savior.

1 TIMOTHY 2:1-3

three

THE TYPES OF PRAYER

God had to teach me some lessons about praying in faith, about understanding that the Holy Spirit was helping me in prayer, and that Jesus was interceding along with me (Romans 8:26; Hebrews 7:25). Two of the Persons of the Godhead are helping me pray!

How often are we to pray? At all times. How are we to pray? In the Spirit, with different kinds of prayer. I believe if we will allow Him to do so, the Holy Spirit will lead us into prayer without ceasing so it becomes like breathing. When that happens we can be continually offering up prayers.

Now I would like to discuss the types of prayer we see in the Word of God. We should be exercising all the various types of prayer on a regular basis. They are simple, can be prayed anywhere at any time, and are most effective when prayed from a believing heart.

God does hear our prayers and does respond to them. That is what makes them so powerful and so effective.

GOD'S WORD FOR YOU

Again I tell you, if two of you on earth agree (harmonize together, make a symphony together) about whatever [anything and everything] they may ask, it will come to pass and be done for them by My Father in heaven.

MATTHEW 18:19

THE PRAYER OF AGREEMENT

First, let me say that I believe this prayer can only be prayed by two or more people who are committed to living in agreement. This prayer is not for people who generally live in strife and then decide they need to agree for some type of miracle because they are desperate. God honors the prayers of those who pay the price to live in unity.

Because our prayer power multiplies when we are in agreement with those around us (1 Peter 3:7), we need to be in agreement all the time, not just when we face a crisis situation. There will be times in our life when what we are up against is something that is bigger than we are by ourselves. At such times, we will be wise to pray together with someone who is in agreement with us in that situation.

If you feel you have nobody in your life with whom you can agree in prayer, don't despair. You and the Holy Spirit can agree. He is here on the earth with you and in you as a child of God.

There is power in agreement! Pray the prayer of agreement, especially when you feel the need for a little extra prayer power!

GOD'S WORD FOR YOU

Hear my prayer, O Lord, give ear to my supplications! Answer me in Your faithfulness, in Your righteousness!

PSALM 143:1 NASB

Oh, that I might have my request, and that God would grant me the thing that I long for!

JOB 6:8

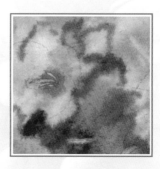

THE PRAYER OF PETITION

This prayer is by far the most often used. When we petition God, we ask for something for ourselves. Another word for petition is *requisition*. It is a demand or request made on something to which a person is legally entitled but not yet in possession of, as in the military when an officer requisitions equipment or supplies for his men. As an officer of the United States Army, he is entitled to that material, but in order to receive it he has to submit a definite request for it.

When we come to the Lord with a petition, we are requisitioning from Him what He has already set aside to provide for us when the need arises. For that reason, we frequently exercise our right to petition God. It is, of course, not wrong to ask God to do things for us, but our petitions should be well-balanced with praise and thanksgiving.

We can be bold in petitioning God for any type of need in our lives. We are not restricted to a certain number of requests per day. We can feel at ease talking to God about anything that concerns us, for He already knows what we need and is willing to grant us our petitions (Matthew 6:8).

When you are in trouble, go to the Throne
before you go to the phone.

GOD'S WORD FOR YOU

Speak out to one another in psalms and hymns and spiritual songs, offering praise with voices [and instruments] and making melody with all your heart to the Lord,

At all times and for everything giving thanks in the name of our Lord Jesus Christ to God the Father.

EPHESIANS 5:19-20

Through Him, therefore, let us constantly and at all times offer up to God a sacrifice of praise, which is the fruit of lips that thankfully acknowledge and confess and glorify His name. [Lev. 7:12; Isa. 57:19; Hos. 14:2.]

HEBREWS 13:15

THE PRAYER OF PRAISE AND WORSHIP

Praise is a narration or a tale in which we recount the good qualities about an individual, in this case, God. We should praise the Lord continually. By continually, I mean all throughout the day. We should praise Him for His mighty works, the wonders He has created, and even the works of grace He is yet to do in each of our lives.

A sacrifice of praise means doing it even when we don't feel like it. We should praise God for His goodness, mercy, loving-kindness, grace, long-suffering, and patient nature in the hard times as well as the good. While we are waiting to see the fulfillment of our prayers, we are to be continually offering up to God the fruit of lips that thankfully acknowledge and confess and glorify His name.

It is not our responsibility to worry and fret or try to play God by taking into our own hands situations that should be left to Him alone. Instead, it is our responsibility to cast our care upon the Lord, trusting Him, praying without worry, avoiding works of the flesh, continuing in obedience, bearing good fruit, and offering Him the sacrifice of praise.

May a sacrifice of praise continually be in our mouths for the marvelous works of grace He has done for us.

GOD'S WORD FOR YOU

Thank [God] in everything [no matter what the circumstances may be, be thankful and give thanks], for this is the will of God for you [who are] in Christ Jesus [the Revealer and Mediator of that will].

1 THESSALONIANS 5:18

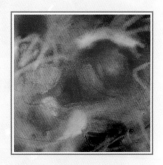

THE PRAYER OF THANKSGIVING

After telling us to pray without ceasing, the apostle Paul directs us to give thanks to God in everything, no matter what our circumstances may be, stating that this is the will of God for us.

Just as prayer is to be a lifestyle for us, so thanksgiving is to be a lifestyle for us. Giving thanks to God should not be something we do once a day as we sit down somewhere and try to think of all the good things He has done for us and merely say, "Thanks, Lord."

That is empty religion, something we do simply because we think God requires it. True thanksgiving flows continually out of a heart that is full of gratitude and praise to God for Who He is as much as for what He does. It is not something that is done to meet a requirement, win favor, gain a victory, or qualify for a blessing.

The type of thanksgiving that God the Father desires is that which is provoked by the presence of His Holy Spirit within us Who moves upon us to express to the Lord verbally what we are feeling and experiencing spiritually.

We are to be thankful to God always, continually acknowledging, confessing, and glorifying His name in prayerful praise and worship.

GOD'S WORD FOR YOU

And I sought a man among them who should build up the wall and stand in the gap before Me for the land, that I should not destroy it, but I found none.

EZEKIEL 22:30

Therefore He is able also to save to the uttermost (completely, perfectly, finally, and for all time and eternity) those who come to God through Him, since He is always living to make petition to God and intercede with Him and intervene for them.

HEBREWS 7:25

THE PRAYER OF INTERCESSION

To intercede means to *stand in the gap* for someone else, to plead his case before the throne of God. If there is a breach in people's relationship with God due to a particular sin in their life, we have the privilege of placing ourselves in that breach and praying for them. We can intercede for them and expect to see them comforted and encouraged while they wait. We can also expect a timely breakthrough for them concerning their need being met.

I don't know what I would do if people did not intercede for me. I petition God to give me people to intercede for me and for the fulfillment of the ministry to which He has called me. We need each other's prayers of intercession.

Praying for others is equivalent to sowing seed. We must sow seed if we are to reap a harvest (Galatians 6:7). Sowing seed into the lives of other people through intercession is one sure way to reap a harvest in our own life. Each time we pray for someone else, we are inviting God to not only work in that person's life but also in our own.

Intercession is one of the most important ways we carry on the ministry of Jesus Christ that He began in this earth.

*We can release God's power in the lives
of others by praying for them.*

GOD'S WORD FOR YOU

Commit your way to the Lord [roll and repose each care of your load on Him]; trust (lean on, rely on, and be confident) also in Him and He will bring it to pass.

PSALM 37:5

Casting the whole of your care [all your anxieties, all your worries, all your concerns, once and for all] on Him, for He cares for you affectionately and cares about you watchfully.

1 PETER 5:7

THE PRAYER OF COMMITMENT

When we are tempted to worry or take the care of some situation in life, we should pray the prayer of commitment. God intervenes in our situations when we commit them to Him.

In my own life I found that the more I tried to take care of things myself, the bigger mess my life became. I was quite independent and found it difficult to humble myself and admit that I needed help. However, when I finally submitted to God in these areas and found the joy of casting all my care on Him, I could not believe I had lived so long under such huge amounts of pressure.

Commit to the Lord your children, your marriage, your personal relationships, and especially anything you may be tempted to be concerned about. In order to succeed at being ourselves, we must continually be committing ourselves to God, giving to Him those things that appear to be holding us back. Only God really knows what needs to be done, and He is the *only* One Who is qualified to do it. The more we sincerely commit ourselves to Him, the more progress we make.

A believer who can trust the Father when things do not seem to make sense is a mature believer.

GOD'S WORD FOR YOU

I appeal to you therefore, brethren, and beg of you in view of [all] the mercies of God, to make a decisive dedication of your bodies [presenting all your members and faculties] as a living sacrifice, holy (devoted, consecrated) and well pleasing to God, which is your reasonable (rational, intelligent) service and spiritual worship.

ROMANS 12:1

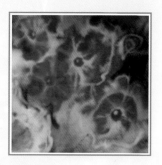

THE PRAYER OF CONSECRATION

Another life-changing type of prayer is the prayer of consecration, the prayer in which we give ourselves to God. In the prayer of consecration, we dedicate our lives and all that we are to Him.

In order for God to use us, we must give ourselves totally to Him. When we truly consecrate ourselves to the Lord, we relinquish the burden of trying to run our own lives. Consecration is a powerful act, but it must be sincere. It is quite easy to sing along with everyone else a song such as "I Surrender All." We may even feel moved emotionally, but the real test is found in daily life when circumstances don't always go the way we thought they would. Then we must sing again, "I Surrender All," consecrating ourselves to God afresh.

Consecration to God is the most important aspect of succeeding at being ourselves. We don't even know what we are supposed to be, let alone know how to become whatever it is. But as we regularly keep our lives on the altar in consecration to God, He will do the work that needs to be done in us so that He may do the work He desires to do *through* us.

When we consecrate ourselves to God,
He makes us into vessels fit for the Master's use.

GOD'S WORD FOR YOU

. . . the Lord is in His holy temple; let all the earth hush and keep silence before Him.

HABAKKUK 2:20

Our inner selves wait [earnestly] for the Lord; He is our Help and our Shield.

PSALM 33:20

THE PRAYER OF SILENCE

I also call this kind of prayer "waiting on the Lord." In our instant and fast-paced society, this spiritual discipline is often lacking. We want it and we want it right now! If we are always in such a hurry, we will miss out on the wisdom God wants to speak to our hearts if we will only be silent before Him.

Elijah was a man who learned the secret of silent, waiting prayer in His presence. After slaying the prophets of Baal, Elijah learned a valuable lesson on waiting on God. The Lord told Elijah to go stand on a mount and wait. A great wind came; then came a great earthquake and a great fire, but the Lord was in none of those. "After the fire [a sound of gentle stillness and] a still, small voice" (1 Kings 19:12).

David also learned to wait in the house of the Lord and "to meditate, consider, and inquire in His temple" (Psalm 27:4). If we want to learn how to pray effectively, then we are going to have to learn to sit in silence and listen for His Word. Waiting and listening takes our focus off of us and places it on Him, Who is the answer to all our needs.

It is often in silence when the power of God is moving the most mightily. Allow the Holy Spirit to teach you how to wait in His presence.

GOD'S WORD FOR YOU

Now when Jesus went into the region of Caesarea Philippi, He asked His disciples, Who do people say that the Son of Man is?

Simon Peter replied, You are the Christ, the Son of the loving God.

MATTHEW 16:13, 16

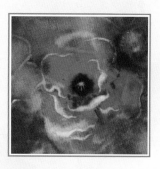

THE PRAYER OF CONFESSION

When Peter made that statement about Jesus being the Christ, the Son of the living God, he was releasing with his mouth the faith that was in his heart. The praying and confession of what we know in our hearts, revealed by the Holy Spirit, is a powerful way to pray and strengthen our faith.

We must understand that we establish the faith that is in our heart by the words we speak from our mouth, as the apostle Paul tells us in Romans 10:10: ". . . and with the mouth he confesses (declares openly and speaks out freely his faith) and confirms [his] salvation."

That is why prayer is so important. Because we establish the things we believe inwardly when we start talking about them outwardly. That is why confessing the Scriptures in prayer is also very powerful. When we do that, we are establishing things in the spiritual realm by the words we are speaking in the physical realm. And eventually what is established spiritually will be manifested physically.

You and I should be constantly confessing the Word of God, believing in our heart and confessing with our mouth what God has said about us in His Word.

We release heaven's power when we confess in the physical realm what God has already done for us in the spiritual realm

GOD'S WORD FOR YOU

Rejoice in the Lord always [delight, gladden yourselves in Him]; again I say, Rejoice!

PHILIPPIANS 4:4

I will rejoice in You and be in high spirits; I will sing praise to Your name, O Most High!

PSALM 9:2

THE PRAYER OF REJOICING

Twice in the passage from Philippians the apostle Paul tells us to rejoice. He urges us not to fret or have any anxiety about anything but to pray and give thanks to God *in* everything—not *after* everything is over.

If we wait until everything is perfect before rejoicing and giving thanks, we won't have much fun. Learning to enjoy life even in the midst of trying circumstances is one way we develop spiritual maturity. Paul also writes that we "are constantly being transfigured into His very own image in ever increasing splendor and from one degree of glory to another" (2 Corinthians 3:18). We need to learn how to enjoy the glory we are experiencing at each level of our development. Let's learn to pray a prayer of rejoicing and be glad in the Lord this day and every day along the way toward our goal.

When I first started my ministry, I depended on my circumstances for happiness. Finally the Lord showed me the doorway to happiness. He gave me a breakthrough by teaching me that fullness of joy is found in His *presence*—not in His *presents*! (Psalm 16:11.)

True joy comes from seeking God's face.

WHY PRAYER ISN'T ANSWERED

There's no power shortage in heaven,
but there is often a shortage
of prayers on earth.

GOD'S WORD FOR YOU

And, beloved, if our consciences (our hearts) do not accuse us [if they do not make us feel guilty and condemn us], we have confidence (complete assurance and boldness) before God,

And we receive from Him whatever we ask, because we [watchfully] obey His orders [observe His suggestions and injunctions, follow His plan for us] and [habitually] practice what is pleasing to Him.

1 JOHN 3:21-22

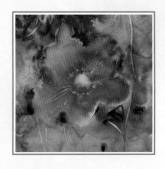

four
WHY PRAYER ISN'T ANSWERED

f there's anything I want to know for sure, it's that my prayers are going to be answered when I go to prayer. For a long time I was frustrated that I didn't see my prayers answered the way I would have liked. I knew that I had a loving heavenly Father Who delights in answering our petitions. But something wasn't working, so I sought the Lord. He began to instruct me in His Word about a number of obstacles that will hinder our prayer life. As I began to line up my life with the issues He showed me, I began to see more faith and power in my prayer life. And more answers to my prayers!

When you go to pray, do you feel uncomfortable? Maybe you're under condemnation, maybe you're not praying as a righteous person, or maybe you're regarding iniquity in your heart.

If we are going to get our prayers answered, then we are going to have to learn how to tap into the spiritual realm and allow the Holy Spirit to show us what obstacles He wants to remove from our lives. Then we must be obedient to what He shows us so that our prayers become fervent and effective for the Kingdom of God.

Allow the Holy Spirit to convict, cleanse, and fill you so that your prayers are filled with faith and power.

GOD'S WORD FOR YOU

And when that time comes, you will ask nothing of Me [you will need to ask Me no questions]. I assure you, most solemnly I tell you, that My Father will grant you whatever you ask in My Name [as presenting all that I AM]. [Exod. 3:14.]

Up to this time you have not asked a [single] thing in My Name [as presenting all that I AM]; but now ask and keep on asking and you will receive, so that your joy (gladness, delight) may be full and complete.

JOHN 16:23-24

PEOPLE DON'T PRAY BOLDLY

Our prayers aren't answered because we don't pray boldly. We need to pray more specifically and have the boldness to come before God and really ask Him for what we want and not be ashamed to make our requests known.

One of the major things that keeps people from praying boldly is they look at what they have done wrong instead of what Jesus has done right. The Bible teaches us plainly that God ". . . made Christ [virtually] to be sin Who knew no sin, so that in and through Him we might become [endued with, viewed as being in, and examples of] the righteousness of God" (2 Corinthians 5:21). Because we are righteous in Him, we can approach the throne of grace boldly with our needs (Hebrews 4:16).

John 16:23-24 tells us we can come boldly before the throne in Jesus' name. The name of Jesus is powerful. When I use Jesus' name in my prayers, it's not like some magic charm that I tack on to the end of everything. When I go in the name of Jesus, I'm saying, "Father, I come to you presenting today all that Jesus is—not what I am."

Don't be vague—be bold! You'll be surprised at the answers you'll get.

God loves to answer our bold prayers made in the name of Jesus.

GOD'S WORD FOR YOU

If I regard iniquity in my heart, the Lord will not hear me. [Prov. 15:29; 28:9; Isa. 1:15; John 9:31; James 4:3.]

PSALM 66:18

We know that God does not listen to sinners; but if anyone is God-fearing and a worshiper of Him and does His will, He listens to him.

JOHN 9:31

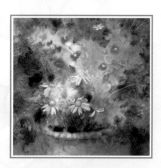

ℐNIQUITY IN MY HEART

Our prayers often do not get answered because we regard iniquity in our heart. David said, "If I regard iniquity in my heart, the Lord will not hear me" (Psalm 66:18). What that means, to put it bluntly, is that the Lord doesn't hear us when we pray if we come before Him with unclean hearts.

If there is sin your life, you will not be able to pray boldly or with confidence. When you're praying and you sense that you're not comfortable, stop and ask God why. Ask Him to reveal anything that's hidden. If He convicts you of something, don't be vague about it. Call it what it is—sin. We get release when we admit and confess our sin and bring it out in the open. He wants you to confess it so He can cleanse you and restore a clean conscience so that you can pray (1 John 1:9). There is power in truth and honesty when we come clean before the Lord and walk in the light.

Make sure your heart is clean before Him so your prayers are alive and energized by the Holy Spirit's power.

*God hears your prayers
when you approach Him with a clean heart.*

GOD'S WORD FOR YOU

For this reason we also, from the day we heard of it, have not ceased to pray and make [special] request for you, [asking] that you may be filled with the full (deep and clear) knowledge of His will in all spiritual wisdom [in comprehensive insight into the ways and purposes of God] and in understanding and discernment of spiritual things. . . .

COLOSSIANS 1:9

PEOPLE DON'T PRAY IN THE WILL OF GOD

Another reason why prayer is not answered is that people don't pray in the will of God. I'd like to say we're all led by the Spirit, and we all hear the voice of God. That's the place we're working toward, but we're not all there yet.

Sometimes it's not all that easy to decipher if what you're wanting is really God's will or just your flesh wanting it. In order to know God's will, you must know God's Word. Psalm 119:105 says, "Your word is a lamp to my feet and a light to my path." We must become students of the Word. Another issue comes into play regarding God's will: God's timing. To be out of God's timing is also to be out of His will. If I try to make it happen right now, then it's out of the will of God for today for my life.

First John 5:14 says, "and this is the confidence (the assurance, the privilege of boldness)." If I'm not praying in the will of God, He is not going to hook up with me and give me the power to pray with that boldness. But if you know the will of God concerning your prayer request, then faith will come out of your spirit to help you pray.

It's amazing what faith can do
when we know the will of God.

GOD'S WORD FOR YOU

. . . *You do not have, because you do not ask. [I John 5:15.]*

[Or] you do ask [God for them] and yet fail to receive, because you ask with wrong purpose and evil, selfish motives.

JAMES 4:2-3

WRONG PURPOSE AND MOTIVES

According to James 3:3, many prayers are not answered because people pray amiss. To pray amiss means we are praying with the "wrong purpose and evil, selfish motives." You could be praying for something that is the will of God, but you're praying for the wrong reason. When you first start to learn to pray, you're carnal, so you are going to pray carnally. You're going to pray many prayers for the wrong reason. We're not talking about what we do but why we're doing it.

Years ago I spent many hours praying for my ministry to grow. I wanted to look good in front of everybody, and I wanted to look successful. I wanted it to appear that I was obviously hearing from God. And I wanted those people to come to my meetings because the more people came, the better I looked.

Now I know who I am in Christ, and I know that my worth is not in my ministry. Back then I was praying with the wrong motive. Do you want your prayer life to be powerful and effective? Then before you go to prayer start checking your motives. Make sure you are praying for godly reasons with all humility.

When God finds humility and right motives,
His grace empowers our prayers.

GOD'S WORD FOR YOU

*Truly I tell you, whoever says to this mountain, Be
lifted up and thrown into the sea! and does not doubt at all
in his heart but believes that what he says will take place,
it will be done for him.*

MARK 11:23

*If any of you is deficient in wisdom, let him ask of the
giving God [Who gives] to everyone liberally and
ungrudgingly, without reproaching or faultfinding, and it
will be given him.*

*Only it must be in faith that he asks with no wavering
(no hesitating, no doubting). For the one who wavers
(hesitates, doubts) is like the billowing surge out at sea
that is blown hither and thither and tossed by the wind.*

JAMES 1:5-6

DOUBT AND UNBELIEF

Another reason why prayer is not answered is that people have doubt and unbelief in their hearts. Doubt brings in confusion and often depression. It kills our faith and causes us to make negative confessions.

In Luke 18, Jesus told His disciples a parable to the effect that they ought always to pray and not to turn coward, faint, lose heart, and give up. He spoke of the widow who continued to plead her case before the unjust judge until he acted on her behalf. Jesus is saying that if an unjust judge can be moved by persistence, how much more will our loving heavenly Father be moved if we won't quit and give up because of doubt and unbelief.

We need to learn to move in the realm of the Spirit through faith, instead of relying on what we see in the natural. "For we walk by faith . . . not by sight or appearance" (2 Corinthians 5:7). Learn to stay in contact with God, always walking in His presence. If you begin to listen to the devil's lies, then soon doubt and unbelief come roaring back. Those fiery darts begin to wage war with your mind. Remember that doubt and unbelief are a product of the mind and our wrong focus.

Looking unto Jesus, the Author and Finisher of our faith, will stop doubt and unbelief.

GOD'S WORD FOR YOU

Enter into His gates with thanksgiving and a thank offering and into His courts with praise! Be thankful and say so to Him, bless and affectionately praise His name!

PSALM 100:4

I will give You thanks in the great assembly; I will praise You among a mighty throng.

PSALM 35:18

ＵNGRATITUDE

Prayer is often not answered because people are ungrateful. There are people who are grumblers, murmurers, faultfinders, and complainers. We have to be very careful that we're not like that. We need to be the kind of people who are thankful for what God is doing. If we are complaining and ungrateful all the time, we are going to have a hard time getting answers to our prayers.

If you want to see God work in your spouse, your children, your finances, your circumstances, or your job, you have to be grateful for what you already have.

God told me once, "Joyce, when people are praying and asking Me for things, if they don't have a thankful heart, that's a clear indication to Me that they're already grumbling trying to handle what they have." The devil's whole plan is to keep you dissatisfied with something all the time, grumbling, faultfinding, and complaining. When you are ungrateful, it holds you back from progressing and maturing in the Spirit.

God wants us to grow in maturity and become more like His Son Jesus. God's answer to ingratitude is a life filled with praise and thanksgiving.

Look for something today to be thankful for and offer up a prayer of praise and thanksgiving.

GOD'S WORD FOR YOU

So shall My word be that goes forth out of My mouth; it shall not return to Me void [without producing any effect, useless], but it shall accomplish that which I please and purpose, and it shall prosper in the thing for which I sent it.

ISAIAH 55:11

For the Word that God speaks is alive and full of power [making it active, operative, energizing, and effective]; it is sharper than any two-edged sword, penetrating to the dividing line of the breath of life (soul) and [the immortal] spirit, and of joints and marrow [of the deepest parts of our nature], exposing and sifting and analyzing and judging the very thoughts and purposes of the heart.

HEBREWS 4:12

PRAYERS NOT BASED ON THE WORD

We also fail to get answers to our prayers because they are not based on the Word of God. The prophet Isaiah says, "My word . . . shall not return to Me void." God says that His Word will always accomplish the purpose for which He has sent it. Learn the Word, speak the Word, pray the Word. Let God know that you are standing on the foundation of the Word.

When the devil tries to lie to you, quote him the Scriptures. The Bible says that the Word is "sharper than any two-edged sword" (Hebrews 4:12). We need to make sure that our prayers are prayers being produced by the Spirit of God and not our soulish prayers. If we stay in the Word, God will teach us when we're operating in the soul and when we're operating in the Spirit. The Holy Spirit uses the Word to judge the very thoughts and purposes of our hearts.

If I'm speaking God's Word in line with His will, then I can be assured that what I'm praying for will not come back empty-handed. God promises to fulfill His Word.

The Holy Spirit will quicken the Word to you to empower your prayers with faith and assurance.

GOD'S WORD FOR YOU

Death and life are in the power of the tongue, and they who indulge in it shall eat the fruit of it [for death or life]. [Matt. 12:37.]

PROVERBS 18:21

He who guards his mouth keeps his life, but he who opens wide his lips comes to ruin.

PROVERBS 13:3

NEGATIVE CONFESSION

If we want our prayers to be answered, we can't pray and then negate them with a negative confession. Let's say a mother is praying for a son who's having trouble in school. So she prays the prayer of faith and believes God for a breakthrough. Then she goes to lunch with two neighbors and spends the next hour saying, "I am so sick of these problems I'm having with this kid. Why me?"

This kind of negative confession wipes your prayer slate clean. You might as well not even waste your time praying until you make a decision to get your mouth in line with your prayers.

When the neighbors ask how your son is doing, say, "You know what? In the natural things have not changed a whole lot, but I'm praying for him, and I have assurance in my heart that God is doing a mighty work in his life."

Once you have laid hold of the answer through faith, then you need to make sure your confession is in agreement with what you've asked God to do. Don't let the devil trip you up when people ask you questions that you could answer negatively. Answer them with a positive confession of the Word of God.

When you line up your mouth with the positive confession of the Word of God, you'll see amazing results.

GOD'S WORD FOR YOU

And the servant of the Lord must not strive.

2 TIMOTHY 2:24 KJV

Let all bitterness and indignation and wrath (passion, rage, bad temper) and resentment (anger, animosity) and quarreling (brawling, clamor, contention) and slander (evil-speaking, abusive or blasphemous language) be banished from you, with all malice (spite, ill will, or baseness of any kind).

EPHESIANS 4:31

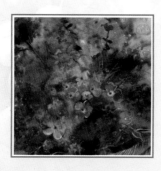

STRIFE

Strife is a thief and a robber that we must learn to recognize and deal with quickly. We must control strife before it controls us.

Strife is defined as "the act or state of fighting or quarreling, especially bitterly . . . discord." It is bickering, arguing, being involved in a heated disagreement, or shows up as an angry undercurrent. Strife is dangerous. It is a demonic force sent by Satan for the purpose of destruction.

Almost any time someone hurts us, or offends us, anger rises up within us. It is not sin to feel anger. But we must not act out the angry feelings in an ungodly way. We must not hold a grudge or get into bitterness, resentment, or unforgiveness.

A judgmental attitude is an open door for strife. We must remember that mercy triumphs over judgment (James 2:13 NIV). Judgment usually leads to gossip. Gossip begins to spread the strife from person to person. It gets us out of agreement, harmony, and unity. It actually moves us out of God's blessings.

When the temptation comes to judge others, and then spread our opinion through gossip and backbiting, we should remember this helpful hint: Let the one among us who is without sin cast the first stone (John 8:7).

Remember: God changes things through prayer and faith, not through judgment and gossip.

GOD'S WORD FOR YOU

And whenever you stand praying, if you have anything against anyone, forgive him and let it drop (leave it, let it go), in order that your Father Who is in heaven may also forgive you your [own] failings and shortcomings and let them drop.

But if you do not forgive, neither will your Father in heaven forgive your failings and shortcomings.

MARK 11:25-26

Then Peter came up to Him and said, Lord, how many times may my brother sin against me and I forgive him and let it go? [As many as] up to seven times?

Jesus answered him, I tell you, not up to seven times, but seventy times seven! [Gen. 4:24.]

MATTHEW 18:21-22

𝒰NFORGIVENESS

One of the greatest reasons why prayer isn't answered among Christians is *unforgiveness*. In Mark 11 Jesus gave His disciples a command to forgive. And then He told them plainly that if they did not forgive, neither would their Father in heaven forgive them their failings and shortcomings. He was blunt with them because He knew what a stumbling block unforgiveness would be for their spiritual life.

It is important to note that forgiveness and having faith to move mountains comes in the same context. There is no power in speaking to a mountain if the heart is full of unforgiveness. Yet this problem is rampant among God's children. If there is anything that will short-circuit God from answering our prayers, it's a heart full of unforgiveness and bitterness toward others. You can't go into your prayer closet and expect God to move mountains for you or on behalf of others when you've hardened your heart with unforgiveness.

Jesus told Peter that he must be willing to forgive seven times seventy: 490 times. Jesus wanted to show His disciples that forgiveness was one of the main keys for unlocking the Kingdom of God in their lives if they wanted to have power in their prayers.

Extend abundant mercy and forgiveness
just as God forgave you in Christ.

PRAYER IN JESUS' NAME

*We have been given the most powerful
Name in heaven and earth
to use when we pray. Let's use it!*

GOD'S WORD FOR YOU

And [so that you can know and understand] what is the immeasurable and unlimited and surpassing greatness of His power in and for us who believe, as demonstrated in the working of His mighty strength,

Which He exerted in Christ when He raised Him from the dead and seated Him at His [own] right hand in the heavenly [places],

Far above all rule and authority and power and dominion and every name that is named [above every title that can be conferred], not only in this age and in this world, but also in the age and the world which are to come.

And He has put all things under His feet and has appointed Him the universal and supreme Head of the church [a headship exercised throughout the church], [Ps. 8:6.]

Which is His body, the fullness of Him Who fills all in all [for in that body lives the full measure of Him Who makes everything complete, and Who fills everything everywhere with Himself].

EPHESIANS 1:19-23

five
PRAYER IN JESUS' NAME

 used the name of Jesus for many years without the results I had been told I could have. I began asking God why I was using the name that was supposed to have power over circumstances that were outside His will, and yet I was not seeing results. The Holy Spirit began to reveal to me that releasing the power in the name of Jesus requires faith in that name, that name that is so powerful that when it is mentioned in faith, every knee must bow in three realms—in heaven, on earth, and under the earth!

Jesus came from the highest heaven; He has been to the earth, and He has descended to Hades, under the earth, and now is seated again at the right hand of the Father in the highest heaven. He has made a full circle; therefore, He has filled everything and everywhere with Himself. He is seated above everything else and has a name above every other name. His name is the highest name, the most powerful name—and His name has been given to us to use in prayer!

What an awesome privilege we have to use the name of Jesus that is above every other name!

GOD'S WORD FOR YOU

A woman, when she gives birth to a child, has grief (anguish, agony) because her time has come. But when she has delivered the child, she no longer remembers her pain (trouble, anguish) because she is so glad that a man (a child, a human being) has been born into the world.

So for the present you are also in sorrow (in distress and depressed); but I will see you again and [then] your hearts will rejoice, and no one can take from you your joy (gladness, delight).

And when that time comes, you will ask nothing of Me [you will need to ask Me no questions]. I assure you, most solemnly I tell you, that My Father will grant you whatever you ask in My Name [as presenting all that I AM]. [Exod. 3:14.]

Up to this time you have not asked a [single] thing in My Name [as presenting all that I AM]; but now ask and keep on asking and you will receive, so that your joy (gladness, delight) may be full and complete.

JOHN 16:21-24

$\mathscr{H}$IS NAME TAKES HIS PLACE

Oh, how wonderful it would have been to have physically walked with Jesus. But He told His followers they would be better off when He went away, because then He would send His Spirit to dwell in every believer (John 16:7).

He told them that even though they were sorrowful at the news of His upcoming departure, they would rejoice again just as a woman has sorrow during her labor but rejoices when the child is born.

He said they would change their minds when they saw the glory of His Spirit in them and the power available to each of them through the privilege of using His name in prayer. He was literally giving to them—and has given to all those who believe in Him—His "power of attorney," the legal right to use His name. His name takes His place; His name represents Him.

Jesus has already been perfect for us. He has already pleased the Father for us; therefore, there is no pressure on us to feel that we must have a perfect record of right behavior before we can pray. Then when we come before the Father in Jesus' name, we can confess our sin, receive His forgiveness, and boldly make our requests known to Him.

When the name of Jesus is spoken by a believer in faith, all of heaven comes to attention.

GOD'S WORD FOR YOU

If ye shall ask any thing in my name, I will do it.

JOHN 14:14 KJV

Then some of the traveling Jewish exorcists (men who adjure evil spirits) also undertook to call the name of the Lord Jesus over those who had evil spirits, saying, I solemnly implore and charge you by the Jesus Whom Paul preaches!

Seven sons of a certain Jewish chief named Sceva were doing this.

But [one] evil spirit retorted, Jesus I know, and Paul I know about, but who are you?

Then the man in whom the evil spirit dwelt leaped upon them, mastering two of them, and was so violent against them that they dashed out of that house [in fear], stripped naked and wounded.

ACTS 19:13-16

JESUS' NAME IS NOT MAGIC

The name of Jesus is not a "magic word" or a ritualistic incantation to be added to the end of a prayer to insure its effectiveness.

In the Book of Acts we read of the mighty miracles that God did through the life of Paul. God honored Paul's faith when he spoke the name of Jesus. Certain Jewish exorcists, however, attempted to use the name of Jesus as if it were a simple incantation to be said. The Bible says the "man in whom the evil spirit dwelt leaped upon them, mastering two of them" (Acts 19:16). The spirit spoke and said it knew Jesus and Paul but not them.

If we are going to pray and use the powerful name of Jesus, then we must be in a living, obedient relationship with Him. Then the power of the Holy Spirit will flow out of our lives and deliver us and others from the devil's bondages.

All Spirit-led prayer involves praying the will of God, not the will of man! It is impossible to pray the will of God without knowing the Word of God. Yes, God certainly pays attention to the prayers that come to Him in Jesus' name, but not ones that are outside of His will.

You must know Jesus as Lord
before you can use His name in power.

GOD'S WORD FOR YOU

Behold! I have given you authority and power to trample upon serpents and scorpions, and [physical and mental strength and ability] over all the power that the enemy [possesses]; and nothing shall in any way harm you.

LUKE 10:19

And His name, through and by faith in His name, has made this man whom you see and recognize well and strong.

ACTS 3:16

THE NAME OF JESUS IS POWER

The name of Jesus is power. No loving parent would release power to a baby, because the parent knows the child would get hurt. Parents don't withhold power from their children to hurt them, but to help them or to keep them safe. Our heavenly Father is the same way. He tells us what is available to us, and then by His Spirit helps us mature to the point where we can handle what He desires to give us.

I believe the power in the name of Jesus is unlimited. I also believe that our heavenly Father releases it to us as He knows we can handle it properly.

When Jesus began to talk to His disciples about the privilege of praying in His name and having their requests granted, He said, "I *solemnly* tell you . . ." I believe that the power of God is a solemn responsibility. God's power is not a toy! It is not to be released to people who are only playing, but to those who are seriously ready to get on with God's program for their lives.

*As you continue to grow and mature in Christ,
you can look for exciting new dimensions
in your walk with the Lord.*

GOD'S WORD FOR YOU

And it shall be that whoever shall call upon the name of the Lord [invoking, adoring, and worshiping the Lord—Christ] shall be saved.

ACTS 2:21

ℐN TIMES OF CRISIS

Years ago before seatbelt laws, a friend of mine was driving with his young son through a busy intersection one day. The car door on the passenger side was not secured tightly, and he made a sharp turn. The car door flew open, and the little boy rolled out right into traffic! The last thing my friend saw was a set of car wheels just about on top of his son. All he knew to do was cry, "Jesus!"

He stopped his car and ran to his son. To his amazement, his son was perfectly all right. But the man driving the car that had almost hit the child was hysterical.

"Man, don't be upset!" my friend said. "My son is okay. Just thank God you were able to stop!"

"You don't understand!" the man responded. "I never touched my brakes!"

Although there was nothing man could do, the name of Jesus prevailed, and the boy's life was spared.

In times of crisis, call upon the name of Jesus. The more you and I see how faithful He is in times of need and crises, the more we witness the power in His name over situations and circumstances, the more our faith is developed in His name.

There is power in the name of Jesus
for every crisis we will ever face.

GOD'S WORD FOR YOU

Let this same attitude and purpose and [humble] mind
be in you which was in Christ Jesus: [Let Him be your
example in humility:]

Who, although being essentially one with God and in
the form of God [possessing the fullness of the attributes
which make God God], did not think this equality with
God was a thing to be eagerly grasped or retained,

But stripped Himself [of all privileges and rightful
dignity], so as to assume the guise of a servant (slave), in
that He became like men and was born a human being,

And after He had appeared in human form, He
abased and humbled Himself [still further] and carried His
obedience to the extreme of death, even the death of the
cross!

Therefore [because He stooped so low] God has highly
exalted Him and has freely bestowed on Him the name
that is above every name.

PHILIPPIANS 2:5-9

OBEDIENCE AND THE NAME OF JESUS

Jesus became extremely obedient; therefore, He was given a name that is above every other name. But let's not get so caught up in the power these verses set forth that we forget the obedience they describe.

John 14:15 says: "If you [really] love Me, you will keep (obey) My commands."

Obedience is important!

Now I realize that the ability is not in us (apart from the Lord's help) to be perfectly obedient, but if we have a willing heart within us, and if we do what we can do, then He will send His Spirit to do what we cannot do.

I am not suggesting that the power in Jesus' name won't work without perfect obedience. I am making a point that the power in the name of Jesus will not be released to anyone who is not seriously pressing toward the mark of the high calling in Christ (Philippians 3:14 KJV), which is maturity—and maturity requires extreme obedience. Extreme obedience requires a willingness to suffer in the flesh, in a godly way, for example, by denying yourself something you want that you know isn't good for you, if need be, in order to know and do the will of God.

In order for us to experience the freedom Jesus purchased for us, we need to be obedient to His Word.

GOD'S WORD FOR YOU

For [instance] a married woman is bound by law to her husband as long as he lives; but if her husband dies, she is loosed and discharged from the law concerning her husband.

Likewise, my brethren, you have undergone death as to the Law through the [crucified] body of Christ, so that now you may belong to Another, to Him Who was raised from the dead in order that we may bear fruit for God.

ROMANS 7:2, 4

But the person who is united to the Lord becomes one spirit with Him.

1 CORINTHIANS 6:17

To Use the Name, You Must Be "Married"!

I was studying about the name of Jesus when the Lord spoke to my heart. He said, "Joyce, when you married Dave, you got his name and the power of all the name Meyer means." He reminded me that I can use the name Dave Meyer and get the same results that Dave could get himself if he were with me. I can even go to the bank and get Dave Meyer's money, because when two people get married, all the property of each now belongs to the other.

Through this example of everyday life, the Holy Spirit was attempting to teach me that although I had a relationship with the Lord, it was more like a courtship than a marriage. I liked "to go on dates" with Him, but when "the date" was over, I wanted to go my own way. I wanted all of Him and His favor and benefits, but I did not want to give Him all of myself.

The apostle Paul tells us that we have died to the law of sin and death and are now married to Another so that we can bear fruit for Him. Remember, you cannot legally use the name until after the marriage to Jesus.

Jesus is the Bridegroom, and we are His Bride.
That is how God the Father has planned it,
and that is the only way His plan will work properly.

GOD'S WORD FOR YOU

Then Jesus called together the Twelve [apostles] and gave them power and authority over all demons, and to cure diseases,

And He sent them out to announce and preach the kingdom of God and to bring healing.

LUKE 9:1-2

EXERCISING AUTHORITY IN THE NAME

As believers we need to recognize that the power of attorney gives the right to *command* in Jesus' name.

We pray and ask the Father for things in Jesus' name, but we command the enemy in that name. We speak to circumstances and principalities and powers, using the authority that has been given us by virtue of the power of attorney invested in us by Jesus Himself. In exercising our deliverance ministry, we don't lay hands on a person and begin to pray for God to cast it out. We command it to come out in the name of Jesus.

Before we can exercise this authority, we have already prayed to the Father in Jesus' name. Now we go and use the power He has granted us, and we exercise the authority inherent in the name of His Son Jesus.

The same thing applies to healing the sick. There are times to pray the prayer of faith in the name of Jesus (James 5:15); there are times to anoint with oil (James 5:14); but there are also times simply to command or speak in the name of Jesus.

Spend time daily with the Lord. Fellowship, ask, pray, seek, and come out of that time equipped for the job at hand.

When you go to do the work of the Kingdom, exercise your authority in Jesus' name.

GOD'S WORD FOR YOU

But Peter said, Silver and gold (money) I do not have; but what I do have, that I give to you: in [the use of] the name of Jesus Christ of Nazareth, walk!

ACTS 3:6

DO NOT BE SELFISH WITH THE NAME

I believe there are those who have heard messages about the power that is available to them in the name of Jesus, and who are busy using that name hoping to get everything they have ever wanted. We certainly can and should use the name in our own behalf, as long as we use it to fulfill God's will for our life and not our own. However, there is another aspect of using the name in prayer: *using the name of Jesus to pray for others*.

That is really what the apostles were doing in the book of Acts. Jesus had sent them out empowered with His authority and His name, and they got busy trying to help others with it. They were using the name of Jesus to bring salvation, healing, deliverance, and the baptism of the Holy Spirit to all those for whom Jesus had died who did not yet know Him.

Take the name of Jesus and love people with it. When you see a need, whisper a prayer in Jesus' name. God has entrusted every believer with two ministries: the ministry of *reconciliation* and the ministry of *intercession*.

So much can be accomplished in the earth as believers begin to use the name of Jesus unselfishly.

GOD'S WORD FOR YOU

Now to Him Who, by (in consequence of) the [action of His] power that is at work within us, is able to [carry out His purpose and] do superabundantly, far over and above all that we [dare] ask or think [infinitely beyond our highest prayers, desires, thoughts, hopes, or dreams].

EPHESIANS 3:20

EXCEEDINGLY, ABUNDANTLY ABOVE AND BEYOND

When I pray about all the people who are hurting, I have a strong desire to help them all. I feel that my desire is bigger than my ability, and it is—but it is not bigger than God's ability!

When the thing we are facing in our life or ministry looms so big in our eyes that our mind goes "tilt," we need to *think in the spirit*. In the natural, many things are impossible. But God wants us to believe for great things, make big plans, and expect Him to do things so great it leaves us with our mouths hanging open in awe.

God does not usually call people who are capable; if He did, He would not get the glory. He frequently chooses those who, in the natural, feel as if they are in completely over their heads but who are ready to stand up on the inside and take bold steps of faith. They have learned the secret of using Jesus' name and depending on that "superabundant" power that works within them.

When our desires seem overwhelmingly big, and we don't see the way to accomplish them, we should remember that even though we don't know the way, we know the Waymaker!

Because of His abundant power within us, God has a way for us to do everything He places in our heart.

GOD'S WORD FOR YOU

And Moses said to God, Behold, when I come to the Israelites and say to them, The God of your fathers has sent me to you, and they say to me, What is His name? What shall I say to them?

And God said to Moses, I AM WHO I AM and WHAT I AM, and I WILL BE WHAT I WILL BE; and He said, You shall say this to the Israelites, I AM has sent me to you!

EXODUS 3:13-14

Jesus replied, I assure you, most solemnly I tell you, before Abraham was born, I AM.

JOHN 8:58

THE NAME OF GOD IS I AM

I have pondered these verses for a long time. To me, they are awesome scriptures that hold much more than we may realize. What was God saying to Moses when He referred to Himself as I AM?

God is saying He is so much, so great, that there is no way to describe Him properly. How can we describe in one name Someone Who is everything? God said to Moses, "I AM can take care of anything you encounter. Whatever you need, I AM it. Either I have it or I can get it. If it doesn't exist, I will create it. I have everything covered, not only now, but for all time. Relax!"

Jesus responded to His disciples the same way God the Father responded to Moses. Revelation 1:8 declares Jesus to be the Alpha and the Omega. That means the first and the last, the beginning and the end. He has always been and always will be.

Our finite human minds cannot expand far enough even to begin to comprehend the limitless power that has been invested in His glorious name.

When we pray in the name of Jesus, we are praying in the name of the great I AM—the omnipotent God of all eternity.

The Lord is the Ever-Present I AM. Always with us.
Everything we need, or ever will need.

JOYCE MEYER

Joyce Meyer has been teaching the Word of God since 1976 and in full-time ministry since 1980. She is the bestselling author of more than sixty inspirational books, including In Pursuit of Peace, How to Hear from God, Knowing God Intimately, *and* Battlefield of the Mind. *She has also released thousands of teaching cassettes and a complete video library. Joyce's* Enjoying Everyday Life *radio and television programs are broadcast around the world, and she travels extensively conducting conferences. Joyce and her husband, Dave, are the parents of four grown children and make their home in St. Louis, Missouri.*

Additional copies of this book are available from your local bookstore.

If this book has changed your life, we would like to hear from you.

To contact the author, write:
Joyce Meyer Ministries
P. O. Box 655 • Fenton, Missouri 63026

or call: (636) 349-0303

Internet Address: www.joycemeyer.org

In Canada, write: Joyce Meyer Ministries Canada, Inc.
Lambeth Box 1300 • London, ON N6P 1T5

or call: (636) 349-0303

In Australia, write: Joyce Meyer Ministries-Australia
Locked Bag 77 • Mansfield Delivery Centre
Queensland 4122

or call: (07) 3349 1200

In England, write: Joyce Meyer Ministries
P. O. Box 1549 • Windsor • SL4 1GT
or call: 01753 831102